SWEPT & GARNISHED
A Royal Academy At Osyth Novel
Book 3

I0652371

Patricia S. Bowne

SWEPT & GARNISHED

DOUBLE DRAGON

Prologue

The sun was just out of bed and still red-eyed, stretching his rays to right and left between the hills, when Mama Simone stepped out of her barnyard onto the path by the hedgerow. Two dozy chickens got in her way and squawked out of it again. Mama Simone walked fast because she had long legs. She stepped hard because she had big feet and wooden shoes, the kind people kick off beside the back door.

Mama Simone walked through the wet grass faster than the sun rose. By and by she reached the shadow side of the hills, and when the sun couldn't see her any longer she felt as if she'd beaten something. She sat down on a log and shook a pebble out of one of her wooden shoes, as if she'd won back the last hour of the night and had it to spare.

On the shady side of the hill it was still spring. The trees on the other side were leafed out, but these still had catkins and flowers. Held back like country girls, thought Mama Simone, whose parents had dressed her like a little girl through her teens. "And not in anything as nice as these," she said to the nearest tree. It quivered its pleated leaves at her and shook a tassel of catkins like spiky green caterpillars. "Sex, sex, sex," was all it would say.

Mama Simone walked toward the hill's edge, where sunrays made a haze up in the trees. The closer she got to the next valley, the further into summer she went. Trees pushed out their leaves, shoved their caterpillar catkins off to curl up on the forest floor, and then stretched their branches out and sighed. "Sun, sun, summer" was what they said then.

Down the valley she went, into a glade that the sun was just peeping into. She made a dark trail across dew-covered grasses to where a big old oak tree stood at the edge of the glade, looking back at the sun. "Hello there, old tree," said Mama Simone.

The tree didn't pay any attention to her, because it was looking at the sun. It sang to itself, long and slow. While she waited for the old tree Mama Simone sat down on one of its roots and pulled her feet up under her skirt. She looked around the glade, then behind the tree into the open space its shade made. She leaned from side to side to look around spindly young trees until a feeling of opening her eyes came over her and she saw four baby oaks with shade-pale leaves standing in what she had thought open space. Here their parent had dropped them, under its sheltering arms; here they had sprouted, and here they would die in its shade.

Mama Simone had the eyes-opening feeling again, as if a question had been answered without being asked. Her nose and the back of her throat hurt as she looked at the little trees that would never grow tall unless the big tree fell. She pressed her face against the old tree, hearing it sing to itself from far up in the sunlight, to far down in the earth, and tears filled her up until she shook with weeping, holding onto the tree as if it might turn and put warm arms around her.

There were six cars and a hearse in Mama Simone's farmyard when she got back to it. People everywhere and none of them feeding the chickens

6

or digging the garden; useless, all of them. People did like that, after a death. They made it an excuse to dress up and do nothing. Her daughter Gretyl was worst of the lot, poking across chicken-mud in her high heels. She was stout, shrill, and important, like a hen with a big worm.

"Mama, where were you? You can't run off in the woods and leave the stove lighted, you could have burned the house down. You knew we were coming! I told you not to do anything till I got here. How do you think I felt, coming here and Daddy dead and you off God knows where —"

Of course I knew, thought Mama Simone. Why else would I run away into the woods? But she thought about the little oak trees. "I knew you'd see to things," she said then. Gretyl got more important and less chickeny.

"I was worried about you," she said. She had a heavy upper lip like her da's, with beads of sweat already standing out on it. The sun dried up grass and made people come out in dew, thought Mama Simone. "People do queer things after a death," said Gretyl.

"Well, why shouldn't they? I couldn't do queer things when your father was alive," said Mama Simone. She washed her face at the pump and kicked her wooden shoes off at the back door, but she didn't want to go inside. She sat down on the bench under the kitchen window and heard the kettle and frypan twittering inside. "Did you make breakfast? I'd like to eat out here. Bread and jam would do."

"You never ate out here before."

7

"That's because your father wanted meat at every meal. You can only cut meat at a table. When you were a little girl, we used to eat apples in the orchard."

"Well, you need more than apples," said Gretyl. She went inside and Mama Simone could smell eggs, coffee, bread. "Who's going to take care of you?" Gretyl said when she brought them out.

"I'll take care of myself," said Mama Simone. "I was taking care of your father until an hour ago, why would myself be any more trouble?"

"Somebody has to be here with you. We've all talked it over."

"Not now," said Mama Simone. "After the funeral."

"Oh my land, I have to go talk to the funeral director," said Gretyl. "Eat up now. I ironed your black dress."

Chapter 1
The Departmental Year in Review

Warren Oldham shut his eyes, the better to pound his head against his desk. It didn't help. When he opened them, the Departmental Year in Review form was still lying there, still blank; no edifying faculty activities had appeared on it, and Warren was no closer to coming up with any. A filtered, rainy light came in from the window behind him and gave the offending document a colder and even more hopeless glow. Warren had walked into work on a dripping Friday morning, for this. A perfect end to the last week of the semester.

He shivered, rubbed his bald head, and glared at the form, growing crosser by the minute — not with the paper, which merely existed, but with the demand it implied that he somehow reframe the Demonology Department's activities into public relations fodder for the Royal Academy of the Arcane Arts and Sciences at Osyth. Warren had many skills, but this was not one of them. Even though someone looking at his round pink face and walrus mustache might have thought him a cheerful fellow, he was more prone to depression than to boosterism, even after a good year; the one just passed had been ambiguous, at best, and required more spin than Warren could muster. He chewed the edge of his mustache in frustration and ran his fingers through the fringe of white hair over his ears.

"To hell with it!" he exclaimed, snatched up the fountain pen he had been given by the International Demonological Association when his term as president ended, and began filling in the form very quickly, as if to get it done before his bad mood ran out. This made it almost illegible, but Warren reckoned that as a plus.

'1. Magisters Oldham and Cinea lost our souls when local demons took over the pentarium and began casting their own invocations,' he wrote in the 'Activities' column. In the 'Implications' column, he wrote: *'We have discovered a new way for demons to steal people's souls and that soulless faculty are as effective on interdisciplinary committees as normal faculty. They are not, however, able to carry out those duties requiring magic.'* He stopped and re-read this. It made him feel much better and, the pump being primed, he went on to fill in the rest of the two columns.

'2. Magister Rho was trapped in Magister Oldham's grimoire with a demon, and emerged without his magic when the grimoire was destroyed. Implication: a second way to destroy employees' talents.' (*And family heirlooms*, Warren thought, but did not write.) *'Temporary (possibly permanent) replacement needed.*

'3. The pentarium was shut down using the emergency switch, after a demon within it escaped from the pentacle. Implications: the emergency switch works. See above, regarding the limitations of soulless faculty. Magister Torecki deserves commendation for throwing the emergency switch.

'4. The department invoked the possessing demon Antimora, which then spoke privately with

each member at the same time. Implication: the repaired pentarium is not as impervious to demons' magic as was hoped.' Or to an exorcist's magic, since the demon Antimora had once been chief of the exorcists — Wilfrid Rosemont, Lord Stimms (that was) — but the Dean knew all about Rosemont's becoming the demon Antimora; it was the only thing the Dean did know about demons, and therefore came up in every conversation Warren had with him.

'*5. Magister Torecki resigned in mid-spring semester. Implication: delay in ongoing research programs including dissertation research. New faculty needed.*

'*6. Magisters Whin and Ligalla pursued the demon Antimora into the Mystic Guild of Alchemists' prison in the netherworld, trapping it therein, but releasing all the imprisoned alchemists. Implication: possible overthrow of existing governmental structures worldwide and disruption of the fabric of reality. Potential lawsuit. MGA will no longer repair our pentarium.*

'*7. Magister Ukadnian loaned Magister Harding's research camera arcana to a priest, who took it to Selanto and used it to record the second coming of the Bright Lady. The camera has been confiscated by the church as a holy relic. Implication:* ' "Damned if I know," Warren said, and after a moment's fruitless thought wrote that down. It was one more thing for Linus Ukadnian and Will Harding to fight about, but the Dean wouldn't care about that.

'*8. Magister Kalin counseled local demons on labor law. Implication: demon unionization,*

11

including demands for library and sports center privileges. Potential delay in or disruption of ongoing research.'

He turned to the second page and listed the faculty, with their status. *Magisters Cinea, Ukadnian, Graham, Whin, Kalin, and Regan, full-time. Magisters Ligalla, Hoth, Harding, and Teale — half time, joint appointments with Department of Public Health. Magister Torecki, resigned. Magister Rho, indefinite leave. Magister Oldham, fed up.* His pen skipped on the last word, which made that part even more illegible than the rest; Warren felt a sneaking relief at this, but shoved it away. He folded the form and put it into an envelope before he could lose his nerve. His computer chimed, a reminder that in twenty minutes he must be in the pentarium, calling up one of the demons that were agitating for use of the Academy's squash courts and swimming pool. "This is not what I went into magic for," Warren said venomously, addressing the envelope. He took it with him and dropped it into the campus mail slot beside the stairwell, and that was that. He was officially fed up.

Regret seized him as soon as he heard the letter whoosh into the void, growing stronger with every step down the stairs that led to the pentarium until it became a kind of cold despair, filling him like ice water. How could he have put such a gloomy face on everything? It wasn't all bad, after all. Nobody had been killed, thanks to Neil's quick work in the pentarium, when Warren and Russell were incapacitated by the loss of their souls. Even that loss, ashamed as Warren was of it, hadn't been as black as he'd painted it. Dozens of people had lost their souls, over the years, but only he and Russell had ever gotten them back, although the charm that did it had been burned with the rest of Warren's grimoire.

Even Rho, who'd caused all the trouble last semester, had tried his best to resist the demon controlling him and had leapt into the grimoire to save Warren's own soul from being trapped therein. He had actually sacrificed himself for Warren … they were all decent sorts, heroes in their own way, and now Warren had let them down. The demon Antimora had been right when it said Warren was past it, in decline, a tool of the administration and a blunt tool at that. He'd accomplished nothing this academic year except mistakes, and now he was failing at paperwork, the defining job of an administrator.

He stopped his descent in the sub-basement, but his heart kept going down. Linus Ukadnian's sharp voice came through the door to the pentarium shower room, Teddy Whin's answering. What had Teddy done but rescue a bunch of people who had been suffering for three hundred years? Yet he had just reported it as a plot against the civilized world … an administrator had no right to indulge his bad mood at faculty's expense, neither when reporting their accomplishments nor when leading them in the invocation of a demon.

Warren summoned all his resources to push depression away, yet even as he put his hand on the door remorse seized him again, an almost physical presence at his side. He stood frozen, a chill deeper than that of Osyth's cold, wet spring striking into him. The *cauld grue*, it was called, and it meant a demon stood beside him, summoning this bad mood and feeding on his soul through it — and had no doubt stood beside him in his office while he wrote, he thought, remembering how he had shivered and grown gloomier by the minute. A demon had come into his office, through the Academy wards and the building wards, and oppressed him as he sat at his desk; it had followed him to the very door of the pentarium shower room, one of the most heavily protected spots on campus; and this, Warren thought, could not be made into anything positive, not by the best spinmeister in all Osyth. Something very bad was going to come of this.

***

Inspector Ric Massey of the Selanto Guard would have agreed with Warren. He would even, had they been intimate enough, have given Warren a sympathetic pat on the shoulder, because Ric appreciated hard-working people who second-guessed themselves. He was that sort of person himself. Unfortunately, the Selanto Guard hired few such people, tending more towards quick-thinking fellows who reacted fast and realized their mistakes afterward.

"I didn't know it was a child!" the patrolman cried in despair. "I thought it was an ape, or an imp, or a wudiwiss!"

Ric wanted to yell at him. What would a wudiwiss be doing in this suburban development? There wasn't an unmanicured plant within twenty kilometers. But it was a reasonable mistake, on

14

some grounds. Daybreak on June first was the prime time for woodland arcana, and the thing that had attacked this patrolman, and now lay bleeding on the lawn, didn't look human. The sorcerer beside it looked up and shook his head. His knees were soaked with blood. Ric heard distant sirens, racing with time. "You have to keep her going till they get here," he said.

"All I can do is freeze her." The sorcerer pulled charms out of an insulated case and began to hang them on the girl.

Ric tried to look through layers of filth and his own rage to see the little girl under the rags, her face pale and glistening with shock. She couldn't have been more than twelve, and the charm straps wrapped two, three times around her bony wrists and elbows. The right side of her chest had been laid open by bullets — how many had the fool used? — and pink froth spilled out of it with every shallow breath. The stink of feces began to go away as her body cooled. *Grue* from the demon inside her ran through him, like ice-water poured into the marrow of his bones. It was too familiar, and Ric shook his own head hard to jostle memories back down into storage.

"How about you?" the sorcerer asked, giving him a sharp look.

"It's not about me," said Ric. "What kind of parents don't report a possession?"

The sorcerer shook his head again. The siren stopped with a squawk as an ambulance arrived. The small crowd of onlookers — neighbors in jackets or golf shirts, wives in suits or housecoats, and a smattering of dog-walkers and commuters — scattered as it pulled into the driveway.

Ric watched paramedics jump out; nobody followed them. "Where's Magister Pasqueflower?"

"In an exorcism on the North Side," said the paramedic. "Can we transport?"

"No." The sorcerer stood up, rubbing his chilled hands together. "We're lucky if we have half an hour."

The paramedic shouted back to his partner, and Ric heard her speaking into the ambulance's radio. But he was distracted as Derek came up beside him.

"There's a window broken at the back," said Derek. "That must be how she got out. Car's still in the garage."

The sorcerer looked a bit taken aback, the usual response to Derek, who was wearing jeans and a tight yellow tee-shirt under a studded denim jacket. His blonde curls reached to his collar in back and his mustache ran down on each side of his mouth. He looked like a teenager trying to look older than he really was, and ironically that made him look younger than he really was. Though they were both in their thirties, people dealing with the two of them automatically turned to Ric, with his narrow face and grey suit, as the adult.

Ric frowned. Did the car's presence mean the girl's parents were still here, in the crowd or walking away?

Derek anticipated this question. "None of the neighbors know the man who lives here," he said. "It was a younger man, no woman. He kept to himself — nobody knew he had a child in the house." He looked at the girl, still and cold, and his

16

mustache drooped further. "This is big trouble," he said.

"Will we save her?"

"I don't know," said Derek. "I can't see enough."

"Will we get the demon out of her?"

Derek shook his head again. "I can see her inside the pentacle, but I don't see an exorcist with her — it's just not clear! This is going to be a big mess."

With all due respect to seers and foretelling, Ric thought, any fool could see that much. "You're right about that. We don't have an exorcist."

"Damn! What'll we do?"

"Lord Stimms is coming," said the second paramedic, appearing behind her partner. "By magic."

"Sweet Lady Jane!" said Ric.

"We'll need all the magicians here for the pentacle," said Derek. "Who's going to take care of his transport?" Not even Lord Stimms could jump across Selanto by magic and still have power enough to perform an exorcism. Somebody else, a transport magician, would have to use up their magic to bring him; and that person couldn't drain power from the rest of them to refuel, because they would all — Ric, Derek, the sorcerer, and the two paramedics — be helping in the exorcism. Transporting magicians had died of shock in such situations. Ric was damned if it'd happen on his watch and, perversely, grateful for this new emergency. It gave him an excuse not to think about the girl and what might be going on in that body, the cold greasy feel of a demon inside you...

"We need crystals," he said to the paramedic. "Pull 'em out of all the equipment you won't need. And you –" the unhappy patrolman looked up, surprised — "You're taking care of the transport. Know the protocol?" The patrolman nodded. "Get every camera crystal those rubberneckers are carrying. Out of their cell phones, as well. And extra crystals anyone is wearing. I mean every crystal!" he called after the man, who had leapt into action to redeem himself. "Anyone who comes away from here with pictures cares more about them than about that transport magician's life, and I'll make sure everyone in Selanto knows it." The sorcerer and a paramedic were already pulling recharging necklaces out of their shirts when he turned back to them. "We'll need a double circle," he said, as Derek collected their crystals. "We'll do it airlock-style."

Derek nodded and jogged away, fishing a box of gold chalk out of his pocket. He and the paramedic began to draw a pentacle on the driveway behind the ambulance. Arguing voices rose from the crowd of neighbors on the sidewalk; the patrolman was being officious, but Ric decided to let it go. The man's career was probably over. Let him get what satisfaction he could out of bullying onlookers and looking after the transport.

"Transport's ready," announced the paramedic with the cell phone. "They're using Gower's Ring."

"Don't tell me," Ric said, nodding toward Derek. "Tell him."

She ran over to Derek, who nodded and drew the Gower's Ring sigil inside the inner pentacle. He was just finishing when Ric reached him; he drew

18

the last line of the pentacle, put one stick of chalk down just outside it, and backed away to where Ric was standing. The patrolman ran up panting, holding a hat full of power crystals and looking better pleased with himself, and they drew the outer circle of the airlock around him and the pentacle so he stood uneasily in the space between them.

"We're ready," Ric told the paramedic with the cell phone. Now he had a minute to catch his breath and get nervous. It would be bad enough to kill any transport magician, but to kill one of Lord Stimms' team! Ric felt sick at the thought.

Exorcists were the ultimate heroes and Lord Stimms was the ultimate exorcist, leader of them all, the one who made new exorcists out of ordinary obnoxious human beings. Being Named an exorcist by Lord Stimms was a bigger deal than being knighted by the king. Ric had seen the old Lord Stimms, Rosemont, at court functions. But Rosemont was gone. He had become the demon Antimora a year ago, and Ric had only once come near the new Lord Stimms, Gerald Manley. That had been the night the God of the Sacred Flame had scheduled its second coming, and he had a private suspicion that Lord Stimms had helped keep that second coming from actually happening. People said, and Ric believed, that Lord Stimms could banish a god if he chose.

This has to go right, Ric said to himself, looking around for any trouble spots, but then his eye fell on the little girl lying beside the sorcerer and shame hit him in the throat. There was no way it could go right for her.

A silver mist filled the inner pentacle, and everyone in the squad stood up straighter. Then the mist cleared to reveal two figures: Lord Stimms, tall and surprisingly young in his red robe, and a stocky, white-haired magician who wavered a moment at Lord Stimms' side and then sat down hard on the pavement. His Lordship opened the pentacle and changed places with the patrolman. It was standard procedure, and they did it smoothly; the patrolman was already laying power crystals across the transport magician's chest when Lord Stimms stood from closing the pentacle and turned toward Ric.

Exorcists never looked you in the eyes. Even Milicent Pasqueflower, who worked with Ric all the time, looked over his shoulder or a little to his right. It was meant to keep you from being defined by their opinions, Ric knew, but it always made him bristle. Wasn't he an equal? Didn't he deserve a little respect?

He might not have felt that way about Lord Stimms, who wasn't his equal, but Lord Stimms didn't look over his shoulder or past his ear. Lord Stimms looked directly into his face with large, dark eyes. The skin around them was webbed with tiny lines. Fragile, Ric thought, and then the exorcist's magic took hold. Ric felt competence flood through him. He ran through everything in his mind, faster than possible yet as calmly as if he had hours, and nodded as he finished the checklist. They'd done everything right. This would work, he knew it — he was going to be safe — and then Lord Stimms nodded as well. He bent to break the outer circle and Ric was discarded, cast back into a maelstrom of doubt. *It's just the exorcist's talent*, he told himself. *It's not about you.*

He held his breath. If there were any flaw in their airlock, this was the moment when he would feel the transport magician pull his own magic out of him. He almost stepped back, but there was no point. None of them were out of range. A mistake would drain all the magicians on the lawn, and then the girl would be lost; she would die with a demon inside her, and it would take her soul with it for whatever it chose to do, forever. This was what he'd been trying not to think about... Lord Stimms stood, and Ric realized the airlock had held. The transport and his need were safely contained within the inner pentacle, and now within the outer circle too as Derek re-set it. Ric took a deep, shaky breath of relief. Then there was no time for thinking, as he raced toward the girl.

Lord Stimms, a few steps ahead of him, was somehow able to run in that robe without seeming hurried or disarranged. He had the kind of dignity, Ric thought that every teen in Selanto wanted; the kind that came from scorning the very concept of dignity. Ric grasped at analysis, as if it would protect him from the confusion inside him. He catalogued the new Lord Stimms' height and youth, his dark hair and weightless run. His face, pale and mustached, was familiar from tabloid photos. Yet in person, Stimms did not look right. There was that fragile something about the eyes... Ric had no chance to gather more data now, for he stood behind his Lordship, at one point of the gold-tape pentacle the sorcerer had laid down around the child, and could see nothing of Stimms but the red robe and dark, feathery hair. Derek, the sorcerer, and the two paramedics stood at the other pentacle points. They held smudging candles and chanted the invocation as his Lordship knelt beside the child. He spat on one pale hand and placed it on her forehead.

Ric almost dropped his candle. He heard Derek choke on his right. An exorcist never touched the possessed! An exorcist spoke to the demon, cozened it, and fooled it into taking his opinion seriously; then he turned that talent for approval and dismissal full on it, making it as weak as he thought it, and lent the victim strength enough to push it aside. Touch was insanely risky. It gave the demon a chance to leap into the exorcist, and turn that power against all around it.

But the girl had opened her eyes, and now Lord Stimms was speaking to her as if to an old acquaintance — no, he was speaking to the demon as an old acquaintance, Ric realized. Exorcists sometimes became that familiar with the monsters. He relaxed a little. If Stimms knew the demon's name, he would have more influence over it. And this proved to be the case, for girl and exorcist had not spoken for more than five minutes when she gave a shudder and lay still, smaller than before. Lord Stimms drew a ward from his pocket and slipped it over her head, to keep the demon from re-entering her, and then leant toward Derek to break the circle and let the banished monster return to the netherworld. Ric saw his profile, and again had the feeling of something not quite right.

"What the hell!" the sorcerer cried, and plunged toward the girl. "That's a summons!" Ric took a step forward and saw for himself. The sparkle of a

22

fading glamour was all around the girl's face, and under it he could plainly see the pentacle drawn on her forehead that had invited the demon into her and trapped it there. Lord Stimms' wet hand had broken its lines. "Somebody gave this child to the demon," said the sorcerer.

Lord Stimms had not risen from his knees, and Derek seemed frozen looking at him. Behind them, shouting began in the spectators around a tall man Ric hadn't seen before. He had the shimmer of a dissipating charm around him as he backed away from the crowd, his hands up in warning. They shouted, he shouted, the paramedics shouted. Even the patrolman was shouting, from where he crouched inside the circle with the transport magician, but through it all Ric could hear the little girl's voice, shrill and desperate.

"Daddy!" she shrieked. "Daddy, Daddy!" The tall man reached into his shirt and stopped — whatever extra power he had counted on was gone with the demon.

Ric walked forward, cautiously. "You don't want any trouble," he said. "Come along quietly. Don't you want to say goodbye to your daughter?"

The man's face twisted, but Ric felt no pity. Ice ran through his veins again. They remembered what a demon felt like, coiling through the blood. His bones knew how it ached in every joint. He could just see the girl on the lawn out of the corner of his eye, the sorcerer and paramedics clustered over her. Even if she lived, she'd never get rid of it. She'd never forget that feeling of no control. *Just this moment*, Ric thought as he reached out toward the tall man. *Just one minute out of control* ..."Daddy!"

23

the girl cried. Too late, Ric realized that he should have felt no *grue*, the demon having been driven out of her — "Daddy!" the voice was from just behind him. The *grue* jarred his vertebrae against each other.

Ric was so close to the demon when he turned that he had to step back, into the tall man, and words froze in his mouth. But the demon was not interested in Ric. It stood within a half-meter of him, nude and filthy, a sexualized parody of the girl it had been called into. "Daddy, don't you love me anymore?" it piped, and the man behind him answered with a groan.

He clung to Ric's arm like a drowning swimmer, and Ric shook him off. Just like that. Just to reach for his gun, though what use was a gun against a demon? Just to put a hand on his ward and reassure himself and just like that the demon reached past him, around his side. Its hair struck sparks off the shield his ward made around him, and just like that it took the man, plucking him from behind Ric as if it picked an apple. Then it and the man were gone, the crowd went silent all around him, and Ric spun to stare at the vacant spot where the man had stood.

He heard Derek cry out and as he turned back things seemed to happen slowly, so that he could watch every detail. He could watch Lord Stimms crumple, not even trying to catch himself, while Derek reached out for him. He could see the hand that had touched the possessed girl land on Derek's shoulder. And then Derek folded forwards too, as if he were emptying something from himself into Lord Stimms, yet his Lordship seemed no better for it,

24

and then they were both crumpled on the ground, the paramedics turning toward them to do what little they could without crystals or equipment.

***

Warren could see steam from the public shower billowing into the right side of the locker room, white against the makeshift individual shower stalls. He had to walk halfway down the room before he was able to see the shower itself past the lockers, a few standing open while demonologists disrobed before them. Teddy was one of the disrobing ones, whatever argument she had been having with Linus Ukadnian muffled by the turtleneck pulled up over her head. Linus was already in the shower, with his narrow backside turned, and Anders Regan was soaping up beside him in a determined I-am-ignoring-this manner. Will Harding was giving himself a vigorous massage with a threadbare beach towel while James Kalin, who abhorred all towels, sat naked on one of the benches to dry off before donning his blue paper gown and booties.

"Where's Russell?" Warren asked, looking for Russell Cinea, the senior demonologist.

"Setting the pentacle," said James. He raked his fingers through the brown beard he grew before every field season, as if measuring it against the days until graduation and faculty exodus. "You all right?"

Warren scowled and fought with his collar button. "A demon's jerking me around," he said.

25

"What? Which one?" Teddy asked, yanking the turtleneck over her curly hair and emerging bright-eyed and curious.

"I don't know," Warren said. "It was bothering me up in my office, and again in the stairwell." He hung his shirt and undershirt in the locker, and began to undo his shoes.

Susan Teale had come out of the private showers and now she hung her towel over the open door of a locker. "Through the Academy wards?" she asked in a worried voice.

"No big surprise," Teddy decided. "With all the wards they passed out while Antimora was in town, you'd expect some fool to have let a demon through one of them by now. Let's just hope it wasn't one of ours." A demon that had gotten through one ward would be able to pass any other wards of that batch. Most batches of wards were small, for that reason and because ward-making was a skilled art, requiring a great deal of magic. Only the demonology faculty made enough wards in a batch for a demons' passing them to pose a serious problem.

"My office?" Warren said, a little nettled. "You know those are our wards. Either yours, or Russell's, or both."

"Ow," said Teddy, as well she might. She and Russell made the most wards in the department, in the largest batches. "It might be easier to just deal with the demon." She had shed the last of her clothes and stepped into the spot Linus had vacated in the public shower. "Hey," she said, at a time when a modest woman would not have called

26

attention to herself, "Shouldn't Russell be out by now? If some demon's getting through the wards."

Every person in the locker room froze, looking at the pentarium door. Behind that door, Russell Cinea was drawing a pentacle of his own blood on the golden floor. He was speaking the charms that set it in place and built invisible walls upwards from every line. He was all alone, in the room in which demons had stolen his soul — and Warren's — not four months ago.

"Crap," said Will Harding, and nobody disagreed.

Warren walked across the room and pounded on the door. Nothing happened.

"Um-" said Anders, sounding querulous, and Warren knocked again.

The door opened abruptly. There stood Russell Cinea, a head taller than Warren, his white cockade of hair as dapper as ever though the rest of him looked ridiculous in blue paper gown and boots. "Um — yes?" he asked, innocently.

"You took your time," Teddy accused.

"My drawing was off," Russell admitted. "We should have grooved floors, like the exorcism suite." He stepped forward, which put him chest to chest with Warren. "Excuse me?"

"Were you in there losing your soul again?" Warren asked, and now Russell did look perturbed.

"Not that I know of," he said. "Let's see." He made a gesture. Warren felt it run warm from the front of his chest to the hairs behind his spine.

"Oh, cool!" cried Teddy and, turning, Warren saw that Russell had stopped the shower. Not turned it off, but stopped the water in its fall, so that when

Teddy stepped aside, transparent rays outlined the spot where she had been. *How beautiful*, Warren thought, looking at the sparkling strands of water. He was not able to do anything like that. They had both been out of their bodies, and Russell had come back doing things like this; Warren had come back the same department head he had always been, no better and perhaps a little bit worse. At least, one grimoire the worse.

Russell waved his hand again and the water splashed through the Teddy-shaped hole. "Guess I'm intact," he said, grinning.

Warren wished he could say the same, but he kept his mouth shut as the demonologists filed into the pentarium and formed their familiar ring around the pentacle. His personal problems would have to wait; and showing weakness to faculty was almost as dangerous as showing it to a demon.

"No general summoning," he announced. "We need to invoke Nezumia and find out what it knows about the demon in my office." Nobody disagreed with this, and within moments Warren had almost lost himself in the familiar syllables of invocation.

Had it been only four months since Warren first saw the demon Nezumia? He found it hard to believe, as he watched the creature's brown hide and three legs solidify in the center of the pentacle. In four months, Nezumia had made itself master and spokesperson for all the demons of Osyth, forming them into a union whether they chose or no. Now it treated the Academy, and the pentarium, as its personal fiefdoms. Even the grue it cast felt familiar.

The demon shrugged its shoulders as if they had grown stiff from disuse and turned a full circle, scanning each of the eleven magicians. "Do you think you can summon me, as if I were a bound demon?" it asked Warren, when its circuit finally brought it around to him. "I have other business than dancing attendance upon you." Its eyes and mouth were tight slits.

"We seek your advice," Warren countered, more politely than he felt. "A demon is passing our wards. It fed on me in my office, and in the hall outside this room."

Nezumia sneered at him. "You lie. No demon feeds here without my leave."

"Yet one was in my office." Nezumia stood silent, its arms folded in disdain. "I don't understand," Warren said in a dangerous, dean-like voice. "Do you expect the perquisites of a supervisory position, while denying any knowledge of what your subordinates are up to?" He didn't know who he was angry with as he said this — Nezumia, himself, the dean or the world; but he did know, suddenly and with relish, that this misery would love company. "If you want Academy employee privileges, you'll have to answer for the other demons supposedly under your control."

Something popped open inside him like the beginning of a new charm, when the first phrases had been said right and magic started to pour out by itself. How long had it been since he had felt that? He listened, curious to hear what would come out of his mouth. "Get used to being summoned. We'll have to get you a beeper," came out. "Unless you have a cell phone?"

This remark startled the demon. It startled Warren. He didn't look at any of the other demonologists.

"You bow to my demands, then?" Nezumia asked. Anybody who didn't know demons would have heard only arrogance in its voice, but Warren recognized uncertainty. "You admit my power?"

"What power?" he mocked. "You obviously can't keep demons out of my office, so how could you interfere with our research? But we do happen to have a faculty position vacant, if you wish to apply and be considered like anybody else." The quality of silence from his faculty changed, but he did not look at any of them. "Two vacancies, actually, but the Academy has only funded one line, so the new hire will teach a load and a half and supervise part-timers to cover the rest. It wouldn't be onerous at all; the only duties would be instructing three sections of Principles of Demonology and an upper-level course in your specialty, coordinating labs and part-timers, and maintaining an actively funded research program supporting two to four graduate students. I assume that would pose no challenge for you. Graduate students are much easier to manage than minor demons. Have you ever written a grant proposal?"

Nezumia looked at him narrow-eyed and flattened its ears, but Warren merely averted his gaze into mid-air, as if reading a heavenly contract suspended above them. "You'd be expected to help with our work in the pentarium, keep office hours, to advise graduate and undergraduate students and to represent the department in interdisciplinary committee assignments. I believe Neil was on the

Student Life and Funded Benefits Committees and Faculty Senate, and helped advise a student group over in Arcane Arts. And of course, he was in the Untenured Faculty Support Group. Do they do much anymore?"

"Um, we have a book club," Isaac Graham ventured, sounding as nervous as might be expected at the prospect of a demon joining his support group. "We hold four in-service lunches a year, and a retreat during winter break. Neil's treasurer."

"Thank you," Warren said. "Now, as for departmental duties, there are of course Department and Division meetings, budgets, writing syllabi, seminar presentations and guest lectures. If you're hoping for tenure, you should get at least four or five publications in the first three years, and as many conference presentations. You'll want to join a few of the most influential professional organizations ... though if you maintain a professional practice, that counts. If you keep your Continuing Education requirements and licenses up to date ... don't feel overwhelmed!" he said, though the demon Nezumia's expression did not look overwhelmed. "It only seems like a lot because you're coming in cold. Most people get up to speed during their graduate programs. Oh, could you drop your résumé off at my office, since apparently demons can get in there? Just a formality, of course, but H.R. has to verify your degrees."

The demon glared at him. "You laugh at me?" it said, its words thin and tight as its mouth. "You will never see another of us in this — playpen! What will you be without us?"

31

"How can you say that?" Warren asked, in mock concern. "I'm offering you as good a deal as any of us have. Did you think we all spent our time reading romance novels? It's even a real management position. You'll get to write ads and interview applicants, and do it all over when they quit a week before classes begin. You'll learn all about how to pretend you have some influence over your subordinates. Frankly, you could improve in that regard. Just claiming to be in control won't cut it, not in the modern academy. You have to come up with something an administrator can act proud of, at the end of the year."

The demon was not the only person regarding him with slitted eyes, after these remarks.

"What, have I left something out?" Warren asked the assembled faculty. "Gosh, I guess I have. You'll get to use the library, and the sports center; and you'll be eligible to buy a reserved parking spot and membership in the Faculty Club. Can the rest of you think of anything? Any other perks?"

"Three months' vacation," Russell said gravely, looking straight at Warren, "if you have sense enough to take it."

Chapter 2
When in Doubt, Obey Your Wife

"That was unusual," Anders Regan *said as the demonologists filed back into the shower room.*

Anders had a masterful grasp of the obvious, thought Russell Cinea. He looked around for Warren, but just caught a glimpse of him going into one of the private shower stalls. Not good. 'Talk with Warren,' Russell put at the top of his mental to-do list, but then Teddy Whin distracted him.

"Would that be your ward or mine on his office?" she asked, shucking her blue gown and stepping into the shower.

Warren slipped out of Russell's mind as if he had never been there. "Yours," he said. "You did all the offices, didn't you?"

"But mine were reassigned," Teddy said, scrubbing her arms and breasts. She always washed herself in the same sequence. Now she bent to run the sponge up and down each leg, and he saw the nape of her neck smooth and vulnerable, at the base of her crisp curls. "I think it's one of yours. We'll have to call up the master list." She straightened up, stepped out of the shower, and shook her curly head like a dog. Teddy dried off with a gigantic bath sheet, which alternately concealed and revealed.

Russell faced into the water and turned its temperature down a few degrees. She was probably right about the wards, he thought, and that was depressing enough to quench any arousal.

He switched off the water, dressed in gloomy silence, and followed Teddy up the stairs back to his office, where he called up the master list of wards on the computer. "Damn. It's mine, all right. Still, it's an old one. I should be able to replace those with no trouble."

The masters for all his wards hung in a special, locked cabinet beside his window, and Russell was not at all reluctant to open it under Teddy's evaluative gaze and let her see how many were inside.

"Holy cats!" she said. "That looks like Will's neck."

"I hope they are better quality," said Russell. While the vampirologist Will Harding wore more wards than anyone else on campus, they were mostly ordered from infomercials, a sign of late-night boredom that also flattered vampires' scorn of magic. It spoke of youth and irreverence, though, and Russell felt the attraction. He had more power than anyone else since his return from being out of his body; why not more youth and vigor? While he would not stoop to Will's nonsense, showing Teddy this cabinet full of wards made him feel good. "This is the one Warren was having trouble with," he said, pulling out a simple gold disc with the Academy's logo etched on it. "One of the old classics."

"How many of those do you have out?"

"Only twenty-four." That was a more than respectable number of wards for one master, and he could see Teddy doing mental arithmetic as she counted the remaining masters in his cabinet. He left its door open for her convenience. "I can re-set it now, if you spot me. What's a nice new charm?"

"Try a skitch," Teddy suggested. "Those are easy to add onto a flat surface."

Russell led the way into his research lab, where he laid the ward master on a specially constructed pad woven of bittersmoke stems. At a word, wisps of smoke rose from the pad and made a dome over the ward, cleaning off any extraneous magic contaminating its surface while Russell drafted the new charm on a paper copy of the ward blank. He would detach the master from the wards it powered and speak these runes onto it while tracing the paper pattern with a special stylus, which Teddy, who was as familiar with his lab as with her own, was now laying on a second bittersmoke pad. When he re-established the link between master and wards the new charm would appear on all of them, a nasty surprise for whatever demon had been getting through the old one.

"How's this look?" Russell asked, holding the draft up for Teddy's review.

"Pretty good. I'd round that off a little there — make it follow the logo more."

Russell made the suggested change. "Ready," he announced. "Will you set up the temp?" He could not suddenly separate a set of wards distributed all across the Academy from their master without providing a temporary backup to power them, a job Teddy could easily handle. She had set up a ward blank while he worked, in fact, and was already unfolding a field charm's silver webbing at the other end of the lab. "You're fast," Russell said admiringly, and she grinned.

"Not as strong as I should be, though," she answered.

"We'll get there," Russell said. It had taken Teddy all of two months to come up with a hypothesis about where his soul had gone while out of his body, and go there herself; he was sure that within the year she would have found out how he'd gained so much power and have as much herself, or more. The thought made him uneasy, and he shook it off. "Ready to tune them?"

When Teddy nodded, Russell went over to the main lab bench . He had inlaid a gold pentacle on the surface, with a continuous groove running along its lines; now he set a ring-stand in the pentacle and hung his original ward on it before he retrieved a vial of his blood from the refrigerator and carefully used a pipette to place it into the groove. It was the work of a moment to set the pentacle and link it to the open center of Teddy's field charm.

She frowned at her ward blank, holding it near the field charm, and suddenly it rose out of her hands, hovering between the silver strands. "I've got it!" she said, her voice a bit strained as she took over the twenty-four wards Russell had just cut off from his power.

He hurried to let down the pentacle and make the needed alterations in his own ward. It took almost ten minutes, but felt longer. When he finally hung his ward back in the pentacle and re-linked it to its copies, Teddy gave a whoosh of relief.

"That was a workout!" she said, shaking herself. "If I'd known that was coming, I'd have had breakfast."

"You knew we were invoking."

"Oh, I can do that on coffee."

36

"Go down to the lounge and have a sticky bun. I'd buy, but I'm giving Rho a lift to the airport. Tell you what — grab Warren, and let him know his problems are solved. His warding problems, at least. Make him buy you breakfast."

"You were right, he needs a vacation," said Teddy, as she preceded Russell into the hall. Warren's office was shut tight, though. "Maybe he's taking one."

***

For the third time that morning Warren had done something impulsive and unprecedented. He had left the Academy in the middle of the workday, without even stopping to file an incident report about the wards or enter the unhappy result of the morning's invocation into the International Demonological Society's database.

He walked across the soggy field that separated the Magic Building from the Academy quad and waited for the light at North Gate; once through the gate and into Osyth proper, he was soon able to catch a bus to the South end of the city center. Here he was among modern castles of commerce, as unlike the mediaeval castles of the Academy as the suited-and-tied businessmen among them were unlike Warren in his rumpled raincoat. His goal was the tallest and most strict-looking of the gray buildings, the Salvation Insurance Corporation headquarters. Within this building Warren's wife, Lilian Oldham, spent her days. He found her in a cubicle on the eighteenth floor, looking intently at a computer screen. A pile of bones and paper strips on her mouse pad showed that Lilian had just finished evaluating someone's insurance application; when she saw Warren she hit 'save' with a surprised expression and got up to greet him.

"Warren! What are you doing down here?"

"I'm having a bad day," said Warren. He took off his raincoat and hung it over the cubicle wall, for lack of anyplace else to put it.

"What — hold on. Digby, can I have the chair?" Lilian brought a slightly larger chair, with arms, back from the next cubicle. She waved Warren to take a seat in it and while he settled himself she walked around the cubicle, sliding plastic covers off the privacy sigils embossed on each panel. Warren saw similar markings burned into the chair's arms. "Now," Lilian said in a businesslike manner, "what's going on?"

"I had the year-end report to fill in."

"Oh."

"Um. Well. I did it before invocation. Thought I'd get it over with. Except a demon got in and — well — let's say it wasn't my best work."

"A demon in your office?"

"I don't think it was a big one," Warren said, taken aback. If he'd thought this through, he realized, he would not have given Lilian that detail. She was looking at him with an expression disconcertingly like Nezumia's.

"So what did you do then?"

"I invoked Nezumia and asked it what kind of union boss couldn't keep its members out of my hair. I –uh— said it should apply for Neil's position, if it really wanted to be an Academy employee."

"No! Did it accept?"

"I don't think it has a résumé, or the degrees listed in the ad," Warren said. "Anyway, we've already made someone an offer. Nezumia didn't know that, though."

Lilian came over, sat down on his lap, and put her arms round his neck. They might have been teenagers again, Warren thought as he embraced her; he kissed her as he imagined a teenager would have done. He was a little breathless when they finished.

"What on earth's come over you?" she asked, concern and admiration mingled in her voice.

"I'm fed up," said Warren.

"Well, thank goodness," said Lilian. "It's about time!" This was not what Warren had expected, but so precisely what he had wished for that his nose and eyes tingled with almost-tears of gratitude. "That department takes you for granted," she went on, "and they have for years. When they hauled you out of hospital to call up Nezumia — that was the last straw. Who else would be expected to get right back to work after losing his soul?"

"Well, Russell did too," Warren said, trying to be fair.

"Russell took himself on a vacation while he was out of his body," Lilian said tartly. "While you worried about everyone else, he made up a tropical island for himself."

That was true. Russell, Warren thought, had a lot of sense. "Maybe I should have done that," he said.

"Vacation without me? Nonsense," Lilian told him. "You'll have your vacation now. We'll take it together. Right after graduation."

Warren's first reflex was to come up with reasons that made this impossible. But, he reminded himself, he was fed up with the department; that erased most of his counterarguments. "How could we arrange something that fast?" was what remained.

"Through the timeshare pool," Lilian answered promptly. "Folks put their unused timeshares up on the web." This wasn't as improbable as it seemed, when Warren considered the tens of thousands of people Salvation Insurance employed around the globe. "If that doesn't work, we'll check other web sites. There's always a room going begging someplace, and a couple unsold seats on some plane at two in the morning. Just leave it to me. We'll leave day after tomorrow, and stay away until I say so."

Warren took his wife out to an early lunch and got back to the Academy by 12:10. By 12:15 he was on the phone with the same wife, trying to undo what had been decided at lunch.

"I'm sorry — I didn't expect anything like this."

"No."

"It's an emergency. We'll have to re-open the search."

"No."

"But, darling –"

"No."

40

If she had said 'you promised,' or 'you need this,' or 'but I've made the reservations!' Warren would have had hope. But all she said was 'No.'

And the truth was, he felt grateful to her.

***

Though Hiram Rho, the junior magician who had lost his powers in escaping from Warren's grimoire, had the best reason to be fed up of anyone in the department, he lacked the talent. Rho had spent years in a state of chronic fed-up-ness, greeting every problem with rage and blame, but in February he had emerged from Warren's grimoire without this ability. His anger had gone, along with his magic and his demon; absent the usual internal chatter of grousing and hostility, Rho felt oddly blank as he taped up the last of his boxes and looked around the tower room he'd lived in for the past four months.

With his clutter cleaned away, Rho might have gone backwards in time to the day he had moved in here. *If I unpacked, would everything else go back to last year?* he thought, with a sparkle of hope. He pretended for just a moment that, if he redeployed his belongings around the room and re-opened his windows, the gift would come back to him. The cooing of pigeons on the rooftops would make itself into words he could understand. He would hear what birds were singing and grasshoppers chirping, and the words to the busy song of bees ... but of course, that was nonsense. You never got a chance to redo things.

Rho would have to live with the winter's foolishness and its consequences. He'd be lucky if he managed to get any of his magic back during the summer and his fall semester's leave, and even that was more of a chance than the Royal Academy owed him. Various administrators had made that extremely clear. Rho shivered when he thought about the Dean of Natural Magic, who had taken a particularly stern line and even shown Rho the curses he was authorized to call down upon faculty who plotted with demons to steal the department chair's soul … Rho tried to put a positive spin on it by telling himself the Dean would have given him the same amount of support, had he been the employee in peril, but his sarcastic half told him that department chairs were far harder to replace than junior faculty.

"At least," he told himself with a little bluster, "they could hardly make me worse off than I am." And in a way this was true; not that Rho's fortunes couldn't fall, for he still had a job to lose, but that they could hardly fall to any lower point than they had been. If Rho had to live on the streets of Kasidora again, he knew how; if they fed him to a demon, he knew how that worked as well. He scowled at the world in general and stacked the boxes in a corner, and then there was nothing for him to do except wait for his ride to the airport. He sat down at the empty table and looked out over the rain-drenched Academy. He had two hours to wait; he could have gone to one of the Academy's cafeterias, or even over to Durrell's restaurant, for a good breakfast, but out of sheer inertia he stayed perched on his straight chair, eating the dregs of a box of crackers he should have thrown out a month ago.

He went over the semester endlessly in his mind, looking for a way to make it sound better when he told his family, whom he had not seen since running away from home at fourteen. There was not really any way to make picking up a demon by mistake at a conference sound less than stupid. Nor letting the demon steal a borrowed grimoire — though that made Warren sound stupid, too, for having loaned it out in the first place. Would it be better for his family to think he was a screw-up, or that all academics were screw-ups? Either way, Rho was not going to get any admiration from the solid farming stock in his hometown. The only thing in the whole story that he could be proud of was that when the demon had tried to trap Warren's soul in the grimoire, Rho had leapt in instead. If he had been a cheerful sort he would have inflated that and made much of his courage and self-sacrifice. But Rho was not a cheerful sort, even on sunny days, and it had been raining for a month. And he had lost his magic. Cheerfulness was not an option, he thought, glaring out at the rain clouds. As if they heard him, they sent down a cheeky bolt of lightning into the canyon between Osyth and the next plateau over, and thunder grumbled around his tower. Someone knocked at the door, and Rho jumped.

"Are you ready?" Russell Cinea said, looking around the room in ill-concealed dismay. "Sorry I'm late; I had to re-tune some wards." His white hair shone as if there were no such thing as a gray day. His raincoat was perfect, his tie old-school, and

43

his shoes were shiny; not a man to carry boxes, Rho thought, realizing both that he himself was scruffy and crumb-covered, and that he should have spent the last hour moving his boxes downstairs. Screw-up!

"No, don't bother," said Russell as Rho threw his poncho over his arm and stooped for the first box. "Allow me — if you don't mind." It took only a wave of his hand for the boxes to lift a little off the floor and begin floating down the staircase. Russell followed them without looking back, a master of tact. Rho couldn't fault his manners, though he dearly wished to; he crumbled the last crackers onto his windowsill, pretending the pigeons might get some good out of them, but he knew they would be soaked into glue and still be there, graying lumps, when he came back. If he came back.

***

Russell felt much dampened as he headed back to his office after dropping Rho at the airport. It was the boy's own fault, he kept telling himself. Senior magicians could not be held responsible for what new hires did at conferences in other continents. Nobody could have expected Russell to mentor somebody when he had lost his own soul. In fact, Russell had not been in charge. If either of them were to blame, it was Warren … thoughts like this consumed him for most of the drive back to the Academy and the entire walk back to his office. He dilly-dallied, hanging up his coat and checking his hair in the mirror behind the door, but that only put off the inevitable moment when he sat down behind his desk and felt the chill drive into him. Would summer never come? Russell thought, and swiveled to look out the tiny arrow-slit window through which long-past inhabitants of this room had defended themselves from the hostile outside world. The hostile outside world looked back at him and sneered; at least, it dripped a single mocking drop of water down the vertical shaft of the cross-shaped window.

Russell shut his eyes in exasperation, and called up the memory of sunlight until it filled his office. When he opened his eyes, the light was there. It wasn't clear where it came from, since the outside world remained as gloomy as before, but when he turned away from the window shafts of sunlight came over his shoulder in several directions, as if a dozen suns were jostling to spy in and get a look at the back of Russell's head. The light hit the crystal wards in his window and sent a score of rainbows glinting through the office. Russell was pleased. *Take that!* he thought to the outside world, and leaned back with his arms crossed over his chest. He still had it. More of it than anybody else in the department, in fact.

Not six months ago, Russell had been in decline. His powers had been fading, though the other demonologists had been tactful about it — loathsome pity! Disgusting respect for elders! He shuddered at the memory. Being thrown out of his body by a demon had been a welcome adventure for the failed magician he had been then, a far better way to go than being eased out of his position to make room for some young stud in his prime. So, unlike Warren's soul, which had hovered around Osyth trying to find out where it was and influence the doings of those left behind, Russell's soul had reveled in its freedom. He didn't even need to shut his eyes to recall the beauty he had created for himself. The crystal seas, the leaping fishes and coral strands ... and hadn't he been right to do so? For Warren had come back into his body as no more than the worried administrator he had thought himself, while Russell had come back the maker of worlds.

A tap at the door recalled him from these musings. Warren was hovering in the doorway.

"Buck up, man!" Russell said expansively. "We thought you'd already left on vacation."

Warren looked a little taken aback. "I have an e-mail from Crayberg, turning down our offer."

"Oh, damn," said Russell. "Why?"

"Social Magic couldn't come up with anything for his wife."

"Did you e-mail Locullan?"

"I left a message, but you know how late it is to be hiring ... the bottom line is, we'll probably have to start another search and I won't be here. I'd like you to step in."

"You won't be here? Why not?"

"Vacation," Warren said sourly. "Lilian's arranging it. By the way, could you give us a lift to the airport Sunday morning? We're taking the red-eye."

"Sure, no problem," said Russell.

"So, will you take over the new search?"

"Why not Anders, or Patsy?"

"The Dean hates them," said Warren. "I might as well ask Linus. You're the best one if we want any chance of getting a second full-time line to replace Rho."

"I thought that was a 'no' already," said Russell.

"It was, but if we have to re-open the search we might as well re-open the question. The Dean didn't say no to you, and you manage him better than I do."

Russell pondered this. On the one hand he was being manipulated with flattery, and for Warren to manipulate him was a role reversal not to be encouraged. On the other hand, everything Warren said was true.

"How far do you want me to take it?" he asked. "Suppose we find a local candidate — do you want a say in the decision, or can we hire before you get back?"

"Oh, hire," said Warren. "I'm just one vote. I can't believe we'll get lucky that fast, though."

"All right," Russell said, "I'll take care of it. You just go off and forget about us."

Chapter 3
Not University-related

Everyone in the factory looked at Ric when they thought he wasn't watching. Patrolmen were worst at it — prone to use gaze as a dominance display, they didn't know how to look at a Detective Inspector they had no issues with — but even the other inspectors were too obvious, over-casual and full of small talk when they would normally have been pumping him about the morning's events. They kept asking him pointless questions like whether he wanted tea. Ric turned this down four times before he realized that only a cup in front of him would ward off his well-wishers, but then they just switched to inquiries about Derek, to which Ric had no answer. He was glad when the chief pulled him.

"Hospital called," she said, as soon as the office door had closed. "The girl's dead. Lord Stimms is stable, and so's Derek. They're saying spellshock — you know what that means."

Ric did. It was like idiopathic or cryptogenic, or any of the other words sorcerers used for a diagnosis of 'haven't got a clue.'"The transport's recovering well. You kept a lot of balls in the air out there."

"Huh," said Ric. "We didn't get the slag."

"The demon saved us all a lot of grief. Check these." She swiveled her monitor.

"That's him!" Ric said, putting his finger on the tall man's picture. "What database is this?"

"University of Selanto's online catalog."

"Duh!" Where else should they have looked?

"Magister Ian Locullan, lecturer in Demonology. The Chancellor's already been on the phone. I'll be talking to the press in fifteen." She looked at Ric, and it was just like being in the outer room. "Porter's SIO on this."

"I'm fine with it."

"I know you are. I'm giving it to Porter."

"You can't keep me off every case with demons in it," said Ric.

"You're still shaking. After two hours."

"I have to get back in the ring. It won't get better for my dodging it."

"Get well first. Nobody expects you to get over being possessed this fast. Guard policy says six months before they even test you." She picked a slip off the desk. "You're in at the hospital at four. Full work-up."

"I don't need it," said Ric, but before the third word he remembered Derek and Lord Stimms were at the hospital, probably in the same demon unit this slip directed him to. His attitude cut off just like that.

Porter came over as soon as Ric had gotten back to his paperwork and his cold tea. "You all right?"

"Yeah," Ric said, without looking up. He didn't have anything against Porter. He had something against not being a hundred percent. The chief had been right, aftershocks were still oozing around inside him; cold tendrils up his spine, down his limbs, swirling around in his belly as if they nested

49

there. But if he were Senior Investigating Officer, he'd be too busy to notice them. How was a man supposed to get well if he had nothing to do but think about himself? "You'll want these," he said, saving the files and opening an email to attach them to.

"Yeah," said Porter.

Ric waited for Porter to move away so he could search the records on Lord Stimms unobserved, but the man hung around as if he needed to make Ric feel better about being taken off the case.

"University slag," he said.

"Yeah."

"We're running an NUR pool," said Porter. "What's your guess?"

Ric fished out his wallet. "Anybody have twelve seconds?"

"It's yours." Porter had barely stowed the banknote when somebody gave a shout and they turned up the television.

The University of Selanto chancellor had unnaturally thick hair that stood up in a pepper-and-salt quiff from his broad forehead. Everything about him was wide, down to the lapels on his gray suit. Even his voice was wide, dwarfing the reporter's smooth baritone. "Magister Locullan was a non-tenured faculty member," he said. "He was finishing his appointment here next week. I cannot emphasize enough that this event was –"

"NOT   UNIVERSITY-RELATED!"   the detectives yelled in concert as Goberman, standing next to the set, clicked his stopwatch.

"Twelve seconds," he announced. "Who's the lucky dog?"

"That's me," Ric announced, pulling out his wallet and taking a glance at his watch. "Pay up. I'm off."

Nobody talked about where he would be off to, at three in the afternoon and without a case to his name. But it was the loudest quiet Ric had ever heard.

Once upon a time, *University of Selanto Hospital* had been in a good neighborhood. That would have been in the days when upper-class ladies had their servants carry in baskets of food for the indigent and someone spread straw along the street every morning to muffle the sound of horse drawn carriages. Nowadays, a guy with a steady job spreading straw would be king in that neighborhood... Ric amended that: a guy with a steady job was reckoned a mug in that neighborhood. The lads he saw lounging outside the rent-to-own furniture place and the corner stores knew steady jobs were just a ploy to keep you out of the man's hair while he screwed you over. Ric wasn't sure he disagreed; either way, he and the lads acknowledged each other with noncommittal gazes as he drove past. He knew what they were, they knew what he was. And the lads disappeared the minute he turned into the lot for appointments. Nobody could get through this lot's warding without a slip like the one in his pocket. Ric locked his car out of habit rather than necessity.

He had to pass through three more levels of warding before he reached the demon wing, and it felt like diving into darker and darker water, colder and colder. He shivered in the final waiting room. It wasn't just cold or just *grue*. It was the dangerousness of life. The demon had been in him for fewer than five minutes, and four months later he was still fighting it.

It had happened too fast for Ric to understand at the time. He had read the reports, though, and knew that if it had been a true possessor he'd probably be dead now. Dead with his own soul, if he were lucky; dead and his soul inside the demon, if it had killed him before an exorcist could get it out. The demon in Ric hadn't been so inclined, though. It had only jumped in to dodge a charm cast at it by one of the police magicians. It had only told Ric what to do until he had walked it out of the room to freedom, and had left him before the rest of them realized the *grue* had gone out with him. They had found him screaming on the sidewalk...

"Fuck," he said under his breath at the memory and rubbed his hands over his face. The other people in the waiting room looked at him cautiously, as if his image was sharp enough to cut their eyes.

"Inspector Massey? Sorcerer Landis will see you now."

Landis' office was oppressively cheerful, with the landscape-photo wallpaper that had been the height of fashion thirty years ago; a bucolic scene of hills, ponds, and happy sheep. Landis herself was a fluffy blonde who probably hadn't been born when the paper went up. "How's my favorite patient?" she asked, as if he were four.

"If you're going to call me that, you have to give me a lolly," said Ric. She opened a bottom drawer, and he groaned; but all she brought out was a scanning pad and a black leather case he was familiar with.

"How've you been doing?" she asked, more businesslike as she plugged the pad into a port on the front of her computer. "You know the drill."

Ric did, and put his fingers into the indentations on the pad. Landis swiveled the monitor so he could watch colors swirl on the screen, finally settling into a dark blue. Landis hit a key and called up a second window, filled with a color between turquoise and teal — his aura, before the demon. Numbers whirred at the bottom of this screen, and a set of scatter plots opened. "Your aura's recovering," said Landis, pointing to a line across the first graph. "Most components are near-normal — you just have some relict shadows."

"It looks a lot darker."

"Yes, but that's not as significant as you'd think. It's the wavelengths we can't see that matter most. How are your glyphs holding up?"

"The ones I can see are fine." This was the part where he had to undress. Ric did it in as matter-of-fact a manner as he could, as if women saw him naked every day.

Landis checked the glyphs written on his body — back and chest, neck, wrists, and just above his privates. "They're a little faded, but I don't think they need to be re-written," she said. "We'll boost them after I've finished your exam. Where are you getting the most aftershocks?" Ric had anticipated this question. He'd drawn them in on a diagram back at the station. She looked it over for a minute before she pulled an adhesive patch out of the black

53

case and stuck it on the back of his neck. "Turn your head right. Fine. — Left."

One by one, they went through the spots where he felt echoes of the demon.

At least Landis wasn't the sort to say 'Hm' and make cryptic notes. "You need to put on weight," she said, "and I don't like this right arm. You're not getting the mobility back as fast as you should."

That was the arm he had fought hardest to control, when the demon wanted it to turn the door handle and sign him out. He'd torn something apart inside his own nerves — not just in the arm, but all the way up into the brain, into the soul — *Fuck*, he thought, and made a fist.

"You're doing a lot better according to the dreamcatcher," Landis went on, calling up another screen. This held records from the dreamcatcher installed above Ric's bed. Not even his dreams were private, these days.

"When can I do without it?"

"You can't. Dreamcatcher's mandatory until those shadows on your aura are gone. Have you had brownouts?"

"Yeah. Last half-hour before I sleep is gone the next morning." That was what Ric hated most about the dreamcatcher — the memory loss. The longer he used it, the worse it would get.

"How are you compensating?"

"Steno pad. And watch sitcoms."

Landis laughed. "That's a good idea! You'll never get bored if you can't remember them."

"Ya think? I need to get off that thing."

"Well, we'll see." She made more notes. "Waking flashbacks?"

54

"Yeah," Ric muttered.

"How often?"

"Just today. The damn thing almost touched me! Anybody'd have flashbacks."

"That's true. Still, I want to put you back on the mobile for a few weeks. Unless you'd rather have it in a glyph?"

"There's no room for another glyph!"

She snorted. "There's always your butt."

"I'll take the mobile," Ric said. If she drew a dreamcatcher on him, he'd never be able to take it off. "Can I dress now?"

"Let me do your glyphs first. Lie down a minute." Landis didn't have to set a pentacle or shielding charm around her treatment table. They were built into the floor, and Ric felt the lines slide across his body as he got onto the table.

He shut his eyes. He would have hung before admitting it, but this was the only place he felt safe shutting his eyes. When Landis draped a blanket over him and spoke the charm that reawakened the glyphs, he felt as warmed and coddled as if he had been wrapped up in fleece. *Like a baby*, he thought. *Should have let her give me that lolly.*

"They were pretty low," Landis' voice said from far away yet very near. "Let's give them half an hour."

Half an hour! Ric thought, in dismay and relief. He couldn't pretend this didn't matter for half an hour.

"My partner's over here," he said. "Came in with Lord Stimms."

"Yes, I saw them. Exorcism recovery room."

"Will I be able to look in on him?"

"Not likely," said Landis. "You know how exorcists are. Sleep for a week after something like this morning. I don't see any of us disturbing Lord Stimms, unless the monitor goes off."

"I'd expect him to have a private recovery suite."

"I'm sure he does in the palace. He'll probably go there as soon as he wakes up."

Ric gave up with a sigh. "Damned if I know how he does it. He touched a possessed girl this morning, and the demon didn't even try to take him."

"He would have made it believe it couldn't. That's their talent. But it's like anything else; you have to learn to use it. Their talent's only as good as their focus and imagination."

"Could we learn any of that in the force?"

"Not the level an exorcist does, but all of us can learn a little of it — the half where we take our own beliefs more seriously. That's what all the truth-focused disciplines are about."

"But would that have kept the demon from using me?"

"Probably not. Demons take over adepts as easily as they do other people. If they have a choice, though, they don't choose adepts. There's less fun in it for them — and adepts suffer less damage afterwards."

"Hm," Ric said. The warmth around him had soaked into his joints. He felt limber and fit. "Do you practice?"

"I used to," Landis said, and leaned back from her desk. "Once you reach a certain point, it starts to eat its own tail. You can't make your own beliefs a god. Some point, you have to be willing to compromise. There's a reason most adepts are unemployable; no code fits them. A true adept wouldn't be a sworn officer, or take the sorcerer's oath. Some point, you have to decide whether what you believe is likely enough to be true to make it worth going on your own and being a nuisance to the rest of the world... I figured it wasn't."

"Wow. That's a little harsh."

"Not as harsh as saying what everybody else believes is wrong." She swiveled back to her computer. "With alchemists and exorcists, anything they believe really comes true. With adepts it's not like that, no matter how well they learn to believe in it. That's a big difference. We're in service professions," she said, and Ric heard the words as if they came through a thick, drowsy layer of sunlight. "Doing something that makes us unfit for service, just on the chance we'll avoid getting hurt — that doesn't sit well with me. How about you?"

"Ask me on a bad day," he said, closing his eyes.

Her laugh was the last thing he heard.

Chapter 4
Home

The six-hour flight from Osyth to Selanto would have been easier to endure without clouds. Rho could have looked down on the mountains, plains, and farmland of one continent, watched the sunlight sparkle on an ocean and the edges of three country-sized islands, and counted the fingers of stone reaching between gigantic fjords that made up the eastern edge of the Selanto plate. He might have seen leviathans, krakens, or other water monsters. Instead, there had been nothing to see but cloud, nothing to read but the in-flight magazine, and somebody had done the crossword puzzle. He had had nothing to think about except Osyth and the failures behind him, home and the failures in front of him, and what his father would say when they saw each other for the first time in eleven years.

When he dozed, he woke up with a start, his father's furious face in his mind and enraged shouts ringing in his ears. He was too nervous to eat the airplane food, and picked his cuticles into a bloody mess while his seat-mate cast him worried glances.

At last he fell into an uneasy sleep and dreamed that it was all over — the reproaches, the fighting. He had apologized, as if it weren't any effort at all! His family had forgiven him. The guilt had turned into relief ... when the Selanto landing announcement woke him to a world in which this all still lay ahead he was sick with disappointment, and viewed everything in the airport through a haze of bitter misery.

Not even a night in one of Selanto's two-star hotels improved his mood, and he switched the television on with no hope of anything cheering. He was right. The Saturday morning news was the same it had been last night, the same Chief Guard being interviewed about the same junior faculty member in demonology who had fed his own daughter to a demon in a bid for tenure. Rho switched away from three versions of it, feeling sicker each time. *At least I never did that*, he thought as he clicked the set off. *Only because you don't have a daughter*, said the cynical part of him, and he shivered at the truth of it. He had not been in control of what his demon did, that was for sure; lucky he hadn't had anything more precious than pigeons for it to tear apart.

He pulled smoke-scented drapes away from the window and looked out onto a dull, cloudy Saturday, Selanto's sky and buildings the same color in diffused light. Swifts raced through the street below in gangs, shrieking, "Hey, c'mon! What's your problem? Get a move on!"

Rho gasped. He had heard them! While he was still looking frantically for the window latch the cry came again, and looking down he saw three boys on skateboards, whizzing down the sidewalk. "I toldja to hurry up!" one of them yelled. "Leadboots!"

Rho stood a moment at the window, feeling as if he were made of solid disappointment, before launching himself into action. "To hell with it," he said, hoping the words would bring back his lost anger, but they didn't; all he could do was distract himself with movement, packing in frantic haste as if he actually wanted to get to where he was going next.

Rho had seen *renting a car* as a declaration of independence when he first thought of it. To rent a car in Selanto and drive to his family's farm north of the Kasidora Range, instead of flying into Kasidora and having someone pick him up at the airport, would, he felt, set the right tone. It would demonstrate that he was an adult now. An educated, well-employed magician and not the fourteen-year-old who had run away from home eleven years ago. Only a competent adult could cope with Selanto traffic, Rho felt. And even before he left the Selanto central carport — as he made his third circuit of the surrounding blocks, having failed for the third time to leave — he found this opinion confirmed.

He had, in fact, only driven twice since getting his license four years ago. In Osyth, he had lived on campus and only been in a car a half-dozen times; now, as he inched along at between five and eight kilometers per hour, reminding himself to keep to the left, decisions zipped up too fast for him to consider them. A road! Was it the right one — well, it was gone, even before Rho could formulate the question over the honking from behind him. He didn't remember Selanto as being so noisy. Shaking, he pulled off to the side of the road and tried to figure out where he was from the map. It was a large-scale map, in primary colors, and looked as if it had been designed for three-year-olds, yet Rho could not make head or tail of it. He puzzled in vain until an official rapping on the window made him jump.

"You'll have to move along," said the guard, bending over to look in at Rho. He was a beefy man, twice Rho's bulk, with an official-looking ward hung around his neck and a large revolver at his hip. "No waiting allowed this close to the capitol building."

"I don't want to wait here," Rho said, trying not to whine. "I've been trying to find my way out for half an hour. Can you show me where I am on this map?"

The guard looked at the map for a minute and shook his head. "You're not on it at all," he said. "You should have turned left here, and gotten out onto Highway 98. You must have turned right instead, and come back to city center."

"What should I do now?"

"You're on the right road, you've just gone the wrong direction. Pull into that parking lot over there and turn around, and go back along this road straight. It ends at the highway. Which way are you going?"

"To Kasidora."

"Really?" The guard gave Rho a look of concern and shook his head, but before Rho could decide whether this was more comforting or insulting he had bent back over the map. "Then you want to turn right on Sarver Road, here, and join 98 after it's gone over the city. Have you done much driving in the mountains?" Rho shook his head. "The best thing for you is just to get in second gear and stay there," said the guard. "Except if it starts running away from you on the downhill, gear down

61

into first. When you get onto flat land, then you can use drive. And whenever you see a turnout, take it and let people pass. They drive like madmen on that road. They'll put it right up your pipe if you let them."

Rho wished he could have gotten this advice without the graphic terminology, but he thanked the guard and began to inch into the endless stream of traffic. The honking began again, reaching a crescendo as he got too far out to be cut off.

Sarver road skirted the Southern edge of Selanto and then joined Route 98 as it headed into farming land, along the edge of a wide valley across which Rho could just see the Kasidora Mountains that lay between him and home. He was on the wrong side of the river, but damned if he'd head back into Selanto and search for a northern route — there have to be bridges, he told himself, and drove on. The road twisted north and east, south and west, through bluffs and foothills until Rho could hardly remember which way he had meant to go. For the first time in months he forgot that he should have been able to sense the ley-line beside him, that he should have heard words in the birdsong outside the car windows.

Four hours into his drive he reached a narrow spot in the valley, where the road finally crossed it on a tremendous bridge and started up the Kasidora Pass. Halfway through the pass, something roared up beside him. He saw big eyes and noses as its rear end flashed by, heard a doleful bawling from cattle crowded together on their way to slaughter. Rho cut his engine and let them get well ahead, sitting with his eyes shut. *If I could still hear animals*, he thought, *that would have run me off the road. If I could still have gotten angry, the carport would have driven me mad. If I could still do magic, I would have killed someone by now...* when he started the car again he drove gingerly, and took three times as long to get through the mountains as he had planned. When he pulled into his family's farmyard, it was empty under a late afternoon sun.

He stopped the engine and sat; his heart pounding. Then he cautiously rolled the window down, as if something outside was waiting to get him, but all that came in was incomprehensible bird song and a smell of manure. Rho sniffed, identifying horse, goat, and chicken. He looked for the farm he had run away from; he looked for the one he had lived on, before he had run away, and disappointment ran down inside him as he couldn't find it. The house was still the same shape, but it had white siding now. The barn had been painted, as well, and the old stone cowshed was gone. The pond he had played in was filled in, and though the woods' edge was still there he couldn't see any of the individual trees he remembered. This was just another farm.

As he sat there, a car pulled in behind him and a stout woman got out. She picked her way up to Rho's window, her expression a combination of officiousness and solicitude.

"Pull back into the field," she said, bending down. "They'll all be back in a few minutes —" she stopped. Rho looked at her as hard as he could; trying to peel the years off.

"Gretyl?" he said, hesitating.

"Oh, my God," the woman said. "Robin?"

Rho got out of the car, slowly. She was still taller than he was. She was sleek and stout, prosperous, and grown up. Was she going to hug him? "My God," she said again, and seemed to recollect herself. "Look at you, all grown up — didn't you know where the funeral was?"

"What? Whose funeral?" Shock thudded into his chest.

"Daddy's," she said.

Relief drove the shock away.

"Oh, here they come," said Gretyl. Rho looked past her to see a procession of cars coming down the dirt road. They came too slowly to stir up the dust. Orange flags waved from their radio antennas. "You really do need to move your car," Gretyl said, her voice unsure, but the first car had already pulled in and stopped.

An old woman in a black dress stepped out of the passenger side, and Rho stopped hearing Gretyl's voice. He was strangely conscious of the air between them as the old woman came closer. It blew sideways, like a river. How had she gotten so old, without changing at all? She was close now, yet the river of air still flowed and they stood on its two banks, unable to cross over.

"Robin," the old woman said, and reached out her two hands. When had she started carrying an old-lady purse? When had she gotten a wristwatch? When had her skin spotted with age and her hair turned gray? He could feel the bones in her hands. She was never getting young again — how dare she do this!

"Mama," he said, but he wanted to cry out to her. *Don't change!* he wanted to cry. *Go back!*

64

***

"Robin's taking care of me," said Mama Simone.

Of course, they all objected. Why? None of them wanted to do it. Gretyl and Willett had their own families, and Lilis had her house and cat to look after. Any fool could see that Robin was staying here, in his old room, and doing his old chores.

"I should have known," Willett said sourly. His black hair lay flat to his head, as if he had greased it down with bile. "Just as if nothing happened."

"No, as if his father just died. What do you want?" she challenged. "Do you want me to bury my husband and turn away my youngest son, all in the same day? Should I just get it all over with at once? I could do that, if you like."

Willett knew when to back down. "That's not what I meant," he protested.

"What did you mean, then?"

"You haven't even asked him where he was."

"Not in front of every gossip in town, no." Mama Simone smoothed down her print apron over her black dress and crossed her stockinged and dress-shoed feet. She had done quite enough for the gossips in town. "We've fed them and let them drip all over us. Now tell me how to get them out of here."

"You don't have to stay downstairs, Mama," said Gretyl, setting a tray of dirty dishes down on the kitchen table. "You go up and lie down. We'll see to everything."

"Well, I will then," said Mama Simone. "I'll make up Robin's room for him."

She heard Willett take a breath behind her as she headed up the back stairs, and Gretyl rounding on him. "I feel the same way," Gretyl said, "but it's the only good thing that's happened to her all spring, and we're not picking it apart today. Have a little consideration, for goodness' sake! Now get out there and talk to Aunt Ada."

Robin's old sheets weren't in the airing-cupboard, so Mama Simone went up into the attic, to the boxes she had put there ten years ago and never looked at since. Now, as she pawed through books and clothes to find the sheets with birds on them, nothing downstairs seemed real. That skinny man with shadows under his eyes couldn't be her little Robin, could he? But he was. When he had his back to her, he was Robin with his straw-dry hair and his two cowlicks. When he ate Cousin Mirelda's marmalade cake in big bites, he was Robin at the holiday dinner table. And he was just as bad at polite conversation as Robin had always been; he didn't seem to have anything to talk about, today, except how bad the Selanto car rental map was. She found the sheets and pulled them out, smelling of mouse and attic. They would have to go into the wash before she could use them. Would he still be here when they came out?

***

Rho was wondering the same thing, minus the sheets. He'd braced himself for paternal furor and sibling resentment, but now he was faced with not

66

only his father's death, which was the kind of relief he knew would turn into guilt later, but a swarm of half-forgotten great-aunts and second cousins, to all of whom his escape from the family seemed the most recent of events. Many of them seemed to think he was still a teen, and had only run away last season. And everybody wanted to know if he had made it up with his father, why he hadn't visited the deathbed, why he had missed the funeral — this was the only question he could answer, thanks to the Selanto map — and whether he was going to stay.

Trapped in a whirlwind of questions, Rho was hard-pressed to do anything more complicated than remember his own name. He sought shelter in the kitchen, but was clucked at by Gretyl; he finally escaped to the pantry, where he squeezed in behind the half-open door and gave a great sigh of relief.

"So, life on your own's not all it's cracked up to be, hey, boy?"

Rho jumped. A balding man, no taller than Rho himself had also taken up residence in the pantry, though he didn't seem to be hiding from anything. He sat on top of the pie-safe, dangling his feet and eating pickled cauliflower straight out of the jar. "Not much o' this in the city," he said, holding it out to Rho.

Rho allowed as how the city was indeed lacking in pickled cauliflower.

"So you've made good and come back to show us?"

"Not especially."

"Degrees? Jobs?"

67

Rho had to admit he had his Magister's degree and a job at the Royal Academy in Osyth.

The bald man whistled. "Not bad for a little spit of a thing," he said. "Always said you'd be the brightest of 'em all."

Rho wished he knew this man's name.

"So, what you study?"

"Incubi in ducks," Rho said. "Animal husbandry."

"Lot o' that goin' round. You come back for the pork operation, then?"

"I hadn't heard about a pork operation."

"Heard! Y'oughta smelt it, if you came in from the east." The man bit into a hunk of pickled cauliflower as if to fumigate his sinuses. "Nasty business, say I. Keepin' clever bits like those in sheds day and night. But who listens to me?" He sniffed, apparently more from vinegar than sentiment. "Thought you'd be settin' that right, when I saw you were back. Don't see how a nervy one like you could stay here otherwise."

Rho almost jumped as he finally recognized the man. It was the neighbor whose pigeons he had watched, as a child; their lullabies had been the first animal words Rho had ever heard, and their mourning the squabs this man had eaten the second.

"I don't have a good track record of influencing people," he said dryly.

"What d'you learn at University, then?"

"How to influence demons," Rho answered.

The man didn't seem disturbed by this, but nodded without looking up from the jar. "Easier to get along with, are they," he said, but it didn't sound like a question.

Rho reached out for more pickled cauliflower instead of answering, and they said no more.

Chapter 5
Graduation

The Royal Academy's faculty made a brave showing in their academic regalia, even to a man who was fed up with them. Warren liked his own garb, a fur-collared velvet robe in deep purple, which lived every other day of the year in the pentarium locker room and smelled of bittersmoke. It had fallen off its hanger somehow, but Russell had been able to get the creases out as he adjusted it. The gold chain that went over it was the imposing square-linked affair Warren wore for invocation, and the hat sat like a purple velvet pillow atop his head. All very splendid, especially when he added the crimson stole he was entitled to as holder of both Wizardry and Magic degrees. The other department members were dwarfed by Warren's glory, except for Cham Ligalla the exorcist, whom nothing could dwarf and who wore a plain black robe and stole as if to point this out.

The Selanto grads certainly could not compete, in their maroon velvet with dragon-skin stoles, and while Anders and Jim Kalin had the same kind of robes as Warren, they were not entitled to the full colored velvet he wore and only had purple cuffs. Competition was stiffer when the demonologists joined the other schools to march, departments like Arcane Arts having the edge in fashion sense (and, Warren suspected, often creating their own regalia), but still, Warren had nothing to be self-conscious about. He held his head high as they processed to the stage and seated themselves in antique folding chairs that looked like thrones but were a touch narrow for the over-fifty rear end.

The Royal Academy's graduation ceremony was enormous, well-attended by family who had been excluded from the more significant ceremonies each school had held during the preceding week. Even late in the programs, there was attrition. Some of the Sorcery seniors had failed their oaths, Warren knew, which lent an extra edge of mania to the crowd who had passed and were now settling into their seats like chattering magpies. All eight of the necromancy students came down the aisle, the other grads giving them a wide berth. Warren smiled at the necromancers, but he was really watching for his own graduate students in the Magic contingent, and was happy to see them all smiling back at him.

Last to enter were the Alchemy students, walking slowly and with great self-consciousness, probably because they were high on pain-killers; it was still an imposing effect that quieted the audience as they passed. Each of those robes covered a fresh Mystic Guild of Alchemists brand — or not, Warren thought, twisting in his seat to look for Vinca and Bill Navanax, the alchemists who had adventured in the Guild's prison with Teddy and Cham during spring break. Not there! The alchemists he could spot were all from the old guard, and all wore very fierce expressions as they stared at nothing in particular. In future years, would there be two classes of alchemy grads — those who accepted the Guild's mark, and another group aligned with the dissidents? He had plenty of time to consider this, for, as always, faculty were seated behind the graduation speakers and could hear them only as distorted echoes. Clicking from behind him told Warren that younger faculty were texting people or checking their e-mails. He, in the front row, could do nothing but twiddle his thumbs and calculate the percentages of different ethnic groups in each class that passed before him.

Though he had been stifling in his robes at the beginning of the ceremony, Warren cooled as he sat watching one student after another march across the stage. The Bachelors of Wizardry came first, followed by an endless stream of Sorcery grads. By the time students he knew began to step up for their Bachelors of Magic degrees, Warren was shivering in his chair, so he was not entirely surprised to see something begin to materialize on stage behind the student who had stopped for a photo-op after shaking hands with the Academy President. Not surprised, yet at the same time not entirely believing what was about to happen, he watched her turn and face the demon.

Even unformed, it was taller than she was. She put a hand on the protective ward her department had given her the previous night and looked past the swirling column of mist to faculty frozen in their chairs. The Dean of Natural Magic turned just a little and glared at Warren as if this were his fault. The President didn't move.

Is he insane? Warren wondered, and then it hit him; the administrators were trying to cover this up. A demon had appeared in their midst, and they wanted the audience to think it was normal! The Dean's face had turned an interesting shade of purple while Warren thought this through, and now he made vigorous gestures with the hand hidden from the audience. Warren put on his most innocent face as he nodded back at this man, who had denied him the funds to replace Hiram Rho. *Don't need a full roster of demonologists, do we?* he thought.

The demon wasn't solidifying very well, on this stage full of warded magicians. Its outline wavered. Anders Regan, next to Warren, tugged at his sleeve. He was shivering too, Warren could tell. "We have to do something!"

"We need to surround it," Warren said, looking back to estimate how many of the faculty he could count on.

"The students are in front!" Regan was a different man when he thought of his students. "It's your call, Minna," he said, loudly enough for the Dean to hear and turn an even more alarming color.

The student's face went blank with shock and then unholy glee spread across it. "Who has wards?" she called in a voice of command, and Warren stood. He felt Russell and Anders get up — the line of folding chairs surged — and heard rustling behind him as many others in the faculty rose, and clicking as others frantically blogged and tweeted the moment.

"Um — cordon it off," the student said, her voice shaky but delight still shining in her eyes.

The faculty and those students already on stage moved as smoothly, Warren thought, as if they did this during every graduation, making a chain of warded bodies around the demon within a minute. Warren held hands with Anders on his right, a Zoomancer he didn't know on his left. The student had said something else he didn't catch, and now

73

her fellow grads were filing onto the stage, laying their own new wards on the floor behind the ring of faculty, their chains hooked end to end. "She's very good," he said to Anders, who glowed.

"They're all doing themselves proud," he agreed.

"Fine batch," the Zoomancer grunted. "Step back."

As one, the faculty stepped backwards, lifting their feet high over the wards, and now the demon swirled within a golden circle. Warren let go of Anders and the Zoomancer and went back to his seat, from which he could see campus security guards talking into their walkie-talkies at the back of the hall. Their distorted voices sounded from the right, where he saw three other guards in the wings with fire-extinguishers; they must have decided everything was under control, for they didn't storm the stage as the students began one of the more recent charms for banishing a demon. A charm of discourse convinced the monster that the golden ring around it was shrinking, and the column of smoke grew smaller as well until it became a thread and puffed out.

"Nicely done," said Russell, clapping his hands. The guards in the wings did emerge, at this, and under cover of applause and cheers they sprayed bittersmoke over the spot where the demon had been. The students who had banished it were putting their wards back on, some with obvious triumph and others trying to look as if they did this every day, until the President took control.

"Let's applaud our Bachelors of Magic again," he said smoothly, "and thank the faculty who took

74

part in this demonstration." The look on his face as he turned to indicate the faculty didn't match his words.

"We should make that a part of every graduation," Russell said to Warren under the applause. "It was certainly better than the speeches."

"Do you suppose it was Nezumia's doing?"

"I've no idea," said Russell. "I thought this building had alchemical wards."

"It does. All the admin spaces do." A quick glance showed Warren several Alchemy faculty with their heads together and worried frowns on their faces.

"Sucks to be them," Will Harding whispered from behind him. If Will could have seen his face, Warren would have felt obliged to frown disapprovingly; but Will couldn't see his face, and this was a festive occasion requiring that he smile. He smiled with pride in his students, with encouragement for the grads, with relief that this was no failing of his department; but he smiled with true delight that at four-forty tomorrow morning, he would be flying away from all of it.

Chapter 6
The Day of Rest

Rho dreamt of walking over a wooded hillside. The trees snubbed him. None of them would admit to having met him before, and even the flowers turned their faces aside ... up and down hill he went, more alone with every step, until he came to a glade with a great oak tree at one edge of it. Somebody had driven a long spike into the oak tree. Rho saw thick blood flowing down from the wound. It smelled like a pig-shed.

He woke with a musty taste in his mouth, and found that he had been drooling onto his pillow.

He could see the farm better from his old window than he ever had when he was a boy. The big maple tree that had shaded his room, so close that he could step out onto its branches, was gone; not even a stump remained, though he kept looking down to see if he couldn't spot a trace of it. Had it ever really been there? he wondered, mistrusting himself. How much of his childhood had he made up?

The yard ran out beyond where the mythical maple tree had been to the edge of the driveway, which Rho could just see if he leaned out the window and peered way to his left. On his right, it sloped downhill into a sort of swale with a drainage tile at the bottom, and along here Mama Simone had always laid out her vegetable garden. Neat stick towers for beans and peas made the garden's backbone, and the dark furrows in front of them were studded with young plants, still small, but prosperous looking. On the other side of the drainage ditch, a pasture had been fenced off to the woods' edge, and a quarter-horse stood idly at the near end, looking at the garden with speculation in its posture. A nanny goat grazed a little further away. No cars passed, no tractors or chainsaws disturbed the Sunday hush.

When Rho faced straight ahead, he was looking at the business part of the farm — the barns and equipment sheds, and the well-worn tracks around them. This was the part of the landscape that missed its owner. The sheds lay in silent mourning, and nothing stirred there except the pigeons clustered atop one of the silos. As if obeying a command, they all took to the air at once and wheeled in a cloud of gray and white, landing on the other silo's roof. Rho, watching, felt the first pang of grief for his father; he couldn't yet have said why.

***

When Mama Simone woke up, her first thought was, *Robin's here!* Her second thought was, *Is he really?* She looked at the ledge above her dresser, where she had tucked the little china robin between two beams and let spiders veil it over, tie it down. It was still there, as if that meant something. The sheets with birds on them were still in her laundry basket below the trap-door to the attic, as if that meant anything ... the house smelled of coffee and burnt toast, and that did mean something. Mama Simone got up and put on her old russet dressing-gown that she had made back when she liked to look romantic, and swept out of her bedroom.

He was eating burnt toast in the kitchen, her little boy who had never wanted his bread any more than warmed in the morning. He had made coffee the way she did, strong enough to trot a mouse. And he had gotten old.

"What happened to you?" asked Mama Simone.

He looked at his hands. "I told you, I'm a Magister now. I work in Osyth."

"You told me that much. There's more to tell."

"I didn't know Dad was dead," he said. "Don't worry; I didn't let the aunts know. They think I came home for the funeral."

"Do you think I care what the aunts think?"

"Probably not," said Robin, "but I figured you'd rather fight with them on your own schedule."

"That's true." She got herself coffee and sat down, pouring condensed milk into it from the can. "Where's the brown sugar?" He knew where it was right away. He moved around her kitchen as if he belonged there, and when she put her hands over her eyes he didn't say anything, just set the sugar next to her and sat down again. When she took her hands down after a while, he was reading *The Minich Township News*. She spooned sugar into her cup and collected herself. "How long are you staying?"

"I wasn't sure," said Robin, without looking up from the paper, "but I'd like to stay till the middle of August. If that's all right with you."

"Of course," said Mama Simone. "If you start to irritate me, I'll pack you off to the aunts. Or Gretyl's."

"I'd never irritate you that much!" He looked around the kitchen like a conspirator. "She's gotten very — take-charge."

"She was always take-charge," said Mama Simone, with a sly smile she hadn't used in years. "She's turned into a chicken."

"She's married?"

"Six years, with two children. So's Willet — eight years last month. He has a boy. You're an uncle, I guess."

"What about Lilis? I didn't see her yet."

"Lilis," Mama Simone said strictly, "was casting the runes and laying the lines. She doesn't come under this roof anymore, or eat our food."

"Did she fight with you?"

"With your father, but we're not angry with each other. She just doesn't come here anymore. She was at the funeral, and she sent over those cookies with the green stuff in them. She's become a hedge-witch."

"Is that what they fought over?"

"No, they fought over the pigs." She took a deep breath. "I'm surprised you're not doing the same."

Robin looked down again. He would know that table by heart, at this rate. "I didn't know about them until Mr. Dilys told me. I can't hear the animals anymore."

"Oh! Robin –"

"Maybe it's for the best." He shut his mouth tight as if biting that conversation off in the middle, and drank the rest of his coffee. He ate the rest of the burnt toast cold, which was closer to how he'd always liked it.

Robin didn't come to church with them, and who could blame him? He was suffering from jetlag, he said, but Mama Simone thought it was aunt-exhaustion. She wasn't sorry he stayed at home, for it allowed everybody who wanted to talk about him to get it out of their systems without scaring him away. But it kept her and the other children a long time at the coffee hour, and she missed Holy Study, which was a shame when one's church had just changed gods. She had a book on the Bright Lady, but hadn't taken time to read it.

They finally got out of the church and over to Gretyl's place, which was where they had Sunday dinner since Lilis had taken her stand against the farm. They settled around the grownups' table with the familiar uneasiness, conscious of things that mustn't be discussed if the family was to have a peaceful meal; but Robin had gone too recently from that list to the list of Breaking News for them to know just how to approach the topic, so there were bound to be false starts. Gretyl's husband and Willet's wife sat at the children's table in the other room, and Mama Simone ought to have viewed that as considerateness. Rats from a sinking ship, she thought, instead.

At least they got everybody served before trouble began.

"He's still lying to us," said Willet, hunched over his plate.

"What? I won't have this," Mama Simone snapped. "I won't have fighting."

Willet glared back at her. "He's lying about something," he said. "I did some internet searching last night. There's a 'Hiram Rho' on staff at Osyth — but the same person's a member of the Demonological Congress, and you can't join that without binding a demon. So he has to have one."

"Who?"

"Hiram Rho! It's the name on his car rental papers."

"You went through Robin's things?"

"Someone had to. The rest of you were too busy with the wake. He's not the little boy you remember, Mama. You don't know what he's been doing."

When they were frightened or suspicious, Gretyl and Willis looked like the twins they were. They looked very like their father.

"You can't be sure about any of that," said Gretyl, in the schoolmarm voice that had always driven Willett to rash deeds. "What do we know about demonologists?"

"It's on the internet," Willet repeated, waving his fork. "It's on their homepage, in big red letters. All Congress members must have bound a demon of their own. It's a listing of magicians who hold demons. And he's been a member for years. A full member since the end of February." Now they looked at Mama Simone. "You can't be alone in the house with someone who has a demon."

"Would I be safer with someone who couldn't command demons? If they're out there, I want them bound."

81

"Mama!" said Gretyl. "It isn't right. We're talking about consorting with the forces of evil." She looked sideways at Lilis, who took another slice of ham. Mama Simone snorted, seeing that. Not so pig-lovey at the table, was she?

"Do you like the ham, Mama?" Lilis asked, too sweetly. "It's field-raised. I got it at the co-op in town."

Mama Simone would have given a sharp answer, if they hadn't been busy with something else. She pushed her ham away untouched.

"There's only one thing demons want," said Willet, single-minded as always. "They want souls. You only get to command them by giving them your soul. Isn't that the truth?"

"More or less," Lilis admitted. "Most folks think they've found ways around it, but who can tell if they're right? For what it's worth, Osyth has a good reputation."

"You're talking about my son," said Mama Simone. *My little Robin!* Heat and cold chased each other through her. The baby she had cuddled, the little boy she taught and comforted, the soul she watched blossom — he couldn't, he never could have cared so little for all that as to give it away forever. "You've made some mistake," she said. "I'm sure he'll explain it to us when he's ready to." Her children looked down at their plates.

Gretyl was the one who said it. "If his demon master lets him," she said, and cut her potato into perfect quarters.

"That's enough!" said Mama Simone. She pushed her chair back so hard it tipped over. "Take me home. I don't want to see any of your faces again until I send for you."

***

When Ric Massey swore, he swore by his cat. In Selanto, home of a hundred competing faiths, the Guard couldn't take sides. But when Ric prayed, he prayed to the Bright Lady, and it was the Bright Lady for whom he had bought freesias on the way home Saturday afternoon, when he heard Derek and Lord Stimms had been released from hospital. He put the flowers into the blue bowl in front of her icon. This was something only over-pious people did, because it made for a nuisance the next morning, when that blue bowl had to have salt and water put into it for the daily ritual— and sure enough, Ric felt a little self-conscious Sunday morning when he had to transfer the dripping flowers to a water glass. He was glad nobody else lived in his apartment except Lady Jane, who viewed all his behavior with the same feline scorn and would not ask incisive questions.

Ric had grown up praying to the Bright Lady. He did it now more for the memories of his mother and grandmother than out of hope for anything in particular. Until recently, after all, there'd not been much chance of the Bright Lady's delivering. Worshipping her had been like following a losing team, or even a disbanded one.

For as long as Ric could remember, Bright Lady churches had been closing right and left and reopening under new management — or the same management, with different jerseys; Selanto priests were nothing if not practical, and the guy who had led you in worshipping Mercy and the Bright Lady in June could be found at the same stall in September, leading the same congregation in worshipping the Glory of the Horseman or the Revealed Truth of the Sacred Flame. Selanto congregations were practical, too. A man must worship, and which was more important: the church you knew, or the god you didn't?

None of that mattered to Ric, who felt wary of joining a church community — police and taking sides, again — so he had gone on worshipping the Bright Lady in his spare bedroom, even when she was likely to be kicked out of the league for missing too many games. But even if Ric had thought of changing teams to a god who might do something about the cold in his bones and the flashbacks, he wouldn't have done it after April. In April the Bright Lady came roaring back, and took the championship.

Ric had not expected the Bright Lady that night. Nobody had. They had all expected the god of the Sacred Flame, and they had a right to. The Flame had been spitting out prophesies, in voices and visions and inscribed on crystals that could be read by any high-end computer, and what more could you ask of your god? Like the Flame or not, this was first-rate service. It had even given a date for its Second Coming, and that was when the Guard began to be unappreciative as millions of believers, seekers, and reporters filled the city. But on the great night, with the Archbishop of the Sacred Flame and his myrmidons prostrate before the Flame in the Square of Justice, what had come out of it? A rag-tag group of penniless old men, the last thing followers of the Flame wanted. Magicians.

Not your ordinary everyday magicians either, who could have been moved around by a god like chess pieces, but alchemists, the kind of magicians who made the world change and might as well have been gods themselves. All kinds of priests hated alchemists. They messed up the categories. And those Sacred Flame prophesies hadn't said anything about rescuing them; to the contrary, they'd promised believers a chance to rise up and burn the Mystic Guild of Alchemists to the ground, the way the Mystic Guild of Alchemists burnt its own members if they got out of line. If the god of the Sacred Flame had really stepped out into his glory, the Guild Council would have been the first people put back into the Flame, in the very spot where Eridanus the Elder had burned their forbears three hundred years ago. Guild first and royals next, according to the visions Ric had been privy to. Whenever he thought about the theocracy that might have been, he made a note to buy the Bright Lady a new candle.

Because she had stepped up. She was the god who had appeared in the Sacred Flame. Not in the Court of Justice, where all the people in fancy robes were waiting to have their contracts renewed, but in a little church in the shabby end of Ric's district, where nobody except two unshaven priests were watching; but they had been watching with a camera, and now every newspaper, commemorative book, and tee-shirt vendor had reproduced their photos. The Bright Lady with her green robe and

85

her blue bowl, weeping for the world's sorrows. The Bright Lady returning as one of those ragged alchemists, trapped for hundreds of years in the Guild's prison behind the Flame. The Bright Lady bending and gathering the Sacred Flame into her bowl, and standing again in glory.

Those were the pictures that had gone all round the world after the Flame went out, and just as quickly the churches had switched over. Where the lamp of the Sacred Flame had stood, now blue bowls sat on altars everywhere: in Selanto, in Osyth, from Kasidora to Sio to the Orren Islands. If you were a corporate sort of priest, cutting your conscience to match your church's official policies, you would wait until the new gear arrived in the mail — a blue bowl with the Archbishop's seal on the bottom, and a lovely tapestry of the Bright Lady with some magic in it that made the flame in her bowl gleam and quiver. But either way, soon or late, you would switch over to the new champion.

Ric had the stubborn attitude of a long-time loyalist, and he had not bought any of the new stuff. He still worshipped the Bright Lady with his grandmother's old icon that had nothing shiny about it except the spot where the paint had worn off and let the aluminum show though. His blue bowl bore the seal of an archbishop from eighty years ago. His candles were not officially blessed, nor was his theology, and he had never joined the crowds of new worshippers who knelt before the Lady beseeching her for this or that. So he felt like a phony as he stood in his spare room on the first Sunday morning in June and messed with flowers in front of his icon. Was he catching the new, cheap devotion? He lit the candles with great misgiving, and looked at the Bright Lady's face cautiously, as if he expected her to frown.

If not for the flowers, habit would have taken Ric through the ritual. That little change, though, made him conscious of every movement as he washed the blue bowl and filled it with water from the silver pitcher his mother had given him. He saw the salt fall into it as if it were the first time he had watched candlelight glint off crystals falling from the silver spoon. He felt every touch as he drew the Bright Lady's circle with the wavery line in it on his forehead and hands with the water, and tasted a drop of it on his tongue, asking that his thoughts and deeds and words all serve Mercy that day. Then he sat on the chair with his hands folded and his back bowed, looked at the light flickering on the painted lady's face, and thought, *What is Mercy?* He couldn't tell, and perhaps he should have worshipped a god he understood better. He felt that keenly today, for no good reason, and before his back could settle into the chair he felt something behind him and jumped up.

There was nothing there. Whatever it was had moved with him, for he still felt it at his back, even more so now that his back was turned to the icon. He put a hand on his ward, but he knew this was no demon. There was no *grue*. Just the feeling, intense and detailed, of hands grasping his right arm from behind; and then he felt his arm move, though looking down at it he could see it was still. He felt it jerk away from the grasping hands and pull its sleeve loose, and that was all. Just like that.

Chapter 7
The Start of a Perfect Vacation

If Rho had waited one more day before leaving Selanto, Warren and Lilian would have been in one of the cars that zipped past him on Route 98. They took the path he had followed; along the Selanto ley-line through industrial outskirts for a nerve-racking forty minutes, during which Warren wasn't able to worry about the department and all they could discuss was navigation, and then along the southern edge of the same wide Kasidora River valley, with the same mist-blue Kasidora Mountains just visible on its northern bank. They took the drive in a different spirit, though, with vacation waiting at the end of it and a good map to guide them; and unlike Rho, they had no concern about when they might cross into those distant mountains. They intended to turn the other way, southwards into the Vinchifer Peninsula.

Fields of lavender and mint stretched as far as they could see, the Kasidora River meandering through richer and richer bottomlands as it headed for the Eastern Sea. Before becoming a dozy flatlander, though, it would split off the more vigorous Vinchifer River, which tumbled southwards along a long, mountainous peninsula to the Ember Sea. At the southern tip of this peninsula the largely marine Vinchifer ley-line, a gold stripe on Warren's map, crossed between one sea and the next. This was their goal, and Warren felt his heart beat faster as they drew closer to it.

The road was in no hurry. It went far out of its way to keep from dipping its toes into the Selanto ley-line, along the sides of ridges and out into the fragrant plain. Warren rolled the windows down and sniffed happily. He was more and more convinced that this vacation was a good idea.

He thought so through the afternoon as they drove steadily east, pointing out scenery to one another and listening to the radio. Around four they made the southward bend with the Vinchifer, away from the valley and the Selanto line. Now they and the river raced through ever-narrower passes. Before the sea came into view, however, they turned west again and headed up into the Vinchifer Range. The sun disappeared behind ranks of evergreens just as the road became challenging.

"We don't have to cross the range," said Lilian, looking at the map with the dome light on. "We just putter along on this side –"

Warren knew that kind of puttering along, on unlighted secondary roads up and down the sides of foothills. If worst came to worst, he thought, they could sleep in the car.

"We ought to eat here," Lilian said as a truck stop came into sight between tall pine trees. "There won't be anything along the back roads, and I don't know what's in the cottage."

"What, no fairy servants with a banquet prepared?"

"That's only if you stay at the lodge."

Warren pulled in between double- and triple-semis. Road trains! Their little car would have fit in the passenger seat of one of these behemoths. "How on earth do they get these through the mountains?" he wondered aloud.

Fistfuls of crystal hung from the trucks' rearview mirrors, too far above his head for him to identify, but he was at just the right height to examine the runes painted on their mud flaps and hubcaps. They were charms of essence, symbols that signified the magician who cast and powered them rather than the function they were meant to perform.

"They must keep a lot of magicians on retainer," he said. "I never thought about jobs in trucking."

"I had a professor who used to tell us about jobs in trucking," Lilian said. "He used it more as a threat than as a promise, though."

The truckers had tan right arms and pale left ones, and they knew everybody else in the joint. Warren and Lilian scooched down as small as their car at a little table and eavesdropped on a conversation about, of all things, wards.

"I picked this up at the goblin market in Sterne," said a woman whose hair was sun bleached on the right side, dark on the left. A blue crystal passed from hand to hand down the counter.

"A goblin market!" Lilian said to Warren. "We're staying close enough to Sterne to go. When is the market?" she asked the woman.

"Odd Tuesdays. You ever been to one?"

"Not since I was a little girl. I have storybooks my grandparents bought me there."

"You know not to buy any food or drink," the woman warned her.

90

"Yes — but it's safe to eat if they give it to you, right?"

"Make sure it's a gift," said the grizzled trucker next to the woman.

"Yeah, get it in writing."

"Better yet, just don't eat any of their stuff. Don't get a taste for it."

"May I see the ward?" asked Warren. He couldn't place it in any of the classes he knew — not a demon-ward, or a rune of protection, a blessing or even an aroynt. He wished he had brought his field charm.

"You in the business?"

"Yes, at Osyth. I don't recognize this, though."

"Osyth! You from the Academy? Know those folks who let the alchemists out of the Flame?"

"Yes," Warren admitted. "Two of them are in my department, and another used to be."

This topic started conversations all around the room. "That was a deal!" said the half-bleached woman, over the babble. "Those strikes could have backed up transport across half the continent."

"Why?" To Warren, safe in Osyth, the Selanto strikes had been the least important part of Teddy's adventures. What had they been about again? Getting the alchemists away from the Archbishop of the Sacred Flame, was it? Without these strikers, Bill Navanax and all the rest would still be locked up as pawns in one of Selanto's ever-simmering religious conflicts.

"All the truckers in the city went out," the grizzled man said proudly. "Eighteen days, and they caved. You know how fast a city like that fills up

91

with garbage? And we would've gone out next — then they would have had food shortages."

"So is your union the one they joined?" Warren didn't see how alchemists and truckers fit together, but then he knew nothing about union politics.

"How do a bunch of ancient alchemists get into a truckers' union?" Lilian asked, her mind running on the same track.

"It's a league of unions," the half-bleached woman explained kindly. "International Brotherhood of Travelers. We have all kinds of chapters — you could form a union at your work and come under our umbrella, whether you're a trucker or not."

"Yeah — the alchemists link in through the airline workers. One of them was a member over in Osyth."

"Oh!" said Warren, the light dawning. "That was Bill Navanax," he told Lilian. "He's done contract work for Angel Air. Now it all makes sense! So now you have an alchemists' union under your umbrella?"

"Had the final vote yesterday. Over eighty percent of them for it," said the grizzled man, nodding.

"Wait a minute. That means you went out on strike for them before they'd joined the union?"

"Sometimes you have to," the man shrugged. "Industries try to stop a vote, if they can. Fire the organizers, intimidate the workers. We took a risk, but we were pretty sure they'd go our way. And they have."

"And that means that the next time you strike, the alchemists might go out in support," said Lilian.

"Yeah, well, we'd have that card in our hand."

"It's not so big a deal as folks thought at first. Everything alchemists do has to be approved by the Guild council anyway, so there's a delay," the half-bleached woman said. "If they did go on strike, nobody would notice for six months."

This statement stopped the conversation, or rather turned it into other pathways; someone from across the room demanded to see the goblin ward, and two other truckers began competing discussions about hubcap runes and the construction project in Waldfild Pass. It was as if Warren and Lilian had come too near a birds' nest, that they would never have known about if the parent birds had not sprung up to distract them. Warren was still pondering what alchemists freed from the Guild's control might do, and for whom, when they found their vacation cottage two hours further down winding back roads.

"This is it!" The clearing Lilian pulled into was just large enough for the car. When she switched off the headlights, Warren saw only blackness between the trees; then a light blinked on, green and close at hand, then another. "Fireflies!" said Lilian.

"Or Will o' Wisps." Warren watched the light jig its way deeper into the woods. The air wrapped around him when he stepped out; dry, chilly at first, but with a warm undertone radiating from the ground below. It was air like wine, he thought, looking up at stars that peeked through the branches above.

"I hope the key works," Lilian fussed, fumbling at the porch railing. She pressed the golden disc into its socket and Warren saw the cottage glow into life, a frieze of lush branches against every window.

Gentle lamplight flowed out through porch windows and the door swung open to reveal a room filled with heavy, comfortable-looking furniture, a fire flickering at its far end. A puff of fragrant smoke made him sniff happily.

"Oh! It's lovely!" said Lilian.

"Look at that bed," said Warren. It was a bed out of fairy tales, built into the wall behind a tapestry that had just pulled itself back to invite the weary traveler. He couldn't take his eyes off those puffy pillows and comforters, and the bed knew it; it stretched and turned down one corner, for all the world like a stripper beginning her act. Lilian and Warren gaped, and both burst into laughter.

"What a strumpet!" said Lilian. "Let's not bring in the luggage tonight. All I want is to get my feet up and my head down — that didn't come out right, did it?"

"I think that bed is going to be a corrupting influence," said Warren.

"Good. That's what we need, thorough corruption." They had washed and brushed and were still giggling like children at a sleepover when the cottage firmly turned down the lights and fire. "Do you suppose it scolds the bed, when nobody's around to hear them?" Lilian whispered.

"Yes," said Warren, snuggling deep into the cool sheets. "It would have to be a very stern cottage, to keep this bed in check."

Chapter 8
The Volunteered

Ric's desk was a complete mess, the type of shambles left behind by someone who didn't care whether the owner knew it had been searched or not. This being the way he had left it on Saturday, he was not alarmed. Derek viewed it with amusement.

"Did you ever find your lighter?"

"In the bathroom sink at home."

Derek's grin got broader. "Now all you have to do is find those Guild wards." They had retrieved the wards in question from a sewer the week before.

"Sweet Lady Jane! Tell me they weren't on my desk."

"Nah, I took them to lockup. How dumb do I look?"

Ric looked him over. "Pretty dumb," he said. "What is this, football thug fashion?" Derek was wearing an ancient jersey with the arms cut off, and trousers three sizes too large over the newest overpriced trainers.

"You're so behind the curve. You could pass for your own Da."

"My Da was a stylish gent."

"So would you be, in nineteen forty-seven. So, what'd we catch?"

"No clue," said Ric. "They took me off the Locullan case. No demons for me. What's on the board?"

"A Grant on Wilms East."

"A Grant!" *Since when,* Ric thought, *do Detective Inspectors deal with ghosts?* Any Special could cope with a Grant. *Oh well*, he thought. *Ours is not to question why…* and out of the factory, he could really talk with Derek. "Has it tasted blood?"

"No, someone got a look in its mouth yesterday."

"Great," Ric said sarcastically, putting his lighter back into his pocket. "You got the kit?"

They drove to Wilms Street, though in Selanto traffic it might have been faster to walk. "What's the deal with Lord Stimms, anyway?" Ric asked as soon as Derek closed the car door.

"Didn't you see it?" Derek asked. "He started to disappear. When I caught him he went solid again, but I think he only did it by draining me."

"Hm. Is that why they kept you in hospital yesterday?"

"Yeah. It happened again while we were in the recovery suite, and none of the monitors went off — so I've been with him ever since, watching. They're trying to keep it quiet."

"You spent the weekend in the palace?"

"Yep. That's some place! The walls have about eight layers of spells painted 'round them. I guess each Chief Exorcist adds his own. It looks as if they keep him safe, as long as he's in there — or it might be that he just doesn't sleep much. He was up at all hours, in the palace." He frowned. "I don't know what's wrong with him, but it looks bad. When I saw trouble, at the exorcism? This was it. And it happened again when he went out yesterday. He fell asleep in the car, and started to fade before we'd gone a kilometer. I woke him up and he started puking like he was paid for it. They ended up giving him an IV and a trank charm."

"So what is it, a demon?"

"I think he knows what it is, but he's not saying," said Derek. "He had some kind of ward around his neck. Exorcist Pasqueflower came over and took it off, and then he slept all right. But about a half hour later he woke up enough to know it was gone, and he raised holy hell about that."

"Did you get a look at it?"

"No. It was really small."

"You should have taken today off, if you've been up watching him."

"And miss this?" Even with his eyes on the road, Ric could tell that Derek was giving him a sharp look. "What are you clammed up on?"

"Nothing. I read up on himself."

"And?"

"I said nothing. There are a hundred reports on the net, and the most plausible are the ones that admit they're fiction. Does he have a scar shaped like a taloned hand on his left thigh?"

"I'm not that far in."

"It's just weird," said Ric, "that the most important exorcist in the world is someone we know nothing about. He shows up out of nowhere and gets Rosemont to take him on, and eight years later he's no closer — far as anyone knew — to being Named. Except Rosemont conveniently becomes a demon — if that's the truth — —and our boy steps up. Self-appointed, or is the demon supposed to have Named him? Why did the others accept him? Not the most biddable people, exorcists."

"Hm," said Derek. "Sounds like you need to ask Pasqueflower. I've got nothing, unless he talks in his sleep."

"There's plenty about that on the internet, as well," Ric said, grimacing as he made the last turn of their drive. "Have you ever heard of fan fiction?" He was able to find parking, as always, by pulling onto the sidewalk in front of a fireplug. A city wraith immediately appeared on the fireplug, glowering at him; he showed it his badge, and it dematerialized with a sour expression.

"Not bad," he said, looking down the street. Wilms would have been wide, if it hadn't been parked up two deep on each side. Identical white row-houses stood up from each side of it; their front gardens, below street level and behind iron railings, sent up flowering vines to curl around the buildings' brass nameplates. An air of placid self-satisfaction lay over the neighborhood.

Ric got out of the car and leaned against it, shielding his lighter from the morning breeze. Derek stretched inside the car. All around, curtains twitched. A perfectly groomed blonde with an attaché case and a small child looked at them suspiciously as she loaded both into her car.

"Must be nice," Derek said, meaning the apartments. They had to be a million each, in this neighborhood. "They'll be calling the Guard on us if we hang around here another five minutes."

"That's why I park at the plug," Ric answered. "They know we're Guards. The wraith would run off anybody else."

Derek snorted. "That just means they have a bigger right to shove us off. Ratepayers!"

"That's the job," said Ric. "The better you do it, the less anybody thinks they need it. What's the time?" He didn't mean the current time, which his watch could have told him. He meant the Grant's schedule. They were punctual monsters.

"Ten to eight. Rush hour."

The kit Derek was opening on the front seat contained an enameled metal bowl with flowers on it, several packets of instant oatmeal, two bottles of water, and a halter woven of maidens' hair and wild grasses. He mixed up the oatmeal into mash and cast a warming charm on it. Ric set out traffic cones across the street and bent over, grunting, to draw a curly pattern on the pavement.

"Which maze?" Derek asked.

"Hmm — the knotted bird."

"Man, you have to learn some new charms."

"Stick with what works."

"I mean it," said Derek. "There's an update Thursday night. Unless you have a date."

"Ha ha." Ric straightened. "Here it comes, right on time."

The creature came out of the middle of Wilms Street full tilt, as if it had been already running in the netherworld. It was black, with a horse's head and glowing eyes, but it ran on its hind legs like a performing dog — if a performing dog had weighed two hundred kilos and barreled down on one like a rhinoceros. Ric stood and watched it with his hands on his hips. "That's sad," he said.

"Yeah, well," said Derek.

The Grant charged toward Ric, ready to trample him, until its hooves hit the tangle. Though it still ran as fast as before, it made no headway. He had

99

drawn a closed maze, and the creature couldn't get through it; its eyes rolled and its breath came in great hay-scented gusts as it struggled.

Ric leaned against the car and had another cigarette as the Grant wore itself out in the tangle. The inhabitants of Wilms Street put their heads out of their French windows and checked their watches.

"We're blocking traffic," Derek said in a sing-song undertone.

"We're the bitch," said Ric, scratching under his jaw. The Grant paused for a moment in its rampaging. Its sides heaved. Derek handed the bowl of oatmeal out the car window.

"Sooey," crooned Ric, who had no experience with horses. Most of the people watching probably had stables outside the city, and could have soothed the Grant better. It shied away as he held the bowl out with both hands.

"That's for pigs," Derek said helpfully.

"What's for horses?"

"For mules, you hiss."

Ric had held the bowl at arms' length during this discussion, and the Grant's nostrils flared. Its great head moved closer. Its teeth were perfect ivory squares. If the Grant had tasted blood, those would be fangs. Now they champed nervously before it dipped its muzzle into the bowl, almost knocking it from Ric's hands. It took only a few minutes to finish the oatmeal, and then it was tame. He stroked down its silken face and held his other hand back for the halter.

"Look, mama!" a childish voice cried from a balcony. "Can't we keep it?"

Ric felt the same way, a little, but he didn't hesitate. He pulled the halter over the Grant's head and it faded, back to wherever the spirits of horses lived. Then he picked up the traffic cones, and scuffed through the tangle before it could trap commuters.

"I wonder if it's happier," he said, pulling out. "Which is better, being a Grant or a beast of burden?"

"There isn't any horse left in it," said Derek. "The horse is long gone to where good horses go, unless it was a bad horse, I suppose. Oh, lookee." There were paparazzi in front of the factory, still astride their motorbikes. "Who's in trouble now?"

"I dunno," said Ric. "Who's been watching the Chief Exorcist sleep, like a perv?"

"Perv yourself. He's not my type."

"Yeah?"

"I like 'em solid."

"Fair enough," Ric allowed. He parked the car in front of another fireplug. The wraith only manifested enough to see who it was before disappearing with a hopeless mien. "That's not too much to ask."

A peaceful morning was, apparently. The first three people Ric and Derek met all told them, with varying degrees of sympathy and relish, that they were wanted in the Chief's office.

The person waiting in the Chief's office was nobody Ric had ever seen before. Short, sandy-haired, with a few freckles on his right cheek and an absent gaze that slid off Ric's face as quickly as it had landed there. *Exorcist*, Ric thought. *Important*

101

exorcist, he amended as the Chief shut the door. Privacy and security charms made the whole room hum. The exorcist pulled a slip of paper out of an inside pocket and Ric's vision swam as the glamour disappeared. When sight came back, he was looking at Lord Stimms.

Damn! Ric thought, his pulse going up a notch. The guilt of meeting someone he had just been gossiping about sparked an irrational fear that the man would see right through him at first glance, to where the memories were; at which thought Ric began to recall the most embarrassing bits of information, or speculation, that he had gleaned from the internet. How accurate were those descriptions of his Lordship's private anatomy and behavior? Ric tried not to wonder, but it was like not thinking of a white bear.

Lord Stimms, however, did not look at any of them. He sat in one of the Chief's armchairs, staring intently at the opposite corner like a cat watching a spider. There was nothing in the corner; Ric looked, and then felt as if he had been caught by some childish game. Without moving a muscle, the man had put him on the wrong foot. *That's a talent*, he admitted sourly, and shared a glance with Derek. Lord Stimms had risen to his feet by then, and Ric felt caught out again.

"Lord Stimms, Inspector Massy. You know Inspector Haaken."

"We have met." Now Lord Stimms looked at Ric with intense interest, as if to gauge the effect of his initial rudeness. Ric bristled. He felt himself unfairly tested. But Stimms said nothing more; he merely held out a large, slender hand.

Ric shook it, taking a silent and somewhat vengeful inventory. Stimms looked taller and younger than he had in the field. He couldn't have been past his late twenties or early thirties. His skin was very pale and his features regular, even pretty. Fine brown hair and a curly mustache gave him a flighty, lightweight air. His robes were the color of dried blood in the greenish light through the Chief's ivy-covered window, and while Ric couldn't see lines around Stimms' eyes in this light, he could see dark shadows under them. Ric looked for the mysterious ward, but saw just the edge of a silver ribbon under the robe's collar. When he looked up Lord Stimms had turned toward the Chief, and once again Ric felt dismissed and inadequate.

"You are just the experts I require," his Lordship said, glancing back at Ric, who stood taller, whether he would or not, from the force of even a moment's regard. "I am apparently in need of Inspection." He gave Derek a sidelong glance, as if wishing to spare him the full effects.

Derek didn't answer; his mouth hung a little open, and he stood staring at Lord Stimms like a dolt for almost forty seconds. Then he came back to himself with a shudder that grew into bone-rattling tremors. The Chief pushed a chair forward, and Ric guided him down.

"My!" said Lord Stimms, with obviously artificial delight. "This is indeed the place to come for Inspection." He turned and Ric thought he might storm out of the door beside him. But he only breathed on the glass pane in it and sketched a sigil in the mist. Ric felt a new privacy charm close around them like a blanket. "Tell me what you saw," Lord Stimms suggested, looking at Derek.

Derek matched his gaze for just a second, and then looked down at his clasped hands. "Blood," he said. "Fire. I saw a demon laughing."

"An Inspector indeed," said Lord Stimms approvingly. "This is just what I need." He sat down in apparent satisfaction.

"Why?" asked Ric.

"It is hard to battle something you can't see," Lord Stimms said mildly. "Even harder, if it attacks while you sleep." He spoke to Derek. "You saw what was happening, though none of the sorcerer's monitoring wards detected it. If not for you, the demon might have pulled me into the netherworld, beyond help." He stretched out in the chair, taking his ease. "It would have been inconvenient."

"You want us — Derek — to keep watch over you while you sleep?"

"That would be delightful," said Lord Stimms. "I so enjoy sleeping. As it stands, I am only safe in the palace; and I have business in Osyth."

Ric reappraised the shadows under his eyes. This man was exhausted, he thought, and less in control than he appeared.

"It should not be for long. I hope to conclude this project within the week; an appraisal my opponent seems to share, if its activity is any indication," said Lord Stimms.

"Which demon is it?" Ric asked.

Lord Stimms looked at him as if he had thought they all knew this. "A salient question," he said, from which Ric understood that the meanest intellect would have already deduced his answer. "Antimora. The possessor."

"Sweet –" Ric said, and shut off at a glare from the chief. "I thought it was locked away in the alchemists' prison," he amended.

"With one of my people," said Lord Stimms. He looked at Ric differently, as if realizing his intelligence. Ric hadn't said anything intelligent, but that meant nothing in the face of Lord Stimms' judgment. He felt as if his brain were getting sharper with every second but, simultaneously, as if he were being managed like a child. It was extremely unpleasant — no, flattering — no, maddening — his Lordship went on talking, as if to say that Ric was not going to figure this out and they had things to do, meanwhile.

"What I will tell you now is confidential." He touched a rune embroidered on his robe — a decoration, Ric would have thought if he had even noticed it, sewn as it was of thread the same color as the fabric — and Ric felt something like a lump in his throat. He looked at the Chief, who nodded; so he swallowed, accepting the geas. "What do you know of Antimora?" Lord Stimms asked.

"Uh — that it was the last Lord Stimms. Rosemont. He went into the alchemists' prison and was changed there. When the alchemists got out, he was left behind. And he did trap one of your exorcists, a Magister –"

"Endamos," the Chief supplied.

Lord Stimms nodded.

"What you don't know is that he also trapped part of me," he said. He pulled the ward out of his robe, and Ric saw that it was a man's ring threaded

105

on a piece of silver ribbon. "I carried the token of each exorcist, so that I could call them back. It was a link between us. The part of me linked to Endamos is still with him; Antimora can reach me through it."

"That's what happens when you disappear," said Derek.

"Yes. If the demon can't get out, it will settle for pulling me in. Misery loves company," said Lord Stimms and relaxed in his chair as if he were discussing the weather. The dreamcatcher around Ric's neck hummed against his skin, and he felt a remote sickness that spoke of flashbacks. He couldn't decide whether he admired or resented Lord Stimms' façade. "The only persons outside the alchemists' prison who have met this demon without my protection and lived are the magicians in Osyth," Lord Stimms went on. "They summoned it into their pentarium, apparently out of professional curiosity, and it spoke with all of them; yet they have suffered no ill effects."

"Selanto has a pentarium," said Derek.

"True," said Lord Stimms, looking at Derek instead of Ric. Ric felt himself set aside. "A less effective one, it appears; Antimora possessed two Selanto demonologists during its forays here and killed both. I will visit Osyth, and pursue Antimora into the alchemists' prison through their pentarium; and I would like to sleep occasionally during my travels. As I said, I require Inspection."

The Chief looked at Ric. "You two will be accompanying Lord Stimms to Osyth," she said with ill grace. Ric could imagine the argument over his inclusion; he kept his mouth shut. "Will you be expecting their help in the pentarium?"

"I doubt it," Lord Stimms answered. "The local exorcist will assist me in that. My challenge is merely to stay alive until then."

"All right," said the Chief. "You're with Lord Stimms for the duration."

"The duration? The duration of what?"

"Until the demon's either won or lost," said Derek. He sat crunched down in his chair, looking at Lord Stimms, and Ric had never seen him look so afraid.

Ric was packing an overnight case with identical shorts and socks when his cell phone rang, with the security icon lighted up. Derek, who had packed the previous evening on the grounds of being a seer, was brooding on the sofa.

"Yeah, Massey."

"Ric."

"Yes, Chief!" Derek mimed surprise and Ric mimed confusion back at him.

"Listen, Stimms is out of here so I can give you your real assignment."

"Our real assignment?"

"Are you going to repeat everything I say?" the Chief asked, irritated. "Does that mean Derek's there?"

"Sir, yes, sir!"

"Anyone else?"

"Sir, no, sir!"

"Twit. Put me on speaker."

"You're on," said Ric.

"Listen up; I'm not going to have another chance to tell you this. You know Antimora's bad news. Stimms thinks he can go in and get this demon, but that means it could come out and get him."

Derek nodded without speaking. Ric had to ask all the questions.

"What's it likely to do, make him rip himself apart?"

"That's what it did to the other victims," said the Chief. "But we have a special alert on this one. There's strong reason to suspect it of planning to take power. If it gets into someone in a position of authority, it just might lie doggo until it can use that person's position to cause the maximum damage."

"Really? Demons don't usually think that far ahead."

"This one does. If worst comes to worst, you may have a bigger problem than just getting an exorcist to take it out of him. You may have to prove it's in him in the first place, and take him out of commission before it can act through him."

"How far out?" Derek asked, suspicious.

"As far as it takes. You're the White Knights, boys."

"Yes, sir. White Knights." Ric felt as cold as if he had walked through a ghost.

"Not without more info, I'm not," Derek said, startling him.

"You took an oath. You don't get to put conditions on it."

"He's not someone you can hold one minute and knife the next," Derek answered. He leaned toward the phone, and Ric was struck by how tired

108

he looked. "He trusts me to have his best interests at heart. I won't be able to hurt him, unless you have something in the sealed reports to convince me he'd be better off dead."

The chief took a moment. "All right," she said reluctantly. "If you tell anyone I did this, you'll be rid of me."

"Yes, sir," said Ric, to lighten the moment. "Thank you, sir!"

"Jackass. It's coming to you as an aura-locked file."

"Derek's aura. Mine isn't back to normal yet."

"Fine. You'll have it in the next five minutes. Haaken?"

"Yes, sir."

"If that's not good enough for you, take yourself out. You might not be able to help Ric, but you can keep out of his way."

Derek stiffened. "I'll do my part."

Ric put the phone away slowly, as if he could put off knowing what he knew. Derek had shut down even further, staring at his hands, and this irritated Ric.

"So I'm at bat for this," he said harshly.

"I'll do all I can," said Derek. "Have you ever killed someone? In cold blood?"

"If the demon takes him–" Ric couldn't finish the thought. His dreamcatcher buzzed again, reminding him to pack the big one from over his bed. By the time he was back, he had himself under control. "Maybe it won't happen."

"Yeah," said Derek.

109

Chapter 9
Visit From a Man-eater

"You can't be serious," said the Dean.

"I'm always serious," lied Russell. He sat at ease in the Dean's guest chair, conscious that he made a more elegant, poised figure than Warren could have, especially at seven-thirty on a Monday morning. "You know how hard it is to handle the major demons, even when we're at full strength."

"You've been calling them up just fine all semester."

" 'Fine'?" Russell shot his cuffs, so the Dean could see the scar on his left wrist as he ticked off points on his fingers. "If you want to call two faculty losing their souls and my hand being torn off 'fine,' "— he waved away the apology. "Even if we let that go, we called up the most dangerous possessor in recent history in April, I'll grant you that. But we weren't able to stop it from doing magic on us, and you know Torecki quit right afterwards. I don't think that was a coincidence. Plus, if we'd been at full strength, we might have been able to hold it in the pentarium longer or get some information from it that would have saved a few lives. Now we have Nezumia threatening who knows what, and ward failure all over campus." He leaned forward, getting his stride. "Everything's always 'fine' until someone gets killed. We've come closer to that this semester than ever before –" he glanced at his wrist — "and that was before we lost Rho and Torecki. When the next demon shows

110

up at a public function, do you want to be the one who explains how much money we saved by cutting demonology? Ours is the last department you should be shorting! A third of our faculty are on joint appointments with Public Health and you only have to pick up half their salaries –"

"All of their benefits," the Dean put in, but Russell could not be stopped.

"— and we're doing better work than any other Demonology department worldwide. You saw the kind of students we're turning out for yourself on Saturday. Warren and I are the only people who ever got their souls back from a demon. You know our graduate applications are through the roof; plus, we're making a name for the Academy in the city. Did you hear about Magister Whin and a couple others clearing a demon out of Durrell's restaurant in the middle of dinner service? When we go out in that neighborhood, people know who we are. They know the Academy's on their side. Tell me that doesn't make administration's job easier when you go up to the Palace to ask for favors."

The Dean frowned. "Two full-time lines."

"One's only temporary," said Russell.

"You hope."

"It doesn't really matter, does it? If Rho comes back, good. If Rho doesn't come back, we keep the temp on or re-open the search — good. Either way, we need a replacement for Torecki, and we need it now. Demons don't go on summer break."

"You sound as if you have someone in mind," said the Dean, giving Russell a shrewd look.

"Let's just say I'll settle for a local search to start with." Russell smiled a mysterious half-smile.

111

In fact, he had nobody in mind for the opening, but one advantage of having a depressive chair was that it had trained higher administrators into a compensatory optimism. Warren was always three times as prepared as he would admit to being, and he would be back long before the Dean could discover that in Russell, he was dealing with another breed of cat.

"All right," the Dean said. "Do your local search."

"For one line or two?"

"You can search for both, but make one provisional on funding. I'll let you know by the end of the week." And that was as close to 'yes' as you got from a professional administrator.

Russell felt smug all the way back to his office. This was how one got things done; no worrying necessary. His phone rang, and he answered it in an expansive mood.

"Cinea, Demonology. May I help you?"

"Russell, it's Cham." Cham Ligalla, Russell knew, began the day even before he did. She put in a few hours at the Public Health building downtown before coming over to campus for nine-o'clock invocation.

"Oh, hullo," he said. "What's up?" Russell respected Cham as a hero who did battle with monsters single-handed, but he did not much like her. They ought to be peers, he thought, all the more since his increase of power; but Cham didn't treat anybody as a peer except, perhaps, Warren. Russell didn't really know what she told Warren in those debriefing meetings after every exorcism. At any rate, Russell decided, it took two to be friends. He would make the first moves and nudge Cham into her role by sheer force of personality. It was hard to take the proper cheery and informal tone when the exorcist was looking at him, but he could manage it over the phone.

"I wanted to speak with you before invocation," she said now. "We have a request to use the pentarium."

"Oh? From whom?" Pentarium requests were no big deal. Warren rubber-stamped them. Russell supposed he would as well; he'd never really thought about it.

"Public Health," said Cham. "We'd like to reserve it for the rest of the week."

"This week? Tomorrow? And you're just asking now?"

"It just came up," said Cham. "We need to send someone into the netherworld, and the pentarium's the best staging spot for retrieval."

"Hm. Fair enough," said Russell, rubbing his chin. "Let me think about it and check the schedule. I don't know if Warren made any other commitments. Can I let you know at invocation?"

"Of course," said Cham, and hung up. Russell was not a peer yet; he could be a nuisance, he thought, but pushed the temptation aside as unworthy of the Acting Chair of Demonology.

Linus Ukadnian and Will Harding were in the pentarium shower room when Russell entered it. "We shouldn't be invoking with Warren away," Linus declared as soon as he saw Russell.

"Bad weekend?" Will asked sweetly, unzipping himself, and grinned into his locker at the sound Linus made in response.

"We'll go on summer schedule next week, after James leaves," Russell said. "This is the only day we'll do regular invocation till then. We have a request to use the pentarium for the rest of the week."

"Oh? Who?" Linus' voice snapped.

"Public Health," Russell said, in a flat tone.

Linus looked only a little suspicious. "What for?"

"They want to send someone into the netherworld, and hope to get him back again."

"Public Health doesn't have a coven's worth of magicians to run retrieval," Linus pointed out. "If they expect us to help them, they should give more than a day's notice. I, for one, am not available after regular invocation hour." He shut his locker door very firmly and stalked into the shower, where he faced the wall and ignored the other demonologists who were assembling behind him.

Russell quite enjoyed morning invocation, particularly today when he was in charge. He ran through a checklist in his mind, ticking off faculty as they came in. James set the pentacle without incident, and there was no more sniping at one another in the shower — first they were all too interested in Public Health's request, and then Cham arrived and nobody wanted to act unprofessional in front of her. They filed into the pentarium without incident, and Russell began his first invocation without Warren in over twenty years. It went smoothly, of course. After an initial

114

abortive swirl and flare, the cold smoke rose up like a fountain. It became solid from the edges in as if the demon it formed were hollow, and indeed the demon that materialized looked hard-shelled, slightly insect-like. Not Nezumia, Russell thought, with a little disappointment. He could probably have handled Nezumia better than Warren had, and cleared up any misunderstandings left over from last week... oh, well.

This demon was new to Russell. Its eyes were shrewd, and it resisted the geas for almost five minutes, stalking the circle to look the magicians over, like a gourmand picking out the biggest lobster. Russell asked its name a third time, excitement bubbling up inside him. The thing turned widdershins, searching for a weak spot in the circle. Its eyes met his with a steady gaze that sent an unexplained qualm into his stomach.

"Xiphister," it said, as if it had chosen to answer rather than being compelled.

Cold speared through Russell's chest, and it had nothing to do with the *grue*. Xiphister! The famous man-eater that had already devoured six magicians when Russell invited it to his defense!

Russell had done his best to forget about Xiphister over the years. Not just because the demon ate people (people he knew), but because he had more than a suspicion that he owed it his degree. The magicians of Selanto would probably not have awarded a Magister's degree to Russell, who had refused to bind a demon, if Xiphister had not sat in the audience three rows behind the Dean of Demonology, and sucked its teeth loudly while Russell outlined his findings about the effect demon-binding had on the practitioner. But this was not a moment for self-doubt, he reminded himself, and snapped back to the present. The faculty were staring at him — or worse, past him at the alchemical safety-switch in the pentarium wall. And hadn't alchemical wards failed at graduation, just two days ago?

Russell pulled a confident expression out of some inner compartment and plastered it onto his face. He switched his thoughts into old Selantese, Xiphister's language of choice. "Greetings," he said to it, in the most formal construction. "We have met before. But why does a demon lord from Selanto choose to visit Osyth?"

"Why not? Magicians visit one another," said Xiphister. Its voice oozed. "For mutual profit and edification. Even the Osyth demons have interesting ideas, on occasion."

Ideas like pulling the souls out of the magicians who studied them, Russell thought despite himself. Ideas like trapping a magician's soul in a grimoire and using its magic to cast the charms in the book. "Really?" he said, making his voice drip condescension. "I've not been that impressed. You must have lowered your standards since we last met."

Xiphister grinned at him, displaying several rows of jagged fangs. "Perhaps I can reassure you," it replied in just as offensive a tone. "Wait and see."

Russell grinned back. "I think you'll be the one waiting, today. I can get back down around noon, and we can talk over old times." He nodded at Cham, who started the final charm that set the pentacle. They would have to leave the room to let the magic establish itself, as they did every morning; but Russell could see tension in all the magicians' backs as they filed out. They had all hoped the catastrophes of spring semester were over.

"A lot of people will be pleased," said Russell, putting a brave face on it as the demonologists all took deep breaths in the shower room. "It's impossible for someone working alone to invoke Xiphister. Folks in Selanto have been trying for years."

Will Harding faced straight into the shower spray, not meeting Russell's gaze. "Are they still trying to find out how it ate its masters?" he asked.

"I expect so. We'll probably get requests from law enforcement."

"What I want to know is whether Nezumia invited it in," said Teddy. "Are they starting to work together? That would mean a basic change in the nature of demons, probably as a result of their interaction with us."

James Kalin looked defensive. "That would apply to all charms of discourse. My telling them about unions would be no different in kind from your telling them they're interested in talking with us," he said.

"Forget that nonsense!" Linus Ukadnian burst out, his face flushed and veins standing out on his temples. "Has any of you supposed professionals checked the safety-switch since the alchemists' wards failed at graduation?"

Russell had never heard the shower room so silent. It seemed as if even the running water was

117

afraid to make a sound. "Fuck," someone said to his left, and he was amazed to see it was soft-spoken Isaac Graham. "It could have killed us all!" Isaac went on, rounding on Russell with real panic in his voice. Then the babble started.

"–absolute irresponsibility," he heard Linus saying.

"For once, I agree," said Patsy Hoth.

Russell felt embattled. "The safety-switch is nothing like alchemical wards," he said defensively. "It doesn't depend on one alchemist. All of them world-wide believe in the principles underlying the pentarium. Still, I'll call Vinca just in case."

"That's not sufficient," Linus informed him. "I will be filing a formal complaint with the Dean, and Faculty Senate. This has gone too far! It was bad enough when you and Warren took risks with your own souls, but putting the rest of us into danger for your research is beyond intolerable. And you can count me out of interviewing any new candidates. I'll have no part of luring someone else into this suicide pact!"

"Well, do what you have to do," Russell said in a stiff voice. "And I will do the same." He took his blue gown off and stepped into the shower beside Isaac, who was obviously wishing he'd never spoken. Being championed by Linus had that effect on people.

Chapter 10
Magic in the Land

Warren slept till six on Monday and then woke up with a jump. Nine o'clock in Osyth, demon-summoning time! For a moment he was disoriented; then he spotted the fireplace and remembered where he was. Birdsong drifted in through the open windows, and a flicker of sunlight danced on one wall.

"What time is it?" asked Lilian, turning over drowsily.

"Six."

"Six! That's what, nine?" She stretched and smiled. Her face was rosy, her white curls tumbled, and Warren thought she had never looked so beautiful. "When's the last time you slept till nine?"

"Our honeymoon, I think." Warren kissed her and leant back on his elbow, admiring everything around him. "Have I told you how much I love you for not letting me cancel this?"

"Not nearly enough," said Lilian, and snuggled closer.

Warren kissed her again. "Allow me to demonstrate, madam."

Neither of them thought about food until a while later. Lilian got up first to forage, and that woke the cottage; Warren lay in bed and watched the fire flicker to life as she padded around the kitchenette in her quilted robe. Nothing missing, nothing needed — his stomach roared, and he gave it a reproachful look.

"What do we have in there? Do we need to go shopping?"

"It looks like I can whip up an omelet. We have eggs, bacon, onions, tomato and green pepper," Lilian reported from the icebox. "Bread, butter, jelly, milk, juice, coffee, and liver treats."

"Liver treats?"

" 'Yummy for your pet,'" she read off the container, holding it in a shaft of sunlight at the window. "Oh!" Warren sat up with a jolt and saw that the aforesaid pet had leapt up onto the outside windowsill, showing great interest in the liver treats. Lilian didn't open the screen without checking the wards, he was glad to see, and what came in appeared to be nothing more than a small gray cat with a stocky build and an attitude of entitlement.

"Yow!" was what it said, but Warren's stomach understood that language. He set the thought of Rho firmly aside. He was on vacation. He lay in bed, concentrating on not thinking, until the smell of coffee lured him out and Lilian set an omelet on the table.

"What's your plan for the day?" she asked.

"Um — I was thinking I'd go out on the line," said Warren. Thinking! It wasn't thinking that ran through every nerve in his body, made his legs jump and his spine hum. It was the magic of a new ley-line. Warren had to go out and meet it. They had to sniff each other.

Lilian laughed at him. "That was the point, wasn't it?"

"Do you want to come?"

"Not the first time. You don't want to be distracted. I brought my own stuff to work on."

"What?"

"I'm making a scrapbook for Angela and the baby. You know you don't want any part of that, so go on. Skedaddle!"

Warren had no use for pinking shears and colored paper, buttons and ribbons and stickers with inspiring words on them. He wanted the wild magic that called to him and drew him out in his shirt-sleeves, with two apples in his pocket just in case. He wanted the breezes that came through the resin-scented forest in ripples, spangled with tree-dust.

He stood outside the cottage and stretched, like a contented householder. The pines dwarfed him, and he had a sudden picture of himself as an illustration in a book of fairy tales, the round little man smoking a long pipe in front of his cottage. First through third sons would pass the cottage on their adventures and whoever scorned his advice would come to grief, whoever took it would prosper... ludicrous! Warren laughed, but the conceit still made him feel happy. He looked up to where sunlight slanted between two tall spruce trees. A light wind swayed pendants of bright green baby needles, each sprig shimmering in a halo of dewdrops. Wild magic flowed through him and out to everything he looked upon, tying them together as he set off on the walk Lilian had promised him three days ago. Like the ley-line, she always kept her promises.

This was the first time Warren had seriously walked a line since he lost his soul in February, and with every step he realized how much he had longed for it. When he was out of his body, the line had felt like the promise of rest and adventure all in one. It had welcomed him in as a part of all creation, not a separate observer but a participant. That was too much to ask of real life, he knew. Yet today, he felt the breeze against his face as if he played a vital part in the world around him. His purpose was to stop the air for a moment, to note it and let everything around him share in how delicious it felt.

The breeze brought him the scent of magic, and he headed into it as if he were following a marked path. Soon enough, he was. He could see it unrolling before him. Herbs shrank back from each side of it, and fallen branches levered themselves away. When he looked back, it stretched behind him all the way to the cottage and the grey cat came walking down the middle of it with her tail held high.

Warren couldn't remember ever having been so welcomed by magic. His breath came fast, and when he bent down to put a palm flat on the path and thank the ley-line it answered with a thrill that went through every bone. He wanted more. He unlaced his shoes and set them on a stump beside the trail, spread his toes, dug them into the cool mat of moss and needles, and went on with the line singing through him at every step. His feet let the forest floor feel itself. His lungs let the air know how refreshing it was. And as he looked around him, everything he saw served the same purpose. How could sunlight know what power and beauty it held, unless trees and his eyes told it? How could stones know how cool and smooth they were, unless his feet and the insects crossing them passed it on?

The path ran between pine and spruce until it came to a damper area where beech trees spread their branches away from smooth trunks. Cushions of moss grew here, cup-shaped fungi and baby trees sprouting in their crevices. Buttercups shone in the sunny glades among waist-high grass heads just feathering out. From here Warren tended upwards again to a ridge where rustling beech-mast lay thick under his feet and not even the gray cat could walk silently. He came out of the woods unexpectedly onto the edge of a great sunny field that sloped down, down, further than he would ever have imagined, to a wide bottomland dotted with white houses and whiter sheep. "Oh!" he said, stopping short, and at that moment he realized someone else was already on the path.

The man on the path was almost a head taller than Warren but thin, with knobby wrists. His face was long, deeply lined and weathered. He wore a cloth cap and dark green jacket, half of it torn away and the remains soiled at elbows and cuffs. Between the cap and jacket, deep-set blue eyes glared out at Warren, the little cat, and everything in the valley below. He looked a little like Rho, Warren thought, unwillingly remembering the days when he had worried that Rho would hit his colleagues sooner than hold hands with them in the pentarium or, even if cooperative enough to clasp their hands, be isolated from them by a layer of grime. In fact, he thought with a pang of guilt, wasn't Rho somewhere around Kasidora? A conscientious chair would visit — *you saw him day before yesterday*! Lilian's voice said in his head, and Warren snapped back to the present. He had been staring at the tall man.

"Good morning," he said politely, stepping aside, but the man glared at him all the more. After

123

an uncomfortable moment, Warren excused himself and squeezed past (for the tall man didn't seem to realize that one stepped out of the oncomer's way). The trail led him back into the woods immediately, as if it had meant to show him just a glimpse of that vista and nothing else.

It kept him just inside the woods, walking parallel to the meadow's edge, until an alder thicket forced them further back among the trees. The thicket ended at the knees of a massive beech, its bark gray and skin-smooth where it wasn't crossed with the scars of a long life. It was almost squat, its roots rising high above the ground and its branches spread out low as if it embraced the alders. Warren walked around to view the other side of the scarred trunk, disturbing a short-tailed squirrel, which leapt onto a low branch and scolded him. Below, he caught just a glimpse of a lame fox limping into concealment and a bird of some sort hopping away from him, one wing dragging as if it meant to lure him away from its nest. Had he come upon some kind of animal hospital? The beech tree had power, he could tell, but it was not any healing power Warren knew. This power was drawn from the earth and given back to it in equal measure. It held firm and did not yield, but it did not rise up either. Musing, he went further around it and was even more surprised to see the man from the path crouched between two roots, imperfectly sheltered by the hazel thicket. The man had his head up like a resting deer, looking at Warren with alert, forest-green eyes.

"Um — excuse me," said Warren.

The man did not reply. His face was brown with white rays around his eyes, as if he had squinted in the sun for days and days. He gathered himself a little together, like a deer ready to leap.

Warren held up an open hand. "I didn't mean to disturb you," he said, to no further effect. This was obviously the wrong language; but the only snippets of other languages he knew were meant for tourists, and he didn't see what good it would do to ask this man where the bathroom was. He knew charms in other languages, though, and blessings. He spoke the first line of one of those, the Kindling greeting, in Old Selantese. "Light against dark, warmth against cold be with this house and all in it." It wasn't quite appropriate, but it made the man smile — he had horrible teeth — and he answered with the next line.

"May the guest be ever welcome, and only well-wishers enter the door." He stood up with his hand on the tree's trunk, and bowed as if welcoming Warren into his home. Then he looked up into the tree and said something else. Warren didn't recognize it; he shook his head helplessly and thrust his hands into his pockets, as if something in there might help. Only a damp handkerchief and two apples he had stuffed in there for munching along the way. He pulled one out and offered it to the man, who took it and bowed. Warren bowed in return. The man bowed to the tree and plucked a leaf off it, scratching it with a thumbnail before he handed it to Warren, who likewise inspected the leaf (he could see nothing on it), bowed again in appreciation, and put it carefully into his pocket, wrapped in the handkerchief. They then stood looking at each other until Warren began to fear the man would think he had to share the apple out of some notion of hospitality. He gestured at himself and then down along the ley-line, and the man nodded and bowed deeply to him again.

"May those who go take strength and courage, and those who come find rest and shelter," he said, from the same Kindling charm, and Warren was delighted to know the reply.

"And may those who dwell be a blessing to all," he answered, and went on along the line. When he looked back once, he saw the man squatting with one of the fox's paws in his hand. Warren would have liked to watch, but the path had grown impatient with his standing around; a tree to his right bent out of his way with a rustle so loud that the man and the fox both started and the animal ran away with no trace of a limp. Warren waved again and set out on the new path.

He must have pleased the line, for it led him into secret, overgrown places he could never have reached on his own. He walked between thorny bushes head-high, the ground sandy under his feet and tiny birds flitting across the open trail or balancing on stems beside it, their feathers glinting rose and green. He peered into thimble-sized nests made of spider web and lichen, and their guardians let him count eggs the size of peppercorns. Then the path turned and he came into taller brush, its new leaves gray with red tips and its catkins golden, with a spicy, dusty scent.

"Whoa!" Warren said aloud, stopping short. His heart beat faster as he fingered a catkin — carefully, for it was hot enough to almost burn his fingers. This was fire-willow, something he had only seen in Anders Regan's greenhouses. The air around the willow thicket was hot and dry, as if Warren had stepped onto another continent. Heat-waves trembled above it and the ground beneath was black as ashes. Warren looked at the path behind him and before, as if to ask the ley-line whether it truly meant to let him into something this magical. Both lay open. The choice was his; so of course he went forward, into greater heat and louder birdsong.

Insects were thick in this little summer. Warren heard them popping in the leaves as he waved clouds of midges away from his face. The spicy smell grew stronger and brighter, less ashy, as the catkins ripened. Now Warren walked through a layer of seed-fluff that clung to the sweat on his legs. The bushes' trunks seeped resin, gold where it came out and white where it had dried or been scraped away. He saw more of the scraped-away places as he went further. At last he came upon a trunk leaning across the trail, the first that had blocked his path. A long white scrape ran down it, and stuck in the resin he saw a phoenix feather.

It could be nothing else. It was dark gray at its heart and iridescent, almost crystalline, at its edges. The down at its base glittered in the wind. Warren stared at it, and then upward and to each side, in a fever to see the bird float above or spy its nest of twigs and resin. When he looked back down, more bushes had ranked themselves in front of him. He could go no further, but the trunk held up that feather as if to console him. Warren bowed to the ley-line. "For this gift, many thanks," he said and pried the feather loose, careful not to lose a single precious barb. He put it into his pocket with the leaf the man had given him, and retraced his steps through the thicket.

The ley-line got Warren back to the cottage by a little before noon, sweaty and covered with debris. Lilian had taken over the dining table and was surrounded with pastel bits and pieces, but happy to tut-tut over his condition and bring him some glassine envelopes from her scrapbooking collection; he put the phoenix feather into one of these, after she had finished admiring it, and then the two of them collaborated on picking all the fire-willow seeds off him and putting them in another. They made quite a harvest, and just when they were done Warren discovered a full catkin smoldering in his pocket.

"Anders is going to love these," said Lilian.

"Anders has fire-willow. There are a lot of other people who'll love these, though."

"What will you do with the feather?"

"Keep it. It was a gift from the line; it'll turn up handy some time or other. If only to fund our retirement."

"Well, that was quite a morning!" Lilian said. "Do you want a shower?"

"I thought I'd have lunch and go back out," said Warren, "since tomorrow's the Goblin Market, in Sterne."

"Oh yes!" She kissed his forehead, probably for remembering. This almost reconciled Warren to a morning at the market. He made them both sandwiches and sat down opposite her, turning her scrapbook supplies over idly as he munched.

128

The bits of cardboard had words on their other sides, he discovered; mawkish, context-less commands like 'peace' and 'joy.' "Why did you lay these facedown?"

"It's like scrying," she answered. "The one I pick up is the one meant to be on the page. Then I can see what else belongs there."

"Ah." Warren thought he might have to view scrapbooking in a different light. After all, Lilian was a professional scryer. If her hunches were good enough to set insurance rates, these books might be more than glorified photograph albums. He turned another of the cardboards over. It said 'Think!'

Warren had gulped his sandwich down by the time Lilian took the first bite of hers. He took down his raincoat, and put his dessert apples into his pocket.

"It's not raining," said Lilian, looking up from her scrapbook.

"I thought that guy by the tree could use it," Warren said, a little embarrassed. "His coat was torn half off his back."

"Oh. Wait! Is there enough for another sandwich?"

"You haven't even started yours."

"Take him one." While Warren fussed with bread and mayonnaise, she filled a bag with slices of coffee-cake and put in a useful-looking plastic container of olives and pickles. "There, that ought to do the poor soul some good." Warren felt absurdly happy tramping off with the sack, like a little boy sent out for an afternoon out of his mother's hair, told to go as far as the line cared to take him and not come back until it told him to.

129

This time it took him downhill, to a riverbank where water foamed over rocks and braided weed into long hanks. He watched the bubbles for a long time before he noticed larger forms under them, swimming upstream. Salmon? They were as long as Warren himself, with red sides and flowing hair. Stare as he might, they paid him no heed, and he could not get a good look at one through the rushing waters. He thought of tossing something in to get their attention, but getting the attention of arcana was not an unalloyed good.

He marched on beside the stream. It grew narrower, a torrent tumbling between steep stone banks, trees with washed-clean roots clinging to them, and he saw no more of the underwater creatures. Intent on the water, he was surprised to come out above tree-line.

Up here, the air was fresh and clear. The stream still raced and leapt, but sun lit every bubble in its froth. Warren heard a 'baa' and bells, and realized he stood on sheep-cropped turf; tiny daisies, pink and white, lay flush to the ground. The only taller plants were gorse bushes, twisted by the wind that pounded at one side of him and roared in his ears.

As he climbed, Warren saw more and more signs of sheep — hoof prints in the stream bank, droppings, and tufts of wool caught on the gorse bushes — but he did not see the sheep themselves. While he continued to hear bells and bleats close at hand, so that he spun round several times to catch a glimpse of the sheep just behind him, they were either sly or invisible. Or Warren himself was invisible, walking through a different pasture than the one the sheep knew. He imagined the shepherd's dog pricking up its ears, staring at his ghost as dogs do, and the shepherd stroking it, saying 'Na there, it's nothing,' as men do. Warren ate one of his apples and tucked the core between rocks where the invisible sheep had trampled most, hoping one of them would find and enjoy it.

The sun was striking him sideways when he came to the place where the stream began, pouring out of a deep cleft in the hill. A path led into the cleft, but Warren didn't have to look twice to know it was not for his feet. The prints in it were child-small, left by soft-soled shoes with split toes, and a branch of gorse tied into a complicated knot hung over the entrance. This was a goblin path. Warren stopped the minute he saw it. He had nothing precious to leave here, but also no boon to ask, so he put the second apple from his pocket on the flat rock outside the cleft and backed away respectfully. When he had gone far enough he turned and went back down the hillside, and although he walked sedately it seemed to him as if he went down it like the water, in leaps and bounds.

When he got back to the trees it was almost dark and he was still carrying the lunch Lilian had packed. For the first time, Warren made a request of the ley-line. He took the beech leaf out of his pocket, pressed it against the forest floor, and asked the line to take him to the tall man. When he stood up and re-stowed the leaf, he walked into the forest with his mind as blank as he could make it; veering this way and that around half-visible tree roots, he soon saw the gleam of birches to his right. Will-o'wisps or fireflies sparkled between them. Out in the meadow he could see their lights taking flight

131

from the tall grass, and ahead of him the alder thicket was lit all over with their flashes. When he went around the big beech tree, however, the man wasn't there. There was only a flat spot between the roots where he had lain, so Warren left the bag lunch there, with the raincoat draped over it, and turned his steps back to the cottage.

"My word," Lilian said, when he interrupted the scrapbooking to tell her about his wanderings, "You're conquering the ley-line with apples! Have you ever taken a pocketful into the netherworld, to give the demons?"

"No," Warren said, picking up a picture of his eldest granddaughter and holding it under the lamplight. "I can truthfully say I have never tried to cozen a demon with apples."

***

For the first year ever, Mama Simone's garden had failed her. When she needed to grub in something, it needed no grubbing. She blamed it, though it might actually be Gretyl's fault. That dratted girl turned her hand to whatever was around! What were the rest of them supposed to do, sit on a tuffet and eat cream? Just as well she wouldn't be here for a while.

Gretyl wouldn't have been out here looking for grub-work, Mama Simone knew that well. Gretyl would have set Robin down and gone over him with a fine-toothed comb. But that wasn't Mama Simone's way. She wasn't sure what her way was for dealing with a son who had run away years ago and might have sold his soul to a demon, but that

132

wasn't it. *I'm slow,* she thought, looking at the garden. *Slower than these seedlings. By the time I know what I think about something, it's over and done. By the time I know what to say, the person I should have said it to's dead.* Unwelcome tears prickled at her eyes and she rubbed the back of her work glove across her face. Robin was somewhere in the house, doing something on his own. Did he see her crying? Did he think he should do something? *He's like me,* she thought. *Slower than molasses.* A snail oozed across her path, and she felt too slow to catch it. Defeated, she turned back toward the house, and the plants shook their leaves at her in mockery.

She found Robin in the kitchen, doing nothing and looking guilty about it. "Um — are you all right?" he asked.

"I'm at loose ends," said Mama Simone, kicking off her wooden shoes before she stepped into the house. "There's not enough to do in June. I wish we still had cows. Then I could at least be milking, or mucking out the shed."

"Why did you stop having cows?"

"We were tired of milking and mucking out the shed." Mama Simone couldn't take her eyes off Robin. She watched every movement he made. Would someone who had sold his soul to a demon still drink coffee? Would he wash the mug? She sighed. "I purely hate being idle! Maybe I should take up quilting, like your Great-Aunt Dismas."

"Um — should we go through father's things?"

"I did all that before the funeral. That's what people were doing in the front bedroom, taking what they wanted. I suppose we could put the rest in

133

the truck and drive it in to the Giveaways in town."
What a wretched chore — the thought strengthened
her, for what was farming except one wretched
chore after another? After the ten-thousandth time,
you realized that wretched chores were what kept
you sane. "Let's do that. I have to visit the lawyer,
as well, and do some grocery shopping; you can
drop in and see your sister, since she wasn't here for
the wake." This sounded better and better to her as
she reviewed it. It would let Lilis get a look at him
without thinking herself officially forgiven.

There was less left in the front room than
Mama Simone would have supposed. Almost all of
what remained had been made by the very Aunt
Dismas she had invoked, a woman of immense
energy and horrible taste. They carried it downstairs
— hooked rugs in orange and avocado, pictures
made by winding wool round hundreds of tiny nails,
crewel embroideries, macramé plant holders with
fishing-net floats trapped in them, mobiles made of
driftwood and bleached shells, crocheted tissue-box
covers, a ruffle-skirted doll meant to sit over the
spare roll of toilet paper, draft-stoppers made to
look like dachshunds, and lamps set in strangely
shaped pieces of driftwood, their shades made of
ironed wax paper with old, faded autumn leaves
between its layers.

"Was this really all father's stuff?" Robin
asked, looking through a box of holiday ornaments
made in cross-stitch on plastic canvas.

"She's his aunt," said Mama Simone. She felt
better with every armload. The rooms were already
bigger, cleaner. Time reeled backwards as layers of
her life in this house peeled away. "Let's not stop,"

she said. "Get it all out! What do we need fifty years of the Farmer's Trivia for? Who's ever going to eat off those flowered dishes?"

"Why not take this load to the Giveaways, and move the next load into the front room so people can pick through it?"

"Because I'm not holding another party."

Robin looked uneasy. He'd only just come back. He wasn't ready for a fight with the relatives over what had become of Great-great's flowered china, and Mama Simone took pity on him. "We'll take this load, and decide about the rest later," she said. "Can you drive a stick shift?"

"No," he admitted.

"That's what we'll do when we're at loose ends," she decided. "I'll teach you to drive." That was when she really believed he was home. She felt relief warm in her bones and found herself thinking about what she would make for supper and how they would talk in the evening, the way they used to do in the good times, when she had children at home and their doings filled the house. The big willow over the driveway looked down at her and nodded its branches in the sun. 'Home home home,' it said.

***

Rho stood outside Giveaways with a desolate feeling as he watched Mama's truck rattle off in a cloud of dust, towards downtown Minich and the lawyer's office. Stupid! You were away from home eleven years without missing it! *he said to himself, but it didn't feel true. For eleven years, it seemed,*

135

he had just been ignoring how he felt. Now the ice had cracked, and would anything seal it again? Did he want anything to?

He turned and walked in the opposite direction, his feet falling silently in the deep white dust. Every plant was coated with the dust, and he could read every traveler in the foot- and tire-tracks. Even bugs made tracks on this road, from centipedes' staccato brush strokes to more organized beetle footprints, like two ranks of tiny soldiers. The roadsides were filled with spring flowers, mostly clovers and vetch — purple, pink, and yellow. Further back, grain stood up in stiff, gray-green ranks. Still further, groves lounged along the hillsides like green clouds come down to rest. Over it all, wispy mares' tails of cloud brushed across the blue sky.

He walked further than he had ever gone before, and people he couldn't name waved to him from their yards and asked after Mama Simone. Rho made the same answer over and over, trying to remember the names he was supposed to give Mama when he got home. When he passed a hedgerow he stepped off to privately write them on the only paper he had in his wallet, a ten-spot. Then the road dipped down through a little glade and over a stream, and he saw a mailbox with Lilis' name on it.

From the outside, Lilis' place looked just like the cottage in Mama Simone's sampler about living by the side of the road and being a friend to man. It had two little windows with diamond-shaped panes, a pointy roof, and iris beside the front steps. Lilis was weeding; she looked exactly like one of those plywood rear ends farmers put in the front garden.

Rho stood by the gate until she straightened up, put her hands on her hips, and looked at him. He expected her to say something along the lines of 'So you're back,' but she didn't. She just stood there in her dark green, shapeless dress and big bare feet. Her hair was big as well, tied back in a wad that might have been carefully designed or might have been just pulled back to get it out of the way. She had a dark streak of dirt across her forehead and another on her chest. The only thing familiar about her was the face; it looked as if his blue-eyed tomboy sister had been conjured into a big, blowsy woman's body and trapped there.

"Um — I'm back," said Rho.

"Yeah, I see that. C'mon in."

Inside, the cottage was a mess, a bigger version of Lilis' bedroom in the old house. Unframed pictures, bundles of herbs and amulets covered every inch of wall space. Incomplete projects were piled, bagged, boxed, on every surface. Rho couldn't see a single thing that was finished; cords ended in a tangle instead of a knot, embroideries petered out in one corner, curtains still had the basting threads in them, uncatalogued collections littered the table. *It looks like my lab!* Rho thought, horrified. A family habit, reaching up from the past to snare him — Lilis had said something, he realized, and was waiting for his reply. "I'm sorry, what was that again?"

She looked at him with interest. "What were you listening to?"

"Nothing."

Lilis seemed unperturbed, but she turned back to the table and crumbled dried leaves into a jar as if

Rho had used up his quota of her attention. "You used to hear animals," she said.

"That's my talent," said Rho, too stoutly.

"Mm."

"So, what's it like being a witch?"

"Dangerous. Too many demons, too little respect." She shrugged. "Of course, if they respected us they'd start burning us again. Have you noticed people kill off the folks they really respect?"

"I hadn't thought about it," said Rho. "In Osyth, they only burn alchemists."

"Osyth is a secular state," said Lilis. "Alchemists are the only people they respect. In Selanto, they burn religious leaders. Folks only bother burning people they're afraid of." She labeled her jar, leaving the top off. "I suppose you could say the world is getting better. They don't burn the freaks just because they can, anymore."

"Not very many people ever did that."

"More than you'd imagine. So what's it like to be a demonologist?"

Rho had to think. "I don't really know," he said. "I've only had the job for six months, and part of that time our department wasn't working. We call up demons as a group, and two of the senior staff lost their souls, so everything was on hold."

"Really? What happened to them?"

"They're fine."

"Nobody gets their soul back," said Lilis. "They must be way ahead of the curve in Osyth!"

"I guess. I suppose someone's going to write it up — but the charm we brought them back with got lost. The whole grimoire is gone."

"Doesn't it always. Well, it sounds like you fell in the pudding. The rest of us are just plodding along, as usual. If you can call any of this usual, which I'd hate to think."

"How is mama, really?"

"I think she could be fine," said Lilis. She picked up a piece of knitting and began to take it apart, winding the yarn back onto a ball. "Or she could get herself into awful trouble. I can't say what's going to happen to her."

"Everyone else is worried."

"They don't want her to stop being wife-and-mother. They can't imagine what else she could be and still care about them, so they're scared. I'm not worried about that, because I'm pretty sure she'd be a witch if she weren't being wife-and-mother, so I don't stand to lose her." The piece of knitting jiggled in the sunlight. Rho watched its green and blue loops pop into nothingness. "Or a woodswife," Lilis added, giving an extra tug at the end of a row. "What worries me is that she might not be a very good witch, starting this late. You can't be impatient in witchery. Fast power is always bad power."

This didn't agree a bit with Rho's recollections of Lilis. He couldn't remember her ever being still, or patient — except, he thought, when she was hunting something. She had been the one of them who caught peepers in the swamp, or dragonflies in the garden.

"How do witches get power at all?"

"The same way everybody else does, from the world around us. But you know how that works — it's faster to take it away from something that's already drawn it together, like the ley-line or a demon. And wherever the ley-line crops up, magicians build on it and turn it into the establishment. So that leaves the demons for us."

Rho looked around. "Do you have a demon?"

"No. I know demons, but I don't bind anything. I'm very careful about that. Everything I do with magic is left open." She grinned. "You always thought I was just a slob, didn't you."

"I — um — I heard a witch charm a demon into being a pig, once," said Rho. "Do you do that?"

"That's one way to make a familiar. The best way, I suppose, but I don't do it. Familiars are bad news, any way you look at them. You always end up killing something you love — and once you have the demon bound, you have to finish everything you start. No loose ends. Nothing undecided. That's the real harm in binding demons," said Lilis. "You can't grow afterwards. You have to stay the same person that bound it, or it'll get away from you. I think that's what happens to the souls they get hold of, too. But you'd know more about that than I would. What did your colleagues say about it, after they got back?"

"One of them says getting near demons was like being depressed. The other says the only demon he saw was himself." Rho didn't need to depend on his colleagues for demon-lore, but he wasn't going to tell Lilis that. "The demons in Osyth have their favorites," he said carefully. "They pick people for character traits they like. If they get any influence over those people, they use it to encourage those traits. So I suppose in a way, they try to keep people from changing. But doesn't anybody?"

Lilis grinned again. "That's why I've never married."

Rho took a deep breath. "Tell me about the pigs."

"Why do you need me to tell you about it? You can ask them."

"I can't, all right?"

"No," said Lilis, giving him a very sharp look. "It's not all right. What's going on with you?"

Rho stood with his back to her, looking out of the window that was half blocked by a jungle of hollyhock leaves. "I've lost my magic, all right? That's what's wrong with me."

He could hear the rows of knitting unravel from behind him. "So that's why you came home," she said thoughtfully. "Does Mama know?"

"Yes."

"And she hasn't taken your head off? Well, you always were the fair-haired boy. But I'd watch out, if I were you. She's mad. She's just not telling you, for fear you'll run away again."

"Is that what you'd like?"

She looked up at him, evaluating. "We always got along all right, didn't we? If you hung around, we could again. I'm not going to waste my time being mad about it, one way or another. So I guess I'd rather you stayed, because it broke Mama's heart the first time you went. It doesn't matter what any of us think. You owe her."

Rho felt rebellious when he heard it stated that plainly. "I can't just hang around sponging off her," he muttered. "I'll have to get back to work sometime."

"At Osyth?"

141

"Not without magic," Rho said.

"I don't see why not. They hire people without magic at Kasidora, at least in the extension departments." Lilis pulled the last row loose and wound it up. "You could teach the theory, couldn't you?"

Rho stared at her. What an odd feeling, to have someone make a useful suggestion for no other reason than genetics. This was family.

"There's a mundane teaching at Kasidora Central College over in Sterne," Lilis went on. "He e-mailed around a week ago, looking for summer adjuncts for the extension programs. You should look him up and ask about it."

Rho had an immediate urge to say this was nonsense, but then he thought again. In his semester at Osyth, the only magic he'd done in class had been to convince students of his bona fides; after he'd spoken to a few pets and revealed a few secrets, none of the students had questioned him, even though he had taught the last two-thirds of the semester without any magical abilities.

"I could see that working with Intro," he said slowly, "but you can't make a career of teaching that, can you?"

"You can in the extensions. They only teach the first two years — and there's one based in Minich, if you're really lucky."

"You're right, I should look this guy up. What's his name?"

"Gordon K. something," said Lilis.

***

142

Mama Simone knew she'd made a mistake the minute she parked the truck in her driveway. She should never have sent Robin to Lilis's place — not because Lilis might tell him anything, but because now she couldn't believe he was really home again. *I should never have let him out of my sight*, she thought, clambering down from the driver's seat. *There's been too much leaving.*

The house was so empty it echoed, and so full it stifled her. She wanted wind! She wanted to throw all the windows open, take the roof off and let the air carry away her life's debris. A person couldn't move in all this! She glared around the kitchen and took a decision. It had to go, now, all of it — at least all that would burn; she grabbed the wastepaper basket and began filling it with everything to hand: magazines and newspapers, unopened mail, bills and mortgage notices for all she knew. Cookbooks she hadn't looked at in years, old yearbooks and yellowed grandkids' art off the fridge and paperbacks nobody had ever finished reading, all of it went into the basket and out back in one trip after another. When she put match to the pile the flame wandered around its edges just long enough to make her panic and want to snatch things out, while she still could; then it took hold and it was too late, and Mama Simone felt as if fire had saved her from herself. The next loads came easier and burnt faster. She began lugging out years' worth of saved plastic containers, all the medical stuff the nurses had left behind, then the foam mattress pad from the hospital bed where he'd lain in the downstairs bedroom. It stank to high heaven, and a cloud of black smoke billowed up.

143

She stood a while watching it. Then she went back into the denuded kitchen and looked around with a lost sensation. Her arms and legs shook with fatigue, and what had been accomplished? The sitting room, where she collapsed in an old recliner, was as full as it had ever been; if glares could have made junk march outside and immolate itself, the glare Mama Simone gave this junk would have done so. But it sat under her glare unmoved. "I can't get rid of things," she cried aloud, not sure what she meant by it, and then she was weeping in earnest — not sure of what she meant by that, either. "It's pointless," she said, and threw the first thing she could reach — an ashtray — into the kitchen, where it hit the floor and went off like a small bomb. "What am I still here for? What am I good for –" the question stopped in her throat as the answer caught up with it. *Robin. That's what I'm here for*, she thought. *That's what I'm here to do, to fix Robin. To get him his magic back. If the thing took his soul, I'll get that back too.*

Chapter 11
Magic in the Air

Ric had never flown on a private jet before and it amazed him. Leather seats! A cabin he could actually walk around in, and a mini-bar, even a microwave! He realized there was no reason for a plane not to have these things. Commercial jets had them for the crew to use. But he couldn't help feeling that as soon as he got out of his seat and wandered around, any more than the bare minimum to the loo and back, the plane would hit dangerous turbulence. If he turned on the microwave, he was convinced at some level below reason, navigation would fail and the whole affair spiral into a cloud and down to the sea. And if he had been as bold as Lord Stimms and lain down on an actual bed, who knew what might have happened! Passenger discomfort, in Ric's personal cosmology, was what kept airplanes aloft.

Derek sat in the private room lounging on a leather recliner next to Lord Stimms' bed. He had left the door open, there being nothing noisier than Ric on the plane, and now Ric leaned against the doorway and looked in at Lord Stimms, scowling more at his own situation than at his Lordship.

The man was easier to look at when he was asleep, but more fragile. The shadows under his eyes looked transparent, as if Ric could see through into darkness inside his head. Derek had taken his Lordship's hand, probably to keep tabs on him while reading the chief's report on his cell phone, and in his sleep Lord Stimms had wrapped his other hand round Derek's wrist. That was wrong in so many ways. *He trusts us*, Ric thought sourly, *and half our job is to kill him if he's possessed.* There was no mercy in that, was there?

He thought about the original White Knights, the elite guard for King Mismas who had turned on him when he ordered the wholesale execution of Selanto's first parliament. Schoolboys argued for hours about the story. Had the Knights broken their vow of loyalty, or kept it? Were they traitors or heroes? Was their execution for regicide justice or a travesty? Boys never solved these problems, but they never forgot them either. The White Knights' faces were carved above the windows in the Justice Building and Ric saw them every day, but he had never thought about their story as something of flesh and blood. It had been a man's body that they killed. Warm arms they had held down, a pulsing throat they had slit. Hands that had clung to them, the way Lord Stimms clung to Derek in his sleep.

Derek had been reading, but now his eyes were fixed on Ric's face. They talked it over in that look, and though Ric could not have put what they said into words, he felt better. He wandered back and took up a station by the window as if it were his job to watch for Osyth; but there was only ocean, flat and blue except where it was bleached by the glare of a sun that fell further and further behind them, the clock turning forward as they raced east into darkness. He was half-asleep when Derek shouted.

Ric didn't answer. He ran forward, pulling his gun out before he realized that shooting a gun on a plane probably wasn't a good idea — as if a gun

146

would help what ailed Lord Stimms — and then he was looking into the room, and saw the blood.

"I can't wake him up," Derek said. He had Lord Stimms' robe in both hands and was shaking him. Lord Stimms didn't respond, or not to that. He cried out, but that would be because of the slash that Ric could see opening down his face, slowly and precisely. It was the third in a series. It came to the top of his eye, paused for an instant, and went on. Lord Stimms arched in Derek's hands and screamed. Derek shook him again, with no result. Ric felt the *grue* as if it were inside him, and the dreamcatcher buzzed against his chest like a live thing. He grabbed a glass from its holder near the bedside and threw the contents into Lord Stimms' face, but all that did was make Lord Stimms cry out again and wash blood off him in a pink stream. The demon had finished its third slash and begun another.

"Sit him up," Ric said. It was hard to move his jaw. His teeth wanted to lock together, and if he joggled anything he would throw up. He forced his hands to the back of his neck, to the clasp on the dreamcatcher. If he opened the plane door and jumped out, it would feel like this... he got it undone, and when he pulled it off his chest the *grue* swarmed into him, like worms crawling through his tissue. His nerves fought every movement as he reached around Lord Stimms' neck, and by the time he clasped the chain again Ric knew he was going to vomit. He used the wastebasket, cursing himself. *White Knight my ass*, he thought miserably. *Fuck, the chief was right about me and demons. Derek better be ready to take care of himself.* Then he

147

realized the room had gone silent. There was only plane engine noise, a steady rumble. Derek and Lord Stimms were as still as if Ric had frozen them.

"What–?" he said hoarsely.

"Look," Derek said, unnecessarily. Ric had taken it in; the clean bed, the unmarked face. Lord Stimms was still stiff, as if his body didn't realize the dream was over, but Ric could see him begin to relax. Derek laid him back down on the bed, on his side, and began to gently rub between his shoulders. He had done that for Ric, after the demon. It hadn't fixed anything, but it had felt good — as if someone cared.

"I think it would have killed him," Derek said. His voice was shaky, as well. "This is why he wanted you along. Who else would have known to do that?"

Before Ric could answer Lord Stimms jerked upright with a cry, his hands flying to his face.

"You're all right," Derek said. "It was a dream."

"Basin —" Lord Stimms gasped, taking his hands down. He was olive-green, his face dripping sweat, and his hands were cold where they touched Ric's on the side of the wastebasket. He vomited, as Derek had reported, with concentration and thoroughness. Not much came up, though. *Not eating*, thought Ric.

Stimms pushed the wastebasket away and stood, leaning over Derek at an alarming angle. He shook his head when they tried to make him lie down. "Not here," he said, turning pale again, and by the time they had settled him in the sitting area, he was dry-heaving once more.

"I've got him," Ric said, holding his Lordship up with a hand on his chest so the dreamcatcher wouldn't get puke on it. "See what's in the galley." He heard Derek opening cupboards.

Lord Stimms finished and leaned back out of Ric's grasp, looking a bit embarrassed. "You have me at a disadvantage," he said, in a pale imitation of his usual manner.

"Good," said Ric. "Maybe I'll get some straight answers." He pulled out his pad and pressed a thumb against a blank page. It glowed for an instant, and his own handwriting began to write the date and time heading of a transcript.

"Ah," said Lord Stimms, with a watery smile. "The bad cop."

"You have no idea." The pad wrote down the words as they spoke. Stimms didn't object; in fact, he seemed to welcome the distraction.

"What haven't I explained?"

"How you're supposed to get someone away from this demon, when it can rip you up inside your own plane."

Derek came past Ric with a damp cloth and a glass of something yellow and fizzy. Stimms took them as if relieved at the excuse to look away from Ric. What had he seen?

"Antimora also has me at a disadvantage," said Lord Stimms. "It has the luxury of attacking a weaker version of me."

Ric didn't feel he had to say this answer was inadequate. He waited while Lord Stimms took a shaky drink.

"The part of me in the alchemists' prison is being subdivided with every minute," said Lord Stimms. "You know about that."

"Tell me."

"Cause and effect don't work in there. In this world, every action you take rules out a host of possibilities, but in the alchemists' prison all those possibilities take place. If you were to jump out of this plane, in there, one version of you would be falling through the air, but another would have changed his mind at the last minute and be clinging to the door. Yet another would never have considered such a foolish action, and would peacefully be sitting in his seat."

"Not rescuing the one on the door?"

"The one sitting in his seat never opened the door. You can only be conscious of one at a time. Though in actual fact, you would find the plight of the faller or the hanger-on more engrossing. One tends to shift one's consciousness into whichever version is having the most exciting time."

Ric pondered this. "Is that what just happened to you?"

"Something of the sort, yes."

Derek spoke from beside Lord Stimms. "So you can tell what's going on in there."

"Only in occasional flashes," said Lord Stimms. "Remember, anything I experience is but one version of events."

Ric frowned at his hands, trying to stretch his mind around it. He imagined himself hanging onto the plane door, falling, hitting the ground, and at that moment leaping back into another version of himself that was doing — what? "There would be thousands."

"At least," Lord Stimms agreed. "With one's magic subdivided among them."

"Why hasn't the same thing happened to the demon?"

"It did," said Lord Stimms. "When Rosemont first found his way into the alchemists' prison, the same fate befell him. But an exorcist's power is to define people, including oneself. We have some ability to pull ourselves together."

"So when Rosemont pulled himself together, he became a demon? Did he know that would happen?"

"That, I cannot say," said Lord Stimms. He sounded like his old self again, in control of what he told them, and Ric realized the moments of unguarded conversation were over. "He came out of the prison often enough and every time remained in his demon form. It was clear what he preferred."

"There's something you're not telling me," Ric accused.

"Thousands of things," Lord Stimms agreed, taking another sip of the fizzy drink. His eyes looked clear and innocent over the edge of the glass.

"If exorcists can pull themselves together in there, why haven't you done it? Are you afraid you'll turn into a demon as well?"

"That," said Lord Stimms, "is the question. Is it not?" He laughed at whatever he saw in Ric's face. "If I had any intention of testing that hypothesis, I would have done it before now. I will wait until Endamos Names me, as I Named the other exorcists

151

who adventured there with me in April. They appear to have emerged human."

Ric thought of Exorcist Pasqueflower, who was certainly not a demon. Demons did not manifest as fat middle-aged women who dressed out of vintage thrift shops.

"What does it mean to Name someone?" Derek asked.

"To tell them what they are," said Lord Stimms.

"Don't you do that every time you look at someone?"

"I would, were I not so obviously unreliable. A formal Naming is more like an exorcism," Lord Stimms explained. "It involves earning the trust of and identifying with the one to be Named, and it's done in the language of an exorcism."

"What is that language?" Ric asked. "I wonder every time I hear it."

"Nobody knows. Speaking it is a mark of the talent. You can't lie in it — but you can be mistaken. That's what differentiates exorcism from enchantment, which is all lies."

"That's harsh," Derek said reproachfully.

Lord Stimms opened his eyes wide. "It's not a criticism. Being told lies by a well-trained enchanter can be better than being told the truth by an exorcist with no insight. So, is that what you wanted to hear?"

"Not sure," said Ric. "How about telling us just how this operation's supposed to work?"

"I'll go into the alchemists' prison from the pentarium. It shouldn't take any effort, given how eager Antimora is to help me ... once inside, I'll reName Endamos, and he'll do the same for me. Then there will only be one version of each of us. Ideally, I should be able to bring us back. Non-ideally, the magicians of Osyth will invoke us, as they would demons." His voice sounded stronger. Ric glanced at his pad, and when he looked up his Lordship was looking at it as well. "Is there anything I need to spell?" he asked.

"No."

"What about Antimora?" Derek asked.

"It might follow us," Lord Stimms admitted. "If we come back with a *grue*, you can assume one of us is possessed. But whether it's in one of us or its own body, the pentarium will hold it, with no place to go except back into its prison. That will make things simple for you, Inspector Massey. Will it not?"

Shock made Ric's breath stop for a moment. He looked an accusation at Derek, who shook his head in denial. When Ric turned back, ready to shoot questions, Lord Stimms' look stopped him. He felt himself steadying under that gaze. Lord Stimms knew what he was supposed to do, and was counting on his being strong enough to do it. *It's all right*, Ric thought, and his nose tingled. He blinked hard. Then his Lordship blinked too, and the moment was gone.

Lord Stimms struggled with a yawn, then hunched his shoulders and shuddered. Any fool could see he was falling asleep again, and frightened of it.

"The dreamcatcher should take care of it," said Ric.

"I can't afford the side effects," said Lord Stimms; but he put a hand on the dreamcatcher as if it were a life-line.

"They don't kick in right away," Ric said. "The Guard let you use one for eight months before you're taken off duty."

Lord Stimms shut his eyes, his body swaying as if he would fall asleep in his seat.

Derek pulled a lever Ric had missed, and the seat tipped back abruptly, a footrest popping up into Ric's shins. "Blankets are up there," he told Ric, nodding toward a cabinet.

As soon as Ric saw the bedding, it was all he could do to keep his own eyes open as he handed Derek a soft throw and a little pillow. He felt as if syrup was flowing into his brain, like a sticky blanket wrapped around his thoughts. *I never read about this*, he thought muzzily; but it made sense, if an exorcist made you believe yourself whatever he thought of you, a sleepy exorcist would — the thought was brilliant, Ric knew, but it wasn't quite in focus … he jerked himself out of a half-doze, standing right there beside the open cabinet. "How're you doing?" he asked, squinting suspiciously at his partner. Was the kid immune to exorcists, on top of being a seer?

Derek pulled the edge of a charm out of his shirt.

"Is that a Wakcy?"

"Yeah. I'll be fine. You can sleep on his schedule, and I'll sleep when he's up."

"Great," said Ric, " 'cause I don't think I have much choice −" He could barely stand up long enough to grab one of those pillows for himself, and though habit made him check his surroundings before sleeping, he knew the things he saw were going no deeper than the backs of his eyes. Helpless, he thought, and then even words deserted him and he had only feelings as he looked at Lord Stimms, half-curled and already fast asleep with one hand on the dreamcatcher, the other in Derek's. Ric felt fear, when he saw his dreamcatcher on someone else's neck. He felt protective when he looked at Stimms' posture and his thin wrists. Then he looked at Derek's hand, closed around Stimms', and felt something he didn't want to admit, between fear and jealousy, but when he looked at Derek's face the feeling went away, anyways. Just like that, Ric felt safe. He could rest.

***

Paperwork, Russell realized, was a man's salvation. He could put off all kinds of unpleasant thoughts, if he did enough paperwork. But this realization came too late, after Russell had spent forty years arranging his life so as to minimize paperwork; after he did all his own paperwork, and then the paperwork Warren had left him, and then the paperwork he imagined Warren might have left him, had either of them thought of it, it was barely dusk and there was still plenty of time to think of Linus or, the lesser of two evils, of Xiphister. He tried to keep his mind on cheerful thoughts, but the only cheerful thought associated with that demon was its appearance at his defense in Selanto.

Russell gave up after a while. He put his head in his hands, shut his eyes, and let himself

155

remember Selanto and his student days. He remembered streets and squares filled with rose-colored dust and the tidy patches of grass in University of Selanto quads, bordered by walkways and colonnades. The studious youth of Selanto were supposed to pace round these, noses buried in their books. Even in Russell's day, this had been a dream of yesteryear and the studious youth had been more inclined to chuck cans of beer to one another across the quads; the first to miss a catch had to open the can and suffer the drenching that resulted.

It was always a summer evening, in the Selanto of Russell's memory, and he was always one of a group. The Demonology graduate students of his day had *esprit de corps*; they felt it distinguished them from their faculty, who were cutthroat psychopaths to a man, so after a day spent pretending to loathe one another they would go out to the graduate student pub together and then sneak back to the Demonology building, there to open labs and lend one another their professors' things. Big jugs of charm-purified water, for instance — somebody's still had always been on the fritz. The students made tea in beakers, weighed out marijuana on the lab balances. Warm air floated outside the lab windows, too lazy to come in. They ate pizza off lab bench tops after midnight, and drank vile coffee reheated over the smudging braziers — it always tasted of bittersmoke. They tagged the unavoidable cockroaches with nail polish and held races.

They'd been like prisoners under sentence, he thought now, but jolly prisoners. How could they have been so happy, knowing each of them had to bind a demon to graduate? They'd all seen what happened to faculty who grew too weak to control their bound demons. It had happened to all of them, except Russell — "Stupid!" he cried aloud, and got up with a vicious jerking motion that made his back twinge. What comfort was there in knowing yourself smarter than your peers, if all your peers had gotten themselves killed?

**

The sun had gone down behind a bank of purple clouds when *Rho turned his steps homeward* from Lilis's house. Dusk evened out the road, making dips and ridges invisible until he stepped on them, a disorienting sensation his legs remembered before his brain did. The road cut off to the left, looping through a no-man's land Rho remembered well from childhood. He had ridden through here a thousand times in the back of the truck, looking with suspicious awe at the hills and valleys of what he now saw to be no more than an old gravel pit, worn shiny by minibike tires. The shack on the edge of it was still as eerie as it had been, and the few chickens picking around it as dispirited-looking. After the shack, though, he went past a beautiful water-meadow, filled with wild rosebushes and the scent of hay, and then the road went straight on under the protection of big old trees with spreading branches. The farms along here were still prosperous, with freshly painted barns and new tractors.

Nobody hailed Rho, it being dinner time, and he hastened his steps lest Mama Simone worry about him. But home was a ways off yet, at least forty minutes' walk, and Rho had to stop at the hedgerow that bounded their land. He had to look at the cart-track between the plowed field and the hedgerow; for the golden grains of sand he had seen in it when he conjured it up, back when he was trapped in Warren's grimoire, the little frog-shaped insects with red eyes and the long-legged beetles that balanced there until they saw him seeing them and flew away. He had to look for this year's toads, black and nimble, struggling out of one rut and into another... but it was June, wasn't it, and none of those things were in the track. Instead, it had wet stones, moss, and daisies. Still, Rho had to collect himself and take a deep breath before walking past that hedgerow to what lay waiting for him. In his vision, everything beyond the hedgerow had disappeared into flame ... the deep breath he took was foul, but Rho didn't register that until he had gone past the edge of the hedgerow and faced the unexpected grassy outer edges of a dike higher than his head. He scrambled up it, the stench worse every minute, and found himself at the edge of a rectangular cesspool, a lake of waste.

"Holy crap!" he said, apt without planning. At the other side of the cesspool, a rectangular aluminum shed echoed its shape and color; also, Rho realized after a minute, its scope. Both were much bigger than he had thought. His family's house and barn would have fit easily into either the cesspool or the shed, and from the shed he heard a continuous grunting and squealing. It was taller than he'd thought, and the upper third of each wall was rolled up like a garage door. While he watched, the walls began to roll down and a door near the front of the building opened, letting out a hum of machinery. Two men in boots came out and walked around the building, making sure all the walls were working smoothly. They came around the other side, got into a red pickup, and drove away.

Rho waited until they were well out of sight before walking around the cesspool and creeping up to the pig shed. The door was locked, so all he could do was stand and listen. He tried to link the different noises to different pigs, or even different ages of pig, but had to admit complete ignorance. His family had never kept more than two pigs, bought as weaners in the spring and fattened up to bacon-size. He was at a loss to interpret what he heard now, except as indicating a lot of pigs. Hundreds and hundreds of them. Something clicked loudly just to his right, making him jump, and a mechanical noise came from above; fans had switched on inside the building. The fans and walls must be on a thermostat, Rho thought, and became conscious of the cooling air. But cold was not all that made him shudder as he went back to the road.

There were lights on in the farmhouse and a different nasty smell hung around the back yard, as if the pigs had called down a curse on Rho's family. Mama Simone called out as he left his shoes outside the door.

"Robin! Is that you?"

"Yeah," he said. "I walked back from Lilis's. She says hello and come to lunch in town tomorrow."

"Not likely," Mama Simone said. "I have things to do."

"What — wow," said Rho, as he got a look at the kitchen.

"What d'you think?" The room was half-empty, counters and shelves bare. Mama was making bacon, from the smell. Rho's stomach growled.

"It looks like it did when we moved in."

"You can't remember that!" she said, turning around to stare at him.

"Why not? I was four."

"So you were, I guess. What do you remember?"

"It was huge," said Rho. "Big and empty."

"That it was. I never thought I'd own enough stuff to fill this house. Nor I won't, neither. Not anymore. Set the table."

"Are you moving out?" Rho asked cautiously, opening drawers as if their contents might leap out and try to escape.

"I haven't made up my mind. They say you shouldn't sell for a year after a death. They don't say you shouldn't throw things out." She dished up a big plate of potatoes and scrambled eggs for each of them, with fried ham on the side. Rho's stomach fought a civil war inside itself, and the pro-ham faction won.

"Are you going to keep the pig farm?" he asked. "Is it ours?"

"It's a joint venture, with a big concern down in Kasidora Springs," she answered. "We could let them buy us out, I suppose. It brings in a tidy sum." They ate in silence. "You're going to be like your sister, aren't you."

160

"Would it matter if I were?"

Mama Simone kept her eyes on her plate, cutting the ham into neat squares. "Don't threaten me," she said. "I was fine the last twelve years without you, and I'd be fine another twelve."

Rho felt it wiser not to answer this. He ate until the tense moment had passed. "What are you doing tomorrow?" he asked then.

"Taking that front room apart," said Mama Simone. "So if there's anything in there that you want, get it now."

***

" — really the Bright Lady?" asked Derek's voice.

"She was an alchemist. Magister Margaret Devitt."

"Everybody knows that. But if she was one of them, where is she now?"

"Dead," said the second voice. "Her body in this world was dead. When she was reunited with it — pfft."

"Yeah well," Derek said, "it's not a real god if it doesn't go pfft, is it? If it hung around, it'd just be government."

"Sober truth, and a warning to us all," said Lord Stimms. "Your partner has rejoined us."

Ric's eyes felt gummy and his neck stiff. He had been asleep with one cheek against the window, as if he didn't have three double-wide leather seats to stretch out on. He felt simultaneously drugged, stupid, and lucky as hell to not have screamed the plane down with nightmares. But what had

161

happened in the half-hour before he fell asleep? He couldn't consult his notebook in front of Lord Stimms.

After downing the cup of coffee Derek handed him, he only felt half-drugged. Lord Stimms looked remarkably well-rested. There were no marks on his pale face. He was still wearing the dreamcatcher; Ric could see its chain at the back of his neck.

Stimms caught him looking, and looked back as if he and Ric shared something important. What the hell had they talked about?

"Did I snore?" Ric asked just to be saying something.

"Like a grampus," Derek assured him. "Only out of one side, though."

"Half a grampus," said Ric, and looked out the window. "Did you get any more sleep?"

"Yes," said Lord Stimms, stretching. "I slept surprisingly well. Apparently confession is good for the soul."

Ric swore, silently. *The loo!* he thought, like an epiphany, and started to his feet. "Loo," he explained, lurching aft to the spacious room, more like a hotel toilet than like the tiny airplane closets he was used to. He hunched on the stool and read the pad, his eyes getting larger as its transcript sparked memories.

"Sweet Lady Jane," he breathed, sitting up straight and staring out the porthole at indistinct clouds. "He as good as said I was supposed to deal with it, if he comes out a demon. He knows all about the White Knights."

He looked out the window, blinking at the last thin edge of sunset and a rush of relief and gratitude

162

filled him. But that brought him back to the White Knights. They hadn't been mere servants to King Mismas. They had loved him. He'd made them what they were. Schoolboys didn't understand that. Ric hadn't understood it until now, and it frightened him more than demons. He put his notebook away and washed his hands, only then realizing that he did need to piss.

When he got back to the sitting area, Derek and Lord Stimms were sitting in a slightly uncomfortable-feeling silence. "You were talking about the Bright Lady?" Ric asked, feeling a little embarrassed.

"We were," said Lord Stimms. "Are you a follower?"

Derek grinned. "Ric swears by Sweet Lady Jane."

"Really?" Lord Stimms raised his eyebrows. "I thought I knew all the gods of Selanto. Foolish of me."

"She's my cat," said Ric, and Stimms was startled into a genuine laugh. Ric glowed inside, as if he had done something unique and important. "I was raised Bright Lady," he confided.

"I didn't know that!" said Derck, a little put out.

"Policc can't take sides."

"We're human. We're allowed to have a religion. I'm Neverending Way, myself," Derek told Lord Stimms. "Um — what do you believe in?"

Lord Stimms raised his coffee cup in a mock toast. "I believe in Inspector Massey's cat — and I believe that is Osyth below us, at last!" Ric saw a spark of light between clouds, the plane tilted

163

downwards, and the planet rising beneath them cut off the sunset.

Chapter 12
The Lady and the Flame

The luminous clock above the door told Ric it was almost six on Tuesday morning, June 5th, when he opened a gummy eye in the visitors' quarters of Osyth's Public Health Building. Sitting up, he discovered he had fallen asleep fully clothed atop the covers. He now surveyed a room painted institutional green. Not that the color mattered. What mattered was the dreamcatcher hung over the head of Ric's bed, the wards inlaid in every door and, in the glimpse he could catch between heavy curtains, worked in wire inside a windowpane — those, and the feeling of never having seen any of them before.

"Fuck," Ric said to himself, hoping he could replace helpless disorientation with bad temper. He put one sock-clad foot out of bed and felt a groove under it: a pentacle scored into the floor around the bed. That would hold blood, if whoever lay in the bed had to be isolated for exorcism. "Fuck!" Ric said again, and this time he meant it. He got out of the bed fast, and made the rest of his survey standing beside the wardrobe.

The room was maybe four meters square, with two doors. One, the apparent exit, was double-bolted and had an extra ward hanging from the chain. The other door only had the inlaid ward. It was wide open, revealing a loo with sink and a shower stall, also open. The furniture was old but not good, with the exception of the hospital-type

165

bed, and there wasn't much of it; the wardrobe, a plastic-upholstered armchair, pressed wood side table and a flimsy floor lamp beside the window. Ric saw a smoke alarm with a green blinking light that told him magic, also, could set it off. He counted five bittersmoke nozzles in the ceiling and a red emergency-looking switch beside the door. What could that be for?

Having inventoried the room, Ric looked for clues to his own activities in it. The wardrobe door stood open — he never left something large enough to conceal a human closed — and his clothes hung neatly inside it. His suitcase lay on the bottom, with his shoes atop it. The bedside light was on. He'd obviously tried to find some way to waste time last night, in this room with no TV, but had fallen asleep before the magic half-hour had passed. Damn! What else had he forgotten besides the red switch's function?

He rummaged in his coat pocket — no notebook. After a few minutes' search, he found it under the pillow. Three new pages showed him unwelcome evidence of a briefing from the night before. Probably in the car on the way here. He read names of Osyth officials — Ligalla, exorcist. Trott, Commissioner of Public Health. He hadn't a clue about either of them. A quick sketch of another room, with a checklist of security around Derek and Lord Stimms, a note that he was expected to meet them at eleven o'clock in Trott's office, and a similar sketch and list of the wards around him. The red switch, he found, controlled the bittersmoke jets. So that was fine, and a quarter hour was enough to spend worrying about himself. Ric put

166

the subject away. He used the loo and pulled on fresh clothing. Then he flung the curtains all the way open and surveyed Osyth.

He was far enough off the ground to look over buildings huddled in a mass below. Their roofs were blue and gray instead of Selanto's terracotta. The buildings ended a kilometer or so away from him, cut off by a city wall, and beyond that he saw a narrow belt of what looked like pine or spruce. Lower, larger buildings lay beyond the trees; the one furthest to his left — to the west, by the light — was an honest-to-God white castle, with crenellations and turrets. A gigantic hospital-looking complex lay a little to the right of the castle. Behind them, more trees stretched out onto what looked like the edge of a plateau, for the woods ended abruptly in nothing except pearly blue space, filled with what looked like an end-of-storm mist with distant pastel mountain peaks rising out of it like islands.

Damn, Ric said to himself. So this was Osyth! Still, better safe than stupid; instead of striding out of his room, he pulled the door open just a crack. There was nothing outside it except a corridor, its walls painted dove-gray and its carpet a shade darker.

Ric spied to right and left. Only doors, but at least doors with nameplates outside them... he turned his head back and jumped. A woman had stepped silently out of the next door to the right and was standing less than a meter from him. She had a northern face, moon-shaped and noncommittal, with smooth black hair swinging along each side of it as she looked at him for just a moment and then let her gaze slide away to the side, like an exorcist. She wore an unflattering brown suit over a white blouse, and in her hand she held a purple mug with poison-green frogs on it. The lettering on the mug read 'Hoppy Solstice.' Ric was sure he knew this woman.

"Inspector Massey, did you sleep well?"

"Uh — yes," said Ric, still trying to put a name to her.

"Cham Ligalla," said the woman, offering a tiny hand. "Osyth Department of Public Health. I'm the exorcist."

"Oh yeah," Ric said, shamefaced. "I remember."

She led him into an office across the hall. A man with gray hair and a red face sat behind a large desk. His windows looked south onto a completely different view, a cityscape of towering buildings, light-filled air shafting down from between gigantic purple clouds. "Inspector Massey's up, Sherman. You remember Commissioner Trott."

"Already? You're tough," said Trott, lumbering to his feet. His hand was as thick as the rest of him and surprisingly cool. The office was oatmeal-colored, its inner wall displaying a gigantic map of what looked like an island, blunt at the base and pointed at the top and glowing with green and blue lights. "We're here," Trott said, seeing Ric's interest. He put his finger on a light near the pointed end of the map. Most of the lights on that end were blue. "Ley-line's across here –" Trott's finger sketched a line across a bit higher, cutting the pointed end of the map off from the rest. "That's the

Academy. Outside the wall, so not our turf. Magister Ligalla's our contact."

Ric didn't like thinking about the Academy and the pentarium below it. Could Magister Ligalla tell? She took a drink out of the silly mug. Her eyes never met Ric's, as if she was too polite to notice his obvious shortcomings, and it had begun to irritate him.

"Well, we're speaking out of turn here," said Sherman Trott, "but what's the chance of your telling us why Selanto Vice is squiring Lord Stimms around?"

Ric thought about it a minute, and took an executive decision. "Derek's fey," he explained. "We were doing an exorcism last week and he saw Lord Stimms half-disappear."

Magister Ligalla went very still. "He half-disappeared?"

"Went transparent. At least, to Derek. He sees things I can't. But I saw something happen on the plane." He could almost smell the blood again as he told them about it. "Lord Stimms says it's Antimora." Ric looked back at the map and the cluster of blue lights at the Academy end of it. "I thought it was locked away in the Alchemists' prison."

" 'Tis," said Trott.

"Pretty active out here," Ric said. He didn't like the look Ligalla and Trott gave each other. "What are the odds of Lord Stimms winning a fight with it in there?"

"Longer we wait, the stronger it gets," said Trott.

"Any of you going in with him?"

"Probably not," said Ligalla. She was looking at him now! "We can't. The Guild sealed it. The only reason Lord Stimms can go in is that he already is in."

Ric frowned in concentration. "Why can't he just use that connection, and pull Endamos out?"

"Endamos doesn't have an anchor out here," said Ligalla. "When Lord Stimms took us in –" *So she had been one of them!* Ric thought, and looked at her more intently. "—he split each of us into two bodies. One went through the Sacred Flame with him, and one stayed behind in this world. When the Archbishop's guards disturbed us, Lord Stimms lost concentration, and the body Endamos had left behind disappeared. There's nothing here to re-unite him with — and with the Flame gone, no way for anyone without an anchor in that world to enter it."

"So how is Stimms going to fetch him out?"

When Ligalla looked away this time, it felt as if she was hiding her own shortcomings. "He's planning to use an alchemical ward," she said. "It puts the wearer into an extension of this world."

"Like a diving bell," Trott volunteered. "Neat little charm. Magister Whin over in demonology makes 'em."

"Alchemy? The Guild alchemists in Selanto wouldn't help re-open their prison," Ric said, thinking aloud and answering his own question, "but your alchemists are leading the union. They're on the other side. "

Trott nodded. "That's my bet." He stood up. "No point wondering. Alchemists never cop to anything, and with Himself, it's strictly need-to-know — if then. You want breakfast?"

"Coffee, maybe," said Ric. "My stomach's not awake yet."

He followed them to an elevator that told him he was on the fourteenth floor. They got off on the twenty-third and went into a cafeteria with windows on three sides and an even more splendid view of the breaking clouds, sunrays driving down between them into a luminous haze.

"Wow," said Ric.

"It's been raining for almost a month," said Magister Ligalla, leading him to the line. "This looks like our best day yet."

Ric turned, splicing these views onto what he had seen from his bedroom and Trott's office. The nearest window looked almost due west, he figured; the spruce trees and white castle were just visible on his far right. The city wall curved around in front of him, a bit further away than it had been from the bedroom, and he could see pedestrians walking along the wall top. The neighborhood of low buildings came closer to the foot of the Public Health building on this side. He saw a few commercial-looking establishments with parking lots, but even from this high up, it looked a slum. Something glinted as he turned his head, and he realized there was a church down there in the slum, just inside the city wall. The Sacred Flame sparkled on its steeple. An answering memory sparked inside him. That priest was from Osyth, the one who'd photographed the Bright Lady.

"I'm supposed to meet Lord Stimms at eleven," he said, making it a question.

Ligalla nodded. "The Sorcerer put him under a sleep charm and your partner's with him. I can't say when she'll clear him for invocation, but we can't invoke at the Academy anyway this morning. They're having the pentarium's safety-switches tested. We'll let Lord Stimms sleep in, and go over to see the pentarium after he's up. Did you want to go out?"

"I'd like to, yes. Anything I should know?"

"Not really. See Miller on four for wards and leave your cell number," said Trott. "If Stimms asks, I'll say I sent you out to get lay of the land."

Ric rechecked his bearings from the window and got directions from Sergeant Miller on four. Within five minutes he was walking through a neighborhood of crumbling two- and three-story stone tenement houses. It smelled wet, but clean. He had to walk around cars parked on the sidewalk, all of them old and in poor condition. The few pedestrians he met were working class, most of them waiting at bus stops and all uninterested in Ric.

The church had a bell, which rang while Ric was trying to decide which way to turn at a five-road junction. Once he figured out the turn, he found the church only half a block away around a deceptive curve in the street. It was small but not tiny, and looked newly renovated — but then, wouldn't all ex-Sacred Flame churches look that way? This one, though, had been renovated just at the wrong time. As he got close enough to make them out, he saw that its brand-new windows showed the prophets of the Sacred Flame being burned in Selanto's Court of Justice. A sad waste of money, that.

He pushed the freshly painted blue doors open and came into an airy, stone-flagged sanctuary, its pews refinished and honey-golden. Someone had been in already, for half the side windows stood open. Window wards hung in all of them and the blue bowl sat on the altar, along with an unlit lamp. Instead of the tapestry he was used to seeing, this church had a mural of the Bright Lady painted in an archway behind the altar. She looked more human and instead of holding the bowl at her chest she held it out toward the viewer, as if offering something other than refuge. The expression on her face invited Ric; he was not sure to what. But it made him feel that this might be the day he figured out what Mercy was, if he kept it in mind.

He bowed awkwardly, not sure how one behaved when meeting the Lady in a church, and walked up to the altar. The bowl already held water, reflecting the gray ceiling, and a sign lay beside it. 'Please wash first,' the sign said; an arrow pointed him to a side table, where he found a bottle of hand sanitizer.

Ric felt very exposed and public, but backing off now would be rude to the Lady, so he rubbed the stuff on his hands and waited for it to dry. Then he dipped his left forefinger in the water and marked his forehead and the back of his other hand; dipped the right and marked his left hand, touching his tongue last. He couldn't focus at all. In apology, he lit two candles on the altar rail, but there was no place to leave money for them. Then he sat in the front pew and the little building's peacefulness began to sink into him. Traffic seemed very far-off, and the air coming through the side windows was fresh.

He had been sitting there for about twenty minutes and the feeling of understanding more had just begun to change into a feeling of understanding less when the priest he had expected to see, Father Rameau, came in through a side door just behind the altar rail. Rameau was as wide-shouldered and brown-haired as he had been in Selanto, but he wore a brown robe instead of the too-small leather jacket he had worn then. He seemed less vague and more focused, here in his own place. He gave Ric a professional glance to judge whether his services were needed and a shocked look spread over his face, followed by a grin. Ric grinned back and stood up to show he was all done praying.

"Inspector Massey!" said the priest. He might have climbed over the altar rail in his haste to greet Ric, except that the candles were burning there. That recalled him to where he was, and he bowed to the altar before coming down its steps. "Whatever brings you to Osyth? Don't tell me the vice squad is still following me around."

"Dunno," Ric said. "Carrying any more prophesies? Photograph any more gods lately?"

Rameau laughed. "No, thank goodness. Come in back and have some coffee. Have you eaten? I make a mean fry-up."

"Don't put yourself out," said Ric, following him out a side door and into the obligate institutional kitchen, with the obligate ancient range and formica-topped tables. "I can get something back at Public Health."

"So you're here on business."

"Yep," said Ric. "I saw the church, and thought that must be you."

"Only church in Osyth," Rameau agreed.

"It's beautiful."

"A little bipolar, I'm afraid."

"Well, people who want Mercy can sit in front, and ones who want Revealed Truth can sit in back."

"True, true. At least until they get the theology worked out at the main office." Rameau poured him a mug of coffee, thick and black. "Cream?" When Ric shook his head Rameau turned a switch and the front burner leapt to life, a salamander just visible racing around the drip-pan beneath it as the priest tied a great apron around himself. He was apparently determined to make the fry-up, and Ric did not try again to discourage him. "You never did tell me what your day job is, when you're not keeping track of Second Comings."

"We're the arcana division of the Vice Squad," Ric said. "Last week we helped in an exorcism, laid ghosts, retrieved wards from a sewer, kept track of stray alchemists, dispelled a Grant; that sort of thing."

"Hm. Angus Line tells me there's quite a controversy over there about those ancient alchemists. Would those be the strays you keep track of?"

"The office does. I'm not in on that, myself. You were there for the strike, weren't you?"

"In the Archbishop's palace," Rameau said, dishing up. It was indeed a lovely breakfast; the eggs piled high with onion, sweet and translucent. "I went down there after you and I spoke, the Night Of."

Ric was so astonished he stopped in mid-mouthful. "How'd you get in?"

"I don't know," said Rameau. "I was led. I took copies of those photos to the Archbishop — not that he was happy to see them, at all." He shivered, even sitting in the warm kitchen, and Ric bet that was an understatement.

"Those would be the visions that showed him burning the royals alive?"

"Mm-hm. Not his best side." Rameau stared into his plate. "He had a right to see them," he said, as if still defending himself. Then he ate eggs for a while. "Angus says the rumor is he had them framed and hung in his prayer closet for a warning. He's a good man."

"So you were in the square when the Flame went out."

Rameau nodded.

"What's that story about a second god trying to come through it? Or is that just internet tripe?"

"That was a demon," Rameau said confidently. "I saw it four times. Twice here, once in Father Line's church, then in the Archbishop's court. It claimed it was the god of the Sacred Flame, but it was a demon. The Archbishop put wards around the flame, and challenged it to come through if it was truly a god; and it couldn't." He messed with the eggs, apparently put off his feed.

Ric chewed in silence, plugging this information into what he already knew. It fit. The demon Antimora had been behind the Flame, feeding on the ancient alchemists in their prison. Lord Stimms had led exorcists in to conquer it, and it had tried to escape into the bosom of the Church.

176

But the Archbishop had not welcomed it, and then the flame had gone out, trapping the demon and Exorcist Endamos. "I didn't know how close the demon had come to getting out," he said.

"There are people who wish it had!" said Rameau, as if letting out a big burst of steam. He bit into his toast with unnecessary force. "There's a group of bishops that claim it really was the god of the Sacred Flame, and would have led us to glory. They say the Archbishop's an apostate, and want him defrocked — if not burned. Not one of them saw it. But they don't care." He chewed viciously and washed the toast down with a gulp of coffee. "Serve them right if they met that demon," he said. "See how they like it face to face."

"There's never been an idea so stupid that six people out of ten don't love it," said Ric. "Working vice teaches you that much."

"Working religion teaches you the same thing."

"They're not all that different, are they?" They clinked mugs and drank together, but Ric didn't know if they were toasting Religion or Vice.

Chapter 13
Near the Edge

Nine o'clock on a Tuesday, and instead of invoking a demon Russell Cinea was pulling his car into the Alchemy parking lot. It gave him an odd, breaking-out-of-habits feeling. He stood a few minutes, savoring the sensation. This was being in charge, being the one who established the schedule instead of the one who slavishly followed it.

Russell made his way into the Alchemy Building with no trouble at all, which would have surprised him a few months ago. Now, he took it as a given that he could walk through any safeguard the alchemists could erect. Magister Vinca's expression, when he opened his door, showed that he didn't take it as such a given.

"I'm sorry," said Russell, "I should have called first." He wasn't sorry, though. If he'd called first, he wouldn't have seen Vinca's expression; nor would the alchemist have known that he was dealing with someone very different from Warren. "I'm here to follow up about the safety-switch in the pentarium. Since the event at graduation, we're skittish about alchemical safeguards."

"Are you chair now?" Vinca asked, opening the door wider and looking up and down the hall.

"Acting chair," Russell said. "And responsible for the facility's safety. We got a maneater in yesterday's invocation, which raised some concerns in the department; and Public Health wants to use the room for the rest of this week. They're sending somebody over to view it this afternoon."

Vinca took off his glasses and polished them, a familiar gesture. "Uneasy lies the head," he sympathized, waving Russell to a seat.

Of course Russell's eyes went to the window first, seeking the changeable scenery of the garden. Time was that sun and rain had looked in those windows together, winter and summer battling in a land where time meant nothing. Trees had sprung where no seed had been sown, and birds fledged without a nest, for in the alchemists' prison neither time nor causation had existed. Russell had never seen that, and he didn't see it now; all the windows showed him was a view across the grassy courtyard to a colonnade with roses growing up it, through which he could see the blue distance off the northern end of the Osyth plateau.

"I had no idea you were so near the edge," he said, to excuse his staring out the windows, which must hold so many unpleasant memories. He turned back into the room, noting the foliage carved into its woodwork and the forest inlaid in its floor, complete with inlaid birds and beasts and people among the branches. These were easy to see, as Vinca's lab was exquisitely neat.

"In more senses than one," Vinca said politely. "The safety switch."

"Ah, yes. Not that I doubt your work, but the faculty are concerned."

"As they should be," said Vinca. "Professionals must be on the alert for such problems. I will be glad to come over and check the pentarium tomorrow morning. I took a look at our own wardage Monday, and all appeared to be in order. It may also reassure you to know that we found nothing amiss with our wards at graduation."

"But a demon appeared right on stage!"

Vinca nodded. "Nevertheless, it did not break through our wards."

"How did it get there?"

"It came via one of us. Someone who had already been admitted through the wards." Vinca polished his glasses again. "Somebody upon the stage had — or has — an attendant demon. Highly illegal — and, I fear suspicion falls at once upon your department."

Russell sat thunderstruck. Where was Warren when they needed him?

***

Ric found Derek in the twenty-third floor cafeteria a little after nine.

"Eating?"

"No, *I ate with Father Rameau.*"

"Oh!" said Derek. "Never thought of looking him up."

"I saw his church out the window." Ric sat down with his coffee. Derek didn't ask him what he'd found out from Rameau; they'd been partners a long time. He knew Ric would tell him anything important. "What are you seeing?" Ric asked.

"A lot of magic," Derek answered, jerking his head toward the window.

"Auras? Thought you didn't see them."

"I don't," Derek said unhappily. "This is more like a sea of magic. It's green, and it goes up and down." He looked a little seasick.

Ric thought about that, stroking his chin. Had he felt any difference from the Selanto streets? He couldn't tell. "Wonder what you'll see over in demonology."

"I'm seeing something now," said Derek, looking past Ric. Lord Stimms' sandy-haired glamour-self was approaching, in conversation with Commissioner Trott.

"How's he look?"

Derek made a 'tell you later' face and they stood up as Lord Stimms joined them. He was shorter in the glamour, and it felt odd to look into a face that would have been chest-level on the real man. He barely glanced at Ric before turning toward the window. That shouldn't have stung, but it did.

"Ah, Osyth," he said, looking at the view. "Isn't it grand? This is a city where magicians work together. Something we from Selanto have rarely experienced," he explained to the Commissioner, "and find both charming and improbable."

Commissioner Trott looked as if Lord Stimms fell into one of those categories, and it wasn't the first. "I'll have to leave you here," he said, looking at his watch. "Cham's getting you a driver."

"Thank you," said Lord Stimms. "You have been more than accommodating." He showed no inclination to sit down, instead looking out the windows with an expression of modified rapture.

"Um — shall I get you some coffee?" asked Ric.

"Oh! No — sit down," said Lord Stimms. "I've been through cafeteria lines before. More often behind the counter than in front. Standards in the peerage have dipped remarkably low," he added in commentary, "though I maintain that we are a sterling last resort for the unemployable. We have an audience with Magister Cinea of Demonology in an hour." He wandered off toward the line, and Ric immediately turned to Derek.

"How is he?"

"He slept fine," said Derek. "No problem, with all those wards. But he looks a little ragged around the edges right now."

"How are we going to do this? When do you sleep?"

"I'll use his room in the afternoons. It'll give us a chance to talk as well."

"What will Stimms be doing then?"

"Exorcist stuff." Derek flattened his diary onto the table between them. Lord Stimms had a full, but mysterious, schedule, most of it indicated by Xs. "I'm with him at night, and we're both on call from nine to noon, if they invoke on schedule. We have until two to eat and confab. Then I sleep and you do whatever he thinks is worth doing."

"Hm."

Derek looked sympathetic. "If the plane's any clue, it'll be something none of us expect and nobody else could handle," he said. He looked over to where Lord Stimms stood in line, teetering slightly as he gazed into the air above those in front of him. They all looked unhappy.

"What was in the file the chief sent?"

"I can't tell you," said Derek. "Geas. I'll have to hold the screen and let you read for yourself."

"You can tell me if it's something worth worrying about."

"It makes me more worried about Antimora," said Derek. "It's not really about this Lord Stimms."

"Oh." Ric chewed that over for a minute. "They were keeping an eye on Rosemont after he started to become the demon, you mean."

Derek hummed two notes going down. This was a code they'd developed in order to get past any attempts to spell them against talking to one another, and it meant 'yes.'

"So the demon was in control of the world's exorcists for a while."

Another hum, this one with four notes in it to indicate the number of pieces of evidence supporting that theory.

"Do they think this Lord Stimms knew about it? — and that he did anything about it?"

Yes to both. But, Ric wondered, what could a student have done about something like that? He couldn't ask any more because said student had rejoined them, carrying a paper cup of coffee by its brim.

"Hot," he explained. Derek handed him a paper napkin to wrap around the cup. Stimms stood looking out the window as he sipped it, uncharacteristically somber.

"Are you going in after Antimora today," Ric asked, "or just getting the lay of the land?"

"The latter. Ah! There is Magister Ligalla," said Lord Stimms. "Excuse me, gentlemen." He strode toward Ligalla and people got out of his way without even appearing to know they were doing it.

Derek looked after him for a moment before getting up. "I wish I could see auras," he said. "Some seer I am!"

"You see more than I do," Ric said, but he knew it didn't mean much.

What Ric saw, as they followed Magister Ligalla into the Public Health Building's basement, was a well-designed parking garage. It had good lighting and wards painted on every post. Somebody had parked illegally in a handicapped spot and a glowering wraith was sitting on the car's dashboard with its upper half sticking out through the windshield, a ticket in its spectral hands. That gave them a chuckle.

Their car was white, with 'Public Health' stamped on its doors over the same ward that was painted on the posts. Lord Stimms, of course, rode shotgun; Ric and Derek had the back seat.

They stared at the downtown traffic, which was lighter than Ric was used to. Skyscrapers quickly gave way to the slum he had already walked through, but after a few turns they were on a commercial main drag that cut through the neighborhood to a triple gate in the city wall. The main arch had a portcullis pulled up over traffic. The side arches were for pedestrians, and a set of stairs ran up from the inner side of each to the wall top. A steady flow of people came down these stairs, heading out of the city through the small arches. Most of them wore blue or green scrubs.

"This is North Gate," the driver called back. "Where all the hospital workers come through."

Then the car was through North Gate, turning left onto a road that ran along the stand of spruce trees Ric had seen in his first view of Osyth. He caught a backward glimpse of the hospital, before it was blocked off by red brick buildings standing between fine, tall elm trees. They went only a little way on this road before taking a hard right into another parking structure. Looking out the other side of the parking structure, Ric saw the white castle.

"That's where we're going," the driver said. "School of Natural Magic."

Ric's throat tightened as he fought down memories.

The castle stood in an unmowed field. It had the remnants of a moat, a grassy rise and dip that made the sidewalk into a mock bridge as it approached the double glass doors. The lobby within was uninviting, obviously meant for people who already knew where they were going, but Magister Russell Cinea was waiting to guide them.

Cinea was as tall as Lord Stimms. He had thick white hair and a patrician face; overall, a slim and elegant man in his late-sixties or early-seventies, even though he was wearing a blue paper gown that stopped at his knees. It wasn't a garment Ric would have worn to meet an exorcist, and he pricked up his ears as the two men approached each other.

"Magister Cinea," Ligalla said in introduction. "Magister Hull." This was Lord Stimms' glamour-self. "Inspectors Haaken and Massey."

Cinea shook hands with a very formal air. "Gentlemen, it is an honor," he said. He had the kind of manners that called attention to themselves — or, more accurately, to the existence of a Code which people of Cinea's stature followed. Ric thought Lord Stimms might have met his match.

"The honor is all ours," that worthy said, very humbly.

Cinea took the homage for granted. His gestures were rather grand as he ushered them to a narrow staircase. "I understand you intend to enter the netherworld," he said without turning around; but his voice echoed in the stairwell, so Ric had no trouble hearing him.

"That is my ambition," admitted Lord Stimms.

"Do you also entertain ambitions of getting out again?" Cinea asked, dryly.

"Oh, yes," Lord Stimms said pleasantly, "I even dream of not being savaged by demons on the way. This is why we came here, rather than using the Selanto facility."

Cinea nodded in a self-satisfied manner.

Clueless, Ric thought, and found he enjoyed seeing someone even less in the know than himself.

"We have a relatively good record," Cinea said in a mock-modest voice. "Two of us did lose our souls in the facility this winter, but we were in there alone. You'd be using a full coven and all the wards."

"You lost your souls!" Derek said, in a startled voice.

"They're back now," Cinea reassured them, as if he had brought the issue up in order to make this reassurance.

186

"Most impressive," Lord Stimms murmured, and Cinea said no more as they went down two more turnings to where the stair ended outside a door with more wards inlaid into it than Ric had ever seen before. He could feel magic all around, a bubbling sensation like being plunged into seltzer water. Cinea muttered words to some of the wards and touched others, and the door opened into a short corridor with similarly warded doors to left and right.

"We are in the ley-line here," Cinea said. "That's the museum's live specimens room, and this is the pentarium. Ah!" He had pushed the door open and almost into a short curly-haired woman wearing the same kind of blue gown. Her face was familiar from somewhere. She had very bright eyes and a curious expression, until she looked past Cinea and saw Cham Ligalla. Then her face went stiff.

"Magister Whin," Ligalla said gravely, introducing them. "Magister Whin has experience in the netherworld and the Alchemists' prison."

That's where I've seen her! Ric thought. This was the face he'd seen on television back in April, the one who broke the news about what was behind the Sacred Flame. She looked smaller in real life.

Lord Stimms bent over Magister Whin's hand like a courtier. "Lord Stimms speaks highly of you," he said, and her face thawed. She stepped back out of the way. The room behind her was large and open, with lockers around it and three shower stalls near the far end. Beyond them it turned into an open shower with tiled walls. Benches stood in front of the lockers. It had a wet feeling as if recently used.

"So what exactly is the plan?" she asked, as they walked past her into the locker room. "How many of you are going in? What are you looking for, and where do you want to go? Do you need maps, or did you bring your own? Who's making up your circle? How long do you plan to stay in there? Do you need to bring anything out with you? What wards are you using? You know, demons will see right through that glamour."

Ric got the impression Magister Whin liked saying things that stopped people in their tracks. She was looking away from Magister Ligalla now, in a good imitation of the exorcist's 'too polite to draw attention to an idiot' manner.

"Only a fool would insist on wearing a glamour into such company," Lord Stimms said.

"What's all this about?" Cinea asked, directing his question to Ligalla. He was trying to speak casually, but his eyes were cold. She didn't even acknowledge the question, and Ric felt a stab of sympathy for Cinea.

Lord Stimms cleared his throat and stood up straighter. "Only a complete fool," he went on, "would take it off." He pulled the glamour-card out and touched it. Ric saw the gold shimmer around him blink off. The demonologists blinked as well.

A broad smile spread across Magister Whin's face. "Lord — hey!" she cried, breaking off in the middle, and looked around as if she could see any spying charms. "Now you've got me being all cloak-and-dagger," she griped, turning back to Lord Stimms. "This is the safest place on campus. The Board should hold their meetings down here. Russell, this is Lord Stimms."

188

"Ah," said Magister Cinea. He bowed, as the Code required of a gentleman; but Ric could tell he was furious.

"Magister," said Lord Stimms, and also bowed. "I appreciate the use of your facility."

"For what?" Cinea asked, his tone dry.

"We need to retrieve an exorcist," said Lord Stimms. "I don't leave my people behind."

Cinea nodded. "Very well," he said, still extremely formal. "What are you using as an anchor?"

"Myself. I have done this before."

"You're going back into the alchemists' prison," said Magister Whin, apparently not satisfied with one conversation-stopping remark. "What about Antimora? Won't that open a path for it to come out again? What's the Guild got to say about your going back in there?"

"The Guild appreciates my venture, as does the church," said Lord Stimms. "They have made every effort to assist me, but have been unable to find any way into the alchemists' garden. It is apparently a most difficult problem."

"But you're going to do it here, with no advance notice."

Lord Stimms clasped his hands behind his back and surveyed the shower room. "Amazing, is it not?" he agreed. "A problem all the powers of Selanto find insoluble is not even difficult in Osyth. I will, of course, require your advice regarding protocol."

This recalled Magister Cinea to business. Ric was glad that he hadn't thought anything too rude about the paper gowns, because Cinea and Whin stood over the three of them until they had put on the same outfit, belted around with gold chains and supplemented with ridiculous paper booties and paper wrist-and ankle bands printed with a wide gold stripe. ("Delightful!" murmured Lord Stimms, and was grandly ignored). Only then did the magicians let them into the pentarium proper. Ric had never seen one of these, and never wanted to. His stomach hated the very smell of it, but he pushed that aside and took a survey.

The pentarium was circular, shiny gold covering its curving wall. It was hard to estimate the room's size, it was so completely reflected in itself, but he got a handle on the gold safety-chain that stretched between poles set in a meter from the walls. The chain was about two meters long between poles, with five poles, which made the room some five meters across, give or take. He noticed a toggle under the light switch by the door and a red button in the wall opposite.

"That's the safety switch," said Magister Cinea, waving at the red button. "It cuts off all the magic in here, if a demon gets loose. The other one starts bittersmoke in the shower room. If we'd been invoking, I would have made you wash and then use bittersmoke to clear off your magic." *Only one safety switch*, Ric thought, *and opposite the door!* Did demonologists have a death wish?

"To get into the netherworld –?" asked Lord Stimms.

"You would have to cross the safety chains and enter the pentacle," said Magister Cinea.

"Where the demons appear?" Derek was definitely shirty about this. He stared at the center of the pentacle, and Ric wondered what he saw.

"Hm," said Lord Stimms. "Would we be able to take our possessions, or must this uniform be maintained?"

"I wouldn't go in wearing a paper gown," Magister Whin said. "I wouldn't go in at all right now, with Xiphister hanging around."

"True," said Cinea. "You realize this is entirely your own responsibility? The International Demonological Association makes no guarantees. I advise against it, myself."

"Of course," murmured Lord Stimms. "A very impressive facility. When would it be available?"

"As soon as you get your team together," Magister Cinea said. "You can't go in without a full circle — thirteen." The very thought made Ric shiver. The sick feeling of having a demon inside him was back; it slid through his arms and legs and coiled in his belly.

"This isn't safe," Derek said suddenly, standing taller. He took Lord Stimms' arm and pushed him into Ric, shoving them toward the door. "Get out. Now."

Ric could hardly feel Lord Stimms over the echoes inside his own body. When he managed to focus, he found Lord Stimms not so much resistant as rubbery. They tangled, trying to get to the door without knocking into the safety chain, as it took Ric a moment to realize that the posts holding it wouldn't tip over. By then, reality had caught up with Derek and a voice was echoing off the golden walls. It was a human voice, chanting an incantation with a strange cadence, as if it were not using breath to power its words. Magister Cinea had taken the rear, and now he stood defending the doorway. Ric peered over his shoulder, almost retching as the *grue* hit him.

The thing that materialized in the pentacle had two faces. The top one mesmerized Ric. It was almost insect-like, with hard-looking skin and eyes that shone deep inside. But it wasn't the one speaking. That was a human face located in its chest; it looked to be a man in his thirties, but absent hair and body Ric couldn't be sure. Eyes closed and brow knotted, that face chanted until the demon was completely solid. Then it opened watery blue eyes and looked at them.

"Russell!" it said, its mouth stretching into the travesty of a smile, as if it were a toy the demon was operating from behind. "How are you, old boy?"

"I am well, Earnest," said Magister Cinea, his voice blank and surreal. "How are you?"

"Oh, topping," said the face. "Well, hasn't it been a dog's age? My word, I often remember those evenings at the 'skeller. As if it were yesterday. We did have the times, didn't we?"

Just as Ric took in this apparently benign insanity, the face twisted into anguish. It howled a long, bubbling, tortured sound like nothing he had ever heard before, and between Magister Cinea backing into him and Derek pulling from behind he found himself in the center of the locker room, looking at the closed pentarium door, before he realized that the demon had been laughing with the face above.

Magister Cinea stood facing away from them, breathing heavily. He swallowed, as if he were about to throw up. "That –" he said, and stopped.

"–was Xiphister, I presume," said Lord Stimms. "Most dramatic."

"You're not going to be able to use the pentarium," said Magister Cinea, very matter of fact and professional, but his eyes looked through them. He took off his gold chain belt and hung it up in one of the lockers. Lord Stimms didn't move. Derek looked back and forth between the two of them.

"But that guy!" he said. "That guy was possessed. This is what exorcists are for, right?"

"That was not a possession," said Lord Stimms, brushing dust off his paper shirtfront. "If the demon were inside the man, it would fall under my authority. Men inside demons are dealt with by some other office."

Cinea's expression gave Ric a rare moment of foreseeing. He foresaw himself standing between Lord Stimms and numerous punches in the snoot. "Do you need a little time?" he asked Magister Cinea.

"I need to see you all out of here," Cinea replied, and his mouth closed tight as a snapping turtle's.

***

Russell sat in his office. Though it was air-conditioned the air felt hot and thick, hard to breathe, and he was trapped in it like a fly in amber, his time long past. He was sitting like that when the department secretary's student assistant rapped her little-girl rap and pushed the door open.

"I'm sorry, Magister Cinea?" she asked. "You said to bring you these resumes."

Russell couldn't imagine what she wanted. "What?" *He looked at her chest but he saw the demon's. We did have the times.* Her face wrinkled up and now it would scream; but she only spoke again.

"The resume file? For Magister Torecki's position?"

"Oh, yes," said Russell. "Thank you."

"No bother." She hesitated just inside the door. "Are you sure you're all right?" she asked, and now her voice was frightened. "Sir! Can I get someone for you?"

"No, no," said Russell. He stood up and turned his back, which was rude, but he pretended to be looking out the window. "I saw a- an old friend today," he said. "He wasn't well."

Chapter 14
Unwelcome Orders

The driver from Public Health apparently had not expected Lord Stimms and his party to be done so soon; at any rate he was nowhere to be found, so Ric, Derek, and Lord Stimms followed Magister Ligalla to a nearly-deserted dining hall on the fourth floor of the Magic Building, where she left them. Ric couldn't tell what Lord Stimms thought as he stood looking out the tall windows and rocked back and forth, making his robes sway. He folded his arms and thrust his hands up the sleeves. "This is a setback," he said mildly. "Trouble everywhere. Is not Xiphister a Selanto demon?"

" 'Tis," said Derek. "For over a hundred years."

"Really!" said Lord Stimms, looking at Derek as if he had never seen him before. "Tell me more."

"It's in the Codex," said Derek. "Five magicians claimed to have bound it, and it claimed to have eaten all five. When we spot it, we're supposed to call your office. Aren't you supposed to know all this?" Sometime during their forced companionship, Ric noted, he and Lord Stimms had dropped the formalities.

"Ah," said Lord Stimms.

"It had that man inside it," Derek persisted, sounding very irritated. "How did it do that? What's happening to him?"

Lord Stimms heaved a great sigh, as if explaining things to a child. "Demons eat souls, but how is one to get a soul? Flighty things, souls … no sooner trapped than gone again, unless they find bodies to nest in. Your possessor slips inside the soul's original body, to feed on it where it lives. That constitutes a trespass, which it is my business to amend.

"This demon had an easier time of it. A bound demon's master has already given it access to his soul. My participation is neither invited nor welcome."

"Then why did it bother to eat his body?"

"He was probably a nuisance. Demons resent interruptions and little demands for this and that, such as ambitious magicians make. But however he played the master, he belonged to it from the moment he bound it. He went into hell on his own; who am I to tell him he must come out again?" He turned a little to watch a butterfly jig across the field below, from one Lady's Lace umbel to the next. "So many people are in hell, and cannot tell it from Selanto. Or Osyth, I dare say." He turned back to them, smiling brightly. "Shall we dine?"

The Royal Academy had beef 'n cheese soup, something Ric had never heard of before. An eclectic bunch of faculty, staff and students came and went, most of them buying the soup with enthusiasm. It was obviously a favorite, though (he judged) an acquired taste; he found it rather like a liquefied cheeseburger, and soon gave up on it and devoted himself to people-watching. Faculty, he thought, were the ones with vague, distracted expressions. Graduate students looked thin and rather desperate.

"Cheese soup!" Derek said to him. "Who comes up with an idea like that?"

"I can't say. How do we spend the afternoon," Ric asked Lord Stimms, "since we don't get to go marching through hell with our hats off?"

"I will leave that to your judgment," said Lord Stimms.

Ric and Derek looked at each other. "I guess you need to sleep," Ric said reluctantly.

Which I," said Lord Stimms, "do not. Magister Ligalla will keep me occupied while you rest." On cue, Magister Ligalla reappeared with the Public Health driver in tow. "Will you return with us, or wander back on your own?"

"With you," Ric decided. He wanted time with Derek. And he knew the wards better in Public Health — an important consideration when you planned to read something classified.

Lord Stimms raised one eyebrow in an irritating manner, but said nothing. Ligalla was just as silent, and the drive back felt strained as a consequence. Getting into a safe room with nobody but Derek felt like coming out of a pressure chamber. Ric threw his coat and shoes across the room to relieve his feelings, and stretched out on Lord Stimms' bed with a whoosh.

"Yeah," Derek said, grinning. "Shove over."

"If I let you lie down, you'll fall asleep."

"Bull. I have to hold this thing. My aura, remember?"

"Does Stimms have any bugs in here? Or Ligalla?"

"No. I did a sweep first thing."

Reading files on Derek's cell phone wasn't the most uncomfortable thing they'd done together, but for the first few minutes it was close. Then Ric got into the meat of the reports and forgot everything else. The file detailed four years of Rosemont's increasingly bizarre, even sadistic behavior. The current Lord Stimms featured as a witness in some of it, as physical evidence in other parts. All of Rosemont's students appeared in the later documents, in which Selanto Intelligence had wondered just what Rosemont taught them. Ric read Ligalla's dossier with special attention. She was not squeaky clean... Derek scrolled down past a section break, and a picture came up instead of text.

"What the fuck?" Ric muttered, squinting. A geas pushed at his throat, and no matter how hard he swallowed it would not go away, because it was meant for Derek and not for him. He felt sick. The picture was a heraldic shield, with a crown and an unsheathed on it. Eight red droplets fell from the sword's blade. "Oh. Crap. Is this real?"

"Yeah," Derek said. "It's real."

"No-one gave me a shield," said Ric.

"You're just a brevet." Derek pressed his thumb over the image and it faded, revealing another committee report from two years ago. But this one had no names of Selanto nobility or noblemen in its header. The names — pseudonyms — in this committee header were of men who had been dead for hundreds of years — as dead as the king they slew.

Ric read the first page in awed silence. "Why the hell would people keep a record of this?"

"To make sure no one of them could be thrown to the wolves, I guess," said Derek. "The chief must be one. How else could she possibly have this?"

"Crap, crap, crap. Damn." Ric held down nausea as he read the minutes of an assassination plot. They'd thought of everything: how every exorcist might react, who might replace Rosemont as Lord Stimms, how many people would be lost to demons if Stimms had no replacement, how long it would be before all the living exorcists were gone and the world left defenseless against possession. His vision swam and his stomach churned. Was it the import of the plot, or the protective charms? "How bad is this?" he asked Derek, shutting his eyes.

"You know what's bad? This time, they were ready to go without a meeting. How long was it between the time she assigned us to Stimms and the time she cleared you to kill him? An hour tops."

Ric rolled over. "If she was a hundred percent into this, she wouldn't have sent you that report." He put his face into his arms, letting his guts settle. "Is there more to it?"

"One more. It's not warded like that, though."

The last report's hospital warding was nothing by comparison. *I'll have to remember that,* Ric thought. *Any jerk with a strong stomach can probably read my health record.* The new Lord Stimms was back in the picture, with injuries that made Ric grimace in sympathy — and then an abrupt end. "What's that date? Oh." Ric searched his memory. "A week before the first Antimora possession."

"Yep. And then the new Lord Stimms, and Rosemont is never seen again as himself," said Derek, snapping his phone shut.

Ric sat up cross-legged and pulled at his pant cuffs. "What are we going to do?"

"I don't know. But I don't see myself sitting back while another Chief Exorcist goes rogue, and then killing him."

"Like so many disposable razors," Ric agreed. "Well, what are we surprised for? That's probably how they feel about us."

Derek's nod was interrupted by a face-splitting yawn, and Ric felt guilty.

"You get some rest," he said, climbing off the bed.

Chapter 15
High Stakes

Russell opened his eyes onto a gray morning. Dismal, leaden clouds filled his window, but he welcomed them. They meant one night between Russell and what he had seen the day before. He stumbled out of bed, and he was old. Old, stiff. Earnest was inside a demon. All his friends were inside demons, some way. Dead, and defenseless against the monsters they had commanded in life. You knew that, *Russell told himself.* You wrote a thesis on it. *But writing a thesis — that was a thing in itself, a chore that dwarfed any mere facts one recorded in the thesis. When Russell had finished that thesis, he'd gone to the Rathskeller with Earnest and Violet, with all the classmates who, according to his thesis, were going to be tormented for eternity by the demons they had enslaved. He hadn't stayed awake weeping over their fates. He'd finished a thesis!*

Heartless, stupid, *he thought.* How many sleepless nights was he in arrears? I'll probably be dead of old age before I've caught up with them. *But he knew he wouldn't. Within a week, he would have reconciled himself to Xiphister, as blithely as that damned exorcist had.* They asked for it, *he'd tell people.* I warned them! They knew what they were getting into. *He stomped his way along the ley-line as if beating a future Russell into shape, and shut his office door with a bang, turning to glare at his desk and his in-basket.* That's what you'll do, *he apostrophized himself.* You'll read resumes, and in an hour you'll be so proud of having finished them off that you won't give Earnest another thought for the whole day. Why, even now you're only thinking about yourself.

He ought to have tipped the basket onto the floor, flung the computer through the window and the chair into the hall. He ought to have howled and wept — he took his coat off and hung it in the closet before opening the first of the resumes. At least I can hire someone into a program where we don't bind them. Twenty years ago you couldn't have found twelve resumes from magicians who hadn't bound demons. Now, we even get grads from Selanto who've refused. *They had some in the department now, in fact. If not for Russell and the International Demonological Association, and the possibility of a job in Osyth, would Teddy have finished her program without binding a demon? Not likely. And then it might be her face looking out of Xiphister's chest.* Bile rose in Russell's throat at the image, and he slapped the second resume down onto his desk.

Russell had finished the resumes and was on his first e-mail when Linus Ukadnian came knocking at his office door, as unwelcome as a cold. *The gleam in Linus' eye* meant he had something unpleasant to report. He had just opened his mouth when a shout from down the hall interrupted them, and Linus scowled. Russell was immediately well-disposed toward the shouter, the more so as he recognized both the voice and the language: Anders Regan, and an incantation of some kind. The *grue* hit him as he ran down the corridor.

Anders' lab was subdivided by bookcases, so Russell had to go all the way in to see what was going on in the space next the window. Linus and Teddy crowded behind him. "Keep the door clear!" he snapped over his shoulder, and that made him realize what he was doing. The Chair, rushing to his faculty's defense! He had five seconds' glow before he saw what he was defending Anders from.

"Holy crap!" said Teddy. She and Linus had cleared the doorway by rushing left into Anders' private office space, and had come out the other end between two head-high filing cabinets. "It didn't look like that yesterday."

Russell recognized at least two of the faces that swam to the surface of Xiphister's torso and submerged again, their mouths gaping as if they drowned inside the demon. But they were gone, he told himself. Dead and gone. And nobody from Osyth would join them, not on his watch. Anders was still shouting, holding up a wooden amulet, and this seemed enough to keep the demon at arms' length.

"What are you doing here?" Russell said to it, in Selantese so as not to distract Anders any more than necessary.

Xiphister didn't turn toward him, but the faces inside it did. They mouthed pleas in his direction. They were male and female, even children.

"I said, what are you doing?" Russell repeated, changing languages. "What business do you have with this man?"

"Leave be," said one of the faces, speaking out of the demon's left buttock. "Oldham can care for himself."

"That's not Warren," Russell said crossly. "Didn't you read the name on his door?"

Everybody in his sight froze.

"Names mean nothing," said Xiphister, speaking out of its own face this time. "Essence is all." But its tone was more arrogant than secure. Its eyes changed color and it looked at Anders again, seeing what? Whatever it saw, it turned away from him and with a rush came up close to Russell. "Where is Oldham?"

"That's privileged information," he was saying, when Linus' voice cut over his.

"You mean your master didn't tell you where he was going?" he asked, in a snide tone.

"What?" said Teddy.

Russell glared at Linus, who glared back. "It followed him into graduation," Linus said. "The auras don't lie. One day he calls up a demon, and the next day he goes off on vacation; I can figure that out, if you can't."

"My master!" Xiphister said, its voice as low and flattened as its eyes. "I have no master. I am the master." Faces rose and fell within it faster than before as it turned its back on Anders and stalked toward Linus, who looked sorry he had spoken. Russell would have done something about it in a minute; he was just going to let Linus have a little lesson; but it stopped its advance when it was a meter away. "You lie. You know nothing."

"I know he left the day after you appeared," Linus shot back. "First thing in the morning. Tell me that doesn't mean something!" he challenged Russell.

"Really," said Xiphister. It sounded as if it was thinking. Russell waited for its next remark, but nothing came; the demon faded before his eyes, and in a moment it was completely gone. Russell turned back to Linus, but he hadn't opened his mouth when Anders — of all people! — jumped in.

"You spiteful ass," he said, and Linus was too taken aback by complaint from this quarter to reply. "We could have kept it here, with people who know it's around, in a building with safeguards. But no, you had to show off and bad-mouth Warren. Now it's searching for him, and he doesn't know to expect it, and we don't know what kinds of wards he's taken with him, or where he's gone. Did he leave contact information?"

"Not with me," said Russell.

"It's probably just as well," Anders said as a parting shot. "Linus would have given the demon his address. Now get out, and let me call security and clean my lab."

The three of them stood in the hallway, and for once Linus had nothing to say. Russell found that he did, though. "Anders is right," he told the geomancer. "If you hate us all that much, you ought to find someplace else to work."

Linus turned his back at this, and stalked away without a word. Teddy, of course, stayed; and as soon as Linus had gone, she began ticking points off on her fingers.

"How can Warren have gone away without leaving a contact?" was her first point. "Somebody must be watching his house, and his mother. If he hasn't bound it, how's the demon going to find him? What does it even want with him? How does it

205

know his essence, and why would it care? And who were all those people inside it?"

Russell didn't want to talk about them. A noise from his office saved him. "Damn, that's my phone."

"Let it ring," said Teddy, but Russell had no intention of doing that.

When he answered the phone he was even happier it had rung just then. Cham Ligalla was on the other end. However miffed he might be with her at the moment, Cham was one of the people who solved problems with demons, rather than causing them. "Cham! I'm glad you called," he said. "We have a problem over here. Xiphister manifested in Anders' lab. It was apparently after Warren, and Linus just told it he was on vacation."

"Really?" said Cham. "Have you called Warren?"

"I don't have a number for him. Do you?"

"No," she said, dropping it. He could feel the letdown that meant she had turned her attention away. "There's not much to be done until we can reach him. I need to speak with you this afternoon."

Great, Russell thought. *You won't help me, but I'm supposed to help you.* "Fine," was all he said.

"Good," said Cham. "Two o'clock."

Russell called Warren's home number as soon as Cham hung up, and answered two of Teddy's questions in one blow when Warren's mother Bosie picked up the phone.

"Russell! Well, for heaven's sake, it's been forever since I heard from you," she said. "You must not get out much these days, dear. I haven't

206

seen you at Durrell's or at the Slap 'n Tickle, or any of the old haunts. What are you doing with yourself?"

"I'm chairing the department, while Warren's away," Russell excused himself.

"Oh, that's right," said Bosie. "Making yourself terribly useful. Warren's grandfather always used to say a useful magician was worth his weight in gold, and far harder to find — though I couldn't ever see what call wizards had to be so judgmental, they're not a whit more useful than magicians unless you want something built. Not even then, half the time. Why, for all his wizardry that old man couldn't drive a nail without hitting his thumb. Warren's grandmother did all the repairs around that house, I can promise you."

Russell had learned, over the years, that to talk with Bosie one must stick to one's point and ignore the flow of the conversation. "Do you have a number I can reach Warren at?"

"Oh, dear, I wish I could help you. I truly do. But Lili didn't give me a number; she said I'd let it out if she did. She bet Warren an awful lot of money that you'd be calling within two days. But they left awfully early on Sunday, and here you've held out until almost eight on Tuesday — I wonder if she was counting from when they took off or when they landed."

"What are you supposed to do if there's an emergency?"

Bosie laughed. "Oh, I have plenty of gentlemen on call for an emergency. You would be one of them, I suppose. Do feel free to stop over for a little drink; I can always use help setting the home-ward."

"I'd only have time for that if I was able to get hold of Warren and hand my own emergencies back to him," Russell said unhappily. "This is important, Bosie. A demon's hunting him."

"I think demons are so misjudged, don't you?" asked Bosie. "Why, you were the one who told me about having them all come to your defense, and how they behaved better than the faculty. Of course, that was Selanto faculty … Warren gets along with demons, you know that."

"He didn't get along with them last semester. Nezumia pulled his soul out of his body and Rho's demon tried to trap it in the grimoire."

"That demon was quite the gentleman," said Bosie. "Not that I have many to compare it with. Demons, I mean; I know hundreds of gentlemen."

Russell felt his brain begin to rotate inside his head. "The demon looking for Warren now isn't a gentleman," he said desperately. "It's a killer, and Warren doesn't know it's coming. He has to call me, right away."

"There, there. I'm sure Warren can cope with a demon. He's taken his wards with him," said Bosie. "The best I can do for you is to tell Lilian when she calls tomorrow to check up, dear; she promised she'd call every Wednesday."

"Every Wednesday!" Russell heard his voice squeak on the last word. "How long is this trip? Warren said ten days."

"Well, that's tomorrow and next Wednesday, isn't it? You worry too much. I know you'll do just fine. Why, someone with your experience should have been chair a long time ago," soothed Bosie. "I don't have a moment's concern about you, or the department."

That, Russell reflected, was certainly true; if not as reassuring as she meant it to be.

Cham Ligalla knocked on Russell's door at two o'clock precisely. When Russell opened it she gave him a quick glance and looked away, as if to politely refrain from drawing attention to something she had immediately noticed. Russell tried to swallow his exasperation, lest he do something that would justify her evident doubts about his character. Besides, he was the one with a grievance!

"Can I help you?" he asked very formally.

"If you have a moment."

Russell stood aside and let her in. "If this is about Lord Stimms and the pentarium, you've wasted a trip," he said. "I'm responsible, and I'm not letting the chief exorcist go into the netherworld while there's one of the world's most dangerous demons waltzing in and out of the building. What would happen if Xiphister got his soul?"

"There's more at stake than the chief exorcist's soul," said Cham. She opened her attaché case and took out a cloth. "May I?" When she spread it out on his desk, Russell saw that the cloth bore an elaborate gold pattern. It was a geas and privacy spell in one. Cham made sure it was lying completely flat, and then looked at him expectantly.

"What makes you think I'll accept that?" he challenged. "You're the one who wants something from me."

"That's true," said Cham. "I want to bring you in on this. I'm alone in that desire."

"Really? You didn't have any trouble introducing Lord Stimms to me under a glamour and a false name," said Russell. "Would you have done that if Warren were here?" Cham didn't answer, which was an answer, wasn't it. "Lord Stimms can't use the pentarium without my permission," Russell said. "It's Demonology's prerogative to decide who uses it, and when."

"It was Demonology's prerogative when Warren left," Cham agreed. "He might come back and find that has changed."

Russell squinted at her. The thing was, Cham never bluffed. Exorcists had to be truthful, so the force of their personalities would remain strong enough to control demons. At least she had the intelligence to realize Demonology ought to be brought in on whatever was going on, he consoled himself, but he knew it was just spin. Defeat was thick in his throat as he put a hand on her cloth and swallowed the geas.

Cham did not gloat. She sat down in his visitor's chair with her feet primly together and folded her hands in her lap. "Do you know how exorcism works?" she asked.

"You establish sympathy with the demon, and then turn on it," said Russell, a little tartly. Everybody knew that.

"How can I turn on the demon, if I am in sympathy with it?" asked Cham.

The question, put so simply, brought Russell up short. Hadn't he just been reminding himself exorcists couldn't be liars? Yet he had assumed she

210

lied to the demon, when identifying with it. "You must draw on a deeper self-image," he said slowly, working it out as he went. "It must be like recalling one's self after being caught up in an enthusiasm."

Cham nodded, and Russell felt validated. Damn! "That deeper self-image is the source of an exorcist's power," she said. "That is what Lord Stimms helps us construct, when we are Named. We must establish a self-image that inhabits the moral high ground, and keep it inviolate, or our powers disappear."

"That's a tall order, isn't it?"

"Yes," Cham said. Russell felt he had been told to mind his own business. "If one of us fails, part of the world is left without an exorcist until a new one is Named. If Lord Stimms fails, no new exorcists can be Named. Lord Stimms is failing."

"Because of what's going on in the Alchemists' prison?"

She nodded. "Magister Endamos is trapped with a demon that feeds on despair, in a place where he can neither escape nor die. Lord Stimms cannot know this and leave him there and still maintain his own self-image as someone with the moral standing to judge demons. Every week, Lord Stimms' powers diminish."

"Then why hasn't he gone in before now?"

"There are people in Selanto who would not be sorry to see Lord Stimms' powers diminish," said Cham. A thrill ran through Russell from heels to head, telling him that this was the real scoop. This was what she'd laid a geas on him to protect. "Lord Stimms can make demons into weaklings and

211

magicians into exorcists. What could he make voters into? Or disciples?"

Russell knew he looked stupid. Part of his mental flooring had just caved in, and he was falling into a new realm; one in which exorcists were ripped from their web of relationships with demons and the possessed, and dropped into a new one of principalities and powers — not only dropped into this web, but landing on their feet at its center, while Russell floundered in the sticky strands around the periphery.

"The world can't do without exorcists!" he protested. "Nobody could be so cynical as to destroy the system just out of fear that Lord Stimms might take political power!" That sounded stupid even to Russell himself. He felt as if he had flopped over in his sticky prison, after supreme effort, and accomplished nothing save to entangle his other wing.

Once again, Cham tactfully ignored his obvious failings. "Between them the Crown, Church and Guild have kept us occupied for over a month with one false promise after another. All that time, Lord Stimms has grown weaker. This is his last option. We must do it soon."

"What makes him think this will work?" Russell said. Something popped inside his head, as if he had burst free of the web. "Vinca's helping him!" he said, awed at his own brilliance. "That's why the alchemical wards failed at graduation, because Vinca's trying to weaken the walls the Guild set around the garden." It was so exactly the kind of thing Vinca would do that Russell could almost see the little alchemist right there in front of him, polishing his glasses and misleading everybody with a combination of old-world courtesy and half-hidden insults

"When can we invoke?" was all Cham said.

"Not today," said Russell. "Vinca's checking the safety-switch tomorrow morning — if we can trust him. And we'll have to get thirteen magicians together."

"Tomorrow afternoon, then."

He couldn't find a good reason to deny her; and for once, Cham's gaze didn't skate off behind Russell's shoulder or ear. She looked at Russell, for the first time, as if they were equals.

Chapter 16
A Visit to Sterne

Sixth sense woke Mama Simone on Tuesday morning — goat sense. Something told her the goat was in the garden. And sure enough, there the old basket was, munching her way along the pea sprouts. "Hey!" Mama Simone bawled out the window. The goat didn't lift her head, but her eyes rolled up and she began to judge just how long it would take Mama Simone to get downstairs and out the kitchen door. *You think you're so smart!* Mama Simone thought as she slammed the window down and ducked behind the curtain. *I'll show you* — the goat went on eating, but just when Mama Simone was about to sneak down the front stairs and surprise her by coming around the house, the kitchen door banged and she took off for the other side of the barn.

Robin came into view, haring after the wretched creature. Mama Simone could see from her vantage point that the goat had doubled back and was crawling behind a patch of burdock that grew along the paddock fence. After Robin had raced past, the goat rose and calmly clambered back over the fence into the paddock, where she began grazing as innocent as a babe unborn while the horse looked at her with mild interest. Robin had disappeared into the field behind the hedgerow; Mama Simone was up and dressed, with plenty time to plan how to talk with him, before he came back muddy and covered with last year's cockleburs.

"What were you racketing round about?" she asked. He glowered at her like a sulky eight-year-old and she couldn't keep a straight face. "Outsmarted by a goat!" she jeered, and Robin glowered harder. "You're not the first. She's had it into everyone on this farm, the rascal."

"Why don't you tie her out?"

"Hadn't thought about it. It's been busy enough round here lately to keep her in the paddock. Now she's up to her old tricks, we'll have to tie her before she climbs on your car."

"I was thinking about that," Robin said. "I shouldn't be just staying here, I mean I shouldn't keep renting the car if I'm just staying here. I ought to either give it back, or use it."

"Use it for what?" Mama Simone asked. Someone who had sold his soul to a demon wouldn't need a car, she was certain. His master would swoop in on its bat wings, and take him wherever it wanted him to go.

"Um — commuting? I was thinking — Lilis told me there were jobs to be had, at the College in Minich. She said there was someone else without magic teaching in the system, teaching theory, so I might be able to pick up something in the summer session. So I went online, and they still have openings — and the session's beginning in a week. I thought I might drive up to the main campus in Sterne this morning and talk with them and fill out an application while I'm there."

She got up and fussed with coffee at the counter so she wouldn't have to look at him. "You haven't been here a week yet," she said. "Why didn't you just e-mail them your résumé?"

215

"I'd rather meet the guy Lilis told me about, before I try to explain — things." He fidgeted with his coffee, swirling it so it nearly slopped over the edge of the mug.

"And you've been here three nights all alone."

"What do you mean by that?"

She braced both hands on the counter. "Willett looked you up online. He says you're a member of the Demonological Congress."

This was the time for Robin to deny it, but he didn't. "How'd he find that out?"

"You rented the car under your new name." She turned around and there he sat stupid as any little boy, outraged at his brother for tattling. "He found out what that group is, too. You can't join it without selling your soul to a demon. Is that what you've done?"

"No!" He looked as if she had slapped him. "You don't have to sell anything to get into the Congress. You just have to bind a demon — and I didn't do that, anyway. I was in the Congress on a student membership."

"Not since March."

She saw his face change as he realized he was found out. "Fuck!" he said.

"Don't talk like that to me. I don't care what you say with your demon friends, but don't talk like that to me."

She had barely seen Robin as a teenager, but the look he gave her then was pure teen. He couldn't imagine, it said, any more ridiculous statement than the one his stupid old mother had just made. "If I had demon friends, my saying 'fuck' would be the least of your problems," he said. "I don't have any demon friends. They sit with the cool guys."

"What's that supposed to mean?"

"Shit," he said, and put his face in his hands. She didn't pick on his language this time. Perhaps he was going to tell her something. Maybe even something true.

"I had a demon 'friend,'" he said after a while, not looking up. "I never bound it. I picked it up by mistake, at a conference in Selanto. It liked me because of my temper, so it followed me back to Osyth, and we used to hang out together. My department chair knew all about it — that's not really true. I told him about it, but he had lost his soul and I didn't know, so all I told was his body."

"You told a dead body your problems." *When you had a live mother!*

"It wasn't — he was walking around and doing all his stuff! He took me home for dinner and loaned me his grimoire. His charm-book. None of us knew he'd lost his soul until later."

Mama Simone sat down with a bump. "Go on," she said harshly, when he looked worried.

"The demon stole the book," he said, "and before I could tell Warren — the chair — we found out he'd lost his soul. And then the demon wanted me to help it trap his soul in the book. Demons can't cast human charms, but if it had a book with a human soul, it would be able to cast the charms in that book. I tried to trick it, and ended up stuck in the book myself, along with the demon."

"So you did lose your soul."

"I got it back!"

She stood up again. "How do you know? You told me your magic was gone. If you couldn't tell your department chair had lost his soul, how do you know you haven't lost yours?"

"Because his body was dead, and mine isn't."

"You just said he wasn't dead!"

"He wasn't *dead* dead," he said, almost whining in frustration, and that was Robin all over. If that wasn't Robin's soul, she didn't know what was.

"What's this demon's name?" she asked. Something messed with her boy; she wanted to know its name. "I want to meet it."

Robin gasped. "You're crazy!"

"I'm not going to make friends with it. I want to see it. Call it up for me."

"I told you, I didn't bind it. I can't boss it around."

Mama Simone felt her eyes narrowing and her face getting the look that told a man just what you thought of him. "Just give me its name, then. I'll do the bossing."

He pulled into himself, sullen and balky. She couldn't hear what he mumbled toward the tabletop.

"What?"

"I said I don't know its name! I never knew its name, all right? Just let it go!" He stomped outside as if the goat would be better company, letting the door bang behind him.

***

It was dew-early on Tuesday morning when *Rho pulled out of his parents' driveway, fuming and*

218

breakfast-less, and drove down the winding roads to the wide Kasidora valley. One minute he was in hills and the next he was among fields flat as green water, on which farmsteads and copses sailed toward him before the breeze. The breeze blew into Rho's face, or windshield, for before him was the sea, just on the other side of the Sterne Range. He had forgotten how the air felt over on this side of the Kasidora River: liquid, as if it were settling on his skin and leaving a layer of brine. He could almost smell the salt.

This range was where the sea air first dropped its moisture, and the woods were lush. Spring was much further advanced than in Rho's hometown. Farmwives here stood knee-deep in their gardens, picking the first crop of potato bugs and dropping them into bottles of gasoline. Rho began to feel better, more forgiving towards his mother. *She doesn't know anything about demons,* he thought. *She means well.*

The road followed the Vinchifer River southwards, with occasional detours up into the Sterne Range's foothills. Bramble and alder grew head-high between the trees; elderberries covered with still-green buds filled every sunny space. Sweetly pretty, Rho's mother had always called this region and its little white cottages with color-filled gardens. Rho saw many more of them than he remembered; he saw day spas and meditation retreats, towns of industrial-strength quaintness, and pretentious signs proclaiming the grand openings of various holiday resorts. He was perversely glad that his destination lay in the factory district of Sterne, which had nothing twee about it.

The University of Kasidora Extension Office was in a low brick building at the end of a campus made of similar buildings, with barely a tree to its name. Over trimmed grass surrounded the buildings, except where it had been removed entirely to make graveled parking lots. Rho left his car in one of these and walked down corridors that reminded him of his schooldays to a room with secretaries behind a long desk. He expected to be sent to the principal's office.

"I'm here to see Magister Gordon Remen," Rho said, wondering if he should still call someone who had lost his magic 'Magister.' That was what it had said in the faculty directory, though, and Remen had not corrected the salutation in Rho's e-mail.

"Oh yes, he's in. Who shall I tell him —?"

"Magister Rho."

The office she led Rho into was neat-ish — not in the intimidating way of Linus Ukadnian's lab or the businesslike way of the vampire lab at Osyth, but in the more sterile and dusty way of an office in which nothing was done except paperwork. The lab sink, surrounded by upended secretarial coffee mugs, was obviously not used for anything except washing-up. Gordon K. Remen had a similarly unused air about him, though that might just have been Rho's imagination. Gordon K. didn't appear to feel any insufficiency. He was stout, wearing a gray suit over a brocade waistcoat, and his blue eyes twinkled behind half-glasses. His gray hair came down in muttonchops on either side of his jowls. He looked at Rho with an expression simultaneously evaluative and encouraging, and under its sway Rho found himself telling parts of last years' story that he had not meant to reveal.

"So," he ended, "I'm at home for the summer and fall term. Hopefully recuperating."

"I understand completely," said Gordon K., looking as if he did. "Sometimes, though, recuperating is over-rated. Sometimes retooling is a more appropriate concept."

"You mean going on as a mundane?"

Gordon K. nodded. "Magic isn't morally neutral," he said gravely, and a little mysteriously. "It's hard to do unalloyed good with magic. Some ways, we're better off without it."

"Really? All the theories I've read hold that it's a force of nature," said Rho.

"Not all forces of nature are benign," said Gordon K.

"If you don't mind," Rho said, emboldened by the man's apparent resignation to his loss, "how did you lose your magic?"

"I used it up," said Gordon K., "and am not willing to do what it takes to renew it." There was something sinister about that remark, and though he went on, as if trying to make it sound better, it didn't. "I have done the things I was born with the potential to do," he explained. "I used up my power, as it was meant to be used."

"I'm not following you. What's the link between magic and potential?"

"Magic is potential," said Gordon K. "It's the pool of potential actions. Every potential action that is never done adds to the pool of magic. That's why the most powerful black magic involves babies or abortions; they have the most unused potential." He

221

steepled his fingers in front of himself in a lecturing manner. "I knew a witch once who maintained her powers by drowning kittens. It's not morally neutral; if you use more magic than you were born with, you batten on the inabilities and losses of others."

"Oh," said Rho. "I've never heard that theory."

"It's a classic," said Gordon K. "You will find it in the Selanto archives."

"One of our theorists went through the archives last month, but all she came up with was a map of the source of magic."

"I remember that map. It's in Lord Cembel's notes. He skirted around the edges of the truth, but never cut across its center." Gordon K. pulled a printout towards him –Rho's resume, it looked like — and —skimmed through it again. "You seem to meet our needs admirably," he said. "We have two sections of introductory magic to staff at the Minich County Extension College. In fact, I'm going out there later this week to make sure the labs are properly set up. If I'd known where you lived, I would have asked you to meet then and saved you the drive."

"Oh, I don't mind. Do you teach them your theory?" Rho asked, feeling inadequate.

"No, we teach them what's in the textbooks," said Gordon K., with a fine condescension toward the unenlightened textbook authors. "Pearls before — well, you know."

Rho, who had vivid memories of Osyth undergraduates, nodded.

"We will need a reference from your current employer, though," said Gordon K.

"Oh. I mean, of course. I'll ask them to send it to you," said Rho.

"Excellent. Would you care to use the spare computer in the outer office?" Gordon K. shook Rho's hand at parting with every sign of great satisfaction.

Rho e-mailed Russell his request for a reference and then, time lying heavy on his hands, e-mailed a summary of Gordon K.'s theory of magic to Teddy Whin. Just e-mailing Osyth gave him a tense, unhappy feeling. He signed off a little more vigorously than necessary, and got up with too-fast, rebellious movements. Why was he putting himself through this? Perhaps Gordon K. was right. *Mundane life isn't so bad,* Rho thought. *It's better than lurking around the edges of magic and trying to fight my way back in.* He strode out of the library onto the campus a free man.

Rho spent as much time as he felt like wandering the Sterne campus. He checked out the library, walked past closed faculty offices and classrooms, and finally found the student bars. One had free wireless; Rho set up his laptop at a table and ordered himself a sandwich and glass of beer, and then another of each, feeling adult and on his own. It was almost two o'clock before anyone interrupted him.

"Excuse me," the person said. "You're Magister Rho, aren't you?"

Rho jumped. There was no good to come from his being identified, he thought at first. He'd applied for the job as 'Rho,' though, and after a moment's panic realized this must be someone from campus. Then his eyes caught up with his brain and he identified her, not from campus but from four months ago at the Demonological Congress. She was the woman who had been speaking on incubi in pigs, at the session when Rho had picked up his demon. Of course she knew him; he'd been the event of the conference.

"*Juliana Evalde*," the woman supplied, extending a large, tanned hand. She was large, smooth-skinned and dark-haired. Her eyes were small, with curved-down bottom margins as if she was always smiling and a sharp glint as if what amused her was not always kind.

"I remember," he said. "Incubi in pigs."

"That's right. What brings you to Sterne?"

"Summer work," said Rho. "My family's over in Minich Township, so I thought I might apply for the opening in the Minich extension."

"I would have expected you to be doing research in Osyth this summer," she said. "Or any of a hundred other places, considering the meeting." Her eyes were bright and her mouth mocking.

"Well, family," Rho said. "Speaking of which, I should be heading back."

"You won't get over the pass," said Juliana, and sat down. "It's been closed for a half-hour. There's rain up on the Stormborn." She pointed out the window. Though the sun shone on the street outside, Rho could see clouds obscuring the mountaintops.

"Oh!" he said, peering. "When will it open again?"

"The storm'll be over in a few hours, but they keep it closed overnight. The hoteliers have a strong lobby."

"The — oh!" Rho said again. "Crap!" He hadn't budgeted for an overnight stay. "Where's the cheapest place to stay?"

"There's no such thing, in Sterne. Two hundred minimum — come out to my ranch for the night," said Juliana. Rho realized that he had never asked why she was in Sterne. From her expression, she had realized it as well; but she didn't tell him. "We have a guest room," was all she said.

Rho was of two minds about this. This woman was sharp and probably a gossip. Could he spend a night without having her discover his loss of magic? Only the thought of his bank account swayed him. "Well, thanks. What brings you into town, if you have a ranch?" he asked.

"I'm based at the Extension Office," she said

"Then you must know Gordon K. Remen?"

"I've met him," she said, without interest. "Dead magician, isn't he?" *Doesn't matter*, said her tone. "I think he was a Natural Philosopher like you, before he lost it."

"He didn't say," said Rho, and fell into an uneasy silence.

Juliana perceived that she had been tactless. "I'm sure he does fine, administering," she said a little apologetically. "He shouldn't be teaching, though. Leave that to us."

"I don't know enough about it to say," Rho said. "Tell me about the Ag program. What are you doing with pigs?"

"We have a nice little 90-sow confinement unit, farrow to finish." Juliana flagged the waitress and ordered herself a beer and a ham sandwich. "The grad students do a little of everything — the coolest

225

thing right now is portals into the netherworld for dust control. Gulpers love the dust from confinement units. We don't have to do any oil spraying in the facility, anymore. We've had good preliminary results with the waste ponds, with even less expense. One of our faculty puts a portal ward in, the Gulpers come through, eat the stuff, and then go back into the netherworld."

"Wow!" said Rho, excited despite himself. "I've never seen a Gulper."

"All I've seen is their tails," Juliana admitted. "They aren't very social. Pigs are way more fun. We have a couple students working on play behavior. You can't find a better job than playing with piglets and beach balls. We have another long-term project on topics of conversation in finishing pens. A bored pig is a problem pig."

"What kind of topics do you give them?"

"We used to use theology, or ethics. Some of the Arcane Arts students developed conversation packets; you can still pick them up at the extension office. AA is invested in those, because they have a joint project with us and Social Magic analyzing the conversations in different piggeries to see how they reach consensus. That's one of the problems, though. Pigs reach consensus in a month or so, and then they don't have anything to talk about unless they start to develop rituals — which can be problematic. So we're moving over to physical puzzles and games. We've developed treat boxes that need cooperative problem solving to open; that doesn't have as big an effect on weight gain, but it reduces tail biting after they've worked together. And I have a new student trying some modified team building exercises from the business literature."

"Very neat," Rho said. He was back in the best moments of graduate school, excited about learning. "Let me buy you a beer."

***

The dust from Robin's car had barely settled in the road when *Mama Simone went to work,* though nobody would have called it work for the first hour. Anyone who'd come by would have thought the widow was setting in the sun for a little rest, leaned back against the house with her eyes closed.

She was cataloguing. She listed all the things she had accumulated since she cast her last charm: clothes, dishes, books, pictures. Medicines and amulets, soaps and perfumes and jewelry. All this stuff, the makings of a life that she had traded her magic for. She listed them all and cut them out of her heart, one by one. It was far harder to cut out her anger at the whole process. *I earned my life!* she thought furiously. *All of this, I earned it!* But the deepest part of her knew that wasn't true, and answered her in a voice like a tree's. *You bought it,* it said, *and now you must return the purchase if you want the price back. Be glad it is no greater.* Mama Simone thought about the great witch-Queens of old, in the stories; the ones who had bought their magic not just with love and home, but with their children. She stopped complaining. And then the clean feeling came along inside her, like a wind off the mountains, and she knew why she had burned up all the stuff in the kitchen. Her heart had known

227

what she was doing before her head. She went back into the house. The front room was waiting for her.

She stood in the doorway staring in, and the room ignored her. It lay there, full of itself, certain that she couldn't make a dent in it. "I'll show you!" said Mama Simone, and strode in with her boxes and baskets. She turfed everything off the top shelf of the nearest bookcase onto the floor, plumped herself down beside the mess, and began sorting through it.

They really did have fifty years of the *Farmer's Trivia* in here. There were a hundred half-finished books, with all sorts of markers in them; school pictures from when Willett was twelve, little embroidered things the girls had made in Home Ec, and the check Dale Tibbett had given them for that bull back in '84. Probably not worth trying to deposit that. Dale had died a year ago ... Mama Simone dumped all of this stuff into the 'burn' box, and after a moment's thought she threw the unread books in too. Why people acted like books were sacred, she would never know. "We could have heated the place two winters with all this," she said to herself, looking around the room.

After that things went faster, with less sorting. The bookcases were all empty by lunchtime, and once they were empty, why keep them? Someone was sure to want them, she thought, but if she thought like that about bookcases, she'd have to start thinking that way about books and the whole system would fall apart. She'd have to find the person who'd want bookcases and that meant stopping to call around and the children finding out — people were gossips. Then there'd be brouhaha, everything being reconsidered, people saying, 'don't throw any of that out without asking me,' and never coming to get any of it. The next thing you knew, you were living in a storage unit. They didn't want the stuff, they just wanted to know it was there.

"Thinking it's there is quite good enough," said Mama Simone. "If I don't tell them, they'll do just fine." She took the axe to the bookcases. Then she was more than ready for lunch. She ate it sitting in the old recliner, and then dragged that out back to the pile, which lay in a long tree-shadow. Then she took to the upstairs, where her own stuff was, and filled basket after basket with the things on her list. It was long past lunchtime. Where had the day gone? No matter; afternoon was the right time to burn things, when it was still light enough to hide the flames.

The fire threw heat along the whole back side of the house and the front side of the barn. It warmed the front of Mama Simone's apron and turned her back into empty chill, and she felt as if the person she used to be was falling out of that cold open backside. She wanted to dance around the fire, singing old songs she hadn't thought about for years.

On these hills, in the old days, people had made fires like this. They had built a cairn over the body, and piled all the dead man's possessions around it. Not just his widow, but his whole family had danced around it, reclaiming the people they had been before they knew the dead man. Treasure went into the flames. Furs and jewelry, fortunes in gold melting into the pile. Even more; in some of the old

229

piles, they'd found bones. One corpse in the middle, but fingers and hands in the edges, cut off and thrown in. Horrible, everyone had said… she stretched her hands out in front of her and saw the light cut them off, front from back, and shook her head. "Not yet," she said. "I'm not sure you deserve all that." But whoever she was talking to did deserve something, or she deserved to do something wild.

The light blazed up, and she saw her garden sickle gleaming in the tool basket. It felt alive in her hand. She balanced on the edge between heat and cold, as secure as if she were lying on bedrock as she tore the golden pins he had given her out of her hair and threw them into the flames; then she took the hair itself in her hand, with one strong twist and one sharp sweep of the blade that scraped across the back of her neck, and hurled it in as well. The bundle came loose and hanks of it soared frizzing into the air, the smell like a live thing. She held the blade out, wet and bright, and laughed. Something flowed into her, filling the empty place, and she knew where she had to go next. Leaving the fire behind her, she went out into the hills with the sickle in her hand.

The sun stretched his afternoon rays out as if he meant to bar her way, but Mama Simone went on with her shadow marching beside her. She took long steps and light steps, up the lit side of a ridge where all the trees said "warm red goodnight" to the sunset and down the shadowed side of the ridge where the trees had begun to fall asleep.

Down the next valley she went, to a glade where it was already twilight except on the top

230

branches of the old oak. The sunlit branches looked at her, so far down. Mama Simone held her sickle in front of her and stood with her feet spread apart, looking up.

"It's me, old oak," she said. "It's Mama Simone again."

"Old cold evening," the branches in shadow murmured, dozing.

"No," said Mama Simone. "I'm going back to what I was. I've given you back all I bought with my old self. Now give it back to me."

The high branches had no time for her. They stretched out toward the sun. "Goodbye warm glory," they said to it, and Mama Simone pounded on the trunk to get their attention.

"Give it back," she said; but the old oak said nothing.

Mama Simone swung her sickle at the lowest branch. The first blow was half-hearted, but the second struck in. The top branches stopped singing. The sunrays stopped in their march up to the sky. The aspens quaked at the clearing's edge.

"Fool fool folly" they said.

Mama Simone struck again and the old oak drew itself up, raising its branch away from her. At the fourth blow, it dropped the box at her feet. After so many years, it was still the same. Its wood was as fresh as the day she had made it; a simple box without any openings, the top shut the same way the sides were fixed to the base, with thin wicked nails.

The trees all around the clearing stopped moving, even though a wind flowed down the cold slope. They stood silent as Mama Simone picked the box up, silent as she walked past them, holding it tight against her chest. It seemed just a step and a hop, going home. The fire was still burning, and she stood beside it for an instant before going into the house for the axe she'd used on the bookshelves.

Her second blow broke the box open down the middle, enough for her to pry the two halves apart like a nut-shell. They rocked open and there, sitting within the lower half, were three acorn kernels with string tied around them. One was large, and two were small ones as alike as twins, all three shriveled, dry, and dark as the place they'd been locked in. That gave her a start, for when she'd put them in they had been bright and plump. Still, she took the largest one out and picked at the string tied around it. The knot was caked together with dried blood, her own blood from so long ago. She had to go in again to get her good embroidery scissors. Did the little nut plump up a bit, once she'd unwound the string? No telling, but Mama Simone didn't let herself hesitate. If she began worrying now, she'd never get anything done. She swallowed the nut and threw the string into the fire.

At first there was no feeling at all, then warmth under her breastbone. Something like opening a new set of eyes began to come over her. The whole world seemed to get bigger all of a sudden.

That's it! thought Mama Simone, and hurried to cut the string off the others, the twin nuts. She spat on each of them and rubbed the moisture in. Weren't they larger? Was it just the firelight and sunset that made them rosy?

Mama Simone did not intend to eat these nuts. They weren't her magic. *They weren't Robin's either*, the tree-like voice said inside her, but she ignored it. She ran inside for the little ceramic robin from her bedroom, stuffed them in through the hole in its bottom, and tore a strip off her skirt to wad in after them. She breathed on the robin, then, and polished it with her hand and all around her the world got bigger and bigger. She would have said spells, but she didn't know any. She only knew the warmth in her breast and the hugeness of the world, and to breathe it into the little figurine while the sun still shone and the fire still burned.

***

Juliana told Rho all sorts of things about Sterne landmarks, most of them scurrilous, until they reached the city outskirts. Then she drove toward the sea's edge in silence. Rho looked out at blonde hills, winds chasing each other across the grass. Air pounded against the car as it raced into cloud shadows and out again. One after another the hills rolled up under them, swooped and crested, breaking at their right into pale cliffs that met the sea below with a crash and tumble until Rho, dazzled, couldn't tell sea from land or speed from wind. The car turned, then, and dove down between two warm, furry hills; the wind broke over their heads, trees rose up to meet them, and they were in cozy farmland, rattling across a cattle guard.

A skinny kid waved at Juliana and pointed to their right. She rolled the window down.

"Park 'round back," the kid yelled. "The milk truck's late."

" 'S'alright," Juliana yelled back. Rho stuck his head out the window and smelled cow.

233

"I didn't think this was dairy country," he said.

"Stock's about all you can do up here. They've tried all kinds of orchard but you can only grow trees in the hollows, and berries want an acid soil." A big dog came over to investigate as soon as they drove behind the barn. "Lazy lout!" Juliana yelled at him, and he wagged his tail as if it weighed a lot. Rho hung out the window, checking the barns and yard. *Dairy*, he thought. *Why didn't I think of that? No plowing, no pesticides.* But there would be mowing, and the bobby calves, and weaning all the time — how they'd holler! *Not that I'd hear them*, he thought, but it was almost offhand. He was still caught up in the landscape's drama, racing cloud shadows through that dancing grass. He missed the first greetings as Juliana's friends came out of the kitchen; they weren't as real as the gold-topped hills around him, until one of them took his hand in a hard grasp that might have been the land's own.

"I'm Eda," she said, grinning with coffee-stained dentures. She was a small woman, about Rho's size, with wiry sun-bleached hair and a rancher's tan. Julianne was handing packages to a tall, narrow-chested woman with black hair who introduced herself as Martina. "You ride?"

"Sure."

"Then saddle up. I'm just heading out for a constitutional before supper." She led Rho to a corral with three horses in it and handed him over to a dust-gray mare.

The horse was bored by Rho. Even without hearing what she said, he could tell. She puffed her sides out under the girth and slapped her tail into his face. When he finally got astride she ambled until

234

he gave her a few good kicks, and then took off with a jerk designed to show the unsure rider who was boss; but Rho was a sure rider, and leant forward along her neck until she tired of the game. After that they got along. He followed Eda down a cow path along streams, over sparkling fords, until they turned back along a fence at the cliff-edge. They had almost reached the farm's out-buildings when she stopped at a broken gate.

"I'll fix this and catch you up," she said. "Nah, I don't need help. It's not much of a job."

Rho headed up the hill looking into the sea-wind, letting it pound at him until his ears flapped. "Hey!" he said into it, feeling the words driven back into him. The horse thought this was foolishness. She rolled her eyes up every time a vulture went over, as if she was pointing something out to Rho. "Yeah," he said to her, "imagine that."

From the top he could see cattle scattered sparsely along the hillsides, black and white among the golden grasses. He shut his eyes and felt the space around him. Then he looked out into the endless air and began to survey the view below, as if he owned it and could take his time. He catalogued the cliffs and coves, the rocks cut off from land by a lace of surf, the red and gold plants sliding downhill; he worked his way along the coast towards himself and tried to make it into a memory he would never lose. So he had been there for a while before he got around to peering just past his own feet, down the shadowed cliff, and saw the cow carcass.

"Oh, crap," he said. It was a brown cow at the bottom of the cliff, bloated and empty-looking all at once, with the shiny surface that meant it was far gone. Rho made a face, imagining how it must smell. But he'd seen carcasses before. What made this one look creepy was that he couldn't see its legs, as if it had bogged down to its belly in mud and died, trapped there. *It doesn't look muddy*, he thought, leaning forward. *Quicksand?* At which the dead cow turned its head and looked at him.

Rho's heart stopped for a second. The cow twisted its head, looking at him from eyes rolled back so far he could see the whites at the front of them, and he saw that it had no ears either. "Shit," he said, meaning it with all his heart. How could something that bloated be alive? But someone would have to go down there and put it out of its misery, and Rho knew he couldn't let Eda do it alone. He searched along the cliff edge for anything like a path; looking back every minute in hopes that the thing would have put its head down so he could tell himself it had died. The cow turned its head to watch him, until the head could turn no further. Then it rolled itself over with a heave. And it had no legs.

Rho looked down at the shiny bulk and felt space rush away from him, as if the world had just doubled in size. The sun felt hot and bright as a fire. The wind beat at him, and he let it roar through his head until his ears stopped ringing; but he kept his eyes fixed on the cow's eyes. He had nothing except his gaze to hold it where it was, whatever it was — to keep it from flying up the cliff toward him. It heaved again, its shiny skin rippling, and opened its mouth. It had sharp teeth.

236

"See how it stares! I maintain, they must think," it said, in a loud barking voice.

"It's lost. It's looking for a land-whale," said a second voice.

Rho shifted his eyes the merest fraction and saw another cow-head bobbing in the ocean. The head's owner heaved itself up onto land, crawling like a caterpillar on broad flippers. Rho caught his breath with a choking gasp. *Seals! And I heard them!*

Joy hit him as hard as the wind, forcing tears out of his eyes to be driven back flat along his cheeks. He gasped again and again, not knowing whether his mouth formed sobs or laughs. The wind blew his lungs full, and he had to force the air out again. The seals watched this with interest. How sleek and smooth they were! They shone with health.

"One could swear that was a language," said the first seal, the dry one. "Have you seen them with their young? They care for one another, I insist."

The second seal snorted. "They're parasites," it said. "They live under the land-whales' flippers. Have you never seen them come crawling out when one stops, and scramble to crawl back in before it leaves? This one has lost its host, that's all. It has no more mind than a sea-louse."

"Boy, that's the truth," Rho said to himself. "How dumb can I be? Seals! And I thought it was a dead cow —!" A vulture soared low over him. "You're out of luck," he called to it, giddy. "I'm only brain-dead!" Then the strange feeling came again, but in reverse; the world got smaller around him, and when he looked down the shingle below

him was empty, with not even a wet spot to show
where the seals had been.

Chapter 17
Goblin Gifts

Lilian got up before Warren again on Tuesday morning. "Oh!" she said, looking into the refrigerator. She closed it with a solid 'thunk' and began making coffee.

"Oh, what?" Warren asked drowsily. He didn't feel like moving. This was vacation! he thought. Instead of getting up half-asleep and making his own coffee, he could lie in bed till he was rested for seven — no, eight more mornings. Shafts of sunlight came through the window, along with sweet breezes and bird-song. He shut his eyes again and sniffed, heard, felt the wonder of it all.

"Nothing," Lilian said. The coffee-maker began to gurgle. She poured herself a cup and sat down beside the window, looking through a magazine.

Warren was happy to let it go, but when he came out of the bathroom, she was looking into the fridge again. "What's in there? A box-imp?"

"No," Lilian said absently. "Well, it'll just have to be what I say it is. Breakfast." She pulled something square and brightly colored out and put it on the table in front of Warren. "Happy early birthday! I hope it isn't an ice-cream cake."

"My goodness," Warren said. "My birthday isn't until July." The cake had thought of that. Its icing said, 'Happy Early Birthday.' "It could be for you."

"My birthday was last month," said Lilian. "It would have said 'Happy Belated Birthday,' for me.

239

Anyway, I was thinking of having your birthday up here. I brought your present along."

"Oh. How — forehanded of you."

"Well, by July we'll be back in Osyth, and you'll be involved in some kind of Academy emergency."

Warren had to admit that was true.

"Besides, I better give it to you before we go to the goblin market, or you'll have bought one for yourself." She pulled down her suitcase and removed a large parcel, wrapped up in tissue paper.

A book, Warren thought as he took it. A large book with heft to it. It was bound in leather, tooled into protective labyrinths and reinforced with gold at the spine and corners. When he tried to lift the front cover the book opened a flame-colored eye above the labyrinth and glared at him.

"Here, let me," said Lilian, and showed it the receipt. "You're for Warren," she told the book sternly, turning it to make it look at Warren. "You're a gift for Warren." Warren put his finger on the center of the labyrinth, and the eye blinked. It gave him one last careful look, and closed. Now he could open the book and turn its blank pages. They were heavy and butter-smooth, edged with gold.

"Lilian!" he said, overcome.

"You like it?"

"Oh, Lili!"

"*Grimoire* magazine said it was the best kind."

"It's the most beautiful one I've ever seen," said Warren. He leafed through every page. He could almost see the magic he would cast into this book. *I'll never write a wicked charm in you*, he promised it. *You'll be a golden grimoire*. He turned the last page and there, written on the inside of the back cover in pencil, was a number. "Oh!" Warren said, and was struck speechless.

Lilian leaned over. "Don't look at that!" she said. "They're not supposed to put the price in it. Let me rub that out."

"No," Warren kept hold of the book. "It's not a price, Lili. It's a 'burn by' date. It means the book's bound in phoenix skin; it has to be burnt every hundred years, or it turns to ash."

"Is — is that a bad thing?"

"No. Those are the most precious grimoires of all. Nobody ever gave me such a gift. Except when you said 'yes'." Warren put the book down and swept his wife up into the embrace she must have expected, yet she was strangely stiff in his arms.

"I thought you could write in it, to replace –"

"I'll make it the best grimoire that ever was," said Warren. He let go. "What's the matter?"

"Let me look at that mark again," said Lilian. "Oh, dear. Promise you won't be angry, Warren."

"Why on earth should I be angry about a wonderful gift like this?"

"It's not this. It's your other grimoires, the family ones." She took a deep breath as Warren looked at her expectantly. "You remember when Bosic gave them to us, after your father died. Well, I came downstairs one morning and Angela had gotten the box open — and she saw they were books people wrote in — and she'd opened every one to the back and colored all over the inside covers. So I cleaned them off. I never told you, because you were grieving and — well –"

"I wasn't at my best," Warren agreed. "It's probably as well."

"The thing is, when I was cleaning off the covers — there was a mark like this, on each of the books. I cleaned them off with the rest of her scribbling. I should have known a four-year-old couldn't write goblin script!"

Warren did quick math in his head. "Don't worry," he said. "Great-grandpa bought those books in — it must have been the eighteen-forties, when they had to replace everything after the flood. The makers would have burned them just before shipping, so Dad must have burned them again about the time I was born. We'll just put them in the fire when I get home, to be safe." Lilian sighed in relief, but Warren felt a shock as the next thought struck him, as hard as a bird flying into a window.

"My grimoire that Rho had!" he said. "Cham's supposed to have burned it up — but if it was a phoenix grimoire –!"

Lilian stared at him. "Where is it?"

Hope, that had blossomed inside Warren's chest, shriveled again. He shook his head. "A phoenix grimoire rises from its ashes. Rho tipped over the dish Cham burned it in, when the bedding caught on fire," he said. "Those ashes are long gone. But I don't need that grimoire. I have this one, and it'll be far better. Far better!"

Sterne lay on the other side of the Vinchifer River deep in the Sterne Range, among mountains high enough to have snow-capped tips and imposing rock faces. Warren and Lilian followed a truck route through dramatic passes until it split in a flurry of blue signs that directed some trucks to the Industrial Loop, some to the Sterne bypass, and some to the Business District. They ignored these temptations and took the narrower way straight ahead as it dwindled into city streets and, then, into brick- and cobble-paved alleys running through an over-preserved Old Town; the sort of place where thatched roofs and buildings with overhanging second stories coexisted uneasily with mountain bike rental and internet cafés.

The goblin market, as if to carry out the theme, took place in a square park with a bandstand and skateboard rink. The vendors, however, had made no concessions. They remained real rather than theme-park goblins. Almost a score of them stood behind tables on either side of the park's main pathway. They were sexless, to Warren's eyes; most stood no higher than his waist and were clothed in grays and browns, with none of the jewelry goblins were famed for. Some wore peaked hats and some had bare heads, showing how far their ears stood up above the little thatch of hair that shaded their beetling brows and tiny eyes. They stood unmoving, arms folded, neither snarling nor jolly but eerily disinterested in their customers.

Warren wondered how the tourists browsing their booths could stand being so obviously viewed as nothing but the carriers of gold. But he was one of those tourists, wasn't he? If he had met goblins in the mountain he would have felt privileged to watch them go about their business, unacknowledged. Here, they watched him go about his business. His fat, idle human business. Consuming. He felt more and more uncomfortable as he trailed after Lilian past booths of gemstones, metal ware, and ironwork. The only things that lightened his gloom were the wards laid out on one of the tables, in row on row of shiny metal and polished stone. These he could evaluate, and found splendid. They were tied directly to the ley-line, without any magician's intervention.

"How are they powered?" he asked the goblin vendor.

"Ward," the vendor answered, giving him a bilious look. "For protection."

"Yes, I know," said Warren. "I make wards. But these are magnificent work! We can't get this kind of power on the Osyth line, even with trained magicians focusing it. This is as strong as an alchemical ward."

The goblin hawked and spat, but in a gratified way. "Alchemist, ptui! Human look in. Goblin look out. Out is stronger than in."

"You mean humans pass the power through themselves, but goblins don't?"

"Human waste nine parts on self. Goblin move power, not eat it." The wizened face grew sly. "Buy goblin power? Goblin strength." The goblin pulled something larger out from under the table, and Warren realized it was a bun, baked almost black and dotted with shiny, burned raisins.

He shook his head. "Do I look like that big a fool?"

"Big," the goblin allowed. "Maybe not fool." It put the bun away and pushed a ward toward Warren instead. "What for, ward-maker?"

It was one of the greenstones, carved into an oblong with concentric circles inscribed on each end. The circles overlapped in the center, their ridges crossing one another in a complicated braid. A ward to trap something; but what? Warren weighed it in his palms, closing his eyes. A jittery, dancing feeling ran through him. He remembered that from his time out of body, when he had traveled along the ley-line in the company of other spirits. "For incubi!" he said, opening his eyes in triumph. The goblin grinned at last, and Warren glowed.

By the time Lilian realized she had lost her escort and came back for him, Warren had a pile of wards beside him on the table. He had learned the goblins' side of several local issues, and turned down a half-dozen offers of food and drink. And he had identified five out of eight wards, but was not much closer to understanding how they worked.

"How much for all of these?" He prepared to haggle, but the goblin gave him a serious look.

"One price. No bargain," it said, and named almost exactly what he had in his wallet. Warren paid up without a peep, and it nodded in approval. "Here, finish ward," it said, beckoning him closer with a long finger. It picked up a strip of silver filigree and held it to his throat, then his forehead, and then under each ear. Then it bent the silver around one of the crystal wards he had just purchased. It took Warren's money in a businesslike manner, and gave him a leather thong to hang the crystal ward around his neck. He was absurdly thrilled by this.

"I am Warren Oldham," he told it, pounding his fist down on the table. This was how goblins exchanged names at the end of a satisfactory interaction.

Caught in the midst of stowing away Warren's money, the goblin looked startled and then wary. Then it pounded its own knotty fist beside his, so hard the table jumped. He felt tingling around his ears. "Ryks Ver Ingerhal-dorstyk," it said. Warren wished it had a business card, for he was sure he wouldn't be able to spell that from memory. He took the pendant and the package of wards, with much mutual bowing, and rejoined his wife.

"So you're having a good time after all!" she said, almost laughing at his pleasure. She held his hand as they walked along. "Oh, look! The bookseller!"

There was a crowd around this stall, most of whom Warren pegged as grandparents. People actually raising young children wouldn't have the money to buy these books, with their leather bindings tooled into mandalas and labyrinths, gold and carved stones set into the power nodes. Warren ran his hand approvingly over the cover of one especially ornate storybook, feeling its pull. Generations of children would lose themselves in a book like this. Lilian plunged into the crowd. Warren knew she had a list of relatives' likes and dislikes in her head that he couldn't hope to match, so he hovered on the outskirts and admired the spellcraft.

As he was following an especially intricate labyrinth, his finger just off the leather to save marring it, he felt a blow to his thigh and, turning, found a goblin at his side. It had a ferocious scowl on its face, and Warren's first thought was that he must have stepped on its toes; a serious offense. "Excuse me!" he cried.

"Trespass!" the goblin shouted. "Trasher!" It was enormously loud, and Warren saw heads turn all around the market. His face burned. The goblin reached into a leather pouch it wore across its chest and pulled out an apple core, which it held out toward Warren. "Fine!" it cried, holding the other hand out in the universal demand for money.

"Oh, no!" Warren said, horrified as he recognized (or thought he did; apple cores were much alike) the rubbish he had tucked under a rock on the mountain. "I'm so sorry. I didn't mean to litter. I thought the sheep would like it."

"Poison sheep!" the goblin cried, as loudly as before. "Fine!"

Warren was in a quandary. Did paying a fine for his own apple core constitute buying food from the goblins? Yet the scowling goblin faces around them bode ill for him if he tried to weasel out of it. And he had spent all his cash for the wards. He didn't know whether Lilian's coming over to his side was a relief or a greater embarrassment.

"Whatever's going on?"

"I left an apple core on the mountain, and this goblin wants me to pay a fine for littering," Warren said miserably.

"Well let's pay it." She began to open her purse.

"Wait!" Warren put his hand on hers. "It's giving them money for food." Lilian froze. "If it's your money, they might get both of us." He squatted to speak to the goblin sheepherder more discreetly, even though this brought him within nerve-racking range of its furious face and big square teeth. "I'll pay the fine, but you keep the apple-core," he said.

"Not keep your trash!" howled the goblin, spraying spittle into his face. Its breath was, unexpectedly, as sweet as the mountain air. Then it looked lower and its face took on an even deeper purple hue. It snatched at the crystal ward around Warren's neck. Its mouth opened in disbelief, and it turned, howling louder than ever.

"Ver!" it bellowed, and broke into goblin language.

The goblin ward-maker stood up at its table and took notice, scowling as fiercely as the goblin shepherd. It replied just as loudly, and at length. They shouted without restraint, hurling boulders of incomprehensible abuse at one another across the sea of wide tourist eyes and round tourist mouths that was the marketplace.

"I'm not giving you any more apples," Lilian murmured to Warren. She snuggled up close to his side and slipped her hand into his, and he felt marginally better. Finally the goblin shepherd turned back toward them, gasping and almost incoherent with rage. "Stinking big perferant, go where want, poison what want! Donghyeat whorkyn, trespass myscrynt –" It hurled the apple core at Warren, landing a squashy blow on his knee, and stormed into the crowd, which scattered before it.

"Oh dear," Warren said, relieved but shamed near to tears. He bent down to pick up the apple core that had caused so much trouble.

"Here," a voice said, and a hand appeared offering him a tissue.

"Thanks," Warren muttered, blinking hard. He wrapped the core in it and put it in his pocket.

"Don't feel bad," said the tissue-giver. He was a tall, lean man with short-cut gray hair and glasses, wearing shorts and an untucked shirt with blue stripes on a yellow background. "That happens all the time. They hang around market looking for hikers to levy a fine on."

"Is it really trespassing to go up the mountain?"

"Of course not," said the woman standing next to the tissue-giver. Her gray page-boy bobbed as she offered her hand to Lilian and then Warren. "I'm Viv Linton, and this is Charles. It's only trespassing if you go past their wards. And it wasn't littering or poisoning, either; I've fed many an apple to those sheep. Don't give it another thought. They're not." The goblins had indeed dropped the subject, Warren saw as he looked around. They were back at the job of selling, and the few that met his eye did so without apparent recognition.

"I'm Warren Oldham, and this is my wife Lilian," said Warren, taking refuge in the niceties. "We're from Osyth."

"We're from here," said Charles. "If you two have finished your shopping, we could show you a nice restaurant."

"Oh, I'm not done," said Lilian. "I have to get books for the grandchildren."

"Fair enough. Why don't you help her, Viv, and Warren and I will have a sit." Warren was fine with this. He still felt shaky, and left to himself he knew he would blow the incident up into a mountain of guilt and shame. "The first time I came here," Charles said as he lowered his long frame onto the park bench, "I ended up paying all my money to goblins demanding fines. I think the last one was for breathing in the smell of a campfire. They were so bad for a while that they got more tourist money than the legitimate vendors, and people stopped coming to the market. Then the vendors got shirty with them, and now it's more under control. That one'll pay a fine himself; he was just wagering he could get more out of you."

"I can see why it'd drive people away!" Warren said, waxing indignant.

"It does at first," Charles said, "but once you know about it, it's part of the atmosphere. How'd you get in with the ward-maker?" Like the goblin shepherd, he indicated the crystal around Warren's neck. "Getting one of those set here is pretty rare. I knew a guy was taken up by a ward-maker like that, and used to be invited inside their hill. His kids played with the little goblins. Went into mining, I recall."

Warren opened his bundle of wards, and they were soon deep in conversation about where the different stones might have been found. By the time the ladies rejoined them and Lilian handed him a heavy package of books, he was able to laugh at his dismay; but he half hoped the ley-line would not lead him up the goblin mountain again.

Charles Linton looked up at the sky. "Looks like weather," he said. "You better head out if you want to get over the pass."

Warren looked up as well. The sky that looked down at him was cloudless, clear and blue. "How can you tell?"

"See the tallest peak, the one with the little snow top-knot? That shimmer over it. That's air off the Ember Sea meeting air from the continent.

250

There's a reason they call this the Stormborn League."

"Stormborn? That's not on the map," said Warren.

"It's on the goblin maps. See?" Charles fished a map out of his glove compartment. Its stiff, translucent paper was bordered with goblin script . He laughed at Warren's lustful expression. "Keep it – I can pick up another. They divide the mountain ranges north to south, not according to the sides of the river. The tip of the peninsula's the Stormborn, right here, and the goblins down here call themselves the Stormborn after it."

Viv nodded. "Any stone that lightning strikes is sacred to them, and any ground it strikes is their home. That's why everybody has lightning rods. You might have seen them standing up in the fields."

"Oh, I wondered about that!" said Lilian.

"It's a lot easier to put up a rod than to renegotiate for your pasture," said Charles. "But anyway, that's a storm starting up in the League. In a few hours, they'll close the Vinchifer pass. Unless you'd like to stay the night at our place?"

"I'd rather head back," Warren said, conferring with Lili through a look. "If we start now, will we have a safe drive?"

Charles nodded. "It's this side that closes. Water runs over the road. Once you get through the Vinchifer pass, you're far enough from the ocean to be safe. It can be pissing down rain here, and droughty over your side."

Warren had enjoyed the new friends, but he felt impatient with the obligatory goodbyes, exchanges of addresses and cell phone numbers. He was ready to be out of Sterne and back to the cottage, where he could examine his new wards and think over the day's adventures.

They reached the top of the pass before the rain did, but not before the clouds. A button on the dashboard labeled 'Fog Guide' lit up as soon as the visibility decreased.

"What d'you suppose that does?" Warren asked.

"I've never seen it before," said Lilian.

There was no reason not to press it, Warren supposed; he did, and almost went off the road in surprise as something appeared on the hood and swiveled its head to fix him with pale, bulging eyes. It was a spindly imp clothed in what looked like rags torn out of a cloud. In one hand it held a lantern. It raised a hand gnarled as a tree branch and Warren stopped the car; the imp rose and walked down the hood, leaped onto the road in front of them, and marched into the mist with its lantern held high. When it had almost disappeared it looked back and hooted at them, a deep foghorn sound.

"Well!" said Lilian. "It's a guide, all right."

The fog guide kept ahead of them, setting a cautious pace, but Warren still found it nerve-racking to poke along behind the creature, trouble lights flashing. Several trucks blared past him and were hooted at.

"How are you doing?"

"I'd be better with something to listen to. Can you get anything on the radio?"

"No luck," Lilian announced after a few minutes' static. "Why don't I read you something out of the book I bought." She settled back and turned a few pages. "Here's a magician's story — Nöon's Glass. Do you know it?"

"No, go ahead."

Lilian used her story-telling voice; Warren felt cozy the minute he heard it, as if he had a little girl on his lap and a yellow lamp beside him.

The Story of Nöon's Glass

King Herrel of Storn was a grown man when he came to the throne, and little joy had he of it, for he was a man without boldness and full of fears. Yet it was boldness that had killed his brother on the jousting-field, and made Herrel leave his books and studies to become King. He worried late into the night over every one of a king's hundred decisions, until he bethought himself of what he had learned during happier days in the castle library, and sent for the great goblin Twerr Nöon Isbelt deer Hogstrun.

Nöon was the wisest goblin that ever lived. He stood no higher than the King's belt buckle, dressed all in gray, and he carried a staff twice as tall as himself. His eyebrows were as thick as brush-tangles, so that his eyes could scarcely be seen. "What want of me?" he asked the king.

"You are the greatest craftsman of all the goblins, oh Nöon," said the King. "I would buy of you a glass such as the books tell of, in which I might see what will come of each decision I am faced with. Thereby I might rule wisely and well, for the good of both our peoples."

"I can make," said Nöon, "but cost dear."

253

"No cost could be greater than what might befall if I rule poorly," said King Herrel.

"Glass will show what life be," said Nöon. "The life not chosen be mine, for my use. But ask one question at a time, no more."

That seemed to King Herrel to be no cost at all, to lose a life he did not choose and that would not even come to pass, so the agreement was soon made; and it was not long before the glass arrived. King Herrel hung it in his most private chamber, and put a black cloth before it that no-one else might look therein.

Now trouble came upon the kingdom, and some of King Herrel's advisors counseled war and some counseled peace. So King Herrel went to the glass and pulled the black cloth away from it. "Show me what will come of this war," he said.

In the glass he saw not his people, as he had hoped, but only the reflection of himself. But what a self! This self had shoulders stooped with toil; he leaned upon a crutch, and his one eye watered — one, for a great scar ran through the empty socket of the other. His face was worn and his hair gray, and he wore not a King's crown but a slave's collar.

King Herrel started back and let the cloth fall upon the glass. "If this is what will come of it, there must be no war!" he cried. And there was none, though his kingdom paid dearly in tribute and the young nobles muttered among themselves.

Many times in his reign did good King Herrel consult Nöon's glass, and many warnings did it give him. He heeded them all, and his kingdom prospered; and in his own country, it is said, the goblin Nöon lived wondrous well, as if he owned the spoils of a hundred conquests and was served by a hundred slaves.

One thing good King Herrel lacked was a wife to sit by his side, and the other was a son to stand at his knee. So his mother the Queen Dowager had brought to her the fairest ladies in waiting from the entire kingdom, that they might be seen by her son. One of them caught the King's eye, a dainty girl from the east. Glances led to looks, looks to blushes, blushes to a brush of the hand, and the King was all a-tremble with the greatness of his love and the import of his decision. He tossed sleepless in his bed until midnight, and then he sought Nöon's glass.

"Tell me, O glass, what will become of me if I do not have her!"

In the glass he saw himself alone on his deathbed, none by except flatterers and toadies.

"Ah, so I feared!" cried the King, not unpleased to see what he had expected. But as he went to let the curtain down, a whim seized him, and he forgot the goblin's warning. "Show me, mirror, what will become of me if I have her," he cried.

In the mirror he saw the same thing! Save only, among the flatterers who turned away from his bed, he saw a young man who tried the crown on his head while they fawned upon him. And this young man was the image of his sergeant-at-arms.

So full of rage was King Herrel that he dashed the lamp in his hand against the glass, and it fell in a hundred pieces to the ground, a different image of the King in every one. There they found him in the morning, lying senseless and still among the shards, and though he still breathed, no-one would have said he had a life after that night.

And to this day, when a man sees closed off a path he might have gone down, he will say 'It was in Nöon's glass.'

"—and there we are, just in time." Lilian closed the book as Warren switched off his hazard lights. He pressed the 'fog guide' button again, and the imp leapt up onto the hood and disappeared to he knew not where.

"That's an interesting story," he commented. "It reminds me a little of the alchemists' prison. The multiple lives thing."

"I've never seen that theme in goblin stories before," Lilian agreed. "The book says these are folk tales from the Sheep League."

Warren shuddered theatrically. "Sheep, again!" but he was only play-acting. "Look that up on the goblin map."

"It's where our cottage is," said Lilian, after some rustling. "The one nearest the sea is the Stormborn League, and right now we're in the Thorn League. Then comes the Windrest League, and then the Sheep League. Pull over — I'll drive, and you can look at the map."

"You know me too well," said Warren, accepting her offer.

A new map was a holiday in itself, and this one was especially interesting. It showed the mountain leagues in such detail that he could identify some individual peaks. The Vinchifer ley-line's course was shown, and its width; he found the phoenix grove, the valley he had skirted, and the mountain with the invisible sheep. Different goblin tribes' territories were outlined in red, and across three of them ran a dotted line he couldn't find on the legend. It ran northeast from the sheep mountain across the Kasidora Valley and what a human would call the Kasidora Range, but goblins named the Calling League and the Falling League; the line wavered across them, as if following a pass, and stopped abruptly just west of a town called Minich.

"I wonder what this is," Warren mused. If he walked out there, would this line be obvious? Or was it a political feature? He looked at the sky and was pleasantly surprised. They had left the black clouds behind them on the Stormborn; the sky above the mountains ahead of him was baby blue, with only the tiniest white puffs floating across it. Before them the road wound between pine-covered hills towards their cottage, supper and rest by the fire, then bed and another morning — and another and another, for eight more glorious days.

Chapter 18
Mixed News

Ric woke early again on Wednesday, as if his body had always been on Osyth time and had only been waiting for him to bring it here. He looked out the window once more, mapping what he had seen from ground-level onto the aerial view. That was the corner with the drugstore on it; that, the three-arched North Gate; that, the field full of buttercups; and that, the Magic Building with the demon in its basement, where they were to take Lord Stimms this afternoon to meet his nemesis. Ric hunched his shoulders as a goose walked over his grave. He checked his watch, wondering whether he had time to run over to the church, and it told him he had hours and hours; upon which, perversely, he no longer wanted to run over to the church but instead went upstairs for breakfast.

Police canteens were never empty, and the Public Health cafeteria was no exception. At this hour, though, there were few conversations. Most folks were nursing coffee and reading the morning paper, waking up before their shift. Ric was startled and flattered when Magister Ligalla hailed him and made room at her table for his eggs and rasher. She wanted his company! Her intent gaze made him feel important, as if the round-faced moon had looked down and picked him out of a crowd.

"Are we still on for this afternoon?" he asked her. "Did you get thirteen magicians together?"

She nodded. "We'll use exorcists and sorcerers. Some of the demonology faculty as well."

"What about Derek and me?"

"You're not cleared for demon work."

Ric poked at his eggs. He thought about Lord Stimms' pale face and the shadows under his eyes. "I'm sure my chief tried to tell Lord Stimms the same thing, but he still brought me along. What do you know about that?"

"He hasn't told me," she said.

"But you have an idea."

"When we were in the Alchemists' garden, Antimora possessed Lord Stimms. He may feel sympathetic toward your position." Her voice was matter-of-fact, but the way she looked away from Ric wasn't. Whatever Stimms thought, she did not think Ric's five minutes' possession significant. He felt his face burn.

"Lord Stimms must have fought Antimora off," he said, changing the topic, "or it would have made him tear himself apart."

"It did," she said, and looked back at her newspaper.

"He's still alive."

"This one of him is," said Ligalla.

"Oh," Ric said thoughtfully, staring at his plate. He could partly understand this. If he let himself really understand it — let his muscle memories and the coiling in his guts understand it — he was going to ralph up his eggs, right in front of her. "How long did it have him?" he asked, hiding in routine questions. Just the facts, ma'am.

Ligalla looked up. She hadn't expected him to take the discussion any further, Ric thought with sour triumph.

"Almost an hour."

"And how many of him would there have been, after an hour?" *Yeah,* he thought at her hesitation, *I know more than you thought.*

"Hundreds," said Magister Ligalla. She, too, seemed happier in 'just the facts' mode.

"So it did make some of him –"

"Yes."

The facts beyond that statement, Ric didn't want. "But he fought it off."

"It fell apart. It fragmented with him, and lost its powers."

"And you exorcists put him back together, the way you did everyone else in the Refuge?"

"We tried. Each of us did part of it. Endamos wasn't able to complete the job, though. The Archbishop's guards interrupted us."

Ric chewed it over. He didn't like the next question, but it wouldn't go away. It was like a lump of gristle. "He doesn't have any injuries as if a demon tore him apart. So you didn't pull the versions it hurt together with him, did you?"

"It's not that simple," she said. "If all the injuries sustained in the garden were retained, nobody could have escaped alive."

"Still. I've read the reports. All those ancient alchemists were hurt. Physical, psychological — nobody got out free and clear."

"Lord Stimms escaped relatively undamaged," she admitted.

260

"So which parts of him are still in there? What shape are they in?" *Fuck,* Ric thought. He didn't like this at all. He pushed his plate away. "Excuse me," he said, and took his throat and guts into the men's room where, like fractious children, they refused to 'go.' It gave him a chance to sit alone and think things through, though. The stall was little and gray. Closed in. Safe. He shut his eyes and let himself understand things.

Out here, Lord Stimms walked around calm as folk. But in the Alchemists' Refuge, other Lord Stimmses lived. Ones who had been possessed for an hour, in many different ways — Antimora was an inventive demon. Ric knew more than he liked about what it made its victims do to themselves. Lord Stimms had cast it out, true; but those weren't injuries one came back from. Those broken versions of his lordship could not have all fended off the demon, since mid-April. It would be going in and out of them, using them as it pleased. Feeding on their despair. What he and Derek had seen on the plane was only the tip of it, and it hadn't been a dream. It had been real, for one of the Lords in the Alchemists' Refuge. Ric's guts whined as he stood up, but he ignored them. They'd had their chance; right now, he needed more facts.

"What's going to come out, if this works?" he said, not even sitting down to the cold bacon at their table. "Is Lord Stimms going to be alive?"

Magister Ligalla looked at him as if he were her equal, at last. "None of us know," she said.

"He chose me. There's some reason I should be here."

"If you weren't here, he would have died on the plane. You can't do what he needs now," she said, as one liege man would speak to another. "This battle is for exorcists."

"You said you can't go in with him!"

"Neither can you. But we can cast the demon out of him, if he comes back possessed."

That brought Ric up short. A weight he hadn't known he was carrying fell off his back with a thud. *White knights*, he thought stupidly, and was filled with relief so strong he had to turn toward the window to hide his face. The exorcists would get Antimora out of Lord Stimms, if he came back possessed! There would be no question of holding him down and cutting his throat... the morning outside was gray, but Ric saw it in a glory of light. He shut his eyes but the glory stayed with him.

***

Russell stepped out into the gray morning and looked around cautiously. The familiar front walk and ley-line seemed vaporous, as if a step onto them would send him tumbling into the unknown. All night he had dreamed of Selanto: unsettling dreams, in which he went back to the buildings in which he had studied and found them filled with new people, all engrossed in research, and Russell an outsider with no projects to talk about, no right to be there. He woke guilt-ridden, with sourness inside his head.

But why? I do more research than any of them! he thought, scowling. *I work with more demons, and produce more graduates. My time isn't wasted trying to protect myself against my own slaves.*

None of my students are ripped apart or eaten by their study subjects!

A shaft of sunlight struck halfway through the mist, not quite reaching the ground. Something rabbit-sized that had been sitting in the tall grass between his house and the line leapt up and bustled away into deeper greenery, and Russell stared at where it had been. It had gotten away. He had gotten away from Selanto. He had never looked back. He had never had a happy dream about going back, or about the people he'd left behind. Yet seeing one of them inside Xiphister — it hadn't been all horror. It had made him remember ... youth. He'd remembered his youth. Its tastes and smells, and this morning he was remembering something else that he couldn't name. It was rising inside him. What would it be, when it reached the surface? Russell felt it welling, springing within him. He walked along the ley-line as carefully as if he held a bowl of water and must spill none of it.

As soon as he entered the lobby of the Magic Building, though, he was accosted by a student.

"Magister Cinea? Is it true you're acting chair?"

"It is," Russell said suspiciously.

"Then maybe you can help me with this issue about my paper," said the student, holding out a sheaf of stapled notebook pages. Russell hadn't seen a paper in longhand for ten years. He had, however, seen Teddy Whin's spiky purple notes before, and the way she double-crossed her effs. "I turned it in yesterday," the student said in an aggrieved tone, "and she hasn't even given me partial credit!"

"Well, um, when was it due?"

"February, but I negotiated an extension with her," said the student. "I was sick."

"For four months? My goodness! Why didn't you negotiate an Incomplete?"

Russell perceived from the way the student looked aside that he had asked a tactless question. *Female problems?* He might have said something hopelessly old-school like 'There, there,' had not a security guard stepped out of the elevator.

"Magister Cinea! There's a flood in the third-floor mens' room. Do you have anybody who can help us with the thing in the pipes?"

"That's corporeal arcana," Russell said. "You want Zoomancy."

"They're all off campus today," said the guard. "Some end-of-term celebration."

"Then Public Health," said Russell. "Is Susan Teale on campus? She'd know who to call." The feeling he'd walked in with was rapidly dissipating and he knew, at some level deeper even than his interest in the thing in the pipes, that he mustn't lose it. "Send me an e-mail summarizing the situation," he told the student, "with attached copies of any emails you and Magister Whin sent one another about it, and your medical excuse. I'll look at them and talk with her."

The student opened her mouth to say something even more mood-destroying, Russell was sure, and at that moment rescue, in the form of Vinca, came into the lobby. Bill Navanax was dragging after Vinca, with his usual fuck-you air. Russell could never pin down just what about Navanax said fuck-you, but it stood out all around him. The man had

264

never gotten over being a grad student — Russell held his breath for a moment. He'd almost put his finger on what was bubbling up inside him. There it was, on the tip of his tongue, he almost had it –

"Ah, Magister Cinea," Vinca said, very formal.

If I move, will I lose it? Russell thought. But he had no choice. "Good morning," he said. The feeling didn't go away. It was stronger when he looked at Navanax and Vinca together. Had Navanax been Vinca's student? In a sense, because all Alchemy students were students of the Mystic Guild. There were no competing schools in Alchemy, as there were in Demonology. No free thought. However fuck-you Navanax looked, if he had ever said 'Boo' to the Guild, they would have burned him.

With that thought, Russell knew what had been haunting him all morning. A door inside him swung open, and there stood young Russell. The guy who'd said *fuck-you* to all the Demonologists in Selanto. Who'd refused to bind a demon, and insisted on his right to graduate without meeting that requirement, and then taken his degree across the ocean to start a whole new, competing school of Demonology. A new International Society to rival the Demonological Congress. A new kind of research. A city with laws against demon binding. Every month he had found another way to challenge his *alma mater*.

Until — *I grew up,* he thought. Not like Navanax. Ten or twenty years into his job, Russell had stopped being a grad student. He'd gotten involved with Osyth for itself, not as a challenge to Selanto, and that was only right. Osyth was worth more than Selanto. But Russell had grown up, and that was the first step into growing old, and he'd stopped fighting Selanto before the battles were all won. Because every student who bound a demon, he saw now, was a loss for his side. Every one of his classmates trapped inside Xiphister was a job he had not finished. He didn't have a right to grow old.

Today, he thought. *Today I start over!* Everything he saw appeared to him in a new light. Surely he'd been named Acting Chair at just this moment for just this purpose — to unite all the magicians of Osyth in his great cause. The two alchemists, the Chief Exorcist, would find themselves his allies. Nothing would stand against him, least of all a mere demon. "This way," he said, and led Vinca and Navanax down a stairwell they knew quite as well as he did. He could have jumped the last half-flight, or swung from the pipes overhead, but he didn't. Let people think he was old. They'd find out soon enough.

Chapter 19
Into the Mountains

The sun was high on Wednesday when Warren rolled over and raised his head from the pillow. In his dreams he had driven all night on mountain roads, guided by a map that changed every time he looked at it, the mountains and roads shifting into a bay and a star-shaped mountain. When he had looked out the car's window, the purple clouds far ahead of them had changed into mountains and the black mountains had become lakes stretching below them. So disoriented was he that even now the marks and knots on the cabin's ceiling seemed to lay out roads and rivers before his waking eyes. He blinked, stretched, and looked for Lilian.

She was nowhere in sight, but then the cabin door opened and she stepped in, followed by a shaft of light. She was carrying something.

"What's that?" asked Warren.

"It looks like the dish you left for the man in the woods," Lilian answered. She opened the square container. "Mushrooms!"

Warren sat up to look at it. Sure enough, the plastic container had been washed, lined with crisp green leaves, and filled with spongy mushrooms. Wide ribs ran out along each umbrella-cap. "Rothecas!" he said. "Those are a delicacy."

Lilian frowned. "It's sweet of him, but I'm not cooking mushrooms until I know they're safe," she said. "What's the best charm to check them?"

267

"I didn't bring very many charms," said Warren. "We can always use the home-ward. It won't let anything malignant into the web."

Lilian brightened. Back in Osyth, they set the home-ward just before supper. They hadn't done it in the morning as well since their honeymoon days, when being a couple was new and delightful. She set out the blue bowl, stood one of their candles upright in it, and poured in cold water until the bowl was dewed over with condensation. Then she and Warren traced the familiar runes on its surface. The candle shone through them in the familiar patterns, making a web of light that shifted and flickered as it spread across the table, their clasped hands, and into Warren's lap. He held tight to Lili's hand, feeling the familiar warmth and joy.

The web of light had reached the floor now, and it spread as fast as tide rushing across a flat. It raced up the legs of furniture, even the bed with personality, and the container of mushrooms did nothing to stop its advance. It did not stop until it merged with the sunlight outside every window and the open door, and all within was safety and peace.

Warren sighed as every lingering anxiety faded in the home-ward's glow. He imagined, so vividly that he could not but think it true, that the ward's light meshed with the ley-line itself. Not only this room was safe, but every place he had walked to. From the goblin mountain to the phoenix grove, he was protected. All Osyth's problems were left behind.

"Why, Warren!" Lili said slyly, "You look relaxed!"

Warren could not deny it. But the spell was a little broken, and he let go of her hand after one last squeeze. "The mushrooms are safe," he said.

"Yes, and I'm sure they meant a lot to someone living rough in the woods. There can't be that much wild food at this time of year." Lilian put the mushrooms in the refrigerator and began to clear away the home-ward apparatus, setting out her scrapbook. "We should thank him."

"At the least, we should give him another meal," Warren said.

"I'll pack something," Lilian decided, "and you can leave it for him with a thank-you note. We'll give him some of your birthday cake."

It was all very well for her, Warren thought, as she began to putter in the kitchenette and left him to create the note. He didn't even know if the man in the woods could read! Within a few minutes, though, he had begun to dredge up all the charms he knew in Old Selantese and chose one, a meal-blessing. Writing it out would be good practice, before Warren set pen to his new grimoire.

"Can I use your paper?" he asked, turning over the sheaf of scrapbook-stuff.

"Sure," said Lilian. "There's some nice, marbled gray with a gold deckle border."

Warren had no idea what she meant, but he found a flat-nibbed pen and some paper almost as soft as his new grimoire's pages. He wrote as laboriously as a schoolboy, chewing his mustache. Then he drew scroll patterns down each side of the paper and cast a fixing charm on it. A little light settled around every letter. Warren was very pleased; pleased enough, in fact, to poke around in the rest of Lilian's stuff for sealing wax to finish his creation.

"What are you looking for?" she asked, immediately alert as any wife is, when her husband starts getting her things out of order.

"Sealing wax."

"Here, I'll find it." Between them they overturned the box of mottoes, and cardboard scraps flew across the table. "Drat!" She wasn't really angry, though. Warren found 'love,' 'trust,' and 'forever' on the floor. He resurfaced with them, trying to think of a non-soppy way to show them to Lilian, and found her staring at the table.

"Warren, look at this."

The mottoes lay scattered in front of her, but they were all face-up. Warren read them to himself. 'Come, help, save, return, stolen, lost, trapped, mountain, help.' "Did they say that when you bought them?"

Lilian gave him a look that would peel potatoes. "Yes, that's what I'd put in a baby book."

"Um — what did they say?"

" 'Joy, blessing, treasure' — it's a set," she said defensively. "Certainly none of this stuff!"

"What about these?" Warren asked, showing her the words he'd picked up.

"I don't think so." They stood together looking at the table. "I think we need to cast them again," said Lilian. She was all business, picking up the cardboard pieces and stacking them. She put the stack back into their box and shook it vigorously, then dumped them out onto the table. Once again, they all fell face-up.

"Save, lost, home," she read, pushing them aside with her forefinger. "Come, mountain, charm, heal, broken, land, help, save, home." She frowned at the table. "Why must sendings be so mysterious?"

"Union rules," Warren said, squeezing her against his side. "It doesn't look that ambiguous to me."

"Oh, I guess not. But if it can change words, why can't it change any of them to prepositions? Are we supposed to go up the mountain, around it, away from it or under it? Be more explicit!" Lilian told the cardboard pieces, and swept them up again. "Say what you mean," she said sternly as she shook the box, and poured them out again.

'Up, sheep, mountain,' they said, obligingly. 'Cast charm save lost home. Mend broken save lost.'

"That's a little better," Lilian said smugly. "We're supposed to go up the mountain and cast a charm. Now perhaps you can add a bit more detail." On the next cast, however, they didn't even get words. They got runes instead. "Bother."

"Pride comes before a fall," said Warren.

"I don't see you interpreting them."

"I know this one," he pointed out. "We draw it on the bowl when we set the home-ward."

"That's true! They're all from the home-ward! Look!"

Between them, they pushed the runes into order, just as they had traced them on the bowl a few minutes ago. *I was right!* Warren thought. The home-ward, the ley-line; they were all one. When he glanced out the window he almost saw the warm, protecting lacework of light spread across the forest floor.

"So we're supposed to go up the mountain and cast the home-ward," Lili said. "And I'm in on it, for once! Not just packing the lunch."

"Darling! I didn't know you felt that way."

"Oh, I don't always. Goodness knows I don't want to juggle all the things you do. It's just — " Lilian stopped for a minute. When she spoke again, there was something wistful in her voice, quite unlike the businesslike tones Warren was used to. "It's just … I use magic at home, of course, but it's the same way I use a computer. Just a tool. I've never had any sign that it *wanted* me, or knew I was there… am I being silly?"

"No," he said, and held her close. "Not in the slightest." *Here I've been playing around with the ley-line as if this vacation's all about me, not giving a thought to what it's like for her!* He felt himself fill with rock-solid determination. Lilian was going to have her adventure, come hell or high water.

Now she was all action. The cardboard pieces went into her daypack, along with the blue bowl and candle-end. "Make us a couple sandwiches," she said. "How far is it up Sheep Mountain?"

"About two hours," Warren said. "But we need more than sandwiches for something like this. We're taking a full field kit. Wards, first-aid — I have it all in my bag."

Lilian pulled on her pack and did a little twirl. "My first quest ever!"

Lilian and Warren took their new map through the woods toward the tall man's tree, and along the

272

edge of the valley. The ley-line opened the path for them, and they reached the stream in less than a half hour. After that they went more slowly. Still, the sun was high over the horizon by the time they looked at it from the high pasture, the invisible sheep bleating around them.

"Oh, this is wonderful!" cried Lilian. "Look at the daisies, Warren! And that twisted gorse bush, and the little stream. It's out of a fairy tale."

It was, Warren had to admit, when he looked at the ground with more attention. The close-cropped grass was studded with pink and white daisies, stones that glittered like mica, and gray, fern-leaved plants that crawled low to the ground except where they put up hairy pods. The little stream Lilian had found was even more sparkling and lively than the one they had walked up beside, and it splashed through a miniature forest of gorse trunks, past a flat stone for all the world like a door-stone. Above the door-stone, the side of the hill had sheared away and left a flat, brown expanse that should have had a door in it but didn't; and sitting at the side of this false doorway, so still that Warren didn't notice until he had been looking for a minute, was Ryks Ver Ingerhal-dorstyk. When the goblin saw Warren had noticed it, it grinned and took a puff from a tiny pipe.

"Back again," it said. "Not enough trouble first time."

Warren flushed. "No apples this time," he said.

"Too bad. Last one good."

"Is it all right for us to come up here?" Lilian asked nervously.

The goblin made a careless gesture encompassing the hillside, stream and sky. "My house your house," it said, and turned a sharp eye on Warren. "Wyf name?"

"Wyf Lilian," Warren said. "Lili, this is Ryks Ver Ingerhal-dorstyk. The ward-maker."

"Ver," said the goblin, pounding its fist on the doorstone. "Line brings."

"It brought you as well?"

Ver nodded. "Magicians?"

"Just Warren," said Lili. "I'm a scryer."

"Seer."

"Not really. I never went that far at school, just the scryer's license."

Ver raised its eyebrows and blinked at this. "Magic not license. Seer, magician. Line brings." It tapped a long finger against a rock meaningfully. "Line wants."

"What does the line want?" asked Warren.

"Lost League."

"What?"

"That's not on the map, is it?" Lilian asked. She handed their map to the goblin, who spread it open on the stone and ran a gnarled finger across it to the dotted line that Warren had wondered about earlier.

"Lost League," it said, tapping the line. "Nöon's."

"No-one's?"

"No. Nöon's."

"No — oh! From the story. Nöon's Glass."

The goblin nodded. "Land of Nöon. Great magician."

"It said he lived as though he had a hundred conquests," Warren remembered.

274

"All here," said Ver, waving its hand. "Sheep League to Calling League, all Nöon's. Lost now. Line grieve. Line always cry for Lost League."

If Warren understood this correctly, it was a bit of a letdown. "How many magicians have come here?" he asked.

Ver laughed. "Hundred hands climb up," it said, spreading a hand and waggling the fingers. "Line call maybe five."

"Did the line tell them what to do?" Lilian asked tartly.

Ver blinked at her and shook its head.

"Then we're a step ahead of them," she said, and poked Warren. "Get some water for the bowl."

Ver watched with interest as Warren and Lilian set up the home-ward on the flat rock. They stood the candle in the bowl and sat cross-legged beside it, drawing the runes on its outer surface until their fingers met and the charm 'took.' The goblin grunted sharply when the lines Lilian and Warren had traced faded into white and candlelight shone out through them. It looked suspiciously at the hand Warren extended. Its own hand was rough and hard in his, strong as the mountain.

The web of light expanded for a minute, then stuttered and halted. The runes faded on one side of the bowl, and no matter how hard Warren pushed at them, they would not come back.

"It didn't work," Lilian said at last, letting his hand fall. She looked so downcast.

"Try again," Warren said.

Three times they cast the charm, and on the third try Warren put every ounce of strength into it. The lines filled with a nasty, gritty flickering. It grated down his spine. He pulled his hands away and wiped his side of the bowl.

"What's wrong?" asked Lilian.

"It was starting to feed back — like a building on the ley-line," said Warren. "You know how wizards put up a life-size charmcast of a building before we break ground? It's to test for that kind of magical interference, and get the thing sited right before we waste any time building it."

"What mean?" asked Ver.

"It means we're not at the right place to cast this charm. The ley-line's interfering with it."

"Where cast?"

Warren looked around. "We need to write these runes on something that'll float."

They found a plant with round, waxy leaves and Lilian scratched the runes on them while Warren filled the bowl with water. When she dropped the leaves in, they scattered like startled fish; then they regrouped, like fish schooling, and nosed against one side of the bowl. "That way," said Warren, standing up and turning to follow the leaves. But there was nowhere to walk to. They were schooling towards the mountain itself.

Ver walked up to the vertical stone face and knocked. It slid open.

Warren held his breath. He remembered what Charles Linton had said. Were they really being invited inside the goblin hill? The leaves danced and quivered against that side of the bowl, as full of nervous delight as his heart and Lilian's face.

"My house your house," Ver said again. "Enter in peace." It held out a hand to Lilian and led her into the tunnel. Warren took a deep breath and went after.

The goblins' passageways were not much taller than the goblins themselves, so Warren had to bend over at a back-breaking angle. Ver and Lilian hurried ahead at a pace he didn't think he could keep up, but he soon realized it might be his only chance to get anywhere before his back cramped. Half-trotting, he raced down the corridor. At first he looked ahead, wondering at the round holes in the wall and ceiling that gave off a greenish light, but he soon found rubbernecking impossible and looked at his feet instead. The tunnel twisted and passed many branches and doorways.

At last he caught up at a doorway a little larger than the rest, shut off by a black curtain. "No noise," Ver warned them, pulling the curtain aside to reveal a stone door with metal bands across it. Something had cracked the door right across, from its lower left to the upper right side of its arch, and the metal bands bowed towards them. Before Warren was able to give this the thought it deserved, Ver touched its pipe-stem to the center of the door, which swung open.

The room within was higher-ceilinged than the hallway, and Warren could stand upright. He straightened up carefully, as if afraid his bones might crack and waken the men who lay sleeping within, each neatly arranged on his own stone slab, like tomb carvings.

The room held nine biers but only eight were occupied. The figure nearest them was human, a tall knight in full armor with a surcoat of some textured cloth, whether embroidered or woven Warren could not tell. His face was long and marked with deep lines of grief. He lay still with his eyes shut, and neither moved nor breathed. In his hands he held a battleaxe, and Warren was alarmed to see Ver lay hands on it and begin to pull it loose.

The armed knight stirred, but did not open his eyes. "Is the time come?" he asked, in a voice like dry leaves. "Has the reborn come again?" The words were in the goblin's tongue, yet Warren understood them. One of the patterns woven into the tunic might be a translating charm; it was too dark to tell, though Warren bent as close as he dared.

"Near, but not yet here," said Ver, tracing a sigil in the air above the man's face.

"I smell my kind," said the knight, his voice wavering. "Surely the time is come, when humans walk the king's hall once more."

"Time near but not yet come," Ver repeated. "Ver of Nöon's line, I tell you. Sleep, until wake in your kingdom."

The knight settled back on his bier, and Ver stood back with the axe.

Warren took Lilian's hand; she looked at him with round eyes, and they both held their breath as they followed Ver past the bier to another door. This one bowed away from them.

As they approached it, the second door stirred. Three eyes, rather bloodshot, opened in its battered center and fixed Warren with what he thought was a malignant glare, though as the door lacked eyebrows it was difficult to tell. Below the eyes, the door opened a mouth which was missing several teeth; before it could say whatever had been in its mind, Ver thrust the pipe-stem between those teeth.

The door shut its mouth in surprise and gave the pipe a tentative suck that made it glow red. It swung open without a sound, and they scuttled through.

"Safe," Ver said, after checking that the door was completely closed. "Talk now."

"Who were those?"

The goblin shook its head. Unwilling to push it, Warren turned around and surveyed the room they were standing in. This, also, was a tall room. They stood at one end of it; four black curtains hung along each of the walls stretching away from them and a ninth hung at the far end. Wards were stretched across each, their chains fastened to gold hooks at each side of the curtains. But Warren could still feel strong magic.

"It's like Nöon's glass," Lilian said in a hushed voice.

"Not touch!" Ver said, indicating the curtains down the room. "Broken. Take away life, like King in tale. Only this one safe." It looked at Warren, frowning, and pointed to the curtain before him. Sure enough, the rune-leaves in Lilian's bowl had clustered at the side next to that curtain.

"This is a way into Nöon's kingdom?" Warren and Lilian looked at one another, and he felt breathless. This was far more than a little adventure up the mountain. But who was he to say Lilian only deserved a little adventure? *She's been behind the scenes for forty years,* he thought. *The line's showing me how much she deserves.* "If we're going in there, we should put on wards," he announced. "We'll do this right." He drew out a sack of wards and pulled out the heaviest. "These are some of the wards Teddy used in the alchemists' prison. They're the strongest wide-spectrum demon wards we have."

Ver hawked and looked around as if not finding anyplace to spit. "Human ward, goat crap." It squinted at the runes, turning the medallion around

"The base is alchemical," Warren said, pointing out the shining silver star that Alchemy used to let people through their wards and into their building. Teddy, who was no metalsmith, had superglued the star and a power crystal onto the front of one of Demonology's golden ward blanks, over the Academy's logo, and then used a diamond-tipped pen or something like it to write a charm of essence around the edges. That was just like her. She doodled on everything.

This charm was shape-based, the runes with the strongest, most controversial meanings written at the points of the star and then filled in between with modifiers and reconsiderations, just the way Teddy talked. Warren could never have written something like this. Yet it was clear what the ward was meant to do — put the wearer into a bubble of reality based on the Alchemy star. As Teddy walked into the alchemists' prison her essence had remained in the world she left behind, protected from even the strongest demons.

For the first time, Warren realized, he was looking at the ward without the sour taste of envy. This combination of magic and alchemy was new. Why hadn't Teddy boasted about it? Had she missed the significance of her own work? *I'll have to push her to publish on this*, he thought.

"Pff," said the goblin. "Might do to keep off demon." It might have spoken in the same tone about a flea powder, Warren thought.

"The main runes are a returning charm," he explained, feeling the need to defend Teddy a little. "We should make sure we know it, before going anyplace."

Lilian read the runes aloud with no difficulty. A scryer knew how to read such things. In fact, her pronunciation was better than Warren's. Ver did not bother practicing the runes; in fact, it listened with a darkening face, and finally pulled a bundle out of its pocket.

"That worried, need *real* ward," it said, unfolding the cloth to poke through a dozen or so wards, all set in silver and strung on cords. The stones it picked out for Warren and Lilian were different; his was green stone, with markings in it like leaf shadows, and Lilian's looked like a moss agate. "No thing touch, with *goblin* ward," Ver said with a superior air. But Warren noticed that it put Teddy's ward on as well, before it pulled the curtain back.

Warren looked into what lay behind. A window — no, a mirror — for his, Ver's, and Lilian's images looked back at him from inside a different world.

"This way," Ver said. It reached out for Lilian's and Warren's hands. Warren snatched up the bowl and stepped forward. Then they were outside again, on the edge of a wide, airy plain.

The place felt more magical than anyplace Warren had ever been. It tugged at him, pulling in all directions until his whole body was humming

281

with it, but he saw nothing out of the ordinary. The forest behind him was filled with fresh-leaved beeches and maples. The plain's grass had just begun to bloom, pendants of blossom dangling from its tall stems. The rune-leaves swam that way, beckoning them out into the sunlight where the land rose in a long smooth sweep. A lone mountain stood up, white-capped, far past the swell of grass. To right and left, Warren saw mountains he recognized from the Sheep League; but they were spread apart, now, as if the new land had opened up right across the range. Right where the dotted red line lay on his new map, he realized. And did that lone mountain rise where the mountain had risen, in his dream? He had the map in his pack, but of course it would show nothing of the dotted line's internal features.

"How wide is this place?" he asked Ver.

"Many mile," was the vague answer.

Lilian had been turning round, and now she looked into the bowl with barely concealed delight. "Well, that way," she said, trying to be businesslike. "Right?"

"Right," declared Warren. "That way."

Chapter 20
Too Much Magic

When Mama Simone woke up, she could feel the magic growing inside her. She felt it solid in her belly and chest, like a tree trunk. It sent smooth supple limbs out her arms and legs. It drew up magic from the earth, like sap. If someone put a spile in her she would bleed power.

She picked up the little robin and shook it, looked at the bit of her dress-skirt poking out of the hole in the bottom, and shook her head. "Idiot!" she called herself, and pulled the cloth out. "Anyone would think you were a city girl." She sniffed at the opening and shut her eyes, and she could smell growing. A farm wife could smell that, any time. "Dirt, that's what it needs."

She went outside even before getting dressed, in her dressing robe and wooden shoes, and took some of the best dirt in the garden from around the bean poles. She spat power into it, rolling it between her hands. Then she stuffed it into the china robin, a bit at a time, shaking it all around the growing thing inside. She planted the robin in the vegetable garden with its beak just showing among the lettuce.

Then she was at a loss for what to do next. The laundry? It seemed an anticlimax, so she made eggs instead, and toast, and bacon and sausage. She made the biggest breakfast she'd had in years. It was only at the end of it that she realized she wasn't expecting anyone to eat with her, and she shouldn't have. She should have expected Robin. She called upstairs, and went up with heavy footsteps, but his room was empty.

I ought to be worried, thought Mama Simone, but she wasn't. She felt as if Robin was really here, safe in the lettuce patch, and the real boy didn't matter at all. She turned to go back down and then she felt it again, just like last night. A power surge, a real one, nothing like the hot flashes women her age joked about. She felt it tingle all through her roots and up her trunk. And had she heard something break out in the garden?

When she got there the robin was split right open, the top of its back and its head pushed out of the ground and lying on its side. The trees growing out of it were leaning away from each other as if to prove they were two separate plants. They were already almost six centimeters tall.

***

The sea-fog, oddly enough, lay in inland valleys rather than along the cliff edge. It made the top of each wooded hill stand out like black lace frills, shot through with the first rays of sunrise, when *Rho went out*, chewing his last bite of toast, to look over the edge and hope for more seals. There were none, though. The mare he had ridden the day before stood in the center of her dew-jeweled pasture with one hind foot cocked, thinking deep thoughts. When he said hello to her, she ignored him. Pretending he had expected no more, Rho leaned his back against the fence and surveyed the territory.

House, barn, and outbuildings all lay in a dip between two grassy hills. It hardly seemed deep enough to call a valley, but it cut some of the wind, even the sea-breeze coming up the cliff on his left. Rho supposed that in rainy times a stream would run down the bottom of the dip, behind the barn, and over the edge of those cliffs into the sea below; perhaps to avoid this, or perhaps to take advantage of it, the owners had planted nut-trees behind the barn. But in front of the barn, and the corral against which Rho leant, there was nothing except a few wooden sheds and the swell of the hill between him and the fence at the cliffs' edge. He shook his head at the outbuildings. You could tell a real farmer by the way he ruined a view.

"It's nice, isn't it?" asked Juliana, leaning against the fence beside him. She held a full cup of coffee, steaming into the brisk air.

"Yes, it is."

"Did you see any more seals?"

"Nope. I thought you had a model piggery out here?"

She shook her head. "That's further inland. This isn't pig country. There's no way we could contain a waste lagoon, out here. Look at that!"

Rho couldn't see a thing until she switched places with him. Then a wavering wraith came into view. The first ray of sunlight had caught it, lit up against the dark wall of the furthest shed. It bowed, and then stretched upright; a long amorphous head or arm shot upwards from it, and then curled back down. Rho laughed.

"You've seen those before," Juliana said, sounding a little disappointed.

"I'm from a farm," said Rho. He took a few steps forward. "You coming?"

"In a minute," said Juliana. "Coffee and midges don't mix."

Rho walked across the springy ground to where the cloud of midges swirled and danced, as tall as he was. There must have been several thousand of the insects. He tried to remember how wonderful it had been to listen to their singing, when he was a boy. He'd have to pretend, now; but just before he reached them, that feeling of something opening came over him once more, and when he stepped into the cloud of insects it was like being swept up in a choir of praise and joy.

"Glory, glory," sang the midges. "Sun, air, friends. Zoom! Dive!" They chased each other, hovered, swirled and sang like sunlight made audible.

Rho gasped, carefully covering his mouth first. He shut his eyes. *It's still back!* he thought. *I'm well again!* He wanted to spin around like the insects, singing, flying up into the air, laughing and dancing, but it would be cruel to break their cloud. He held his breath instead, stepping out of it, and grinned at Juliana as she came up.

She grinned back. "Great, huh?"

"Nothing like them," said Rho, not lying. They stood grinning foolishly at one another, and he thought he loved her. She understood. Then he heard another voice.

"Mamma," said the voice. It sounded young, and hoarse, and without hope. "Mamma mamma mamma mamma mamma..." It went on without stopping, an insane babble.

"Crap," said Juliana. "Let's go over here."

"What is that?" said Rho, cold running through him. Other voices had joined the first one, now. They spoke over each other, worn and plaintive. They came from the sheds beside him. "Are those – ?"

Juliana had walked away a little. She looked back, defensive. "You have dairy, you have veal," she said.

"Mamma mamma mamma," said the weary voice in the shed nearest to Rho. The other voices had stopped.

"He's new," Juliana said. "He'll stop fussing in a few days."

When Rho didn't answer she turned around again and walked away. She was probably offended, he thought, but the concept was faraway and unimportant. Because it was all true, what Gordon K. Remen had said. About magic coming from lost potential. The only reason Rho had heard the midges, the seals, was because of these calves tied into dark crates too narrow to move in, all their running and playing over. The calf nearest him went on and on. Its voice cracked. Now it only said "ma—ma—ma—ma—"

He stood there, between the midges and the shed. He wanted to scream, to dash his arms through that cloud of oblivious insects. He wanted to knock the veal sheds over and take every calf home with him, and make it up to them. He wanted to run at the cliff and throw himself over the edge. But all he did was blow his nose and walk back to the barnyard.

Nobody else seemed to notice any change in Rho, or maybe they thought he was depressed about

287

having to leave. He fielded invitations and goodbyes with noncommittal answers, but when he was alone in the car with Juliana he couldn't bring himself to say anything. What could he say, that wouldn't make things worse? And talking about anything else, changing the subject, frivolous small talk — that would be obscene. They rode for most of an hour in silence. The road swooped and dipped as it had before, the air sang around his ears, but there was nothing beautiful in any of it.

She spoke at the first stop light at the edge of Sterne, without looking at him. "You'll never make it in farming if you're not ready to do what it takes," she said.

Rho hadn't thought of worrying about this, and took a minute to figure out what she meant. "My family never crated calves," he said. "We sold them off."

Juliana snorted. "What d'you think the buyers did with them? There's a demand for veal and people are going to raise it, whether we study it or not. Somebody has to do the research, or they'll just use whatever methods give the most profit."

Rho had no answer to this remark. It was probably true, he thought. But it seemed completely irrelevant to the voice from the shed.

"You have to do what it takes to fund a program," said Juliana, sounding angrier. "You can't just study the pretty parts of farming. There's no grant money in midges."

Again, Rho had nothing to say; but now he felt nervous about saying nothing. He scanned the roadside as if it could save him. Liquor stores, strip malls — "Oh!" he said, his tongue loosed with relief. "That copy shop — I have to pick something up. You can drop me here; I'll find my own way back to campus."

She looked at him this time. She wasn't buying it. "Campus is four kilometers away," she said.

"It's okay, I can use the walk," Rho said, hastily bundling his stuff together. When he'd gotten out, he felt guilty. "Thanks," he said awkwardly, leaning back in the window. "You were really nice to me. I appreciate it."

"Yeah, sure," she said. "It's not me, it's you, etcetera." She put the car back in gear and drove away.

Rho took a shaky, decompressing step toward the copy shop. He didn't really have any reason to go in there. In fact, he wasn't sure he could. Getting away from Juliana had put the first chink in his false front; now he felt his breath coming fast and his eyes tingling. He looked around desperately and there was an alley, a blessed alley, the place you ran to when you were going to cry or be sick. He made himself walk like a grown-up with business and turn into it as if he were checking the gas meter, or something like that; it had a dumpster, large enough to sit behind and cry in privacy. He let himself remember the calf's voice and cried every tear it must have shed, he cried calves and calves worth of tears, and it didn't get any better. Then he cried because of what a monster he was, to gain power from the calves' suffering and walk away without trying to do a thing to help them. Then he got disgusted with himself for sniveling in an alley.

"Right where you were eleven years ago," he told himself, "hiding from real life in some alley."

He cried a little out of sympathy for the little boy he'd been back then, and a little more out of chagrin at not having known where his family's bobby calves went. Finally he achieved a kind of dry, stupid peace. He sat with one cheek on his drawn-up knees, looking sideways at the alley, and wondered if Juliana would make Gordon K. fire him. It didn't seem likely. Rho mopped his face with a smeary handkerchief, picked up his backpack, and started the long trudge back to his car.

He made it in less than an hour, astonished to find it still morning on campus. Coffee time, from the people ambling past him with paper cups. None of them seemed surprised to see Rho. A campus, he thought dully, was a good place to be disheveled in. Everybody thought you were a graduate student.— He found his car where he had parked it the day before, with a ticket on the windshield, and had just picked the thing off when a voice hailed him.

"Magister Rho!" said the voice, big and cheerful. "Were you caught by the rain yesterday? Give me that. The department will take care of it."

"Oh!" said Rho. "Thank you." He was struck by how wide Gordon K.'s hand was, as it took the ticket out of his own. Wide and white and warm. Why did it make him feel as if things could be all right?

"Did you stay at a hotel?" Gordon K. went on, looking at the ticket. "I don't know if we can cover all of it, but let me have the bill and we'll do what we can — what's wrong?"

Rho couldn't answer. He'd thought he was all cried out, but now his eyes were full again and his nose ran.

"What happened?" asked Gordon K., sounding a little panicked. He looked around. "Here, get in." Taking the key from Rho's hand, he unlocked the car door and pushed him onto the driver's seat. He went around and let himself into the passenger side, by which time Rho had put his head down on the steering wheel. "Now. What is it?"

Rho took a few deep breaths and told him, making his account detailed and clinical. Every word took him further away from tears, further into a dry, hard place. That was life, really, and you had to walk through it. You had to keep going on. "So you were right," he said at last. "I am a monster. I should take up drowning kittens."

Gordon K. put a warm hand on his shoulder. "We're all monsters," he said, with bitterness in his voice. "Some of us just know it."

It was surprising how much better Rho felt.

Chapter 21
A Familiar Face

Ric felt as if he'd spent all of Wednesday morning watching the clock, trying to steel himself for this moment when they would pile into a Public Health car and drive toward the Magic Building in nervous silence. He expected to head straight down to the pentarium, but instead Ligalla took them up a flight of stairs and along a corridor *to Russell Cinea's office.*

"Oh, come in," said Cinea, looking up from an almost bare desk. Ric, Derek, and Lord Stimms sat down while Cinea turned to take papers off a computer printer.

Cinea's desk was wide, clean, and bare. He had only one window, a cross-shaped arrowslit, but light streamed in through the arrowslit at a dozen angles as if from floodlights outside. A small jungle of plants stood on a bench under the window, thriving in the unnatural brightness. On the wall to Ric's left, Cinea had overstuffed bookshelves; to Ric's right, he had a wine rack full of scrolls in tubes, every tube's cap ornamented with labyrinths, runes, and tassels hung from cord woven into complicated knots. Ric couldn't interpret any of the knots or labyrinths. The effect was both festive and intimidating.

Cinea turned back and handed each of them a printout. It contained a diagram of the pentarium with names printed around the edges. Below, a charm was printed in phonetic rendering.

"You two will be seated behind the circle," Cinea told Ric and Derek.

"No," Derek said.

"What?" Cinea acted as if he had never heard the word.

"We're inside the circle. So we can get to him without breaking it."

"Oh. Well, we can manage that. Anyway, you need to learn this charm. Line by line." Cinea led them through the pronunciation several times. Lord Stimms sat silent, but gave the impression of being mightily amused.

"What's it do?" Ric asked.

"Protects the speaker and anyone he's touching from demons. Specifically, from Xiphister." Cinea frowned. "Don't use it unless I tell you to. It's only a millimeter away from demon-binding, which is against the law here. Also, you don't want this demon for a personal enemy."

Ric nodded.

"Do we have the coven assembled?" Lord Stimms asked casually, looking at the sheet.

"Almost. Cham had arranged two sorcerers, but one's stuck in surgery, so we're waiting for his replacement to get here from the hospital," said Cinea. "And one of the magicians we were counting on missed his connection coming back from a conference, so Magister Whin is fetching a backup. We'll work as two teams — one sorcerer for you and one for Endamos. The magicians indicated with stars on the diagram will be concentrating on you, those without, on him. Cham, of course, will be watching you both for possession. "

Lord Stimms nodded. He was still wearing his glamour, but it hardly mattered now that Ric was familiar with his mannerisms. He leaned back in his usual mock-relaxed pose. Ric was reminded of a snake, or a reptile of some kind; not ready to strike, but noticing things.

Magister Whin stuck her head through the doorway. She wore what looked like a man's short-sleeved shirt under an embroidered vest, trousers that buttoned round her ankles, and felt clogs. "Oh, good, you're here," she announced unnecessarily. "Are you wearing that glamour into the netherworld?" Ric grinned despite himself. She sounded like a mother commenting on her daughter's makeup.

"Not if you advise against it," Lord Stimms said formally, rising. "You remember Inspectors Haaken and Massey."

"Sure," said Magister Whin, and shook hands. "Everyone calls me Teddy." She had an energy about her much like a small rodent; Ric wouldn't have been surprised to see her jump onto Cinea's desk and begin shelling a nut. "Still waiting for the sorcerer, huh?"

"Apparently."

Teddy began to count on her fingers. "There's Cham and me, Russell, Anders and Patsy Hoth. Bill and Vinca from Alchemy. Neil, if we're hard up. Sue and Will, two sorcerers, and Inos. That's it."

"You can still put this off," Cinea said to Lord Stimms.

He doesn't mean that, thought Ric. Why? Something had changed about Cinea. He seemed — more solid. Bolder. Less burdened.

"Delay is not an option," said Lord Stimms.

Teddy gave Ric another computer printout. "You won't have to use this, but you might want to look it over. It's the recalling charm we'll use to bring him back, if we need to."

Ric knew the charm. He'd known it since he could remember. It was a little incantation about finding one's true self, between a blessing and a prayer. His mother had said it with him every night — so had every mother in Selanto, he would have wagered. "This is a kid's charm!"

"Those are the important ones," she said. "Things you learn before you know what truth is have real power. They tap into parts of yourself that you can't reach any more. That's why children are so sought-after in black magic. Here, just hold these for two minutes." She handed Ric and Derek each a ward blank with a dull, discharged power crystal in the center and turned back to Cinea, as if struck by a thought. "Oh, yeah! Two guesses who I got an e-mail from."

Cinea gave her a look.

"Sorry," she said, not really quelled. "It was Rho!"

"Rho? He's back in town?"

"No, he emailed yesterday from Kasidora or wherever his home base is. He's run into a fellow pushing the unused potential theory of magic. Have you ever heard that?" she asked Lord Stimms.

"It is not unfamiliar to me," he said. Something in his voice made Ric's spine tighten.

"Did you know anything about it?" Cinea asked Teddy.

"Not as a serious theory, but I've been on the internet ever since. It's black magic, but that doesn't mean it's all wrong."

"Where did Rho find this?"

"He got it from a guy who claims he found it in the Selanto archives, but I'd swear there's nothing like that in there. All that stuff was purged under Chancellor Spurges, back in the seventeen hundreds. Thing is, this guy claims to have evidence for it. He's lost his own magic, and claims he did it by using up all his potential. That's odd, isn't it? How could anybody use up all his potential? I mean, whatever you do, you haven't done something else — oh. Oh, crap!" She stared at Cinea with her mouth open. "This guy's been in the alchemists' garden."

"That fits with what the ancient alchemists say about the garden, does it not?" Lord Stimms asked, so idly that Ric knew he was very interested. "Because people trapped in there could live all possibilities simultaneously, their magic became divided between all the possible versions of them until no single version had enough power to use."

"Who is this guy?" Ric asked. "One of the ancient alchemists?"

"Can't be; he's been working at Kasidora for years. His name's Gordon K. Remen," said Teddy. "I checked out his website — no publications to speak of, just a few notes on teaching. It says he graduated Selanto a few years after you, Russell, but from Social Magic. I've never heard of him before."

The ward Ric was holding began to buzz, making him start. He handed it back to Teddy, who squinted at it in an expert manner and nodded, then repeated the process with Derek's ward. "You've been close to a demon," she said to Ric, not a question.

"Possessed for a few minutes, back in January."

She opened her eyes wide with enthusiasm. "Which one?"

"We didn't get its name," Ric said in a shutting-down voice.

Teddy Whin frowned at the ward. "What's your sorcerer say about your working with demons?" Ric looked at Lord Stimms helplessly.

"Here," said Lord Stimms, and produced a folded paper from some hidden pocket. He handed it to Teddy, who opened and scanned it.

"Okay," she said. "I guess you're cleared."

Ric intercepted the document as she handed it back to Lord Stimms. It was heavy, on such thick embossed paper that it seemed a sin for Lord Stimms to have folded it up and jammed it into a pocket. But, Ric supposed, he could do as he liked with his own — for the seal pressed into this paper was Lord Stimms' seal, and the signature at the bottom was his signature. The parts in between were Ric's. At least, they outlined his and Derek's privileges as deputies of the Chief Exorcist. Working with demons was the least of them, not even mentioned except under 'such duties as approved by the Chief Exorcist;' more interesting, to Ric, were the other details. He had jurisdiction to arrest people in every country signatory to the Treaty of Hands, which he had never heard of. He could requisition assistance from the police in any of those countries, as well and emergency transportation within and between them ... Ric stared at Lord Stimms, who looked back with a very innocent expression, his hand still outstretched for the document. Ric folded it and put it into his own inside breast pocket. Stimms smiled and turned his attention to Russell Cinea, who had ignored all of this and was still looking at his computer screen.

"Did it have a picture?" Cinea asked.

"What?" said Teddy Whin. She had one of his printouts pressed against the doorjamb and was jotting notes on it, revising the arrangement of magicians in the circle.

"Remen's website."

"Oh. No, I did an image search first thing. I know so many more people by sight, especially the ones who aren't publishing." She snapped her fingers. "I should try the networking sites."

Magister Cinea gave her a look that indicated she should know he knew nothing of such things, and she went around the desk and shoved him away from his own computer in a manner that bespoke long friendship.

"Here, let me sign in," she said. "One of the alums friended me last year, but I've never had time to putz with it — here!" She clicked at the machine for a few minutes, and a set of pictures flashed up. "Here we go, college picnic. Looks as if he advises some student group." She frowned. "I don't know him. I'd remember that face."

Lord Stimms craned forward, and Magister Cinea obligingly turned the monitor around. The mysterious Gordon K. Remen did have a distinctive face. It was square, with jowls fluffed out even further by gray mutton-chop whiskers. His blue eyes twinkled behind half-glasses. He wore an old-fashioned brocade waistcoat and a bolo tie. Still, there was something familiar... Ric looked at Derek, who shrugged. Magister Cinea was about to turn the monitor back when Lord Stimms leant forward. He put both his index fingers on the monitor, laying them over the whiskers. He put his right thumb over the bolo tie.

Ric gasped. "Sweet Lady Jane! That's –"

Lord Stimms spoke as if nothing could have mattered less to him. "That is Rosemont."

Chapter 22
Lord Stimms Adventures

"Rosemont!"

"Who?" Magister Cinea asked, sounding irritated at the distraction.

"The last Lord Stimms!" said Teddy Whin. "Antimora!"

"Oh!" said Cinea. Now he was interested enough to swivel the monitor back for another look. "Hm! Not much resemblance. How does a demon come to be advising the Future Magicians' Social Union?"

Teddy Whin grinned. "Perhaps their chair threatened him with a faculty position." An apparent in-joke, this startled Cinea into a snort.

"This is not the demon Antimora," said Lord Stimms. "It is doubtless the part of Rosemont that returned to this world, while the part that became the demon remained in the alchemists' prison. It hardly takes a whole exorcist to make a demon."

"What's the ratio?" Teddy asked him, not entirely joking.

"What should we do about it?" Ric asked. "All this talk about anchors in this world — Antimora has one now, doesn't it? If it reunites itself with Rosemont, it's free!"

Lord Stimms nodded, and Ric felt very intelligent.

"We should get him into custody," Ric said. "Warded against the demon."

Derek pulled his cell phone out and flipped it open. "Protective custody –" Then he stopped and looked at Ric, and Ric knew he was thinking about the minutes their chief had sent him. Was there still a contract out on Rosemont? What kind of protection would he get in Selanto? And would his dead body be less, or more, available to the demon Antimora? "Kasidora police," Derek said. "Under the name Remen."

Ric nodded.

Derek's thumbs danced over the phone's keyboard.

Cinea's phone rang.

"Hello?" he answered it, distracted. "Oh, good! We'll be right down. I'll meet her in the lobby. Our sorcerer's here," he announced, hanging up.

"But what about Rosemont?" asked Ric. "If something goes wrong, everyone who knows about this will be on the casualty list."

The demonologists both looked offended. "Here," Cinea said crossly, and wrote a note in red marker on his legal pad. He held it up for Ric's perusal. 'Rosemont is Gordon K. Remen of U. Kasidora at Sterne,' it read. "Will this suffice?"

"Add 'tell Kasidora police,'" Ric said grudgingly. He truly couldn't think of a better solution. He watched Cinea lay the pad on the exact center of his desk and weigh it down with a glass paperweight shaped like a dolphin.

"Ah," said Cinea, rising. "Here's Cham."

Magister Ligalla had four people with her. One, a slender middle-aged man, wore a Public Health badge that proclaimed him a sorcerer. The others were badgeless; one was small and round, in his fifties and dressed in an old-fashioned suit. He wore pince-nez, over which he looked in a benign manner as he teetered back and forth on tiny feet in gleaming shoes. Ric had seen this man before, he knew. The others were familiar too; one was Derek's height and age, with red curls topping a snub-nosed face. While he didn't look happy at the moment, Ric felt he was basically a cheerful person. The third man looked content enough, but gave the impression of being basically sardonic. There was something likeable about his face when he grinned at Teddy. This man would be an amusing, if profane, drinking buddy. His hair, eyes, and suit were all the same brown, and a big triangular nose stuck straight out from his long face. Connecting them with Teddy, Ric began to place the three. They were Osyth alchemists, the ones who had gone into the alchemists' prison with her and now led the union challenging the Mystic Guild.

Ligalla had been making introductions, and Ric stored the names away to look up later. The sorcerer was Klimt, a slim man in his late fifties with glasses and a narrow, nervous face. The three alchemists were named Vinca, Torecki, and Navanax. "Do we have everybody?" Ligalla asked, directing the question at Cinea.

"Sorcerer Pim's waiting for us in the lobby with Susan and Will," Cinea said. "Let's go down. We'll be able to brief people better when we're in the pentarium."

Ligalla turned without answering. Ric followed her and Lord Stimms toward the stairwell, eavesdropping on Teddy Whin and Torecki just behind him.

"Old home week," she said.

"I didn't think I'd ever have to go into that pentarium again," Torecki answered unhappily.

"Hold on a tick," said Teddy. "Inos! We're heading down."

Another magician came out of one of the offices and joined them. He knew Torecki, because they said hello and made polite inquiries about each other's work. Inos apparently worked with Seelie-stones, and Torecki did art. Not an alchemist after all? Then the conversation turned, more interestingly, to the ancient alchemists who these people had rescued from the garden last spring. Inos knew a lot about them. He knew, for instance, that four of them had left the Archbishop's palace. That wasn't public information in Selanto, so how had he found out? Yet Ric found it hard to keep his mind on Inos, with a demon-filled pentarium coming closer every step. When he tried, he almost fell down the stairs. *Idiot!* he scolded himself, and put a hand on the paper in his pocket for reassurance.

More demonologists joined them on the ground floor. They had names he recognized from Public Health — Teale (ghosts), Hoth (incubi), and Harding (vampirology). Teale was a hefty woman with long brown hair, perfect skin, and a friendly smile. "How's it going?" she asked, when they'd been introduced. "Are you in the circle?"

"Inside it," Ric said, showing her the printout of the pentarium.

"Oh," she said. "You're right in front of Will."

"Great, I can barf down his back if I see a demon," Harding groused, twisting his too-handsome face into a theatrical moue. "Why I waste money on food when we're invoking... who'm I next to? This is a weird circle. What's Bill doing in it?"

"It's all the people who've been in the alchemists' garden," said Teale. "That's probably smart ... you're between Neil and Vinca."

"That's safe enough. Neil saved all our lives last year," Will told Ric as they jostled through the sub-basement's warded door. "Good instincts."

That wasn't as reassuring as he seemed to think.

They all had to shower and put on the blue paper gowns except for Lord Stimms. As the adventurer, he wore his usual robe and an impressive assortment of wards, which Teddy Whin explained carefully to him as he put each of them on. Lord Stimms listened with a too-intent face, like someone having pretend tea with a small child. That changed when Teddy demanded to see his link with Endamos.

"No," he said, a remark so straightforward Ric did a double-take.

"Don't be silly," she said, holding out her hand. "If you get lost in there, we don't want our only link to him gone as well."

"I need it to find him."

"I'll give it back," she said. "Honestly!"

Lord Stimms gave in, looking unhappy about it. All she did with the ring was press it against the center of a star-shaped ward and mutter a few words over it; greenish-gray smoke arose, with a nasty smell of burning herbs. She repeated the process twice with two other wards.

304

"Now I want something of yours," she said, giving the ring back. Lord Stimms passed her his seal ring, which she pressed against another three wards. Instead of giving the ring back, though, she threaded it on a length of silver and handed it to Ligalla, who somehow took it and put it around her neck without acknowledging Teddy Whin in any way at all. Rick's internal alarms buzzed. Would this discord cause a problem in the pentarium? Probably not, he decided. Every team had a sore spot; best not to poke at it. He looked around the locker room instead, reviewing names. It was easy to do, as almost half of the magicians were using the shower stalls, or waiting to get into one.

The team members in the public shower, which Teddy Whin had just hopped into and out of again with dispatch and a startling lack of modesty, included Harding (vampirology), Cinea, a long-nosed, potbellied man named Regan, the alchemist Navanax, and the mysterious Torecki. Sorcerer Klimt joined them with a very matter-of-fact air. Sorcerer Pim, a tall round-faced woman, came out of the first shower stall while Ric was still making his inventory, and Ligalla took her place. The other stalls were, he deduced, occupied by Inos, Teale (ghosts), the alchemist Vinca, and the little blonde Magister Hoth (incubi). His inventory was interrupted by Derek, who had finished his shower and put on the blue gown.

"What do you see?" Ric muttered to him.

Derek shook his head. "Nothing," he said, unhappily. Ric pulled off his clothes and headed into the shower himself. He used the public side, the better to keep an eye on Lord Stimms.

305

"Whoa!" said Teddy Whin, and Ric turned to find all eyes upon him.

"Some glyphs," said Torecki, in explanation. "Can I see your back? Oh, that's well-done. Who wrote these?"

"Uh — Eve Landis."

"I've never heard of her, but this is nice work. What's that one for?" Torecki poked Ric's right deltoid.

"Demon damage," Ric said, and covered it with lather. Torecki whistled, but he apparently got the message. He didn't ask any more questions. After all this, Ric felt entitled to openly look at other people's bodies, and at this closer range he saw impressive scars. Torecki's face and arms shone with fresh charms, and the skin beneath was new; that meant recently healed burns. Cinea had a narrow, ragged scar round his wrist from a wound that must have almost taken his hand off, and when Navanax turned Ric could see thin white lines on his chest in a runic pattern. *Flesh magic*, he thought, and revised his opinion of the Osyth magicians downward. He felt less secure as he stepped out of the shower.

They had almost all suited up by now, and Cinea and Regan were passing out the paper wrist and ankle bands and the gold chains. Teddy Whin handed Lord Stimms another of the wards she had used to check Ric's and Derek's magic, and it buzzed almost immediately. She took it back and looked at it carefully, then passed it to Ligalla without looking at her, in a good imitation of the exorcist's own manners. Where did exorcists find friends? Ric wondered. You wouldn't ask one to the

306

pub for a pint. Lord Stimms didn't look as if he cared for such things, as he stood smoothing down his robe and arranging the golden chains.

"Inspector Massey," he said suddenly, putting both hands to the back of his red robe. Ric didn't know what he expected, but Lord Stimms merely undid the dreamcatcher and handed it back. "Thank you for the loan," he said gravely.

Ric held it, feeling stupid. It was like a farewell. What Lord Stimms was about to do suddenly felt real.

"Come in with me," Cinea said to Lord Stimms. "You need to get a feel for the space."

Ric glanced at Derek, who followed the two of them into the pentarium, looking as if he had a bad feeling about the whole enterprise. Ric swallowed his own feelings and put the dreamcatcher around his neck.

"We're as ready as we'll ever be," Teddy Whin announced, looking around the group. "I want everyone to go through the recall charm. All together."

Ric read from the card, but before he was halfway through he was reciting the charm from memory. The syllables slid out of his throat before his brain had a chance to second-guess them. The second time, he could tell that all of them were doing the same. They were adjusting to speak in chorus, the demonologists setting the pace as if practiced in it. The third time, Ric was able to ignore the mechanics and lose himself in the charm. It wasn't just words; it led him into an inner inventory, a ritual he had performed every night as long as he lived with his mother and grandmother and then immediately abandoned when he went off to school. Why? Ric wondered now whether he had retained the wrong childhood traditions.

"Walk around inside yourself, take note of what you find," he chanted, and felt the old combination of bedtime safety, repentance, and amendment. Today might not have been so good, but tomorrow was a clean slate. "Feel the inside of your skin," he went on, hardly hearing the words. "See your soul and meet your mind." He relaxed, watching neon circles expand within his eyelids. The inner circle grew and shrank, then filled with gold and blue; the Bright Lady's image opened out of the darkness. He felt it again, the thing behind him. He couldn't move or turn as it pressed against his back. It was as warm as his body. It clung to a sleeve he wasn't wearing. Now Ric felt demon-cold at his chest, as if he stood between life and death. And he felt himself wrench his sleeve out of life's grasp. He felt himself pull away from life's warmth, and death reach around him and take it away. Just like that.

And just like that, the Bright Lady's image was gone; the chant was ended, and the magicians were shifting, dusting themselves off, and trying to look professional and unaffected. Ric took note of them not as he normally would but in a desperate, fingers-in the-ears attempt to keep from thinking about what he'd just experienced. *La la la, I can't hear you*, he said to himself. Ligalla didn't meet anyone's eyes after saying that charm, but then she never did. Torecki and Navanax were looking at each other as if they knew what it was like in one another's skins. Inos looked pensive and unsurprised, as if his sins were old news to him. But now Teddy Whin was shuffling them into order, and there was no more time for inventory.

"All ready?" Whin asked. "Anybody got issues? Need the bathroom? We could be in there a while."

Nobody admitted to issues or bladders. "Hope she has chairs," Torecki said from behing Ric as they filed through the door into the pentarium.

"Please," replied Harding. "That would be organized… I'll be damned, she did get us some."

They were the folding metal kind that people usually didn't sit on in thin paper gowns, but Ric was glad to get off his shaking legs.

There was no pentacle on the floor, only another chair right in the center of the room. Lord Stimms was already sitting in it with his eyes closed, his hands folded in his lap. He was almost lounging in the chair, but Ric could see through that by now. He gave Derek a worried look, and Derek made a worried face back at him.

"All set?" Cinea asked Teddy Whin, and she nodded. He looked the same question at Ligalla, and she looked at Derek and Ric. Derek looked at Lord Stimms, took a deep unhappy-sounding breath, and nodded in his turn.

"All right," said Cinea. "Folks, we're just on watch. Lord Stimms can take himself into the netherworld. We won't do anything unless he needs help getting out again. He'll let us know through the link Cham's holding. Until then we wait and watch. Are you ready?"

Lord Stimms nodded without opening his eyes.

"Wish I'd brought paperwork," said Torecki. Looking across the room, Ric saw that the little blonde — Hoth (incubi) — had! She set a briefcase beside her, and her neighbors looked jealous. Didn't demonologists take this seriously at all? The sorcerers and Vinca had settled down as if they were used to long waits, and Inos put his hands on his lap and shut his eyes just as Lord Stimms had. Teale (ghosts) did the same. Minutes ticked by and still Lord Stimms sat unmoving in the center of the pentarium, and nobody seemed willing to be the first to say this was a wash. Then Teale (ghosts) started, so noticeably that Ric sat bolt upright with his heart pounding. She poked Hoth (incubi), obviously demanding pen and paper, and wrote a note that the demonologists began to pass toward Ric. Most of them read the note, raised their eyebrows, and looked intently at Lord Stimms. Every time they did this, Ric could feel his blood pressure get a little higher.

Finally the note reached Derek. *"No aura!" he whispered to Ric* as he passed the note along. Ric read it with a sick feeling. He looked across the circle at Teale and she made emphatic 'pass it on' motions; apparently the note was meant for Cinea or Teddy Whin.

"What should we do?" he asked Derek, passing the note along.

"I don't know. Maybe it just means this is working, and he's gone into the garden." Derek watched the note's progress around the circle, his face worried. Cinea frowned over it, and Whin shrugged her shoulders. Neither of them seemed to know whether it was a good or bad thing.

"Hey!" Derek yelled, and a ripple of exclamations ran round the circle. Ric looked back into its center and leapt to his feet. Lord Stimms was no longer alone.

The man standing beside Lord Stimms holding one of his hands was out of focus. Ric could tell he was short, with gray hair and a narrow face, but nothing else showed clearly. He blurred, came clearer, blurred again, and grabbed Lord Stimms with his second hand like a drowning man. Ric heard a gasp from the other side of the circle and saw blood patter on the floor under the two men. He started to his feet; Harding took hold of his arm from behind, holding him back, and Ric nearly screamed with a mix of rage and fear. Now he could see that both men were wounded with long ragged slashes, four at a time like the claw-marks of a giant cat. Ligalla and Whin exchanged looks across the circle, and Whin nodded. Harding let go, reached past him, and undid the gold safety chain, and Ric stepped into the circle.

***

Russell didn't realize, until the exorcists' rescue went wrong, that he hadn't entirely wanted it to go smoothly. He didn't have time to analyze the mix of excitement, malice, and triumph with which he stepped over the safety chain. Nor, he thought, was he alone. Teddy wasn't even trying to hide her enthusiasm. After all, they'd just given up an afternoon's work for the two men who were appearing in the center of the pentarium, and if they had not even been called upon to assist it would have really been a waste. *And now he'll be even more in our debt,* Russell thought. He wouldn't be approaching Lord Stimms as a supplicant, when he'd designed his plan for overcoming Xiphister. He'd be calling in a debt.

Also, he had to admit, he didn't mind the prospect of telling that smug Lord Stimms to look around inside himself. He'd taken a dislike to the man almost the moment they met, at least the moment they met without the glamour. Exorcists were entirely too manipulative and superior. Stepping in to rescue one would be sweet — but, not having thought this through beforehand, Russell had put himself on the team caring for Endamos. He felt a pang when he realized this, but set it aside and grasped the gray-haired man's arm. The flesh felt mushy under his hand, and blood dripped down his fingers. The man clung to Lord Stimms as Russell checked his own team and led them in the opening lines of the charm.

It worked! Triumph bubbled up in his chest as the man became solid right before his eyes. The blurring faded away; the arm seemed to knit together. Now it felt strong, if thin. Its muscles were hard and its ligaments tense against Russell's grip. The hands holding Lord Stimms' arm were in focus now, tanned and filthy. One of them wore a ring, startlingly bright and clean against the dark skin, with a silver ribbon trailing from it. Russell recognized it with a start as the one Lord Stimms had worn around his neck. That part of the plan had worked … the gray-haired man let go of Lord Stimms and stood up, shaking himself loose from Russell's grasp.

"I'm fine," he said impatiently, as if being saved were a nuisance, and looked Russell up and down with a combination of disbelief and disdain. He was an exorcist all right; Russell immediately became conscious of his knobby knees and pale shins.

His self-consciousness was interrupted as the gray-haired exorcist folded at the knees and waist. "Hey!" Russell shouted to Will Harding, "Hand me that chair!" He swung it into position to catch the man.

"He's stabilizing," said Sorcerer Klimt, running a diagnostic amulet over the man's chest. Was it a good thing for a necromancer to say one was stabilizing?

"Magister Endamos?" Cinea asked, and the man nodded.

"You should lie down," said Klimt. "Over here."

"What about –" Endamos gestured toward Lord Stimms.

"Is there anything you can do for him?" Klimt had a good bedside manner, which surprised Russell.

"I did what he told me to," said Endamos. "I Named him." He stood up, shaking in Russell's grasp. "If he's not right, it means I Named him wrongly. It's my fault!"

"Fainting on top of him won't help, will it? Come over here and recover, then maybe you can be useful."

Now Russell had time to look over at Teddy's team, around Lord Stimms, and see that his lordship remained a blur — and all the time that blood, dripping and spattering onto the golden floor.

Chapter 23
The Forgotten Man

Warren, Lilian, and Ver had followed the swimming leaves for a few kilometers across the prairie, and were down in a deep hollow from which he could only see swells of green grass against the sky, when Lilian stopped. "I smell burning," she said, looking up at the sky — impossibly blue, amazingly huge. "I don't see any smoke, do you?"

"No," Warren said. "It smells more like cooking than like a grass fire, doesn't it?" His stomach rumbled.

"That way," Ver said, gesturing up the slope to their right. They crept up through a patch of thigh-high goldenrods. Something long with eight pairs of sparkling wings rowed itself past Warren's ear. The smell grew stronger, as if somebody was roasting a haunch of meat over a campfire. Warren's mouth watered. It was already getting cold — had the day gone faster in here than outside? — and he shivered, thinking about the warmth of a fire. Hair stood up on his forearms and his hand grew clammy in Lilian's … he stopped with a jerk, pulling her down with him under the goldenrods.

"What?" she whispered.

"*Grue*," Warren whispered back. "Demon."

They froze, listening. *What was I thinking!* thought Warren. *I should never have brought her in here!* He heard no footsteps, but something rustled through the tall plants over near the stream.

"No, no," said a voice, and Warren felt horror wash through him. There was no other voice like the demon Antimora's, with its gentle chiming sound or the way it twisted his insides into a cold knot. He felt Lilian tremble but was too afraid to put an arm around her, almost too afraid to breathe. *We're in the alchemists' prison?* He thought, and looked around frantically, as well as he could without moving his head. *It can't be — this place isn't changing!* But the demon was speaking again.

"We are not going over to the stream," it chided. "No water. Move along — you're doing so well. You've lasted much longer this time."

Warren felt sick as well as cold. He snuck a glance at Lilian, who had gone ghost-white. If she threw up — something large fell into the plants, maybe ten meters away over the crest of the rise, and Antimora spoke again.

"No no," it said with the same encouraging tone. "No lying down. You know the rules. No resting, no water." Warren heard a hissing noise and smelled cooking meat again. Another voice cried out, more of a croak than a scream, and the plants rustled as if an animal were struggling to its feet … Warren was on his own feet before he knew he was going to do it, blood hot in his face and singing in his ears. He went forward in big strides, too angry to even feel the demon's chill.

"Get away from him," he shouted. Then the demon Antimora rose from an area of tumbled grass, surprisingly close to him, and Warren's anger deserted in the face of the enemy. He caught just a glimpse of its rear end as it ran away.

Antimora looked just as it had when Warren saw it in the pentarium. It was man-shaped, slender and graceful, with a long gray robe and great feathered wings. Its beauty was only slightly marred by its being on fire, outlined by a halo of blue-gold flame.

"Why, Magister Oldham," it said. "It's been months since I have seen you. I should have known you were the sort to visit those in prison. And you have brought friends."

It looked past him, and Warren knew from the sinking feeling in his heart that Lilian and Ver must have revealed themselves as well. He would have looked, but this close to the demon he dared not turn away from it.

"Take this over to the poor soul it was tormenting," he said, reaching a hand back with one of Teddy's wards in it. A hand took the ward and Lilian came into his field of vision, walking a large arc to avoid Antimora. She walked like someone on a balance beam. "Don't listen to anything the demon says," he told her, remembering how it had sowed dissension among his faculty, speaking to them all separately as they stood around it. It could be talking to Lili right now, telling her — what? *It doesn't matter,* he told himself. *Nothing could drive us apart.*

Lilian reached the tossed grass and looked down into it, her face white and set. Antimora would only have to step sideways to be between them … as if it read Warren's mind, it did so.

"How delightful to see old friends and make new ones," it said. "And how wise of you, to bring someone along to provide the motive force you so

316

often lack. Professional experience so often makes one over-cautious. Left to yourself, I'm sure you would have come up with so many reasons not to venture here — at least, not without a significant force at your command."

That's true, Warren realized with a shock. He would never have done anything this stupid, if he'd been at home. It was Lilian and Ver — *and the scrying, and the ley-line*, he told himself fiercely. He was following the ley-line. He trusted it.

Lilian had knelt down, her face tight with disgust, and was talking to someone in the grass. Warren tried to ignore Antimora and listen to her instead. How could such an angry face produce such a soft voice? "Put this on," she was saying. "It'll be all right. It's not going to hurt you anymore. Here, drink some of this." A water bottle glinted in the sunlight, and Lilian's head disappeared below the leaves.

Warren felt proud of her. However big a mistake the quest turned out to be, Lilian was doing it right. He walked around Antimora, which made no move to approach him, and over to the trampled grass.

"That's Antimora," he told Lilian. "It'll try to set us against one another."

"Yeah, I got that," she said, a bit sharply.

"And if it succeeds –" Warren waved at the figure she was holding. It was a slender man in a maroon-robe. He looked young, in his late twenties, and had flyaway dark hair and a curly mustache. *I know that face,* Warren thought. Images from a photo spread in the student newspaper popped into his mind. He'd remembered it because of the man's

317

lazy, affected air — like a cat, Warren had thought then. Lord Stimms, the new chief exorcist, the paper had said, and Warren had wondered how Cham would get along with her new boss.

Lord Stimms didn't look sleek and superior now. His eyes were sunken, his face drawn, and burns like fingerprints dotted his face and neck. He lay against Lilian's knee, letting her give him water without trying to help himself, and Warren understood why when he looked at the way each of the man's wrists was twisted backwards.

"I know that too," Lilian was saying, really crossly this time, but Warren cut over her.

"I think his arms are broken."

"What?" She had regained some color with irritation, but went pale again as she looked.

"Arms and wrists," Antimora corrected, from behind Warren. "One a day. There must be rules, you know."

"Rules good," said another voice. "Head first." Warren felt a swish in the air behind him, but that wasn't half as shocking as the sudden disappearance of the *grue*. He twisted to see Ver lowering its axe, with a disappointed frown. "Stupid talking," it said, as if scolding itself. "Got away." There was no sign of Antimora except a shimmer in the air.

Warren stared at the goblin. "If you'd hit it, you would have let it through our wards!"

Ver lowered the axe. "Goblin not stupid," it said, pulling the ward Warren had given it out of a pocket. "Took off human ward. Not need such junk." It tossed the ward, not too gently, at Warren's head. He caught it.

"Thank goodness!" said Lilian. "Not that you missed, but thank goodness that nasty thing's gone. Now I can hear myself think. And I can think, I'll have you know," she said to Warren, "even if I'm not one of your demonologists."

Warren put up his hands. "This is what I meant about it turning us –"

"You don't need to tell me everything three times. Where's that first aid kit?"

Warren felt unjustly accused, but he held his tongue and dug out the kit.

Lilian and Warren worked on the exorcist in an uncomfortable silence, slitting his red sleeves to bandage the twisted, swollen arms. Warren was not silent for lack of things to say — he could think of a lot of things to say — but for lack of trust. Every time a remark sprung to his mind, so did three reasons it would make his wife angrier. He began to feel angry himself. What right did she have to be so difficult to get along with? It was her stupid quest, anyway. He shouldn't have let her talk him into it. So he kept silent, except for the charms he had to speak over the exorcist's fractures and burns. Nor did Lilian speak, except to ask him to pass things in a tone that made it sound as if he were being obstructive. Even the exorcist kept silent, but he had a better reason; as soon as Warren put a pain-killing charm around his neck, he had fallen into something between unconsciousness and sleep. Ver prowled around them, axe at the ready, but said nothing.

"I think that's it," Lilian said at last. "Unless — unless he has internal injuries."

Warren had been about to say that, but had felt sure she'd take it as insulting negativity. Now he was the one who felt irritated.

"We have to stop this!" he said, his own voice loud and offensive in his ears.

"Stop what?" she bristled.

"Stop not talking and then getting mad when we do talk. Since when do we treat each other this way?"

Lilian turned away and messed with the first-aid kit. "Maybe since forever. Maybe we just haven't seen it."

"When did I ever act as if you couldn't think?"

"Well, when did I ever ignore your warnings about demons? And don't you dare say when I brought you in here," she challenged. "You were just as ready to come in here as I was."

Warren caught her hands. "Lili, what did the demon say to you?"

She tugged, half-heartedly. He could hear tears in her voice. "It said I'd brought you in here for it, when it could never have gotten you on its own — because you were too cautious, and your colleagues were too intelligent, and you would never have come in here without them."

"Do you think that's true?"

"Well, isn't it?" When Warren pulled this time, she didn't resist but collapsed against him, crying.

Warren pressed his face down into her curls. "Honey, neither of us knew this was the alchemists' prison. How could we have known? It's not changing — it's nothing like the way it used to be."

"Goblin ward," Ver said. "No magic pass goblin ward."

"There, you see," Warren said, holding Lili tighter. "There was no way we could have known. And I was so caught up by the ley-line, I thought I was in a fairy tale and nothing bad could happen. So I brought you in here."— "Waking up," Ver said, poking the axe-handle toward the exorcist. He was indeed waking, and unhappily, from the whimpering noises. Warren let go of Lilian and they hurried to his side.

"Don't move your arms," Lilian said. "They're bandaged."

He opened his eyes wide, staring at them with a look of desperate surprise. "What — who are you? Where's Rosemont?"

"Who?"

"The demon? Where's the demon?"

"Don't worry about the demon. We gave you a ward against it — and Ver chased it away."

"What — no!" he croaked, struggling to sit up. "I was keeping it busy!"

"You were letting the demon torture you on purpose?" Warren said, with a sinking feeling. "Why?"

"So I could save Endamos without it interfering," Lord Stimms said, collapsing back against Lilian's arm.

Lilian looked at Warren in confusion.

"You mean another version of you is escaping, while this version keeps the demon busy?" Warren asked. "You remember everyone in here fragments into multiple versions of themselves."

"Yes, you told me," Lilian said. "There's no point arguing. What's done is done, unless you want

321

us to run after the demon and invite it back." Lord Stimms shuddered and shook his head again.

"Who are you?" he croaked, squinting up at her.

"Lilian Oldham. This is my husband Warren — he's a demonologist from Osyth. And that's Ver."

"How did you get in here?"

"Well, we're on vacation, and Warren was walking the ley-line –" she gave Warren a hopeless look. It was pretty complicated.

Lord Stimms turned his head and threw up the water Lilian had just given him. "Vacation," he said in what might have been a bitter voice if it were stronger.

"I think we should have given him something with sugar in it," said Lilian. She felt his forehead and frowned. "He's getting awfully cold."

"It's his arms," said Warren. "All his energy's going into healing his arms." He checked one of the bandages. It had been the color of a bruise when he wrapped it around the broken wrist; now it was paler, and the power crystal he'd fastened to it right over the break had gone dull. Warren could feel it pulling at his magic. "He's used up the first crystals."

"How many do we have?"

"A box full." Warren fastened new crystals to the bandages and put the old ones into a necklace of plastic loops, like the kind people put on key-heads to tell them apart. He hung the necklace around his neck and tucked it inside his shirt, so the crystals could recharge in contact with his skin.

"How long is that likely to take?"

"Recharge? Maybe three hours."

322

"No, fixing his arms."

"The bandage box said it could take all day."

"Well, what are we going to do? We can't just leave him here. Should we take him with us?"

"I'm not sure where we're going, any more," Warren said slowly.

"Cast charm," said Ver. "Where leaves want to go?"

Warren took a deep breath. "You saw that demon. It's trapped in here. Can we take a chance on letting it out again?"

"I tell you, goblin take care of demon."

"Fine," said Warren. "You take care of the demon then we'll cast the charm you want."

"What charm?" asked Lord Stimms.

"It's supposed to lift the curse on this place and give it back to the goblins," said Lilian.

Lord Stimms almost smiled. "This is your idea of a vacation." Warren had the distinct feeling that his attention was elsewhere. "I — ah!" He smiled for the first time. "You need not worry about Endamos. He is himself again."

"You mean the other version of yourself has finished what you came in here to do?" Lilian asked.

"Yes," said Lord Stimms. "And he will now return the favor."

The eyes looking at Warren didn't change much, but the face around them grew blurry, as if a hundred pictures of Lord Stimms were being projected over one another; pictures of him well and ill, scarred and whole, angry and happy and sad. He stood up straight, the remnants of his red sleeves hanging from his shoulders like wings; *his bandages had turned snow-white* and the healing crystals on his arms and wrists brightened, recharging themselves second by second until they blazed like stars.

"You — look a lot better," Lilian said lamely.

"I appear to be myself again," Lord Stimms answered, shaking his robe into place. "I rather expected to be myself somewhere else, though." With each word, he became a bit less imposing. He was just a human, Warren realized, powerful but also young. Still, the crystals and bandages retained their mythic grandeur, enough to make Warren shiver — no, he realized, that was the *grue*. The demon Antimora had returned.

The demon seemed a commonplace figure, compared to Lord Stimms. It stood a little ways off, to Warren's right, in an attitude of surprise. It leant forward, and actually seemed to push its cowl up to get a better look at Lord Stimms, and then it began to laugh; not a sniggering or malicious laugh, but a full-bellied laugh of pure amusement.

"What in the world!" it said. "What is this, one of those avatars out of a North Sio tapestry? When do you descend to earth and start seducing milkmaids?"

Lord Stimms looked self-conscious for a moment, but then he half-closed his eyes and put on an air of detachment. "I didn't think we would see you again," he said. "You didn't like the axe, as I remember."

"What, that thing? You did not really believe the goblin could hurt me, did you?"

Lord Stimms folded his arms. "Let us experiment."

The demon disappeared abruptly, and Ver's axe came whizzing through the place where it had been. "This can become even more amusing," the demon said, this time from Lilian's left. She gasped, and Warren pulled her close. "We can play at this until the little thing tires, or strikes one of its own allies. Whatever can happen will happen in here. As you know."

"True," said Lord Stimms. "Even you might err."

"At what? There is nothing here that can destroy me," said Antimora. "They are no threat, and you cannot destroy what you yourself created."

"What?" asked Lilian.

"Has Gerald not told you why he is so determined to overcome me? I imagine he feels a personal obligation," said the demon. It spread its arms and wings, and disappeared. Ver, behind it, lowered the axe.

"Is the demon claiming you created it?" Warren asked Lord Stimms, in the moment of silence. "That might give us some insight into its weaknesses."

"How wonderfully non-judgmental you are," the demon said from behind him. "The perfect middle manager. Of course he made me! Three times he followed me into this place. We did interesting things, here where there were no consequences. It was the third time when he turned upon me, his teacher. He stood no further from me than he stands from you, weeping with rage, and said to me *'You're a demon,'* and behold! I was as you now see me. Or would, if you turned."

By the time Warren had turned, though, it was gone. The voice went on from behind Lord Stimms.

"I knew, though, that I was leaving the world's exorcists in good hands. In powerful ones, at least. Unless he grows angry again, and turns them all into demons, or pudding, or suchlike.

"But don't feel bad," it said tenderly to Lord Stimms, "You gave me all this — power, freedom, prey — and I will forever be grateful. You will have the hearts of all my kills. It will be a delicious irony, will it not? The Chief Exorcist and his demon confidante."

"What silliness," Lord Stimms said, stifling a yawn. "You sought me out, and stole my potential to boost your own fading powers. Now, like any abuser, you say I made you do it." Something about his voice made Warren's ears prick. He looked more closely. Lord Stimms' face was darker than it had been. The hand that covered his mouth trembled.

"Ah, but you did," said the demon. "I perceive that you know it yourself. The moment you heard of me, you set me upon this path. You never wanted a teacher. You wanted someone strong enough to punish you. Shall we tell them what for?" It turned to Warren, its eyes wide in false innocence. "What could an exorcist possibly do to deserve punishment? Such a little talent. No ability to change anything, except what people think they are. What could he have done, that might only be expiated by changing the world's greatest hero into his personal sadist?"

"Demons lie," Warren said. He said it to Lilian, but he was reminding himself as well.

"This is nonsense," said Lord Stimms, but Warren could tell it was not. It was real, at least to

326

Lord Stimms — more real than his broken arms had been, to judge from his tone.

"Alas, if it only were," the demon said, shaking its head sadly. "What I have suffered at your hands!"

"That *is* nonsense," Lilian said fiercely. "You were the one hurting him!"

"True," said Antimora, nodding. "Has he thanked you for rescuing him? Or did he reproach you for interrupting us?" It looked from Warren to Lilian, and whatever it saw in their faces made it nod again. "This is your story, is it not, Gerry? You remake the strongest people you can find into things that can punish you, and then you need more punishment for having destroyed them.

"But now that you are chief exorcist, who can punish you? No power has ever challenged Lord Stimms. In my day, the world agreed on only one thing — that they needed exorcists, and the one who could make them. Whatever wars raged, Lord Stimms was held untouchable. Is that still the case? Or will your pitiful needs leave the whole world without exorcists, in the end?"

Lord Stimms shrugged his shoulders. "If I had any such needs, they'd be fulfilled by now. You can dish out enough abuse for any one," he said, in an attempt at nonchalance. His voice trembled, though. Did his half-closed eyes cover tears of rage?

"Ah, so true." Antimora sighed. "I was a good man, once. I would still be a good man, if you had never heard of me. How many people would be good, if they had never met you?"

Lord Stimms flushed a sudden, alarming red so dark it was almost purple. "Have it your way, then,"

327

he said, and there was nothing urbane or self-conscious in his voice at all. This harsh, shaking cry was raw power, Warren thought; the kind of passion that reshaped worlds. It wiped Warren's vision away for a moment, and what returned was tentative, not to be trusted until Lord Stimms told him it was true.

"You think you were a good man before I met you? Find out for yourself what kind of man you were, then. You never met me," Lord Stimms said. "Nobody ever met me, I never existed — will that satisfy you?"

***

Warren felt odd, and a bit foolish. Why was he clinging to Lilian like this, stiff as if they'd been standing still for half an hour? Why did he expect to see a demon, when there was no *grue*? Why were his nerves on edge?

"Goodness," said Lilian, letting go of him, "I feel all un-nerved. Do you feel it too?"

"We must have walked through someplace especially magical."

She took a deep breath. "Do the leaves want us to stop here? No - what a pity."

"We'll have to go on." Warren loved the touch when his fingers met hers on the cool surface of the bowl. But he could not help thinking he was forgetting something important.

Chapter 24
Just For a Moment

"One more time," said Teddy Whin. Ric hid his expression behind the sheet of paper with the charm for knowing yourself written on it.

Ric had heard about the changes people went through after they returned from the exorcists' prison, but never seen them. He'd thought he knew what was happening, as Endamos' and Lord Stimms' faces blurred like an out-of-focus photograph. Then there had been the blood, and everything had gone wrong. Well, maybe not everything. Endamos was in focus, but not Lord Stimms. Ric couldn't see through the blur sitting in Lord Stimms' chair. He couldn't even tell what it was doing, except that it rose and sank in a thick, oily way that made him seasick.

The part of it nearest Ric rose, and he reached out for it. None of the magicians reproached him, but *Ric couldn't tell what he had grasped*. It changed under his hands; now warm, now cold, now hard and now soft. Under it all was a loose feeling, as if whatever he held were boneless or fragmented under the skin.

"This isn't right," he said, as soon as they finished the charm.

"It helped the other one," said Derek, looking from Ric to Endamos, who was now completely solid. "What's wrong?"

"I think he's fighting it," said Teddy.

"But can he live like this?" Derek asked, looking at the blur that had been Lord Stimms.

"I don't know."

"Move," said a new voice, and Cham Ligalla ducked under the sorcerer's upraised arm. She took what might have been Lord Stimms' hand in both of hers. Ric felt like a piece of furniture, so entirely did the exorcist ignore him.

"Gerry, come back," she said, and Ric thought even a dead body would be unable to ignore that command. He felt Lord Stimms come together under his hands. Bones became long and hard, muscles fastened to them, skin closed it all in solid as a sausage, and Ric held a whole man; blurry, as Endamos had been, but whole.

Ric had expected Lord Stimms to return bloody and bruised, perhaps even lacking a limb. He had nerved himself against the possibility of a demon looking out of his Lordship's eyes, and having to play the White Knight if Osyth's exorcists failed to banish it. He hadn't imagined Lord Stimms' coming back with a tan.

The new Lord Stimms had, besides the healthy glow, a wide white scar running down the left side of his neck. The sleeves of his red robe were slashed, hanging loose from his shoulders, and the arms beneath were covered by snow-white bandages. Bright lights shone from his wrists and his lower arms, and Ric had to squint to see that they were power crystals.

Lord Stimms looked over Cham's head, as if someone taller were standing behind her. "This is nonsense," he said, but Ric could tell it was not. Whatever he was speaking to or about, it was serious. He had never heard Lord Stimms sound serious about anything before.

"Gerry!" Magister Ligalla said again. "Gerry, do you know where you are?"

Lord Stimms flushed dark red, almost the color of a bruise. "Is that what you want?" he cried to whatever he saw over Ligalla's head, and the cry ran through Ric like fresh water, as if everything in him could be washed away at this moment. "You think you were a good man before I met you?" Lord Stimms cried, and Ric thought *yes, I do*. He had no choice.

"Find out for yourself what kind of man you were, then," said his Lordship. "You never met me. Nobody ever met me, I never existed — will that satisfy you?"

Exhaustion flowed over Ric like melted chocolate. He felt himself dissolving in the sticky heat of it, and his arms relaxed despite his efforts. Then there was nothing to see, and anyway Ric was too asleep to see it.

Chapter 25
Caretakers

It showered Wednesday afternoon; good for baby trees. *The saplings had grown* another ten centimeters by the time the rain ended and Mama Simone could go out to check on them. They leaned further away from each other, tugging against their own roots.

Looking at them took Mama Simone back. She felt again what it was like to have two babies in her belly, each pulling away from the other. How they had fought being twins! When they kicked, Gretyl and Willett had kicked each other. Even when they were born, Willett had held back long enough — past midnight — to give himself a different birthday. And after — she put those thoughts away. She'd taken care of them, after. She was still taking care of them all, and she hadn't brought these little trees back for Gretyl and Willett. Fight as they might, these trees were rooted where Mama Simone planted them — in the ceramic robin — and there they would stay. The sun broke through between clouds and blazed off their wet leaves, as if to say amen. She could feel its strength inside her, where the acorn's magic had started to grow out along her nerves. The little trees stretched and she could have sworn they grew taller, stronger, right before her eyes.

Mama Simone turned to go back into the house, and that was when she saw the goat.

The goat had reared up and put her front legs on the next-to-topmost rail of the fence, just to remind Mama Simone what a joke fences were. Her eyes were fixed on those little trees at the end of the garden. She moved her jaws as if she were already chewing something.

Mama Simone went cold all down her back. "Oh no, you don't! Don't you dare!" she said. The goat looked up at her with eyes that oh yes, dared. She didn't even dodge when Mama Simone pounced on her and snapped the chain onto her collar. Why should she? The trees would still be there the day Mama Simone forgot to tie her.

And now, wherever Mama Simone turned, there was something just waiting for a baby tree. Deer in the woods, rabbits in the field, gophers under the barn, moles in the lawn. Cutworms, grasshoppers, and aphids. Clueless children mowing the lawn, or weeding the vegetables. In the fall, rakes and snowplows — "and how I thought I could grow two full-sized trees in my vegetable garden!" she cried aloud. "What kind of fool am I turning into?"

There was no place, no place at all on the farm where little trees could be safe, even if you girded them round with hardware cloth and mulch. No place, unless something guarded them day and night ... Mama Simone almost ran as she fetched the bucket and spade. She dug as deep as she could. Their roots were already almost as long as the bucket was deep, and pieces fell off the ceramic robin as she pulled it out. The sun slanted over her at an evening angle, getting in her eyes as she walked toward it, and went back behind a cloud just as she stepped into the edge of the woods.

***

Rho dithered at the traffic light in town. He surprised himself by turning east into little built-up streets instead of onto the road that led home. Within a block he recognized where he was going. Lilis' place.

She was out in the front garden, just as she had been before, though she wasn't weeding this time. She sat on a glider, drinking something amber and watching the sunrays beam through a bank of purple clouds.

"Hey," she said when he got out of the car. "Want some wine? It's elderflower. A good year."

"No," Rho said. He trudged across the yard and sat down heavily beside her, making the glider bounce and sway.

"What's eating you?"

"I went over to Sterne to talk with Gordon K."

"No job, huh?"

"No, he hired me," said Rho, with a bit of a start. "I start at the extension college next week!"

"Then why do you look like the dog ate your wooden leg?"

Rho kicked at the ground, making the glider jerk so much that Lilis drank her wine off in one gulp, as if to keep it safe. "I heard animals again. Seals and midges."

"Nice combo," she said. "That's great, isn't it?"

334

"No," he said, and told her all of it. Gordon K.'s theory, the veal sheds. "Is it true what he said about a witch that killed kittens?"

"I've never heard that one. The stuff about babies and abortions is true enough, though. Even mundanes know how powerful the cells from abortions are." Now Lilis was the one kicking the ground. She frowned at her feet. A hummingbird flew over them, trying to get its beak into one of the swaying honeysuckle blossoms; it made a tiny, industrial whirring noise, then flew away with a frustrated cheep. "It's an easy theory to test, I guess. Just go out to the pig barn, and see if you hear anything — hey!" She lifted her head. "Look, it's black magic, right? Torturing another creature to get its magic — that's illegal everywhere."

"Yeah, I thought of that," Rho said sourly.

"Torturing another creature for its milk, or eggs, or meat isn't illegal. That's just farming as usual. But if those factory farms are supplying the magic for the regions around them, they're illegal under the black magic laws!" She jumped up. "*We could get them banned*, the whole industry!" When Rho didn't respond, she put her hands on her hips and glared at him. "This is a bigger issue than your magic."

"They'll just make it illegal for magicians to go near factory farms."

"How, by locking them up? When they haven't done anything wrong?" She shook her head. "You can't lock up innocent people wholesale, even if you're King. Let alone magicians. The Mystic Guild alone — magic's bigger than agribusiness."

335

"But won't the magicians side with agribusiness, if that's where they're getting magic?" There was no point warning her, he could see. She had that look in her eyes, the one that came right before she moved her Queen all the way across the board, flung all her toy armies against one enemy, or threw back all five of her cards in draw poker. The 'shake the box and see what falls out' look.

"We have to verify it, first," she said. "Not just your magic. We need more cases — go home by the pig barn, and if you hear them we'll invite Gordon K. out. And if he gets his magic back, we'll talk to some lawyers I know at Defense of Life. Well, what are you waiting for?" She kicked the glider so hard it rattled.

Rho felt put upon by a sister who had yet again missed the point. He rose with a sulky face.

"It's not about you, Robin," she said, wheedling. "I'd give you my magic, if I could. Some of it, anyway — but this could save millions of animals, don't you see? This could really do something good."

As if a film reel had just been turned on, things began to happen in the garden around Rho. A fat bumblebee lumbered her way out of a foxglove butt-first and tried to turn around on its inadequate lip. She fell, bouncing off two leaves before she got her wings going fast enough to barrel her away through the swaying stems. Three sparrows began clamoring in the hedge and a dragonfly darted past his face, its wings flickering. A squirrel scolded from the nearest tree, and a swallow went hawking along the edge of the road, so low its wind ruffled the grasses. All around him creatures went about their business. None of them were locked into dark crates too small to turn in. None of them were crowded into metal sheds without sun or rain... "You're right," he said, and found that he meant it. "Not your idea — that could be a pipe dream — but you're right that this is more important than I am. I'd rather never hear them again than listen to them crying –" his voice stopped without warning, and Lilis gave him a too-big, too-soft, too girly hug.

"Do you want me to come along?"

"No. I'd better get going." He went back to his car as if he were walking to an execution.

The pig barn was pale and featureless, the same color as the waste lagoon. Rho wondered sourly if they had a gulper in the lagoon, but he couldn't stand and stare for long. Who knew when the men in the truck would come back? Looking both ways, he skulked up to the side of the barn

Rho heard nothing at first except the soft grunting of many pigs. Then the sun broke through the cloud layer and the fields and barn suddenly turned golden against a slate-gray sky. The landscape seemed to open again, just as it had before he heard the seals and the midges. He took a big breath and leaned against the metal wall, and heard a voice.

"...late with food," said the voice in the pig barn. It sounded heavy, a grumbling grunting sort of a voice. But nothing answered it, not really. Rho heard grunting, squealing noises, but so few of them resolved themselves into words that he started back in alarm, afraid his power had gone.

337

It hadn't; he could hear everything around him, even the mosquito at his ear. "Sweet blood, hot blood," the bug sang.

But the pigs made no more sense when Rho put his head back against the shed wall. He caught a few words — "food," "stop!" and "move!" but nothing more complex. It was like listening to roaches.

A cold deeper than the night air struck through Rho as he remembered the conversations he'd had with their farm weaners. The little pigs had been curious about everything — brighter than goats, without the attitude. He leaned his forehead against the metal and sniffed back tears. The world felt small around him; the sun had hidden itself behind clouds low on the horizon, and night was coming on. He had to go home, and only now did it occur to him, horribly, that Mama Simone might have expected him the night before.

By the time he got back to the farmhouse, he had his story worked out; but he didn't need it. Mama Simone was nowhere to be found. Her truck was in the driveway, but she wasn't in the kitchen.

"Hello," Rho called, stepping into the dark hallway. Because the blinds were down, it took him a minute to realize that things were different in the sitting room. He felt around where the lamp used to be. By the time he convinced himself it wasn't there, his eyes had adjusted and he could see that nothing was there. "Whoa!" he said to himself, and backed out of the room. "Mama! Where are you?" No answer. As he went up the stairs, light spots on the wainscoting stared at him. Hadn't there been pictures there?

Her bedroom looked almost as empty. The bed was still there, but hardly any dresses hung in the closet. Was that normal? Rho only owned one suit himself. The dresser drawers, the jewelry chest, were almost empty. Her toothbrush was still in the bathroom. Nothing in Rho's room had been touched, as far as he could tell. He looked out the window and saw the goat tethered to the paddock fence, which she was chewing in an absentminded way. The spade was lying down in the garden, among the lettuces. That was the first time he thought something might have happened.

"She's gone for a walk," said Lilis. "Like she did the day Daddy died. She gave Gretyl six fits."

"But the sitting room's empty," said Rho. "It looks as if she had a giant bonfire out back. And she left the spade lying in the garden."

He heard Lilis pause in the middle of a breath. Whatever argument she'd been meaning to give him never came out. "We'll be right out," she said.

"Who?" Rho asked, his heat sinking.

"Me and Gretyl and Willett."

"Do we have to tell them –?"

"Yeah, because if we don't I'll never hear the end of it."

Rho didn't even want to hear the beginning of it.

"You have it coming," said Lilis. "Bite the bullet."

"They'll blame me."

"They have a right to. Take it like a man. Make some coffee — that'll help a little."

They erupted out of the car like thunderstorms; two thunderstorms, one cloudbank. Rho had never seen gumboots as big as Willett's. *The better to kick me with,* he thought, but Willett didn't even look at him.

"Her clogs are gone," Willett said to the girls. "She's off in the woods somewhere."

"It'll be dark soon," Gretyl answered. They'd apparently made a pact to ignore Rho completely. She tromped over to the garden, picked up the spade and something from beside it. "She dug something up here." The fragment that finally made its way to Rho looked like pottery; unglazed on one side, brown and shiny on the other. It was curved, with part of a drainage hole cutting into one side.

"It was hollow," he said timidly. "Not meant to hold water, though."

Nobody paid any attention to him. Willett was raking through the ashes of her big bonfire. "What's this? Hair?"

"We have to find her," Gretyl said, and suddenly rounded on Rho. "You were supposed to be taking care of her! Where were you while all this was going on?"

"I went to Sterne for a job interview, and got caught by a storm on the pass," he said, finally getting to use his story.

"And you couldn't call any of us? What did she sound like when you told her? Was she upset?" Rho couldn't answer. Gretyl stooped and glared into his face. "You didn't call her? You let her think you'd run away again—" She stopped and took a firmer grip on the spade handle. "Keep him away from me," she said, turning to Lilis. "You're so fond of

340

him, keep him out of my reach. You thoughtless, heartless, self-centered ass!" Rho, who had thought himself done with, jumped. "Irresponsible, selfish, no-good –"

"What did you expect?" Willett took Gretyl's arm and led her a little away, out of spade-length. "You know what he is. You read the web page." He kept a hold on Gretyl's arm while she breathed heavily, her color gradually going back to normal.

"What web page?" Rho said indignantly. "What am I?"

"Some demon's bed toy."

"I am not!"

"Boys!" said Lilis. "After we find Mama, I'll personally set up a cage match for you. Right now, can it." She picked the frizzled hair-ends out of the pile and whispered to them. Then she breathed on them and pulled her hand back. They rose, sparkling in the evening-orange sunlight, and began to drift toward the woods. "Hurry up. We won't be able to see them for long."

Chapter 26
The House in the Book

Warren carried the bowl along until his arms grew tired, but still the leaves schooled at one end. Lilian took a turn. Ver was carrying the axe. The sun crept down the sky, and Warren began to worry about spending the night here. How had so much time slipped away? When Lilian suggested a lunch break he objected.

"You eat while I carry it," he said. "Then I'll eat while you carry it."

She handed the bowl over without any argument, and dug in her pack for a sandwich. "Hey," she said, her face still half inside. "Have you been messing around with my backpack?"

"I haven't touched it."

"I thought I packed better than this. The first aid kit's supposed to be in the outside pocket, and here it is all mixed in with the lunch." She pulled the kit out and opened it. "The bandages are half used. And we're missing eight power crystals — almost the whole pack!"

"I have four of them," said Warren. "They needed recharging."

"But I thought we put a full pack in, back in Osyth."

"I have no answers," Warren said a little desperately, because the conversation was making him want to gesture and he couldn't, without spilling the bowl.

Lilian took pity on him. "All right," she soothed. "Do you want ham and cheese, or turkey?"

"Ham."

"Ver! Sandwich?" The goblin came over cautiously. "Free, a gift," said Lilian.

The ground tended downward now and the leaves quivered as if trying to swim through the bowl's rim, to go faster than Warren could carry them. A cold breeze blew along the bottom of the valley they had descended into. Here the leaves turned right, leading them along a stream at the bottom of the dip. Warren squinted his eyes against the wind, which whipped grasses against his shins. The leaves quivered even harder, more eager the nearer they drew to their destination.

"Warren! What on earth is wrong with you?" Lilian took the bowl from his hands, and only then Warren realized he had almost dropped it. His arms and fingers were cramped, frozen. Lilian set the bowl down and tried to rub warmth back into them, to no avail. "Is it the *grue*?"

"I didn't think there were any demons in here," Warren said between chattering teeth. Famous last words, he thought as something large and dark materialized in the mouth of the valley. The frozen wind howling off it took his breath away

The demon had two faces, the top one rather insect-like. The second was a human face, male and middle-aged, looking out of its chest. The human face looked at Warren and Lilian, and its features twisted into despair. "No, no," it mourned. "Not more. No more!" Tears ran out of its blue eyes, and then something seemed to pull it into the demon. "No," it cried, and choked as its mouth went under

343

the demon's surface. "Please, no –" it gasped, tried to scream, choked, and was gone. Warren saw it submerged inside the demon's black, translucent flesh. Were those other figures around it? His own breath stuck in his windpipe out of sympathy. Lilian's hands were cold on his arm.

Warren forced air into his tight chest and prepared to address the demon, but it addressed him first.

"You are Warren Oldham," it said. "Of Osyth."

Crap, Warren thought, fervently. *I got Lilian into this. Damn, damn!* The thought felt re-used, as if he had thought something just like it a moment before. But who could have expected a demon here, inside the goblin's realm? He began to frantically run through the Infernal Lexicon in his mind. What demon could it be? *You know the man-eaters!* he scolded himself. The name was on the tip of his tongue.

"Leave us be," he said to the demon. "We're warded against all your kind."

The demon took a step forward. Something new was pushing out of its chest, and as Warren watched the protrusion began to look more and more like two human hands, holding a large book. "I am already within your wards, Warren Oldham," said the demon. "How can I not be, when I carry your essence within me? You let it blow disregarded on the wind, ashes of power for any with the wit to collect it."

Cold seized Warren from the middle of his chest, like a black hole sucking him into himself. He had barely time to pull his hand out of Lilian's before he seemed to squeeze through the center of

344

his own body; then he saw her from a different angle, as if he stood where the demon stood. She was calling his name and frantically feeling the air, grasping at nothing.

Warren was trapped, stuck together, tangled. But one thing had sprung loose. He remembered the demon's name. He pushed and struggled, freeing his mouth enough to call Lilian, and saw her turn. He saw horror on her face. "Run!" he screamed. "Tell Russell — its name is Xiphister!" Then the demon's substance closed over him, cold and foul. Pain seared through his eyes and ears and chest, and she was gone.

Warren's brain screamed for air, his chest heaved and burned, but there was no relief; neither breath nor death. He pushed frantically against *the viscous stuff that surrounded him*, fighting toward its surface. Each movement burned, deeper into his limbs, as if his efforts helped the demon seep into him. *Lili,* he thought, *this can't be happening to Lili, it can't — I have to stop it!* He forced his eyes open, desperate to see if Lilian was safe outside, but that let the burning into his head. He shrieked. A sound like a thousand voices screaming filled his ears. For a moment, there was nothing but the pain and noise.

Somewhere deep inside himself, though, Warren found he was recording what had happened. The tiny observer inside him had studied demons for thirty years, and had categories for what he was now experiencing. *Like a surgeon being dismembered, or a cook being burned*, he thought, and a second little observer told him that these

345

analogies were both horrible and unhelpful. Warren marveled at the existence of these analytic homunculi. He lost touch with them as another wave of pain wrenched at him, but they came back. They didn't care much about what Warren was feeling. To them, he was a measuring instrument — *a better analogy,* said the second observer. Warren grasped at it, clutched it, fought to perceive rather than suffer.

Warren had always tried to perceive what was real, and not to make things up. Even when demons lured his soul out of his body, back in February, he had tried to map out the world around him. *How's that working for you?* asked a new voice inside his head, observer three. He thought of Russell, who hadn't given a minute's thought to what was real when he was out of body. Russell had used that time to explore his fantasies, and had come back with his power increased tenfold.

True, Warren admitted to himself, and yet … fantasizing inside a demon, that was just wrong. Trying to comfort yourself with pretty visions, while the creature outside you ate your wife; could that be justified at all? *Only,* said the voice, *if it makes you less useless than you are now.* And since Warren could not be any more useless than he was at the moment, he was forced to agree. He was inside magic, soaked through with it. It tore at every nerve and pushed aside every cell; and Warren had spent his life studying how to use magic.

He knew just what he would conjure up if he had his heart's desire. Home, a refuge, where the demon couldn't hurt him or Lilian. He would have knitted his brow and gritted his teeth in concentration, if he could; as it was, he set his mind, and tried to feel in his body the sensations of safety and home. He let himself feel every agony, in careful observant detail, and imagine how it would feel to have that ebb away, to be replaced by comfort and love. He knew he was crying, from the way pain seeped in around his eyes. He knew he was screaming, by the way it stretched his chest from inside. But after a while his left foot stopped hurting.

The foot felt warm, as if it were stretched comfortably up toward a cheerful fire. It felt softness, as of a nice wool sock and a padded footstool. Warren tried mightily to move his other foot toward it, and succeeded; now comfort covered both feet and halfway up his shins. As he concentrated it crept further and further up his legs, his hips, his arms and chest — he would have held his breath in anticipation, if he could have — and now the fire in his lungs became sweet warm air. Warren gasped in as much of it as he could possibly hold, sobbing with relief. Then the comfort flooded over his eyes and ears and he saw, heard what he had dreamed up.

He was in his living room, in his chair with his feet stretched out to the fire. He had on plaid slippers with blue piping around them. His feet were very small. What he sat on was very warm, and wrapped around him on both sides. He had a large book on his lap, his lost grimoire, and as he looked at it in wonder a hand turned one of its pages, moving without his volition as if it weren't attached to Warren at all. The hand pointed to a sentence, running its finger along below the words.

"Go on," a voice said behind Warren's head. "Read it."

He turned his head far as it would go and saw a face with long cheeks, a round chin with a dimple in it, and a hawk's beak of a nose. The face's eyes were hazel and looked at Warren through metal-rimmed glasses much like his own. The face smiled. Warren gasped.

"Dad!"

Warren's father tightened warm arms around him. He smelled of aftershave and pipe tobacco. Warren could see nothing but those eyes and smile. The wool dressing-gown was soft under his hands, and the fireplace's heat struck against his back. Long-lost sensations attacked him from every side. They blocked every thought and filled him up, pouring out his eyes and nose in hot tears.

"Dad!" he choked, in a piping child's voice. He gulped and sniveled like a baby, buried his face against his father's chest, and when those arms closed around him he gave up fighting his sobs. "Oh, Dad," he wept. "The demon ate me, and it might be hurting Lilian, and there wasn't anything I could do about it!"

His father held him tightly, a warm hand rubbing up and down over his shoulder blade. "Poor Scooter," he said. "It's all right. It's all right, Scooter." As the passion died down he shifted and reached into his pocket, handing Warren a handkerchief. "Poor Scooter," he said again, using his thumb to smooth out the worry lines that had been on Warren's forehead even as a child. "We get a lot of dings in life, don't we."

348

Warren blew his nose, feeling stupid. "It's important," he protested into the kerchief. "Lilian might get hurt!"

His father kissed the smoothed-out spot. "Never ignore what you feel," he said. "It'll only sneak up on you later. Right?"

Warren sniffed

"We'll do everything we can for Lilian. You're only eight. You'll have all the time in the world; don't hurry it."

This confused Warren, and he was sure it was incorrect. He pondered it while he scrubbed the tears away from his burning eyes. "Why am I only eight? I wasn't before."

"I don't know, punkin. I just work here."

"Then — you're not real," Warren said, afraid the words would make it all go away and send him back to the horrors he had just escaped. But nothing changed except that his father held him more tightly and more tears sprung to his eyes.

"Well, that's a big question. Where would you say we are?"

"Uh — inside a demon. It wanted to trap me in your grimoire."

"In this grimoire?" He shifted under Warren, picking the book off a side table.

"Yeah." Warren touched it gently. His lost treasure.

"We are inside it," said his father. "This is just a model of it. A memory."

"Then — did the demon eat you? That can't be it," Warren said, shaking his head. "I was there when you died." He ran his fingers over the book. When had he seen it last? The day before Cham burned it up to release Rho's soul from it. He remembered how he had turned the pages, saying goodbye to the memories of his father. These memories. "You're my memory. I've made you up."

"I think I'm more than that," said Dad. "Of course, I would. If I were just your memories, though, why would he be here? You never met him."

"Who –" twisting around, Warren saw a figure standing in the shadowy hall. It looked very large, dark and menacing. He clutched at his father's dressing-gown, and was relieved when Dad put an arm around him.

"Father," Dad said formally. "You've not met your grandson. Warren, say hello to your grandfather."

Warren's heart pounded. Grandfather was an ambiguous figure, at best; the charms he'd put into the grimoire were, if not black magic, a very dark gray. But, Warren thought, that might be just what he needed now. He watched with mixed hope and fear as Grandfather stepped out of the hallway; a stocky man, younger than Dad, with black hair and pale blue eyes like a Husky's. The combination made him look insane, which matched Warren's presuppositions.

Grandpa grinned unpleasantly. "Think you made us up, do you?"

"Uh, I guess not," Warren said. He looked to Dad for reassurance.

"He's right that we haven't got souls," Dad said, standing up for him. "Nor real bodies, or we could have cast some charms ourselves."

"I know what we are," Grandfather said, dismissing the topic. "What I want to know is what you are. Hey, boy? What are you? Another essence?"

"I'm a whole person, I think," Warren said. "The demon sucked me in whole –"

"At eight years old?" Grandfather challenged.

"At sixty-three," said Warren.

"You've regressed."

Warren felt his face burn. "I didn't plan to be eight," he said hotly. "Anyway, what's wrong with being eight?"

"The last thing we need is a weeping child," said Grandfather. "Or another mere essence. You can't cast charms with dream-stuff like this." He swept his arm out, scornfully dismissing the room and fire.

"I –" Warren's hands flew to his sides. Did this little body have any of the things he had packed for his adventure? *Of course it does!* he thought. *The demon didn't undress me first!* And sure enough, he was wearing the same pants, unwieldy with pockets, and the same backpack. He stood up, the better to reach into them, and when his feet reached the floor his slippers turned into hiking boots, the right size for an eight-year-old.

"Um — I, um, have a few things that might be useful," he said, looking down. "I'd better not take off the wards, but I have — apples, a scone, spare power crystals—" sneaking a glance upwards, he saw that the two were not impressed. He pulled out his wallet and his trump card.

"Money will hardly suffice," Grandpa said dryly.

"How about a phoenix feather?" Warren asked innocently. "And some fire-willow seed?" As he took them out, his fingers brushed something cool and smooth. It was the beech-leaf the tall man had given him. His fingers closed on it, but something made him stop before pulling it out. *Come and help me,* he thought, as loudly as he could, clasping it hard, and almost blushed at the childishness of it; but he closed the wallet without revealing the beech-leaf.

"I told you," Dad said to Grandpa.

"Where in the seven realms would you get a phoenix feather?"

Warren couldn't decide whether Grandpa had put the emphasis on 'you' or 'phoenix'. "The ley-line gave it to me."

"Which line? There are no phoenixes in Osyth, or Selanto."

"The Vinchifer line," Warren said, a little smugly.

Dad sighed. "Would you two either have your battle for dominance, or agree to put it off?" he asked, leaning his head on his hand. "Let's get this out of the way one way or another."

"It is," Warren said, though his ears were burning. "I'm the one with the phoenix feather."

"So what do you intend to do with it?" Grandpa challenged. "Any fool can carry things around."

352

Chapter 27
Fire and Blood

Something woke Ric. He blinked at the ceiling, wondering what it had been, when it came again — a rapping on the door.

"Hold on," he called. When he undid the locks, Derek was standing in the hall with his hands in his pockets. He rocked back and forth, looking large and happy.

"Hey, sleepyhead," he said. "It's almost five. Are you gonna doze away all of our free time?"

Ric grinned back. "You should talk. You and your afternoon naps."

"They paid off, didn't they? *We saved an exorcist!*"

"Yeah," Ric said. He didn't remember how he got from the pentarium to bed, but the image of Endamos coming together was clear in his mind. Triumph! He couldn't stop grinning. "We're the bomb."

Derek shouldered his way into the room. "You have a better view than I do," he said. He stuck his arms straight up, stretching. "Man, I feel like I've had my first real sleep in a week. And the rain's stopped!"

The sky over Osyth was indeed a clear, vivid blue, the west just beginning to turn pale with approaching sunset. Sun glinted off a window in the next building over, making Ric blink and rub his eyes. "What do you want to do?" he asked.

"Ligalla says we can't take Endamos back to Selanto till the hospital's cleared him. How's about we see what the rest of the team's up to? I thought I'd corner Magister Hoth and talk about the Hoth protocol."

Ric groaned. "Incubi!"

"Prude."

"I'm too old for incubi."

"You're only as old as you act," said Derek.

"I never acted young enough for incubi." Ric was fully awake by now, his face washed and his shoes tied. They bickered amiably all the way to the cafeteria, where Magisters Teale (ghosts) and Harding (vampires) were seated at a table by the western window. The sun slanted in across them, glaring off Harding's wardage. He must have had twenty metal or crystal amulets hanging from his neck.

"Hey," said Teale, smiling happily. "How are you feeling?"

"Grand. How's Endamos?"

"Cham says he's doing well. Stable, and his magic's already starting to come back. They'll want him in hospital for at least a day, though. What's your plan?"

"I don't know. How do you celebrate when something goes right? Derek wants to talk incubi."

"What, with Patsy Hoth? She's probably at the Academy. You can call her on my cell if you'd like."

"Thanks," said Derek, leaning close to Teale as she showed him how to work the phone. That left Ric with Harding. The man looked tired but cheerful, his blonde hair unnaturally bright in the sunlight and his weak, handsome face just starting to show its age — late thirties, Ric decided.

"Nice," he said, indicating the sun, and Harding nodded.

"The clouds blew off around an hour ago. They can stay gone for all of me."

"So, you do vampires? I didn't think they were a problem over here."

"Off and on," said Harding. "That's what I'm for — to keep them from being a problem."

"We use hunters."

"Yeah, and you catch what — two, three vampires a year? And lose a dozen victims?"

"More than that. Close to fifty kills last year. They're catching up with the drug dealers."

"We've kept it in single digits for two years," said Harding, "and one of those was suicide by vampire."

"Wow," Ric said. "That's pretty good."

"I should write a book, like Hoth's. Then people would be wanting to talk to me about the Harding protocol."

"You should. Vampires kill a lot more people than incubi."

Harding shrugged and leaned his chair back on its hind legs, folding his arms over his chest. "I've published everything," he said. "Selanto could do just what I've done, but they won't. It would mean giving up the idea that vampires are evil. Accepting them as citizens."

"Aren't they evil?"

"Oh, yeah." Harding thumped his chair back down. "Look, you want to come out with me

355

tonight? Meet the Queen, see how we do it on this side of the pond? I promise, no blood required."

"Hmm." Ric thought about it. "Hey, Derek! You up for a vampire bar tonight?"

Derek grimaced. "That's how you guys celebrate, after breaking through alchemists' magic to save an exorcist? You go to vampire bars?"

Harding grinned. "It's all in a day's work, for us. Meeting, rescue exorcist, dinner, vampires. No rest for the wicked."

"He's right," Teale chimed in. "I'm going home and maybe ordering a pizza before I buckle down to the paperwork. We ought to have some kind of protocol for triumph, oughtn't we? I don't think we even recognize triumph, half the time."

That's how it is, Ric thought. When saving people was your job, you stopped celebrating it. "You could come to the vampire bar as well," he suggested, only half joking.

Teale shook her head. "Not my scene," she said firmly. "I'll get hold of Teddy and Russell and make them go over to the faculty club, where we can look ostentatiously unimpressed with ourselves."

"There you go," said Harding, getting up. "We'll all do that. And if you're still game afterward, vampires!"

They didn't have to go anywhere near the Magic Building on their trek from Public Health to the Faculty Club, which turned out to be an old house among birch trees in the east end of the campus. The people trailing out of buildings in this area were secretaries and administrators, with only a smattering of students. Broad swaths of lawn glowed in the slanting sunlight, spangled with pink and white flowers. *This is a bit of all right*, Ric thought. Teale signed them in and led the party to a patio table. Ric could feel himself walking through security spells like beaded curtains as he followed her across the dining room. He exchanged impressed glances with Derek. Then they were back out in the sweet air, settling at a table with snowy linens and heavy silver. *Nice!*

"Champagne, shouldn't we?" Teale asked. She had a determined air, as if she'd read up on celebration and intended to do it right. Ric didn't really like champagne, but felt some pressure to go along with her. Harding had no opinion, it seemed; he was taking a handful of pills.

"Iron," he explained when he saw Ric watching. "Iron, folic acid, and B12. Tools of the trade."

"I thought you said there wouldn't be any bloodletting tonight."

"Not from you," Harding said. "Not unless you want to."

Ric didn't have anything to say about people who wanted to donate to vampires. At least, nothing he wanted Harding to hear. *Sick!* he thought, and was glad to see Cinea and Teddy Whin come onto the patio.

" — tonight," Teddy Whin was saying, but Cinea shook his head.

"We won't have a coven," he said. "I'm not up to it myself, either."

"Up to what?" asked Harding.

357

"I want to try summoning Xiphister again. Since Linus told it Warren was off on vacation, we might do our part by keeping it occupied here."

"The demon with the face in its chest?" Ric shivered at the thought.

"That's the one," Whin said with enthusiasm. "Hey, after today there's nothing we can't handle! Let's give Warren a nice peaceful vacation."

"You just want to talk with that demon," Teale said.

"Are you in?"

"Yes! But not tonight. That would be asking for trouble."

"You brought me over here under the pretext of celebration," said Harding. "Are we just going to talk shop?"

Whin and Cinea vetoed champagne, Cinea tactfully promising something even more festive. The bottle that arrived was triple-sealed and, when it was opened, sent up a cloud of vapor shaped like a tiny dragon.

"Wait!" said Cinea, cutting off the admiring babble with a raised finger. The cloudy dragon had not dispersed, and when their waiter had poured the amber liquid into glasses — cut glass, fragile as a breath — it swooped low over them, shooting a cloudy flame into each. The drink flared up like a furnace, and when it subsided it was the color of rubies. More magicians had arrived at their table meanwhile, and the waiter repeated the ritual. Ric caught movement inside the building. Faculty were standing at the windows to watch.

"Drink up!" said Cinea. "We have to finish the bottle. You can't put the imp back inside."

They clinked glasses and sipped. It was like drinking life straight from the ley-line. *Glory,* Ric thought for no reason, and his nose tingled. Cinea refilled his glass, and the cloud-dragon flamed it again. Ric couldn't feel the chair under his rear end after the second glass. If he'd found himself floating six inches above it, he wouldn't have been surprised. Looking around the table at flushed faces, glowing with the drinks' light as well as sunset, he loved them all. *Pals, buddies. Nothing we can't do, if we put our heads together.*

"Another," Cinea said, pouring. The dragon swooped, the light blazed, and Ric floated higher.

By the end of dinner, the floating had been replaced by a solid glow just in front of Ric's spine. He sat between Harding and Neil Torecki, talking about art. "Church murals up the wazoo," Torecki said with a theatrical moan, when Ric inquired. "I'll spend the rest of my life painting church murals — up side is, it takes us to some nice vacation spots."

"So churches in the snow belt will have to do without your skills," Harding teased.

"Damn straight. I've done three, and accepted six more commissions. But more requests come in every day. I dread the day I get one from the Archbishop's palace," he confided. "I don't know how I'd turn it down, but I don't know how I'd drag myself back in there. Let alone Bill."

"It's gonna come," Harding assured him. "You're the only artist who ever met her in the flesh."

"Met who?"

"The Bright Lady," said Harding, with a malicious grin. "You didn't know that? Neil moves in exalted circles."

Torecki looked abashed. "Yeah well, that's why I was willing to help today," he said. "I was in that garden for months. It sucked."

"How'd you get in?"

"Through the alchemy building. We came out through the Sacred Flame, though." Torecki looked at the fresh skin on his arms, not as if he meant to, and dropped that topic of conversation. "So what's the news from Selanto? The Griffins taking the cup this year?"

Harding covered his ears theatrically. "When we have nothing better to talk than sports, the party's over. You coming along to the *Brace and Bit*?"

"You've got to be kidding," said Torecki. "Wild horses."

"Not you. You have a man to get home to. I was talking to the detectives."

Derek looked up from his conversation with Magister Hoth (incubi). "I'm going to check out the venery lab. See you tomorrow."

It said a lot about the little blonde Magister Hoth that nobody even raised their eyebrows as she and Derek headed out together. There was more joking when Ric left with Harding, who lurched against him when they stood up.

"I won't be bleeding tonight either," he said. "Vampires hate fire."

"What was that stuff, anyway?"

"Fire."

Harding led Ric into a bad neighborhood just inside the city wall. He walked fast and straight, hands in his pockets —*Not as drunk as he'd seemed*, thought Ric —and finally stopped at a boarded-up building with a sign swinging over the door. Sure enough, there was a picture of a brace and bit on the sign.

"You met vampires before?"

"No," Ric admitted.

"She'll want you to kiss her hand. They like doing that, because touching them scares you."

"I never heard that," said Ric. "I thought it was –"

Harding grinned. "The bite is. The only vampire you're not scared of is the one biting you. You good with being scared?"

"I guess so," Ric said. "I've had practice. Is there a back door?"

"Smart," Harding said, and led Ric into the alley beside the pub. "Back door here. And here –" he put a hand on one of his wards — "a bolt-hole to campus. See it?"

Ric could just see a shimmering circle, on the ground beside the door. If Harding hadn't pointed it out, he would have thought it the mark left by a garbage can. He nodded.

"Don't use it unless you see blood on the floor," Harding said. "Better take a piss now, as long as we're back here. So you don't wet yourself."

Ric thought, *you have to be joking!* But Harding looked serious.

The first thing Ric noticed was the smell. They smelled of death: not decay, but stable death. Finished death, unchanging death. *Grave-mold*, he thought, not sure what that was.

They were young. He hadn't expected that, but it made sense. Only young people would think staying as they were was worth giving up life, light, love. Only good-looking young people. The vampires were good-looking, if you could get past the smell. They had perfect faces and figures. Their skin was flawless. Their chests were still. Not a sound of breathing except his own and Harding's; not a heartbeat. Ric had never known he could hear heartbeats. He missed them.

Their eyes moved like live things in their too-still faces, like worms twisting in empty sockets. Their eyes moving as they checked him out made Ric taste sick in his mouth.

"Milady," Harding said to one of the youngest-looking vampires, a girl of maybe eighteen. You could tell she was the blood's Queen by her position at the central table, and by her posture and the way she looked at Ric, as if she would make decisions about him. She wore full Goth with a lot of bosom, a chandelier of jet jewelry draped over it. "This is Ric. A visitor from Selanto," Harding said.

The Queen held out a slender hand, covered by a black lace fingerless mitt. She wore rings — wedding rings, two or three to a finger. Her nails were painted black and edged in silver. Ric took her hand and bent over it.

Panic flooded over him, the body's response to taking its own death by the hand. His heart jerked and his lungs and chest fought each other as every

362

muscle tightened. He panted. Cold terror poured out of him in greasy sweat all over his body. *Don't squeeze her hand,* was all he could think. *Don't scream. Don't throw up.* He bent further. The Queen's hand swam toward him, meaningless. Nothing except his heart and lungs meant anything. His guts had stopped, his bladder loosened. He put his lips to the back of her hand, cold and hard. *Now you can let go,* he thought, but the Queen gripped him. Her face smiled, as a torturer might smile at a flayed victim. Ric dared not pull away from her.

"We've been drinking Fire," Harding said casually, sitting down. He pulled out the chair next to him, away from the Queen.

"Selanto," she said to Ric, still holding his hand. *I'm going to die,* he realized. *I'm having a heart attack. This is what it feels like.* "A Selanto slayer?"

"Get real," said Harding. "He's a pal of mine, and I'll thank you not to give him ulcers. Siddown," he told Ric.

This time the Queen let go. Ric almost fell over when the fear drained out of him. *Damn you,* he thought when he looked at Harding. *You bastard!* It wasn't real anger, just the automatic response after a shock. He sat down next to the bastard as if there was no other safety in the world.

"Why would you drink Fire?" the Queen asked Harding. She looked as if she were trying to be interested. But all the time those eyes moved, alive in her dead face.

"We had a good day," Harding said. "Got an exorcist out of some trouble. Did you have a chance to check the website? I put up the informed consent

363

forms. Just have to get a few bugs out of the interface with Public Health and you'll be able to issue donor cards."

Ric sat in a daze while Harding talked about web page design with the Queen of the Osyth vampires. *Web page design! Donor cards! Sweet Lady Jane!* Around them, the other vampires went back to whatever they had been doing before Ric came in. Some were playing cards, some talking in companionable groups, some hunched at the bar over glasses of what looked like hard liquor. The ones at the bar were gaunt, their faces blue-shadowed as if blood had died there. They huddled inside layers of clothing. Wherever they turned their faces, their eyes were always watching the Queen. "Starvelings," Harding murmured, seeing where Ric was looking. "Slept cold last winter."

Just then the door opened and a man in dark glasses lurched up to the bar, knocking one of the huddled starvelings off its stool.

The man was a few inches taller than Harding, but looked taller yet because of his slight build. Willowy was the word. He had curly brown hair, so fine it floated away from his ears, and the light ran around its curls. His mustache was curly as well, perched like a butterfly on his upper lip; he had one of those pointy Selanto chins, and his tan skin was flushed with drink and reddened over one cheek by a fresh bruise. He was clad from the waist down in expensive tailored trousers and glossy shoes, from the waist up in a cheap dress shirt and vest, a ripped necktie wrapped around the collar and fastened in a lopsided knot.

The man caught his balance and looked 'round the bar, the dark glasses hiding what must have been glassy eyes. "Sorry," he said to nobody in particular, belched, and began to grin. "Hey, 's this what I think?"

"What do you think?" the Queen asked dangerously. The vampire he had knocked into had risen and moved behind the man, in position to loom over him if he turned to escape. But its eyes were still on the Queen.

"Ti — hey," the man said, turning and being loomed over, as arranged. "Pew!" he gasped, waving a hand in front of his nose. "Tick bar, all right." He laughed, right into the starveling's face. Ric looked at Harding, who shrugged.

"Do you want to get hurt?" the starveling said. Its eyes stayed on the Queen, asking. She nodded.

The man in dark glasses had watched this, and now he laughed. "Yeah," he said, pushing past the starveling toward the door. "Sorry I bothered you. 'll find someplace else." His tone wasn't the near-panicked attempt at polite escape it should have been, in Ric's opinion. It was more like an insult or a dare. What kind of person insulted vampires, when he should have been near screaming?

"We can accommodate you," said the Queen.

The starveling put out an arm to block the man's path, at which he turned to look back at the Queen's table. Ric felt a surge of *déjà vu* as the man looked at him.

"You think so?" the man asked, Selanto-nobility arrogance surfacing through his drunkenness. "How much do you charge?" He stepped forward, pulled out his wallet, and riffled through it, finally dropping a five onto the Queen's table.

Damn, Ric thought, *I like this guy's style!* Before he had finished the thought, the Queen had nodded again and starvelings piled onto the man. Ric's heart jerked again, in sympathy. He started to his feet, and Harding's hand closed tight on his arm.

"He asked for it," Harding said. "He paid for it."

Ric shuddered. "You sit there and watch this?"

"Yeah," Harding said, holding his eyes. "That's what I do."

Ric could barely imagine what the man in glasses must be going through. The terror he'd felt before, magnified tenfold —the thought made his head swim. But as soon as the man was hidden by starveling bodies, Ric began to forget about him. It felt like having his mind bleached.

"Do you want them to kill him?" Harding asked the Queen quickly.

"What?" she said, as if startled. "Who?"

"Him," Harding said, gesturing toward the feeding frenzy.

"Oh. No," she said, as if pretending she knew what he was talking about. "No kill!" she called sharply, and the starvelings moaned in protest. "No kill," the Queen said again, her voice more commanding. "Is that yours?" she pointed to the five on the table.

"Don't think so," Harding answered, checking his wallet. "Yours, Ric?"

Ric couldn't remember putting any money out, but he checked his wallet anyway.

"Nope? Guess it's yours," Harding told the Queen. "Finders keepers."

She picked up the money with those black-and-silver fingernails. *A foregone conclusion,* thought Ric. Then she waved scornfully toward the feeding pack. "Enough!" she called, and resignation rippled through the starvelings. They reluctantly withdrew from their prey. "Throw it out in the street."

It was odd, and a little worrisome, that Ric couldn't remember the face of the man they were dragging across the threshold. He had a wiped-clean feeling about it, as if even his worry about forgetting the man had been muted. The door banged, but it was only a starveling slouching in from the street, sullen and dissatisfied. Its foot hit something that rattled —a pair of dark glasses — and it peevishly kicked them toward Harding. He picked them up.

"Sunglasses," he said to the Queen, turning them over in his hands. Expensive ones, too. "Not a hot item in this company."

"They're yours," she said indulgently. "Finders keepers."

The street outside was sweet, even with slum smells wafting up from it. The clouds had blown away, and Ric looked up at a sky so high and full of stars that it put him off balance. Harding straddled his legs like a sailor on deck, looking up into the warm summer night; he hung his leather jacket over one shoulder with a jaunty air.

"So, vampires!" he said to Ric, as if pointing out a museum display. "And you came out with all your blood, too. Can't do *that* in Selanto, can you?"

"Not hardly," Ric agreed. Relief, escape, exhilaration all made his limbs tremble as he turned toward the Public Health Building and Derek. But he nearly tripped over something. There was a body lying in the street just down from the *Brace and Bit*.

"Whoa!" said Harding, his good cheer barely dented. The body was a young one, a little longer than Ric's own and dressed in good clothes, though the shirt and vest were torn off to the waist and marred by dark stains. "Sucks to be you," Harding said to it, and immediately corrected himself. "Nah, this is the suckee."

Still alive; the pulse thrilled against Ric's fingertips, too weak and rapid for him to distinguish beats. Shallow, alcohol-laden breaths made the body's mustache ripple. Fine dark curls were plastered against his forehead and cheeks. While Ric was taking this inventory, the body opened eyes as dark as the pavement beneath his head, as if two holes had been cut in the pale surface of his face. Ric could not believe a person was inside there. He was looking into emptiness, or at most into something that might reflect him back. He felt absurdly self-conscious, glad he was hidden in the darkness.

"Not a tick," the body said in a hoarse whisper.

"No," Harding said. "You neither."

The body heaved a deep sigh. "Guess not," he said.

"Here." Harding squatted beside the body. He pulled a charm out of the jumble around his own neck and slipped it over the body's head. "Give this a few minutes then we'll take you somewhere to sleep it off."

Ric couldn't look away from the body's eyes. He felt responsible. *Why?* "You should see a sorcerer."

The body shook his head. "Not in the cards," he said with no apparent concern. "Got a smoke?"

It doesn't get stranger, Ric thought, but he pulled out his cigarette-case and lighter.

The body smoked like someone from Selanto, looking around for something to drop the ashes into. Ric handed over his ash-box.

"Ahh," the body said. "My first in six years." He shut his eyes. "Mmm. Better than sex." Ric looked around the darkened streets and the body faded a little from his mind, so that when he looked back and saw it, he felt surprised. *Smokes the same brand I do,* Ric thought. *From Selanto.*

"Or maybe my memory's playing tricks on me," said the body, his voice lowering. He gave Harding the sort of look that got you punched, in a lot of places. Ric had a sudden feeling he'd thought this before. He imagined himself standing between — who? and a punch in the snoot. He came back to himself with a start. The body lying between himself and Harding hadn't been punched. It had bite marks on its neck and wrists, and it was smoking a cigarette with no signs of concern. *My brand,* Ric thought. *Wait, my ash-box! I gave him that?*

"Ah well," said the body, as if they were in the middle of a conversation. He stretched, laying his arms out to each side and his head back onto the stone street. "I'll have to settle for talking. Do you know how long it's been since I could really talk to someone?" He mumbled a bit, around the cigarette.

Raised a hand and took it out of his mouth, the better to talk, but to whom? His gaze was fixed on the stars above.

"By the time I could talk, they were already paying too much attention to whatever I said. Not that I minded. What two-year-old would? I have family who'll never be the same. I've made people feel so worthless they killed themselves. I'd say it wasn't on purpose, but it was."

Even as Ric gaped at this confession, he felt the words slipping away. An anonymous body in the streets, vampire-bitten. Smoking a cigarette, as if it had been a pleasant evening.

"It was coming to this," the body said, still looking upwards. "Power like that eats the world, or itself. Got another?" He lit a second cigarette from the first one and put his butt into Ric's ash-box. "It's why I put up with so much crap from —my teacher. I thought it was an ordeal. Purifying, you know, my penance for past misdeeds. What a laugh! It was all about him, all along. He told me I had potential; he just didn't tell me which of us was going to use it.

"Ah well," he finished, his eyes almost shut. "We deserved each other. But that's all over now."

It took Ric a minute to react. Then his heart skipped a beat. "Did you kill your teacher?"

"No," the body replied. "I thought I'd have to, but no. In fact, I think I gave him back his life. Funny how things turn out, isn't it?" He stared upwards, smoking quietly, and Ric lost hold of why he had been alarmed. *Nothing dangerous here. Just some poor devil had a run-in with the vamps. Lucky they didn't kill him —*

"Shouldn't you report this?" he asked Harding.

"What?" Harding looked down as if he hadn't seen — what? *A body! No, not dead,* Ric thought with relief. *Bitten.* Harding bent down to examine the body, one hand on its bloody throat. "We'll take him to a safe house. They'll get his info and call the police."

"Who's Lord Stimms?" the body asked, out of the blue.

"Say what?" said Harding.

"Who's Lord Stimms?" the body asked again.

"Is that one of those trick questions?"

"Rosemont," said Ric. "If we can find him. Been missing for a year."

"Rosemont, hey?" said the body, and took a long puff of his cigarette before grinding it out half-smoked and dropping it into an ash-box. *My ash-box!* thought Ric. "What would you do about that?" the body asked him. His eyes were as dark as the pavement beneath his head, as if two holes had been cut in the pale surface of his face. Ric could not believe a person was inside there. He was looking into emptiness, or at most into something that might reflect him back.

"About what?"

"If you knew where Rosemont was," the body said slowly, as if talking to a child, "what would you do?"

"I'd tell me," said Ric.

"Ha," said the body, and closed his eyes. "Easier said than done."

When Harding hauled him up, he stood. Ric took the other arm and between them they ushered the body along the dark street. Ric felt more

371

competent and in charge by the minute. By the time they stopped, he was master of the night

Harding knocked at a door in one of the tenements. "It's Will Harding," he said into the intercom. "I've got one for you."

The man who opened the door could have passed for a dwarf. "What's his issue?"

"Drunk, and drunk from," said Harding. "Give him a bed, will you?"

"Who got him?"

That made Harding stop and think. "Could have been Evan and Victoire," he said. "Everyone else was in the *Brace*."

"Oh yeah? If it's Ev and Vic, they've got themselves an army."

In the light from the open door, Ric could see at least eight separate bites on the body's neck and arms.

Harding could apparently see the same, because he pursed his lips in a silent whistle. "Give me a call when he's up, will you?"

"Sure," said the faux dwarf, manhandling the body into the corridor. He shut them out into the sweet night, under a sky so high and full of stars that Ric almost overtipped as he looked up and felt the warm summer air close around him. He looked down and followed Harding toward Public Health.

Chapter 28
Following the Trees

When the sun got high enough to shine over the hill *Old Oak began to wake up*, top branches first. "Sun, sun, come," they sang, far up in the air. The lower branches joined the chorus, minute by minute. Mama Simone lay on the leaf-mast at the bottom of the tree and listened to the song coming closer and closer. She kept one stiff arm curled around the bucket with the little trees growing in it. At last the lowest branch had sung, and then Old Oak was awake all the way.

"Old Oak!" said Mama Simone.

The branches went silent.

"Old Oak!" She sat up into the sunlight and put her hands on the trunk. "It's me, Old Oak! It's Mama Simone."

The branches shivered. Old Oak kept silent.

"I have them with me," said Mama Simone. "The seeds you kept for me. My babies. Look at them, how straight and strong!"

The branches rustled as if a little breeze ran through them. "Shade, shade, sorrow," they said. Mama Simone looked back under Old Oak's sheltering arms and saw four baby oaks with pale leaves. Here their parent had dropped them, here they had sprouted, and here they would die in the shade.

"Then show me a safe place," she said fiercely. "These are ours, yours and mine. Show me where they can live for a hundred years." But Old Oak turned its leaves away from her. Sunlight caught on the gash she had cut in its bark and made the sap sparkle. Every tree in sight turned its leaves from her, and their silver undersides glistened.

She could be sad or angry. She chose angry. "All right, be that way," she said, gathering herself up. "See if I attend any more of those 'save our greenspace' meetings!" She began to stalk away in disgust through the still air, batting lazy midges away from her face, and then stopped. The air was still. Why were the leaves moving? She looked back at Old Oak, and from out here in the clearing it was easy to see. Every leaf pointed south.

Mama Simone walked south all morning, from one deer track to another through the foothills, but she never got tired or hungry. Magic grew bigger and bigger inside her. All it wanted was sunlight. She came to the edge of the hills, where land sloped down to the Kasidora River and the farmed river valley stretched far off to her left toward the Eastern Sea. Just here, though, the valley was too narrow for farming. Sheep grazed on this slope and at its bottom the Kasidora plunged along a chasm that had broken, eons ago, to let the rollicking Vinchifer River escape southward. Looking west, she could just see the big bridge over the Kasidora; listening, she could just hear traffic from the highway that followed the Vinchifer southwards to Sterne.

She looked back at the trees. "Are you serious?" The nearest one waved its leaves at her, pointing south yet again. The sun felt good on her head, and she was tempted for just a minute to stop, planting herself and the treelets she carried here at the forest's edge. But there was even more sun down below, so she began taking big steps down into the sheep field.

She went straight toward the river, for only there would she find more trees to advise her; willows, with enormous warty boles and limber twigs as long as her arm. They clustered around the water, gossiping to one another so loudly she could hear their voices from half a field away, but when she came near they fell silent.

"Willows!" she hailed them. "I bring you greetings from Old Oak of Fairtree Hill."

The willows quivered their trailing branches. "Old Oak. Old, slow, dry," they whispered to one another, and dabbled their lowest leaves in the river. "Bright, fast, wet. Sun sparkle." Mama Simone felt they had a point. Yet bank-willows, for all their size, could not live as long as Old Oak. Generations of bank-willows would grow, split and tumble down beside the water while Old Oak kept his quiet watch atop the hill.

"Which way should I go, Willows? I seek a home for my children." She held out the pot with the two saplings leaning away from one another.

The willows whispered and murmured in the endless river breeze, and then their branches trailed out across it, pointing to the far bank. "Dry, hard, high," they said, and that was certainly what it looked like, over there. Cliffy, dotted with brush. Mama Simone looked at her treelets doubtfully, and they pointed their baby leaves in the same direction as if they were just learning to wave. "You," she said sternly, "are too young to know what's good for you." Still, she went that way.

The river ran narrow in this spot, which had made it a natural place for the first bridge-builders. No cars passed Mama Simone as she walked across the ancient stone bridge. The old road led nowhere in particular, nowadays; towns that had once sprouted up along it had withered just as quickly when the highway and six-lane suspension bridge stole away their traffic. But that made it a pleasant walk in June, its hedgerows filled with hawthorn and the racket of small birds. Mama Simone followed it up a break in the steep river bluffs. The hedgerows grew shorter as she neared the top, sheared off by a hundred harsh winters rolling down from the mountains ahead. She stopped and took her bearings, remembering a time when she had known every peak in the Sheep League. There was Pasture Rock, and High Dingle, and Nöon's Castle. But before she reached any of them there was an expanse of sheep field and wooded foothills that she hoped would show her someplace else to go, for none of the mountains seemed good for baby trees.

She crossed the field on a rutted farmers' lane that ended behind a family of aspens. They were really one plant, sprung from the same roots and bickering like siblings; when Mama Simone spoke to them they answered in unison. "Not this land," they murmured. Aspens, with their giant root systems, felt they owned everything. "No room here. Follow sun," they said, quivering their leaves southward, so Mama Simone did that, into the deeper, older parts of the forest. She felt happier among the big trees and away from the know-it-all aspens.

In here, trees didn't speak to her. When asked, they waved southwards; but they were lost in their own thoughts, as really old people often are, and she felt shy of disturbing them. The sun was just starting down from noon when she came to a clearing with something different in it.

The tree was a pagoda dogwood no taller than Mama Simone herself, its branches spread out in tiers and its leaves held neatly horizontal. It reminded her of a set of shelving. Someone should come along and put knickknacks on those perfect flat surfaces. In fact, someone had! She was close enough now to see little items sitting among the leaves, and they weren't birds, for they didn't fly away at her approach. Nor were they wood-sprites, though one of them looked a bit — no, it was really a knickknack. It was a statuette of the shivering princess, just like the one Gretyl had given her for a May Day long ago.

Mama Simone felt a pang. She had burned that statuette, along with everything else. She went round to the other side of the tree. There, she found the lumpish something Willett had made out of clay from where they'd dug out the root cellar. And the buttons her husband had whittled for her, and the brooch the children had given her for Wintertide. Here were the old Kindling lanterns, strung along the branches... all the lost things. Seeing them again, here, hurt more than putting them into the flames had. Tears blurred her vision, and she almost stretched out a hand to take them back — to take her life back — *Stop!* she told herself, and put her arm down by her side. *A bargain's a bargain.*

And now, as if the tree had just been waiting for her to confirm something, she began to see her lost, burned-up clothing among the knicknacks: first undergarments, then slips and dresses and jackets and shawls. Spread across the branches at first, then hung upright, then drawn closer in to the trunk, a trunk far too wide for such a small tree; and the branches were far too short, too drawn in, and thicker than they should have been, and instead of boughs they bore only twigs now, a handful of leaves at the end of each branch until Mama Simone was looking not at a tree, but at a dumpy figure like a poorly-carved woman. Wearing her clothes! She drew back in alarm, but the tree continued to become a woman. Its top drew in, upper branches curling and reshaping themselves into hanks of hair. Its bark became smoother and a warmer color flushed through it. And finally it began to tug at its roots, trying to pull them up out of the earth; at first slowly, as a tree in a windstorm leans from side to side, and then more vigorously, like somebody tied up and trying to get loose. It twisted its torso and jerked its trunk from side to side, the movements under the skirt more and more like two legs.

Mama Simone clutched the bucket to her chest and backed away. Too late. The tree-woman had seen her, and now it fixed her with what might have been a stare. It didn't have eyes yet, or much of a face, yet it pointed what it had in her direction, and stretched out one of its limbs toward her, waving the twig-fingers. It took a moment for her to realize that it was waving the ring finger, in a demanding gesture. She looked at her own hand and saw the glint of her wedding ring. She hadn't thrown that into the fire. She closed her hand into a tight fist.

"What are you?" she said, but the tree-woman made no answer. It gave up gesturing and went back to twisting at its roots, and now one of them was coming loose. Mama Simone could see the earth cracking around it. A rue plant tumbled down, knocked sideways as the tree jerked up the soil. The tree-woman took a half step towards Mama Simone, stretching its hand out again. It was still anchored to the ground by one root.

Mama Simone stepped back, her heartbeat making the pot clutched against it shake. "What do you want?" she cried. The tree-woman twisted its bark where a mouth ought to be, and bits fell off. It would open — the places where there should have been eyes would open — the second root would come loose from the ground, and the thing would be upon her — Mama Simone's nerve broke, and she ran. Big trees loomed up in front of her and fell off behind as she dodged around their boles. The bucket bounced in her arms. She ran until breathlessness and shade had taken all the run out of her, and then she walked on berating herself. She called herself a coward, fool, all manner of harsh names, but none of them could make her turn back. None of them could even make her slow down.

***

Willett walked so heavily, for a moment Rho thought it was his father's tread. Gretyl sat down with so much creaking of the kitchen bench it sounded like their father coming in from the fields.

Rho's father filled the house, as if he had only been waiting for Mama Simone to leave before he took it back.

"Did you find her?" Willett asked, not looking at Rho. The kitchen felt clammy, though it was not all that cold outside. Late morning sunlight painted the top of the barn. Dew had dried off the plants outside the window.

"No."

"Then what are you doing in here?"

"Same thing you are, I guess." Rho looked out past the barn to where the woods stood, tall and featureless. Nobody came out of them.

Willett stared across the kitchen, to where there was nothing posted on the refrigerator. "She's left us."

"You knew she was going to," said Gretyl. "We just let ourselves hope, when the fair-haired boy came home. She wouldn't have stayed for any of us," she said to Rho, "but we figured she would, for you. I guess your running off again put paid to that."

"I didn't run off! I went to a job interview."

"And stayed overnight, and didn't call."

"I'm not used to having anybody to call," muttered Rho.

"And whose fault is that?"

"I didn't say it was anyone's fault," he cried. "Will you give it a rest?"

"Half her stuff is gone," said Lilis, standing in the stairwell.

"What?"

"I said half her stuff is gone. Dresses, shoes, jewelry. She hasn't run off in the woods; she's packed her stuff and gone somewhere. Probably with someone."

Willett rose to his feet. "What are you saying? She's run off with some man?"

"I don't know. Did she have a man?"

"You know she didn't!"

Lilis shrugged. "All I know is that we've been running around the woods all night, when we could have seen it was no use if we'd taken ten minutes to look in her closet. I'm going home to get some sleep."

Willett rounded on Rho. "You didn't even look in her closet?"

"Yes, I did! How was I supposed to know how many dresses she owned?"

"Oh, give it up," Gretyl said tiredly. "He couldn't have known." She stood up and pulled on her jacket. "I have a family waiting for their breakfast, and you have a job to get to. You" —she pointed at Rho — "stay here in case she calls. We'll check back in this afternoon."

They hadn't been gone a quarter hour when the phone rang. Rho jumped and ran to get it.

"Yes? I mean hello," he said.

"Magister Rho?" asked the voice on the end. Rho felt himself warmed, relaxing, even before he recognized it. "This is Gordon K. Remen."

"Oh," Rho cried in relief. He was transported, in that instant, from one world to another. No longer the ungrateful son, incompetent caretaker, hated sibling; now the qualified, worthwhile professional.

"My secretary said you had called," said Gordon K. "I was planning to give you a call anyway, just to see how you're holding up."

There in his mother's kitchen, it was Gordon K.'s voice that made Rho feel as if he'd come home. What kind of fool had he been, plotting with Lilis against magic? *Magic is the only thing I have going for me,* he thought.

"I'm doing all right," he said to Gordon K. "I had wanted to know when I should come back to Sterne to get set up for class, or if you're going to e-mail me the syllabus. It does start a week from Monday, doesn't it?"

"Good, good," said Gordon K., his voice warm. "I was actually planning to come down to Minich this afternoon and make sure the lab supplies are all in order. I'll bring your contract and the syllabus with me. Perhaps we could meet there, and have supper at the Rosewood Inn? My treat, of course."

"Oh," Rho said again, and began to fear he was sounding like an idiot. "That'll be fine," he added hastily. "I'll be looking forward to it."

"As will I," said Gordon K. "I anticipate our working together with the keenest pleasure. You have tremendous potential."

Chapter 29
Mothers

Warren laid his supplies out on the dining room table, everything from his pockets and backpack except for his wallet with the beech-leaf in it. The three magicians sat around them, staring. Would nobody say something? *Lili*, he thought, flooded of a sudden with despair and fury.

"Lilian's out there! We have to do something for her!" The grimoire's pages were smooth, thick, familiar in his hands.

"What do you think you can do for her?" asked Grandfather. "You don't even know if she's inside the demon."

"She's not," Warren insisted. "She was wearing a ward." — *The same ward I'm wearing*, a thought that froze him to the heart. *A ward the demon's eaten. How can that protect her?* "A calling charm," he cried, shuffling through the book again. "If she's in the demon, she needs to find this place. If she's not, she needs to find me again after she's gotten help. *Please, let her be out of here, getting help. Russell, or the alchemists.*

Grandfather shrugged. "Destroy the demon, and none of this is necessary," he said. "I'd use page seventy-one, myself."

You would, thought Warren. Page seventy-one was certainly a destructive charm, as likely to destroy the caster as the target. "We don't have the stuff for it."

"We have enough for page eighty-three," Grandfather said, as smoothly as if that were the charm he'd wanted to cast all along.

"Someone in our department cast that a few months ago, and lost his magic," Warren said. "Getting out of the demon won't do us any good, if I have to face it without magic right afterward."

"What happened to your colleague?" Dad asked, before Grandfather could riposte.

"He's still magic-less," said Warren. "He'll probably lose his job — oh, you mean then. He had all of us around him, plus the hospital wards. Plus, a different demon came in and drove his away. It was probably this one! That has to be how it got my grimoire." He'd found the charm he was looking for, and flattened the book on the table. "Are you helping me with this, or not?"

"We are but essences," Grandfather said.

"You can at least hand me things!"

Warren built a calling charm out of what he had. Salt and paper, with runes squeezed onto the table surface from a tube of antiseptic cream. First-aid crystals at each corner of the pentacle. It shouldn't have worked except that it was Warren calling Lilian, and that was the real magic, that made the crystals blaze and the salt flash rainbow colors. But when it was cast, nothing happened. They sat staring at the door, waiting for somebody to knock, and nothing happened.

"She isn't in the demon," Warren said, looking at Dad and Grandpa, daring them to disagree. "She got away. She'll be calling Russell. He'll come after me."

384

Sheep Mountain was just as steep this afternoon as it had been the morning Mama Simone climbed it to see sunrise after her high-school graduation dance. It was the same rough walking, with sheep trails eroded into little gullies. The top was the same jumble of goblin doorsteps. A woman her own age was sitting on one of them crying, and that was different.

"What's your trouble?" Mama Simone asked, perhaps a little roughly; but she was too busy worrying about the tree-woman that might be following her to really care for someone else's problems.

The woman lifted her blotchy face off her knees and glared upwards. She was one of those pink and white women, with a city haircut and tourist-style hiking clothes. "A demon ate my husband, if you must know," she said bitterly, "and the goblins have thrown me out while they argue about whether they'll let anyone try to rescue him." Hope lit up her face. "Do you have a cell phone that works here? Do you know how I can get help?"

"Sorry," Mama Simone said. "Nobody's cell phone works up here." The bucket had gotten heavy during the climb, and she was glad to set it down. "How'd you get in? Won't whoever took you in help get him out?"

"That's who threw me out!" the woman wailed. "It'll take hours to go down the mountain and find the police — what can I do?"

Why ask me? thought Mama Simone. "Can you get them to come out and tell you anything?"

385

"No," the tourist woman said. "I've been banging on the door, but nothing happens." The rock face was solid as the rest of the mountain. It had marks on it as if somebody had pounded it with a softer rock, and Mama Simone saw the pieces of the softer rock around her feet when she looked down. *Not very smart. She needed a harder rock...*

"Well, I guess you wait until you think they're not going to come out again, and then head home." *Or I could,* Mama Simone thought suddenly, as if she was already out of practice at solving random folks' problems for them. *That's what she wants. I could climb back down the mountain and get help.* She looked at the trees in her bucket. They pointed to the goblins' door, quivering like the hands of children who knew the answer and wanted to be called on.

When she looked up, she was surprised to see the tourist woman staring at them, her face white. "Are you following those leaves?" she said.

"Yes."

"That's just what we were doing when the demon got Warren! We tried to cast a charm, but Warren said we were in the wrong place. So he wrote the runes on these leaves, and floated them in this bowl — and they all swam to one edge, and we followed them. Just like your trees."

"Hmf!" said Mama Simone, looking at the blue bowl. She was thinking about all the trees that had pointed her this way. *What were they up to?* She thought about the tree-Mama Simone again and gave her saplings a parlous look, wondering if they meant to lead her into a demon's maw. Before she

386

could decide, rock rattled off to her left and a man came around the edge of the nearest boulder.

He was a tall, dirty man with deep-set green eyes, swamped in a rain jacket that matched Lilian's but looked better used. It had obviously been made for a much wider person, with shorter arms; this man had zipped it up, but it still draped over him like one of those shepherd's smocks from old paintings. What she could see of him was filthy, as if he'd been living rough, and he carried a spray of waving beech leaves in one hand.

"Well," Mama Simone said, "Welcome to the club."

The tramp put out a filthy hand, laying it flat on the goblin's door, and twiddled his fingers. Then he pounded on the door, put his ear against it and listened, and then he sighed and put one hand in his pocket. When he pulled it out, he was holding a jack-knife.

"Good luck with that," Mama Simone said to him, but he didn't attack the stone. He cut his own arm instead, a long slash that made her heart jump up into her throat and the tourist woman jump up from the doorstone. Blood began to run in rivulets across his grimy skin, but the tramp showed no alarm. He dipped a forefinger into it and began to write runes in his own blood on the goblins' door.

"For goodness' sake!" the tourist woman scolded, pulling a box out of her backpack — "Oh, for — someone's put an empty box of bandages in here." The tramp had finished with his writing and sat down on the doorstone's other edge, holding his arm, by the time she found a roll of gauze to wrap him up with.

Mama Simone retrieved the empty box and stood turning it over in her hands, remembering times at home when she had found the bandage box full of toy soldiers. What was it about bandage boxes? The air felt chillier, so she leaned against a clean part of the warm stone door. That was how she felt the movement, like heavy footsteps. An elephant or an army.

"Hey!" she said, standing back, and the goblin's doorway slid open. It was man-height and a man stood in it, a knight in dusty armor. The sunset light glittered on his chain-mail, his helm, and his thin bearded cheeks. It ran down the edge of the sword in his hands, and pooled at the tip.

"The time is come," the knight said. He looked past Mama Simone as if she weren't there.

"What?"

"The time is come. The reborn King reclaims his own." He strode past her and fell — no, he'd gone down on one knee before the tramp, and pulled his helm off and bowed his head.

"Oh," said Mama Simone. She could see more knights-in-armor inside the passageway, still as statues except for their glittering eyes. "Whatever you say," she said.

***

Worry about where Mama might have gone, and with whom, made Rho slow as a computer running too many programs. He should have set off for Minich Extension half an hour ago, but he was still doing the chores, heavy and slow. Every creature on the farm had something to say this morning, and their lively chatter made him think of the silent pigs in that shed. Guilt grew inside him, another thing to drag around as he tried to get the work done —and *the goat had just dodged out of the paddock.*

"Get back in here, you stroppy old basket!" he howled, and she stopped to look at him with those oddly blank horizontal pupils. One could never tell what goats were thinking.

"Can't catch me," the goat said gleefully, and gave her tail a little flip.

"Don't want to," Rho said back in her own language, a lie which nevertheless made her jump with surprise.

"It talks!" she said, dancing a little on dainty hooves. "Give me something. Apples, cheese." She sidled closer, but Rho knew how that game worked. Snatch and Run Away, it was called.

He folded his arms and stared at her disdainfully. "You give me something," he said.

The goat had obviously never been addressed in this manner. She stopped and thought, chewing. "Why? I got out."

"I let you."

"You're slow and stupid," said the goat. She bucked her rear end up into the air and trotted in a semicircle. "Slow and stupid," she sang. "Na na nanana."

"Whatever you like to think," said Rho, and went back to feeding the chickens.

"Hey, hey," yelled the rooster, as the hens darted past him. "Order, order!" He hadn't a prayer. His words were lost in the gabble as the ladies discussed their supper, mainly complaining that it was late. Rho didn't try to defend himself against hens, but he still felt a little bruised inside. How unappreciative farm animals were! Didn't they know it was work to take care of them?

The goat was bored with baiting someone who ignored her. "Where's the old woman?" she asked, looking sideways at the garden. "Where's the old man?"

"He's dead," said Rho. At the words, he felt something unexpected swell up inside him, taking the space he had been using for air. His eyes prickled.

"Dead and butchered?" asked the goat, stopping her dance.

"Dead and buried," said Rho. He sniffled.

The goat gave a prance. "He gave me apples and cheese," she said. "He let me in the kitchen. She made us go out again."

Rho dumped out the chicken feed and hung the bucket bale over a fence post. "Come on," he said gruffly, and led the way into the kitchen. "I said come in!" She was skittish at first, stretching her face into the doorway from as far away as she could reach, but then she clattered gingerly into the room. Rho cut an apple and some cheese, and set two plates at the table. They ate together in thoughtful silence. He felt the swelling in his chest get smaller with every bite.

Rho finished before the goat, who had trouble getting her last piece of cheese loose from the plate. As if in revenge, she bit a chunk out of the plate itself. "Don't eat the dishes," he said absentmindedly. Then he saw the time. "Darn, I'm late! Come on." The goat let him grab her collar and put her back in the paddock, though she crapped on the kitchen floor. He'd have to clean that up later.

He almost drove into the ditch at the end of Minich Extension Road, where it hung a sharp right to go between the old clapboard labs. How could someplace be fifty years old and still have no trees at all? Generations' lack of forethought had left the extension campus a barren, dusty semicircle of barracks-like buildings, its signage faded and the buildings furthest back boarded up with plywood. Rho pulled in beside the only other car, which was empty, and went searching for Gordon K.

"Halloo!" he shouted into one empty lab after another. They were depressing, deadly, dusty rooms with board tables and benches, but Rho could imagine them alive and filled with students. He'd seen people make nests in alleys, after all. He was standing in the end of one lab, thinking about his syllabus, when Gordon K. found him.

"Ah, Magister Rho! I thought I heard you," he said cheerfully. His old-fashioned outfit looked just right in this old-fashioned room.

"Sorry I'm late," said Rho. "The goat got out."

Gordon K. nodded. "Goats, like copiers, can tell when their behavior will have the most impact," he said. "Were you able to hear her?"

"Yep. We had quite a conversation. Goats are the best to talk with," said Rho.

"Excellent, excellent," said Gordon K., rubbing his hands together. "So your access of power was not limited to veal calves, after all."

Rho's good mood evaporated. "Guess not," he said, looking down. If Gordon K. noticed, he said nothing; instead, he sat down at one of the dusty tables and opened his briefcase. They went over the syllabus together. It was old and boring, its mimeographed sheets faded.

"Um, is there any leeway for updating this?" Rho asked, and immediately realized this might have been tactless.

Gordon K. merely chuckled. "Every teacher's first question," he said. "It speaks well of your pedagogic instincts. Unfortunately, the curriculum is set in Kasidora. Ours, I fear, is not to reason why."

"It's just that there's a lot more students could be doing. When I took intro magic, I was casting charms by the third week. You learn it a lot better if you practice."

"Kasidora again," Gordon K. apologized. "This facility isn't licensed for anything beyond the very basic magic. Why, they might even be perturbed if they knew you were hearing animals on campus. Are you?"

"Not at the moment," said Rho. *Too far from the pig shed*, he thought glumly.

"Ah. Let me show you your supplies." Not even Gordon K's enthusiasm could make the scanty stockroom look anything but pathetic. Rho was polite, not wanting to lose this job before he'd started it, and eventually the tour of campus was over. They stood together beside their parked cars and looked across the flat landscape.

"Shall you follow me to the inn? I usually stay the night there when I come over this late in the day," said Gordon K. "Aging reflexes and mountain driving ... one must make the best of one's limitations."

392

"All right," said Rho, but he hesitated. The sun setting behind the Kasidora Mountains cast a deceptive, temporary glory over the extension campus. "Does anybody who trained here go on into magic?"

"Not in my brief experience. Our students, however, could not be said to have much potential."

Dinner was more pleasant. Rho had never been to the Rosewood Inn and found its food well up to his standards, which were admittedly low. Gordon K. was a better friend with every glass of beer; he gave Rho inside tips about negotiating the system and told amusing anecdotes about the misdeeds of past extension faculty. Rho realized he should be grateful. Against all odds, he'd stumbled upon someone who identified with his plight and saw something worthwhile in him! He felt a muddled pity for Gordon K., who was dealing with his own losses so gracefully.

"Did you go out to the veal sheds?" he asked.

"I have not yet had that opportunity," said Gordon K. "I receive few invitations from the full-time faculty. There is ill feeling..." He explained why, a story involving egregious, yet hilarious, misbehavior on the part of several adjuncts hired by his predecessor. Rho found himself laughing until tears came, though beneath his laughter he felt a wincing suspicion that his own interactions with Juliana had been added to her list of adjunct atrocities. "I am the more anxious to visit there," Gordon K. finished, "given that the effects appear to be so long-lasting. Perhaps you can put in a good word for me."

"Probably not," said Rho. "I got a taste of that attitude." He took a breath, stopped thinking, and plunged on. "I don't think it lasted this long, though. I wasn't hearing anything when I first got home, but then I went out to our pig facility and I've been hearing animals ever since. You can come out and visit it, if you like."

Gordon K. looked surprised by his kindness. "That is a very handsome offer!" he said. "I shall certainly accept. When will be convenient?"

"Whenever works for you, I guess."

"Admirable!" said Gordon K. "Unfortunately, I have to return to Sterne first thing tomorrow. I have another meeting in the morning, and a conference call from two to four. Might I come day after tomorrow — say five p.m.?"

"Fine," Rho said. He drew a map on the napkin. "Here's how to find it. I'll meet you there; that's easier than your coming out to the farm first."

"Excellent," said Gordon K. "I look forward to it with great anticipation. Another round?"

It was late dusk by the time Rho headed homewards. He was surprised to see a light on in the kitchen. *Damn, they're back*, he thought; there was not a one of his siblings he wanted to see. But it was a different figure entirely in the kitchen, stretching up to put cookbooks back on the top shelf. At first, Rho thought it was a tree that had walked into the house. *What?* He blinked, and it was Mama in her print dress and apron.

"Mama!" Even thunderstruck, Rho could see that she'd put the kitchen back together just as it had been before the big clearing-out.

Mama turned around —again, like a tree swaying —and put her hands on her hips. "Robin Earl Jeffries, did you let that goat into my clean kitchen?"

Chapter 30
Through the Looking-Glass

Mama Simone could tell the goblins were angry by the smell. It hung thick in the dark tunnels, a harsh musky odor like the smell after you ran the plow over a garter snake. It closed in all round her, and every hair on her neck stood up straight. But the saplings in her bucket waved her on, and she'd come this far. *No turning back now!* she thought, and hurried after the knights.

They scuttled through a backbreaking length of low corridors into a big room with stone tombs scattered around it, and ended in a semicircle facing a battered door. It blinked at them, scowling. When the man she had been calling a tramp — *the King, I'll have to call him*, thought Mama Simone — when he stepped up to the door, its scowl went away. The door grinned in delight, showing broken teeth and bloodshot eyes. The man put a hand on it, beside its mouth, and blew on its face; and maybe it was the light, or Mama Simone's eyes, but were the door's teeth straight again and its eyes clear? No time to find out, for the door swung open and they were hustling through.

The new room was long and lined with black curtains, one set pulled back to uncover a picture — no, a window — no, a mirror. Mama Simone stared at herself standing in the picture. Sweat stained her collar and underarms and her hair was falling down about her face. She looked like a sheep that had just come through a hedge.

"This is where we go in," said the tourist woman.

Any fool could see that, thought Mama Simone. "What's your name?" she asked, abruptly. *I'm sick of thinking 'tourist woman!'*

"Lilian," said the tourist woman, looking surprised. "Lilian Oldham."

"I'm Mama Simone," said Mama Simone, and that was that. Now she felt stupid. "What do we do after we get inside?" she asked.

"I don't know!" said Lilian. "I thought the goblins were going to help us." She looked around the room. "Ver's axe — where's Ver?" she asked the tallest of the knights. "Where's your axe?"

"Here," said a voice from behind them. The musk and burnt-sugar smell of cross goblin grew stronger. Mama Simone knew what she'd see when she turned around. The little goblin was scowling, and it had a huge axe. When it saw the King, it yelled a stream of goblin-talk fit to deafen a body.

The King stood quite still under this harangue. He didn't look kingly, but he looked more dignified than the screaming goblin. When it had finished, purple-faced, he pulled something out of his pocket and held it out, balanced on his open hand. He spoke, and again Mama Simone could understand nothing. But she could see that he was holding out a shard of glass, like a piece of a broken mirror. The goblin's face grew even darker, and the smell stronger. But the King ignored it. He turned to one of the knights and held out the shard, and as the knight touched it Mama Simone heard a clattering, breaking sound from behind one of the black curtains. Its folds stirred, as if in a breeze from behind, and the knight strode toward it without hesitating. He pulled the curtain aside and climbed into the mirror it revealed, and then the picture shimmered, solidified; it was a portrait of the knight in his prime, his armor bright and his face at ease.

One by one, the King turned to the knights and let them touch the piece of mirror. One by one, they stepped into their own portraits, until there was nobody left in the room except Mama Simone, Lilian, the goblin with the axe, and the King. *I would have held onto those knights a little longer,* Mama Simone thought when she looked at the scowling goblin.

Lilian spoke to the goblin. "You liked Warren," she pleaded. "Help me bring him back! We only went in there to help you!"

The goblin spat on the floor. "Help?" it said. "Not goblin's place to tell master what to do in his kingdom. Goblin dirt on floor to great King."

"Forget about him! What about Warren?"

"See if great King care," said the goblin. "Nöon's tale ended." It turned away and went back through the open door. *It's going to —* thought Mama Simone, and before she could even finish her thought, the door had slammed and she heard a bolt slide across it.

"Well!" she said. "There's no going back now."

Mama Simone didn't like the ward Lilian gave her. On general principles, she didn't like wards. "I've never needed this kind of stuff," she said, the way she would have said she never needed bug spray or sunscreen, as if it were a point of pride, which it was. People who needed to be protected from the world should just stay in their cities. When she saw the King put on the ward she figured she might as well, just to be polite.

The mirror felt cold and tingly, like stepping through soda water. Mama Simone caught her breath. Her vision blurred for an instant, and then she was standing in the deep grass of a prairie's edge. Wind hit her from one side, and then a surprising gust of snow. The light changed, from clear to cloudy without any in-between. She turned a bit further, and behind them was the mirror they'd stepped through. She could see through her reflected self into the goblin's cave, as if it were one of those tinted windows.

Seeing the mirror helped. It was something stable, in this shifting world. She looked at the saplings again, and they pointed away from the mirror, down a path trampled down in the grass. At least, sometimes.

"Why does everything keep changing?"

"I can't see that," Lilian said. She stood for a minute, and then pulled a ward off over her head. It was a moss agate set in silver. She froze, holding the ward in her hands, and stared straight ahead.

"Oh! It's just like Warren said!"

"What? What is it?"

"Didn't you read about it in the papers?" Lilian asked. "It's the Alchemists' prison."

"I don't read about that sort of thing," said Mama Simone. But she'd heard about it at church. *That was when I didn't have magic,* she thought. *When I was trying not to care about it.*

"The things in this garden — they're not really changing every minute, they're splitting into all the

399

possible plants they could be. I mean, that plant —
there's a bare one, and a dead one, and a blooming
one. They all exist; we just see one of them at a
time. There's no time here, no cause and effect.
Warren got to see it once before. A couple people
from his department came in here in April, and let
the alchemists out again. It was the biggest news in
magic since I don't know when."

"So are we going to turn into lots of different
people?" Mama Simone asked. She wasn't sure she
minded that. Getting to be more than one person at
once. Having it all. Women talked about that, didn't
they?

"Not as long as we're wearing these wards,"
Lilian said, touching a silver-star ward like the one
she'd given Mama Simone. She set her pack down
and rummaged in it, pulling out a blue bowl, a
baggie full of leaves, and a plastic water bottle. The
sort tourists left all over. Trust city folk to make
even water into litter! But Lilian put the bottle back
in her pack after she had put its water and the leaves
into the blue bowl, which was a point in her favor.

For a moment the leaves in the bowl lay like
any set of waterlogged leaves, and then they moved.
Like a school of fish, they nosed up to one side of
the bowl. "We should follow these. They'll at least
take us to where we met the demon. I don't know if
the demon will still be there, though."

Mama Simone had no problem with that, as
long as Lilian's leaves pointed in the same direction
her saplings pointed. The beech twig in the king's
hand was pointing the same way. *All the trees
agree*, she thought. *What do they want?*

400

"How will we find our way back here? Leave bread crumbs?"

Lilian looked around. "I don't know," she admitted. "The goblin brought me out."

"Well, that could be a big problem."

The King was looking from one of them to the other as if he wondered what their issue was. "Look," Mama Simone said to him. "Can you understand a word we're saying?"

"Yes," he said simply. "Some."

"Well, how do we find our way back to the mirror?"

"I do not know."

"Oh!" Lilian said. "I know! One of us has to stay here."

"How's that help the others?"

"No, I mean one of each of us," said Lilian. "We take off the wards. There'll be a whole bunch of us, all different. So one of each could go back and wait in the goblin's hill. Then after we've found Warren, we put the wards back on and we'll be pulled together with the one in the goblin hill."

"You're kidding," said Mama Simone. "It's that easy?" *We really can be more than one person? And stop being more than one, whenever we want to?*

"Yes, I read all about it. That's how they got the alchemists out! But I think we have to be apart for a second to do it. You can't be with two of me at a time. Just go over that rise, and I'll try it out."

Mama Simone didn't get this at all, but she took the King's arm and urged him off behind a swell in the prairie. After a minute Lilian called them out again. She was still standing, just as she had been, except that she had the star-shaped ward in her hand rather than around her neck.

"It didn't work?"

"Yes, it did," said Lilian. "Just wait a minute. I'll show you." She walked round the rise herself, out of sight, and a movement from the other direction caught Mama Simone's eye. There Lilian was, waving at her from the goblin's mirror. The Lilian in the mirror was wearing the ward.

"Get out," said Mama Simone. She ran up the rise and looked where Lilian had gone. There stood Lilian. Mama Simone went back and looked at the mirror, and Lilian was in there too.

"You can only see one of me at a time," Lilian said, coming back. Sure enough, mirror-Lilian was gone. "But there are more than one of me now. More every minute. And one's safe behind the mirror, and if I put this ward on I'll be put back together with her, and I'll be safe."

"I'll be jiggered," said Mama Simone. But she felt excited. This was the most magical magic she'd ever seen, unless you counted the tree-Mama Simone, which was creepy. "I just take this off and go?"

"Yes, but do it when you're not with us." Lilian gestured to the King, who walked slowly away with her.

Mama Simone faced the mirror and took off the ward. *I'm magic now.* She didn't feel any different. The Lilian in the mirror waved at her again and stretched out a hand, so Mama Simone reached into the mirror and took it; then with a step and a swirling light around her, she was through, back inside the goblin hill.

402

"Did it work?"

"You tell me," said Lilian. "Is there another of me in there?"

"Yes. On the other side of that rise."

"Then it works."

"So what do we do now?"

"We wait, I guess." Mama Simone put the ward around her neck, but nothing happened. She sat down on the floor, there being nothing else to sit on, and looked at the knights' portraits. "This is going to be a bore. I thought I was going on an adventure!"

"You are. It's just another one of you going on it."

That wasn't what I wanted! thought Mama Simone. *Magic is just a cheat.*

"Were you always magical?" she asked Lilian, who nodded. "Are your children magical?"

"No," Lilian said. "At least the girls aren't. The grandbabies are two, too young to tell."

"Not for all kinds, they aren't."

"I guess. I started looking for the girls to be wizards when they were two. It's just as well they weren't," Lilian said, and laughed. "The terrible twos are hard enough without their levitating beams and shifting foundations."

Mama Simone looked at the mirror. The person who tried not to care about magic looked back at her. *But that person's gone.* "I knew someone who had twins — twin exorcists," she said. "A boy and a girl."

"Oh my! That's what we're all afraid of. What was it like?"

403

"Like going crazy, she said. Thinking you're whatever the baby thinks you are — one minute you're god, the next minute you're the devil."

"They say a lot of those cases where women kill their babies, the babies are exorcists," Lilian said uneasily.

"They say that."

"What happened to your friend's two?"

"She did everything for them. Nothing could please them. They hated each other; you know how children can hate. Whatever she did for one of them made the other hate more," Mama Simone said to the woman in the mirror. The one who had done everything, even black magic, illegal rites — who'd ended up cutting her own magic out to pay the trees for taking her children's powers. The one who'd spent the rest of her life pretending she didn't care.

The woman in the mirror looked back at her with gray eyes. *You can't have everything,* she said.

Lilian sounded nervous. "Did it turn out all right in the end?"

"What? Oh, they grew out of it. Still judgy, though."

"I didn't know they could grow out of it," said Lilian.

"They're better off, I'd say."

"Are any of yours magic?"Mama Simone had to stop a minute to make sense of this. *Of course,* she thought, *that exorcist stuff happened to someone else. Didn't it.*

"One hears animals, and one's a witch," she said to Lilian. "The others are just regular folk." Having run out of family conversation, they lapsed into silence. *Recipes come next, I suppose*, thought

404

Mama Simone, but damn if she was going to start that ball rolling. "What do we do, just sit here?" She got up and paced back towards the mirror. She put out a hand to touch it, and something reached through it and grasped her.

"Oh!" Mama Simone pulled her hand back, with difficulty. The king came into the room, holding to her. She'd forgotten all about him! "Oh," she said again. She was ready to apologize, but pulling him had put her off-balance; her other hand flailed through the mirror, and she was back in the mirror-world.

In this world, Mama Simone walked down the prairie path, Lilian in front of her and the King behind and his eight knights in single file behind him, silent as children playing scouts. She was carrying the bucket of trees, and their leaves pointed straight ahead. The light was changing as it did in there, light to dark to light again, and the plain around them flashed from spring to winter, fire to freeze.

Well, I'll be, Mama Simone said to herself. "Are you back, too?" she asked Lilian, who gave her a frown.

"I've been here all along," she said. "So've you."

"Oh." *All right then*, thought Mama Simone. She wondered if the other Mama Simone and Lilian were still in the goblins' hill.

They walked a good ways in silence, probably eight or ten kilometers. If they were still heading south, they'd have come out on the dry side of the mountains by now, and been looking over foothills onto the Liger marshlands. But in here, they were just coming into a wide river valley with a ford. Way down to the east she could see a big mountain standing all alone on what looked like the other side of a lake. The mountain's top was white, and greenery covered its ridged sides.

"We were near the water when we met the demon," Lilian said, her voice tense.

Mama Simone began to look out more carefully for any signs of a demon, but there weren't any. She was getting a little bored, in fact, when they went up another rise and found a village just ahead, not a hundred steps away. The village didn't seem to have more than a few dozen houses in it, with a stockade wall around them and a big gate. The wall and gate kept changing — sometimes tall, sometimes squat, sometimes open, sometimes closed. Behind them, house roofs bobbed up and down like girls curtsying.

"Look!" Mama Simone said. The trees in her bucket were almost leaning over, as if drawn to the houses and wall.

Lilian looked, not happily. "That's not where the demon was when it took Warren. We have to go down that way."

"My trees want to go to the village," said Mama Simone. "What about your leaves?"

Lilian looked into the bowl. Sure enough, her leaves were swimming toward that side of the bowl. "Darn," she said. "That means they're not leading me to Warren at all!" Her voice had the beginnings of tears in it.

The King had been watching the village with them, but now he grabbed both their hands and pulled them down into the grass.

"What —?" Mama Simone said, but the thing he pointed at shut her mouth.

The gate was open at that instant, and she could see into the village street. Something was coming out from behind one of the houses, way too close to Mama Simone for comfort. It was man-shaped, the size of a cow and shiny black, like polished glass. It turned its head as if it were hunting … it had a thick neck and an insect sort of face. Its long arms had too many joints and claws. Mama Simone felt a cold chill run down her spine. She knew, as if she'd been born knowing it, that this was a creature to stay away from.

"That's it!" whispered Lilian. "That's Xiphister! That's what ate Warren!"

Mama Simone snatched at Lilian and held her down. *What in the world was I thinking?* she asked herself.

The little trees in the bucket beside her quivered, pointing at the demon. They shook their leaves, like children trying to get a teacher's attention. *You little beasts got me into this*, Mama Simone thought, hating them. *You couldn't kill me when you were babies, so now you're trying another way!* But it was far too late to run now … as if of its own will, her hand reached into her pocket where the star-shaped ward was. Slip that over her head and she'd be back in the goblins' hill. The thought calmed her; grasping the ward with one hand and Lilian's coat with the other, she looked between clumps of grass at the demon.

She couldn't tell whether its hide was hard or just filled to bursting with fluid, like a rotting carcass. Its color shifted, as if there were thick, oily currents in the stuff within. Mama Simone stared. Who knew demons were filled with fluid, like water balloons? She saw a paler eddy in the stuff within the demon. A hand reached up, or congealed just under the thing's surface. It scrabbled at the underside of the shell, like a man drowning under ice, and Mama Simone thought she heard a tiny voice cry out.

It took a minute for her to realize what she was seeing, and for that whole minute the hand inside the demon fought to get out. It was a little hand. Its nails were broken and its knuckles barked, like a little boy's hand.

Mama Simone shut her eyes for an instant, but that didn't get rid of what she'd seen. Her heart raced and her hands shook. *A child inside that demon. Some child's soul. Robin's soul.* The demon moved to one side, then the other. What was it up to? *Hunting something*, Mama Simone thought. The demon stepped out of her sight, back between the village wall and the cottage, and she relaxed — for just an instant, because the man it had been hunting stepped out from the cottage's other side.

He didn't look very tall or strong, though it was hard to tell because he wore a gray robe with its hood pulled up. There was something shimmery about the robe that made him hard to see clearly; but Mama Simone could see that he hadn't a clue there was a demon hunting for him by the incautious way he walked. He looked absentminded, distracted; gazing round him like some sightseer, and all the time a predator waiting just around the corner!

Someone has to warn that poor fool, Mama Simone thought. She even took a breath in and opened her mouth to do it, but just then the man turned and she saw two big gray wings sticking out of his back. The breath caught in her throat with surprise, and before she could recover the demon had jumped right over the cottage onto the gray-robed man. It jumped like a spider, straight up in the air and down with its legs under it. The man didn't even have a chance to scream. It landed right on top of him, and Mama Simone saw blue flames go up all around them. She gulped.

Lilian lay so still beside her, Mama Simone had to glance to see if she was still breathing. She was; her face was turned away from the demon, white and set.

Mama Simone put a hand on her arm. "It'll be all right. We'll get them back out again." It felt like the biggest lie she'd ever told.

***

"She's back!" Rho said triumphantly into the phone.

"What! I'll call Gretyl and Willett. We'll be right out."

Rho was alarmed. "Why do you need to do that?" he asked.

"Because they'd never let me hear the end of it if I didn't call them," said Lilis, "and wild horses couldn't keep them from coming, once they know;

and I'm assuming you'd rather have me come if they are, am I right?"

"Yeah," Rho muttered.

They all came out, of course, even though it was past suppertime and children needed to be nagged into brushing teeth and read their bedtime stories. But then, they were the children, weren't they? Rho was unused to thinking about that and it led into dangerous territory, so he put it aside.

Mama Simone didn't answer any of their questions, but she did cook supper for all of them; a real supper, not the sandwiches she had been feeding Rho since his arrival. For the first time he felt as if he were back in the home he'd left, with all of them around a loaded table. He found himself looking for his father, for just an instant, and that put up the 'dangerous territory' flags again. Being home — really being there — getting used to it, remembering things he had liked about it, all were dangerous. He looked at Willett's five o'clock shadow to remind himself things had changed, and felt firmer.

"It's just the way it was," Gretyl reported, looking back into the shadowed living room. "Right down to the dust. That's magic."

"It's grime," said Mama Simone, shaking her head. "I'll get to that in the morning. I've been letting things go."

"I'll say you have," Lilis said dryly. "There was nothing in that room last night. Where was it?"

"I don't know, dear. It's been here every time I was. Are you sure you weren't mistaken?"

They looked at each other, weighing the thought of a shared hallucination. "What would

410

make us — it's you!" Willett said, turning on Rho and breaking the uncomfortable rapport. "It's that demon of yours."

"I don't have a demon! Why are you always blaming me? Didn't anything bad ever happen while I wasn't here?"

"Nothing magic."

"Nonsense," Lilis said, taking the last corn muffin. "He wasn't here when that two-headed cow came into Mr. Dilys' yard."

"Two-headed cows aren't magic. They're just freaks." Willett glared at Rho all the more, as if 'freak' also applied.

"Children, I've had quite enough of this," Mama Simone said in a tone that brooked no argument. "This is not how well-brought up human beings treat one another."

None of them had ever been referred to as well-brought up human beings before, from the way they stared at her. Rho had been looking at her ever since she came back, but now he saw her clean apron and sensible shoes as if for the first time. Her hair was neat. There were no smudges on her hands. "You've had a good life," she said firmly. "Your father worked hard to make sure each of you had the best life he could manage, and I won't have you throw his efforts away in nasty, jealous bickering. You know how human beings ought to live. Grow up and do it. It's not as if you have forever to do it in."

Her children stared at the table.

"She has a point," Willett admitted. "We're not getting any younger."

"We're family," agreed Gretyl. "No matter what." She got up and began clearing the table. "It's a good thing you came back," she said as she passed Rho; he wasn't sure if she meant it for him or for Mama Simone, but he took it as an olive branch and passed her the salad plates. "It's the magic," she went on as she walked behind Mama Simone. "We're jealous of the magic."

Nobody moved, any more than if she had dropped a lit bomb onto the table.

"We think you love the ones with magic more than you love me and Willett."

Rho snuck a look around, peeking up through his eyebrows. He caught just the edge of Willett's glance and they both looked away.

"And we think that now Daddy's gone, there's nothing to make you stay with us ordinary people."

"Yet here I am," said Mama Simone. "I seem to have made my decision, don't I?"

Chapter 31
Giving Demons What They Want

I thought being eaten by a demon would be worse than this, Warren thought. *I didn't imagine a family reunion...* This was selfish, he knew. The other people eaten by Xiphister weren't having a good time. If Warren listened hard, he could hear them screaming outside the house. But here inside, it was no louder than wind howling in the eaves; easy to forget.

"Why haven't the rest of them come in here?" he wondered aloud.

"The demon wants you in here," said Grandfather. "That's what it ate you for, isn't it? To cast charms it can't cast. Believe me, boy, it won't leave you alone for long. You'll have to pay your way, if you want to stay cozy in here with us."

Warren bristled, but a new sound distracted him. Someone — something — was scratching at the front door. Cold terror ran through Warren; he froze, staring at it.

"And it begins," said Grandfather, leaning back on the sofa. "You going to get that, boy?"

The doorbell rang now, loud, imperative. Answering it was the last thing Warren wanted to do — *but it might be Lilian!* he thought, and leapt up.

When he swung the door open, though, nobody was there. He could hear the screaming clearly, though — five, ten, a dozen voices, all pleading and gasping. *That would be me, if not for this book,*

Warren thought, and held tight to the doorknob. *Those are real people, really hurting! And here I am, almost forgetting them* — The bell kept ringing, in jerks. What was wrong with it? Warren turned to the door, and there were two hands grasping the bell. They were long-fingered hands, with a fading nicotine stain on the right forefinger. Their knuckles were white as they twisted the knob.

"Who's there?" Grandfather asked, as if he didn't really care.

"Um —" Warren reached a finger out toward one of the hands. He touched the wrist, as light as a breath, and saw a soiled sleeve cuff come into being under his finger. "I think it's —" he began, and stopped, because he really had no idea what it was. But it was solidifying, and Warren had to step back to make room for it. Now the hands twisting the bell belonged to a thin brown-haired man, with a narrow face and a widow's peak. He looked awfully familiar, but from where? Then Warren placed him.

"Magister Locullan!" The magician Warren had interviewed last month and e-mailed just a week ago, offering him the position Crayberg had turned down. No wonder he hadn't answered!

Locullan looked down at Warren without recognition, his face white and eyes staring. The bags under them were dark purple. *I'm only eight,* Warren remembered, and flushed. This wasn't how one wanted to appear to a potential junior faculty member — *who got himself eaten by a demon,* he told himself. Locullan was in no position to judge. Nor was his judgment the issue, right now. "Come in!" Warren cried, pulling the door open further.

414

"And shut the door," Grandfather put in. "You'll let demon into the hall."

Locullan let go of the doorbell and stepped in. But he never stopped looking down at Warren. His face was even paler, and his eyes filled with tears. Then he looked away, as if to hide them. *Anybody would cry*, Warren thought sympathetically, but he was still embarrassed ... turning away from Locullan's discomfiture, he caught Grandfather's eye and, for the first time, found it comforting.

"So, now we have two real magicians and a pack full of supplies," Grandfather said, looking at Locullan. "What shall we do next? I know some lovely charms, if we only had the blood of a murderer."

Warren felt talked-over, like — like an eight-year-old. Something told him, though, that he did not want to tell Locullan who he was. The man hadn't looked up at Grandfather's words, and now he reached back toward the door handle, abruptly.

"Hey!" Warren piped, hating how high and scared his voice sounded.

"He's right," Locullan said. His voice — his voice was flat. His expression was flat, when he looked down at Warren. His other hand reached out, as if he wanted to stroke Warren's hair, and pulled back, as if he dared not. "That's where I belong."

"No," said Warren. "Now you're here, you have to help me."

"Do what?"

Warren knew that voice. He'd heard it a thousand times, in his office — the voice of hope. There was life after the current catastrophe, that voice said. There was something to do next. "Well, to start with," he said, reaching for the grimoire on the coffee table. "We're going to tranquilize this demon."

The spell required wholesome food, preferably dairy; Warren was relieved to find a crumb of cheese in an empty sandwich bag. He and Locullan drew a circle around it with wax driblets from one of the candles, scratching symbols in each drop of wax as it solidified, and the moment the circle was complete a wave of something clean and restful passed over him.

"Eight must have been a good year for you," said Grandfather. Warren had to look up a long ways to scowl.

"Stop it," Dad said. "You don't know what you're talking about."

Warren felt unsafe, suddenly. He felt afraid to be grown-up with responsibilities, but also afraid to be eight and find out what Grandfather didn't know. It wasn't fair! He hadn't asked for secrets and guilt … "I think it worked," he said hastily, looking away at the walls of the living room. "Listen, there's not as much screaming."

Grandfather waved a hand dismissively. He never looked away from Dad. "Eight's young," he said.

"He was ready," Dad said defensively.

"Ready for what?" Warren asked.

"See? He doesn't even know what you made him do!" For the first time, Grandfather's voice was not unkind when he spoke to Warren. "To cast your essence into this book, boy. Eight is too young. A child needs all his essence."

"He was ready," Dad said again, his voice tight.

"Don't say that," a voice said, and it took a moment for Warren to realize it was Locullan who had spoken. "Never say that again," he said. His voice was a warning. Warren wanted to take a step closer to — who? Who could he trust?

"I think I'm a judge of my own—" said Dad, but Locullan cut him off.

"Just shut up," he said, and even Grandfather obeyed.

Dad glared at Grandfather for a moment. Then he turned and left the room, going up the stairs. *What's up there?* Warren wondered. *My old room?* He didn't want to find out. The screaming was up there, above the house. Locullan went the other way, toward where the kitchen should have been. That left Warren alone with Grandfather, a place he didn't want to be. He held tight to the grimoire.

"Bring that here, boy," said Grandfather, patting a spot beside him. "Come on. Move your carcass." His tone was friendly, for Grandfather. Still, Warren felt wary as he stood up, hugging the grimoire to his chest. "Show me what you cast into it," Grandfather commanded.

Warren leafed backwards from the last filled page. He'd cast a lot into this grimoire, over the years! But Grandfather didn't care about any of that.

"Show me the first one. When you were eight." He picked the book up and held it at arm's length as if he needed glasses. "Hmpf!" he said. "Since when does an eight-year-old need to know a high-octane anxiolytic charm? I thought you were a magician, not a sorcerer. Who'd you cast this charm on? Your mother?"

"For her headaches," Warren said defensively. "What's wrong with that?"

"Never mind, any fool can see why he did it. He didn't want to cast the damn thing himself. If I'd been alive, he'd have tried to saddle me with it."

Warren was enraged, as he hadn't been since childhood. He'd forgotten how helplessness and lack of status worked on the emotions; his chest heaved as if his heart were boiling with no outlet save explosion. He put all his strength into answering like a grown-up instead of a whining toddler.

"What do you mean?"

"He's my only son," said Grandfather. "Guess that counts for something. Never did a thing in his life that I didn't have to clean up after, till he married that stripper. But if I'd lived I'd have had to clean up after that as well, I see now."

"She wasn't a stripper! She was a dancer."

Grandfather gave Warren a stern look. "If you're really older than eight, you know that's not true."

Warren was abashed. He looked down. "I guess," he mumbled.

"That's why eight is too young to be casting charms," said Grandfather. "Eight-year-olds believe whatever line you feed them." He nodded at the book. "This emptied out her head, all right," he said, looked at Warren's dumbfounded face, and scooted to the right. "They teach spellcraft in Osyth, don't they? Look here." Warren sat beside him. Grandfather flipped to a different page, far back in the book. "See this charm? Know what it's for?"

"We used it when Russell and I got our souls back."

"What!"

Warren felt a lot better. "The demons tried to steal our souls, but we got them back with this charm. We're the only people who've ever done that."

Grandfather raised his eyebrows. "I'm impressed," he said. "Truly impressed. The screw-up gene must have skipped a generation. Keep a close eye on your children. Did you ever analyze this charm?"

"How could I? The demon had the grimoire."

"Well, look here. See this sequence? Now, this –" he flipped to the page Warren had written at eight — "it's a modulated reversal of the same charm. A Linden braid. Doesn't show up on first read, because it's syllable-based rather than sign-based — you getting any of this?"

"Only the terms," Warren admitted. "I'm not a spellwright." *I should show this to Teddy*, he thought.

"One draws your soul closer, the other sends it further away," said Grandfather.

Warren sat very still, thinking about this the way a rabbit thinks about a fox. "You mean I was casting charms to send away Mom's soul?" He hated the little voice that came out.

"All magical charms work on the soul. If you could cast charms on anything else, you'd be a wizard or an alchemist."

"I am a wizard," Warren flared up. "I had tenure in wizardry before I moved over to Magic."

419

"Without learning the theory, eh, and still did well enough to get your soul back? Maybe Sonny was right to split you up early. Anyway, yes, this sends parts of your soul further away from you. The parts that are anxious. Everyone did it, in my day."

"Everyone took laudanum in your day," Warren said tartly.

Grandfather laughed and ruffled his hair. "Smart mouth. That's my side of the family coming out." He grew serious. "There's nothing wrong with shoving part of your soul to one side. What d'you think meditation does? Or education, for that matter. You don't learn to manage your soul, you end up –"

"A stripper?" Warren asked dryly. "With anxiety attacks?"

"I was about to say, dependent on someone else to manage it for you. Maybe even on your eight-year-old."

Warren sat wrestling with his feelings. Had he really sent his own mother's soul further away? *But she's full of soul!* he thought. *She's more herself than anybody. She's knights and trumpets and adventure and courage!* He felt Grandfather's arm come around him. It was thin, hard and strong.

"You're some kid," said Grandfather, in tones of grudging respect. "You're the kid I'd send to do a man's job."

Warren didn't like Grandfather, so why was this hug safer-feeling than Dad's? "Why didn't Dad want to cast it himself?" he asked finally. It felt treacherous.

Grandfather must have known this, because he gave Warren a squeeze and answered without looking straight at him. "Caretaking sucks you in," he said. "Put too much of your essence into something like this, and you'll go through life seeing how people feel and thinking it's your job to do something about it. That's why folks in my day made sure to teach little girls these charms, and keep 'em away from our boys. In between our doses of laudanum, that is."

"So if Dad had asked you, you wouldn't have done it?"

"I would not. He chose her; it was his duty." Grandfather pulled his arm away and handed the book back to Warren.

Warren stared at the lines of that first charm he had ever cast. *I'm stuck with it*, he thought. *Stuck as a caretaker, middle manager, babysitter of adults for the rest of my life …* he shook himself. *Think about something else!* But that was wrong. That wasn't how you solved a problem like this. What advice would he give a faculty member with this problem? *To do something where it would be an asset*, he thought. *Knowing how people feel is an asset. Being motivated to do something about their problems is an asset.* But how was it an asset here? The people trapped in Xiphister certainly had feelings, and problems. But Warren couldn't help thinking he was missing something else.

"I'm taking something for granted," he said, frowning at the book, "but I just can't figure out what it is."

"You have a forehead like a basset hound," said Grandfather. "That must come from your mother's side."

There was no reason for that remark to shake Warren's thoughts loose, but it did. "Demons!" he said. "What are their feelings? What are their problems?"

"That's taking caretaking too far."

"No, it's not!" Warren was so excited he jumped up. "We can work the rest of our lives trying to keep ahead of them — generations of magicians can try keeping ahead of them — but when have we had someone who understands what people feel actually look at what they want? All the girls you taught this charm to, did they go on to become magicians?"

"That wasn't the purpose. They went on to become wives and mothers."

"And you didn't teach it to the boys, who did go on to become magicians. I remember a book Bosie read me when I was little, about the wicked magician who tried to curse his enemies, but he knew so little about what they wanted that he ended up giving them their hearts' desires by mistake. That's the truth, isn't it? Most magicians don't know a thing about other people's needs. But I do!"

"Oh? Tell me, then." Grandfather leaned back, folding his arms. "What do demons need, oh, wise one?"

Warren stopped. He took a deep breath and shut his eyes. He imagined himself in his office: the computer, the cross-shaped window, the cluttered desk, and sitting across the desk from him, Xiphister, or any of the demons he'd called up in the pentarium over the years. But because this was an imagined demon, no *grue*. *What does it want?* he thought, and the imaginary demon sneered at him. *What does it do?* Warren asked himself, and made a list out loud.

422

"They come into the pentarium, and into the classrooms," he said, "even though they know they'll be trapped there. They like the contest; they like figuring out how to escape. They prowl the city looking for souls to feed on. They try to trap me. Two of them have tried that, now — and what they wanted was my soul in the grimoire, so they could cast the charms in it. They want to be able to compete better in our world."

"What else does anybody want?"

"No, this matters! Why would they care to compete in our world, when they can reshape their own into anything they want?" Warren answered his own question. "Their own world is too easy. They're immortal, they all know each other; the pecking order must have been established a thousand years ago. Demons want a challenge, something that'll notice them and fight back. Everything they do to us is to make us fight back. They do worse and worse, to keep us fighting back." He opened his eyes. "Haven't you ever known someone like that?"

"Ha! I am someone like that."

"I've supervised people like that," Warren said. "But they're cowards when it comes down to it. They pick fights with their colleagues, but they cry when we give them what they're asking for and hit back. And they won't try the really hard battle, the one to make everyone a winner."

"Hm," said Grandfather.

"If you really want to work with something resistant, just try making people happy!" Warren said, waxing hot.

"Not all of us have your ambitions."

"I wouldn't, except that I cast this charm a hundred times when I was a child. Now Xiphister's eaten me so I can cast the charms in this book for it. Suppose I give it what it's asking for? What happens to it if I cast this charm a hundred times?"

Grandfather frowned. "I think you would have to alter the charm a bit, to make sure it affects the demon's essence."

"Show me how," said Warren.

Warren had to cast the charm himself, which didn't surprise him; Dad and Grandfather were mere essences, after all, and Locullan hadn't come back from the kitchen. Warren didn't care about that, either.

"Are you sure you wrote this right?" he asked Grandfather, worried. "It's not making me any more caring."

"I'm sure," said Grandfather, without looking up from the fire he sat staring into. Its yellow glinted in his pale eyes. "Being a caretaker doesn't make you a fool. That man killed his own child."

"You don't know that!" Warren said. He felt sorry for the libeled Locullan, but if it were true …

"Ha! He's been wailing about it ever since the demon ate him, if you had ears to hear." Grandfather shrugged. "Either he killed her or he let something else do it … either way, he's useless. Finish your business, boy. Of course it's not making *you* a fool; I set it against the demon."

Warren sighed, and cast the charm again. It came back to him easily, the bits of paper and runes written in water and smoke. He had to take care to make sure he cast Grandfather's new version and not the old one, and even so he thought of Bosie as he pronounced the words.

He thought of her as she had been when he was eight, beautiful and exotic. Once he had gone to the club with Dad, and seen her in gauze and sequins. That memory, of lovely women and poles and smoke curling through shafts of light in the dark room, was mixed in with other memories of the time; the circus, where a lovely woman in gauze and spangles had ridden upon a white horse that turned mid-circuit into a dragon and soared above the delighted crowd. A strip club based on Warren's memories would indeed be a grand and glorious thing! And whenever he cast this charm as a child, he had thought of the woman riding the dragon. How much strength she would need. What great deeds she would accomplish, when he had given her the power to master her steed. It was almost as good as riding a dragon himself, Warren had thought.

Now he thought of his mother as older, even stronger. He cast the charm for her courage as she faced widowhood and aging, for the way she had faced Rho's demon as she helped Lilian get Warren's grimoire away from it back in February. Then he cast the charm for Lilian, over and over: for Lilian setting the home-ward and scrapbooking, holding him in her arms, understanding and supporting him. He cast it for his children and grandchildren, that they might never be anxious about their choices in life. He went through the members of his department one by one, even the ones who would have been furious that he was trying to take away their edge. He even cast it for some of the demons he knew. Weren't demons often anxious? The little ones certainly were, but it was with good reason, and a calming charm might do them more harm than good. In fact, was this doing any of its recipients any good?

Well, he thought, it's not supposed to. It's not as if casting a charm for people when they're on another continent is going to do them any good! They needed to hear the words, smell the smoke; what he was doing now was only supposed to affect the demon Xiphister. Warren refocused his efforts on the people Xiphister needed to feel protective towards. Ver the goblin wardmaker, the magicians it had eaten, the questionable Locullan, whomever it might encounter in this garden. And always, Lilian. Lilian, always and foremost.

**

Looking at Lilian didn't make Mama Simone happy, so she watched the demon Xiphister. It hadn't spent more than a minute crouched over its prey, and when it stood up the grey-robed man was completely gone. *Inside it*, she thought. Would the demon start hunting them now? No; it stretched instead, and yawned. When it turned towards her and Lilian, it didn't move like a hunting creature. It ambled instead, out of the village gate and to the left, where a branch of the road went across a little stream, sometimes with a bridge and sometimes without. The demon reached the stream at one of the without-bridge moments, and splashed through the water. It climbed halfway up the bank and then it sat down, in a little grassy dip. It nestled down in the dip and closed sideways-moving eyelids over its big black eyes, and took a nap.

A nap! It just ate someone alive, and it was going to sleep the sleep of the just — *That tears it*, thought Mama Simone. *That's the kind of world this is*.

"Why don't we just cut its head off while it's asleep?" she whispered to Lilian.

"Because that wouldn't hurt it," Lilian whispered back. "Its body doesn't matter to it. We might cut the people inside it, but not the demon."

When Mama Simone looked down the rank of knights, she saw heads nodding in agreement. She imagined them standing over that body, hewing its head off in triumph, then seeing the person they'd come to rescue lying there headless as the demon dissolved away — *Robin*, she thought. She almost saw him lying before her. Not the man who'd come home, but eleven-year-old Robin. Her vision blurred for a moment.

The saplings shook their leaves toward the demon as if to say 'hurry up,' and she felt madder and madder as she looked at them. Years' worth of mad had crept up on her, and now she hardly dared speak for fear she would scream or cry.

She shut her eyes, and saw the hand inside the demon again. Nails broken, knuckles bleeding as if it had scrabbled against the monster's shell for hours, years. How often had she taken that hand, or one like it? It would curl up its fingers inside hers, resentful. How warm and alive it was, like a little animal … her nose tingled.

"Enough!" she whispered. "Either we do something, or I'm leaving."

Lilian looked round with squinty eyes, like a hedgehog. "Where do you think you'll go?"

"Back home," said Mama Simone. "I'll put on the ward, go back to the goblins' hill, and take myself and my trees back where we belong." As soon as Mama Simone spoke she realized leaving the goblin hill might be harder than it sounded. Weren't they locked in? And hadn't it been a maze of tunnels to get to the room with the mirrors, in the first place? "We have to do something!" she cried in a whisper. "Are you going to spend the rest of your life sitting here?"

The king made a noise and held a hand out, gesturing her to keep still. The demon was moving.

It rolled over, stretching out its arms and legs, sighed loudly, and subsided back into sleep. This should have pleased Mama Simone, since it had now exposed its soft underbelly; but it had also increased in size as it spread out, so much that it now filled the little dingle it had been curled into. The demon's belly was black and shiny as tar, with blue flames flickering above one side. It bulged and fell as creatures — people — struggled under its surface. Stabbing at it was obviously more likely to hurt those inside than the demon itself.

"You're right," Lilian said, and stood up. "We have to do something. Or at least I do — it's really not your problem." She took her hand out of her pocket, where she'd probably been holding on to her ward, and picked up the blue bowl of water and leaves. Mama Simone could see the leaves still schooling at the edge of the bowl nearest the demon. They quivered, just like the leaves on her saplings. "I'm going into the demon. Warren's a

428

magician. He'll know what to do to get us out, or I'll stay in there with him." She stared at Mama Simone, her face white and her chin quivering. "I won't come this far and then turn back and leave him," she said.

Any fool could see she was trying to talk herself into this, and it would only take one word of common sense to turn her back; but she was looking in the wrong place for that word of common sense. The shock that ran through Mama Simone was a shock of recognition. This was what you did when you'd lost your husband! You burned your old life and did what only somebody with nothing to lose could do. She imagined herself wading into the demon, grasping that little warm hand, pulling it out again — or herself in; she didn't care. "Wait a minute," she said, and stood up herself. "I'm coming in with you."

"Really?" Lilian was so shocked, it was obvious she had been counting on Mama Simone to talk her out of going into the demon.

"My trees want to go in there, don't they." Mama Simone nudged the bucket with her foot. "I can hardly watch you walk into that mess alone, can I?"

"Well — do you really think we should? Warren will be furious, I can tell you that much."

"I don't see him doing anything. Like you said, we've come this far."

"That's right. Well ..." Lilian sniffed hard and took a firmer grip on her bowl. The water inside rippled as if there was a storm brewing.

That was when Mama Simone remembered the knights. They were standing up as well, gathered around the two women. *Look at that!* she thought. *We two making the decisions, while men stand around letting us talk.* That was when she really knew she was in another world.

"What about all these?"

The knights, she realized hadn't been silent out of respect for her and Lilian. They were looking at the King. He raised his beech-twig, and it pointed toward the demon as well. The knights' faces were solemn as he spoke in a language Mama Simone didn't know.

"We will come after you," said the knight they could understand. "In three hours, we will hew it open and pull you out. Dead or alive."

"What? Do we get any say in this?" asked Mama Simone.

The knight just looked at her. Apparently she did not have any say in this. *Not such a different world, after all,* she thought.

Lilian stepped forward. "Are we doing this or what?"

"We are!" said Mama Simone, picking up her bucket. "Lead the way."

Lilian took a deep breath, squared her shoulders, and marched forward into the tarry black edge of the demon, not pausing when it overflowed into her shoes. But her hands were white against the bowl, and the water within sloshed almost up to the rim with every jerky step. Mama Simone's own trees trembled like a windstorm as she followed.

Chapter 32
Reunion

Walking into a demon as if it were a lake had to be the strangest thing Mama Simone had ever done, but she kept her eyes on Lilian and followed. The demon was squishy under her feet. Then it was over her shoes, and she felt as if she had no feet. "Oh!" she said and tottered, and the King took her elbow.

Now her feet hurt, like they were burning up all the way into the bones, and Mama Simone would have yelped except that Lilian hadn't. *I'm as brave as any tourist!* she thought and clenched her teeth — then, just before she began to cry from it, the pain stopped. Her feet felt as if something had taken them over and was trying out to see what they could do. They went hot and cold, they itched, and then she could feel no pressure on the soles; it was like walking on cloud, or in water that held up her body weight. And the strange feelings had moved up her legs as she waded onward, though there were fewer, less dramatic, shifts in them. By the time Mama Simone was knee-deep in demon, it felt as dull as sticking your tongue out the window. She had time to think about what she was doing and how purely stupid it was. She caught up with Lilian, who had forged onwards without hesitating, glanced sideways, and saw Lilian's face frozen in an expression of intent terror.

"I can't believe we're doing something this stupid," Mama Simone offered.

Lilian gave a gasp of relief, but didn't say anything in response. Tears ran down her face and she glared at the blue bowl as if it was the only thing in the world.

"I wouldn't have done this for my husband," said Mama Simone, looking at the bucket she was carrying. The little trees shivered their leaves like children outside an ice cream shop. "Well, maybe I would have. Do we just keep wading across it?"

"I don't know! It sort of rose up and sucked Warren in."

"It was awake then, wasn't it?"

"Maybe we have to dive in — I'll spill my bowl if I do that."

"We better keep together, whatever we do," said Mama Simone. "How about we hold hands or something and then just sit down?"

Lilan had stopped. "This is just plain ridiculous!" she said.

"What isn't?"

The King came up behind them, and only needed a little gesturing to understand that he was the only one with enough free hands to hold on to both of them. He took Mama Simone's hand and Lilian's elbow.

"Ready?" Mama Simone asked Lilian.

"I'm never going to be ready for this," said Lilian, and sat down on the demon.

Mama Simone followed suit, and then she was sinking into it; it felt sort of gluey under her rear end, a little cold around her waist, like absence as it came to her heart and lungs and she couldn't feel their movement any more. She just had time to think, *I won't be able to breathe!* before it closed

432

over her face and true enough, she couldn't breathe — but she had to breathe — she had to get out!

She started to her feet, but there was no getting out; her head didn't break the surface, and then she had to breathe and inhaled a chest-full of hot-cold-freezing demon stuff. She was smothering. The choking, dying feeling wouldn't stop; she yelled and nothing came out, gasped and nothing came in. *I'm going to die,* she thought, and knew she was crying — and then the choking feeling ebbed away. She was breathing air. It smelled and tasted wrong, but it moved like air in her throat. With every breath it got better. She was reminded of the way her feet had felt, as if something was trying to figure out how they worked.

A little encouraged, she opened her eyes. They burned, and of course she saw nothing, but now she knew to wait while the demon, or whatever was inside it, tried her eyes out. She saw colors, flashes, speckles like what appeared at night inside her closed eyelids. *There's only so far this can go*, she thought, *unless there really is something to see in here*. Did it have guts? She began to look around, for what she didn't know. *Organs. It has to have something in here — Lilian! Lilian and the King. Where are they?* She couldn't feel anything useful in her hands until she concentrated, and then it did seem something was holding the right one. As if her thoughts were creating them, Lilian and the King appeared. The three of them stood as they had before they sat down, one of the King's hands in Mama Simone's and the other on Lilian's elbow.

"This isn't at all what I expected," said Lilian, looking around.

433

"What did you expect?"

"Blood and guts, I guess," she answered. "Or else the people it ate."

That's right! Mama Simone thought, with a start. *That child's in here somewhere.* She looked around the grayish void, straining to make him appear, but no luck. Only the swirling grayness. "Maybe we just can't see right."

"Then why would we be standing here just like ourselves?" Lilian asked, and shook her head. "Don't you get the feeling that it's sort of — trying us out and figuring out what we are? The longer we're here, the more normal it feels. Like breathing — I couldn't breathe at all, at first. Now it seems to know we need something like air."

"I guess ..." Mama Simone said doubtfully. "It does seem to be giving us what we need. I thought demons were supposed to be wicked."

"They are. But this one's asleep — maybe it doesn't really know what it's doing? I need Warren!" Lilian called, so abruptly that Mama Simone jumped. "I need to find my husband and take him home again. And his grimoire, while you're at it!"

The grayness roiled little, as if the volume of Lilian's cry had disturbed it. Now Mama Simone could hear other noises, that might have been birds or might have been people, crying in the distance.

"Hush! You don't want to wake it up, do you?"

"Oh. You're right."

Something was definitely happening. The grayness looked like fog now, eddying and dispersing. Was it growing thinner above them? It was, and a shaft of sunlight came through and lit up

434

the trees in Mama Simone's bucket. "That must be up," she said. But she couldn't see any sun up there, just the light that made her little trees stand up straight and quiver their leaves. Mama Simone gave up looking for the sun and gazed around her instead. The fog swirled around them. Dark things loomed up behind it. Tall, pointy things. Reflective things, like gigantic eyes — square eyes — "Windows!" Mama Simone exclaimed. "That's a house!" And it was; a two-story house with dark gray painted shingles and a steep roof that hung over its upstairs windows like a forbidding brow. Its lawn needed mowing.

Mama Simone followed Lilian up a perfectly normal-looking concrete walk to the gray house's door. *Lilian rang a perfectly normal-looking doorbell.* "This place looks so familiar," she said to Mama Simone, half turning away, and just then the door opened onto — nobody. Mama Simone looked into a hallway with striped wallpaper, an oval mirror on the wall, and a three-legged piecrust table. A choking noise made her look down and discover that a child had opened the door; her heart froze for a second before she saw it wasn't Robin. This boy was eight or nine, with tow-colored hair over an earnest little face with glasses. His eyes were wide and his forehead creased into folds like one of those puppies with the floppy skin.

"Lilian!" he cried. "It got you as well?" The horror in his voice wasn't childlike.

Lilian was looking down at the boy with confusion. "I'm sorry –" she began.

"It's me, Warren," he said. Just then a man with a long nose and glasses came up behind him. Lilian looked up and gaped.

"Arthur!" she cried.

"Why, Lilian," said Arthur. "What a surprise. Do come in."

"Arthur? But you're dead! Oh!" Lilian pressed a hand to her mouth. "Warren –"

"Warren is quite alive. I am but an essence, cast into the grimoire," Arthur said politely. "And as always, delighted to see you."

The little boy had come forward, and now he put his boy hand, with its barked knuckles and chewed nails, on Lilian's arm. Mama Simone stared at the hand and fought down tears. "I'm all right, Lili," the boy said. "I just look eight. That's how old I was when I cast my essence into the grimoire."

"What?" Lilian said. "What about the grimoire?"

"This is it," said the man she'd called Arthur. He gestured around them at a perfectly normal-looking living room. Mama Simone peered around with interest. She'd heard of grimoires, but they were books; not houses.

The living room had the same striped wallpaper, a shabby rug, and a fireplace without a fire. It contained a few armchairs, a loveseat, and the same armoire that had been in Mama Simone's living room, before she took the axe to it. There were two more men in it, one of them a long-faced sad sack of a fellow in his thirties, and a coffee table with candles burning on it and a bunch of odds and ends laid out in what even Mama Simone could tell was charm-casting.

It all crashed onto her at once. She was inside a demon — a demon! And she'd walked in of her own free will, and it had all been a stupid mistake. What had made her think the hand she saw was Robin's? He wouldn't even have still been a little boy, by the time he sold his soul to the monster. Mama Simone couldn't see for a minute, she was so overcome with her own stupidity. Then the last person in the room stirred and cleared his throat.

He was a solidly built man, forty- or fifty-odd years old, with black hair and challenging pale blue eyes. He stared at Mama Simone from where he leaned against the wall by the fireplace, and did not bother to introduce himself. Then he stared at her chest, to which she clutched the bucket of saplings. Mama Simone glared at him, but he did not care.

"I thought you got away, Lili," the little boy mourned. "I shouldn't ever have brought you into this."

"I'm the one who brought you," Lilian said, and her voice broke. She bent over and started to spread her arms in a hug. "Oh, the bowl –" Arthur took it from her and put it on the armoire. Lilian didn't give it a glance. She was on her knees with her arms around the little boy.

"Oh, Lili," he said into her neck.

"I'm so sorry," Lilian said, rocking him as if he really were a child. "It's all my fault."

"No, I should have known better."

"You can tell they're married," Mama Simone said to the sad sack, who was standing nearest to her, but he didn't seem to be paying any attention.

437

"The bedroom's upstairs," said the pale-eyed man, though since he never took his eyes off Mama Simone's chest, his meaning was not really clear.

"Do you mind!" she said to him.

"What? If you bring those in here, they'll command attention," he said. Insolent!

"I'll show you commanding," Mama Simone said fiercely. She had to admit, she was enjoying this lout. He wasn't bad-looking at all, but what a scoundrel!

"Where are my manners? Have a seat," he said, patting the back of the loveseat.

"Oh!" said Lilian again, pulling away from Warren. "This is Mama Simone. And you know –" she indicated the king, who advanced gravely and bent over to shake Warren's hand. "Mama Simone, this is my father-in-law Arthur Oldham — I'm afraid I don't know —?"

"Lees," volunteered the dark-haired man. "Your grandfather-in-law. And that is Locullan, suffering the pangs of remorse. Sit!"

As if I were a dog! Mama Simone thought, and sat. Her heart beat hot and merry. He'd pay for that!

"Where's Ver?" Warren asked Lilian.

"We'll talk about that goblin later," she said.

"I'd hoped you'd gotten away," he said. "Wait a minute! Where did Mama Simone and — where'd they come from?"

"Outside, on the mountain. After the demon ate you, Ver and I ran back into the goblin hill and they put me out on the mountain to wait while they argued about whether to do anything. That's when Mama Simone came up, and him — he's the king of

438

this place, according to all those old knights in the mirror room."

"Those knights woke up? Where are they?"

"Waiting outside. We came in after you. They'll give us three hours before they hack it open."

Warren stood silent for a while, holding both her hands. "So you did get away — and then came back into the demon after me."

Mama Simone didn't like the undertones in his voice, not one bit.

"I left part of myself outside, in the goblin hill," Lilian defended herself. "We all did. So if this didn't work, we could put the wards back on and be pulled together. Like you told me Teddy did to get out of the garden."

"Neil did that, not Teddy," Warren said. He looked past Lilian's waist toward the far wall.

Mama Simone had a feeling he knew a lot more about what might be happening to the other parts of herself and Lilian than he would ever tell them.

"Touching," the pale-eyed man — Lees — murmured into Mama Simone's ear. "True love and all that, but what brought you on this adventure?"

Mama Simone felt herself flush a little. "I'm looking for a safe place to plant these," she said, indicating the saplings. "They led me here."

"A safe place? Inside a demon? Let me look at these little suicide plants." Without even asking, he picked the bucket off her lap and began to put his hands all over the trees; caressing their leaves, running his palm along each little branch. They ignored him, still stretching upwards into the sunlight. *Sunlight inside a house?* Mama Simone

439

caught herself. It wasn't a real house, was it? And whatever, the sunlight followed the little trees wherever Lees moved them. They basked in it. Had they already grown?

Lees stroked down their trunks and laughed. "Hah! A couple of little exorcists. What do you expect from them? They're hunting."

Now Mama Simone was truly flushing, and there was no hiding it. She was angry, too. She snatched the bucket back. "Did your mother ever teach you to mind your own beeswax?"

"No," Lees said, his eyes laughing. "Why, have I let the cat out of the bag?"

Mama Simone couldn't look at him, she was so angry. She looked away instead, and met Lilian's sympathetic gaze.

"I don't know if it's any of your business where someone stores a magical artifact," Lilian said briskly.

"Ah, is that how it is," said Lees. He leaned back and laughed silently. "What haven't we done to this poor thing?"

Warren grinned, a little shamefacedly.

"Why? What have you been up to?" asked Lilian.

"I've only cast a relaxing charm on it –"

"We saw it go to sleep. Right after it ate — somebody."

"And then I cast some well-wishing charms. Thinking it could use a bit more charity toward the world."

"He's been building the poor thing a conscience, making it into a copy of himself!" said Lees. "And now you've brought it two internal

440

exorcists — what will you do to it, man? Sorry, your Majesty."

The King answered, surprising everybody; but Mama Simone couldn't understand what he said. Lees listened intently. Then he replied in the same language, and grinned even more broadly.

"What did he say?"

"He's reclaiming his kingdom, and his life," Lees said. "First he lost it to Nöon, that old scoundrel, and then Nöon's grandchildren sold the whole lot to a bunch of alchemists. Alchemists weren't into slave-trading in my day."

"Oh! He must be the King from the story," Lilian said. "Good King Herrel."

The King's face lit up. "Herrel!" he cried, putting a hand on his chest. He bowed to Lilian.

She put a hand on her own chest. "Lilian," she said, and bowed back.

Lees was bored. "Well, what are we going to do next, eh? Unless the lovebirds want to go upstairs first."

They all looked at each other. Then Lilian started. "I've brought the bowl! It led us in here. This must be where we ought to cast the charm." She got the bowl off the shelf where Warren had put it, and set it carefully down on the coffee table. Mama Simone leaned forward to look at the leaves floating in it. They were no longer nosing up to one side of the water; they'd arranged themselves in a pattern like a lace doily, all with their heads toward the center and their little stems outward.

"Hm," said Lees. "A home-ward? Inside a demon?"

"The one we set every night," said Warren.

"And that's going to undo the alchemists' strongest charms? We can hope," Lees said, grinning. He stood up and stretched, all in one movement. "Now are you going to cast it, or sit around talking about it?"

"Aren't you going to help?" Mama Simone challenged.

"I am merely an essence," he said, pretending to be humble. "Charming, but unreal and without power."

"What is an essence, anyway?" Mama Simone challenged.

"A part of his soul," Lilian said with some asperity. "Presumably, a part he thought he could do without. Are we casting this charm, or not? Who's helping?"

"I'd help, but I can't read the runes," Mama Simone said. "And I've never cast a charm before."

"Hold my hand, then," said Lilian, "and repeat what I say."

King Herrel sat down where Lees had been and took Mama Simone's other hand. Sad Sack sat down on her other side.

Lilian had been scribbling on the table top. "Can you read this?"Mama Simone read. "O-on-ga-thee-ka."

"That's right! Go on." Luckily, it was a short charm.

"I guess I can do that," Mama Simone said after a run through.

"I need a candle," Lilian said, looking at the water-filled bowl with her brow knitted in thought. She and Warren conferred over their backpacks, and ended up cutting one of those stupid water bottles into a candle stand with a votive balanced atop it, just at the surface of the water. The leaves nosed up to the water bottle. The four of them took their places around the bowl as Lilian lit the candle and began to recite the charm, drawing on the bowl's outer surface with her finger as she did so. Warren was doing the same thing on the other side of the table, and Mama Simone began to see light coming through where their fingers had gone, as if they had wiped away the bowl's color and solidity. The light made a pattern on the tabletop, like a lace doily. When Lilian and Warren had finished, the pattern was complete, spreading all round the bowl. Sad Sack and King Herrel took Mama Simone's hands.

"Say the charm, and pull it toward you," said Lilian. That seemed like nonsense at first — how could she pull light? — but as Mama Simone spoke the words, she began to feel the web of light in her mind, and it seemed she could imagine pulling it towards herself, as if she were stretching out a lace tablecloth. But it wasn't near the edges of the table when something like an earthquake tremor made them all stop chanting and look around in alarm.

"I think our host is waking up," Arthur said from behind Lilian.

"Your charm doesn't like it," Lees added.

The charm had definitely suffered from whatever the demon was doing. Its lacelike tracery was lopsided, fading away before Mama Simone's eyes. The bowl was becoming solid blue again. She looked into the bowl and sure enough, the leaves had swum away from the center and were clustered at one side.

"Oh, damn!" Lilian said. "What's it doing? Where's it going?"

Nobody tried to answer, not even Lees. Who knew what a demon might do? Then a shrill noise cut through the room, and Mama Simone jumped. The noise came again. A bell! One of those old-fashioned doorbells with a knob you turned. It rang again, and now they were all twisted around staring at the door.

"Is anybody going to get that?" she said.

Arthur stood up; so did Warren, but Arthur gave him a look. "My house," he said like a stern father, and Mama Simone heard Lees snort. Arthur stalked to the door and threw it open. "Yes?" he said, as a wave of cold air flowed into the room. Mama Simone saw Warren clutch Lilian, and felt herself draw tight against the chill. The demon Xiphister stepped into the hallway and stood, looking at them all with unblinking insect eyes.

444

Chapter 33
Memory

"So how were the vampires?"

It was hard for Ric to believe in the vampires, here in the cafeteria full of morning sunlight, with Derek's scrubbed face and yellow mustache across the table.

"Scared me sick," Ric admitted. He wouldn't have said this to anyone but Derek. "Would have pissed myself, if I hadn't just gone."

Derek raised his eyebrows. "Guess Harding's got something going for him, hey?"

"Why, you heard otherwise?"

"Not in so many words. Hoth doesn't have much use for the others, that stands out."

"Heh! How was venery?"

Derek shrugged.

"Yeah," Ric jeered. "That's about what everybody thought."

"We weren't sent here to play around," Derek said, defensively.

"Yeah — what's the news on Endamos? We heading back today?"

Derek nodded. "Tonight. We can sleep over the ocean."

Ric thought about the Chief Exorcist's plane. Luxury! "You can't make me mad about that," he said. "How many beds are on that thing?" But there was something uneasy at the back of his mind. An image — one of the beds on that plane, filled with blood. *What's that about?* "Maybe they'll send us

445

to find Rosemont next," he said, seizing on the only thing worrisome about the plane. The Chief Exorcist had been missing the best part of a year. *They'll have to name a new one soon,* he thought, and Cham Ligalla's moon face floated into his mind. She wasn't squeaky clean.

"We could be the exorcist squad," Derek said. "Get them out of trouble." He leaned back, nursing his coffee.

"Better than our usual job." Ric hadn't thought of the possessed girl in weeks, was it? No, just a few days. *Wouldn't mind if I never saw something like that again.* He leaned back too, almost bumping his chair into a woman as she passed behind him. "Sorry." His sleeve had caught on the woman's purse, and she stopped to free herself, tugging on it.

The girl. The demon had come out of her. The tall man had clung to Ric's sleeve, and Ric had pulled away, and the demon had taken him. Just like that.

"Damn," he said, leaning forward again and looking down. He didn't want Derek to see his face.

"Say what?"

"I just remembered something I have to take care of."

"Yeah?"

"Sure," Ric said, pushing himself to his feet. "Listen, I'll take care of that thing I have and meet you back here at — when d'you want me?"

"I dunno. We're not leaving till five."

"I'll call you." Ric avoided Derek's eyes. The sunlight that had been so cheerful pressed against him now, and he could hardly breathe until he was in the elevator, alone.

446

Don't be an idiot, he scolded himself. *Don't be superstitious* — but he couldn't turn it off. The hand grasped his sleeve, and he pulled away. Then death reached past him, just like that. The Bright Lady had been warning him, and he'd taken this long to catch on. He'd been fooling with vampires and demons and now airplanes, while all the time the Lady told him death was reaching past him. "Idiot!" he said, and almost punched the elevator wall; the door opened, so fast that he feared the people waiting for it must have heard him, but they got on with blank, polite faces as Ric got off.

It only took Ric ten minutes to reach *Rameau's church*, now he knew the area. The building was open; he pushed through the big doors and then stood with his back to them, defiant, waiting for the Lady to appear and have it out with him. Nothing happened. After a while Ric began to feel stupid and to wonder why he had come. He finally went up to the altar, with a sullen feeling of having been scolded into it, and did the familiar ritual. It calmed him a little, and then he felt even more stupid. Had he really thought the Bright Lady would punish him for letting the demon take that slag Locullan? That was insane, even for a man who didn't understand Mercy.

He sat glumly in the first pew, wondering not about mercy but about what else this foreboding might mean. *Damn this memory!* he thought, and beat his fist against his leg. He pulled out his steno pad, but it was on the fritz; the letters blurred no matter how hard he blinked at them or how much he rubbed his eyes. Giving up, he leaned forward to put

447

his head in his hands, pulling his sleeve out of a ghostly grasp from behind him. His fury felt old as a stretched-out sock, his resentment stale with no crunch left in it. *Whatever*, he thought to the Lady. *Have it your way.*

At this edifying juncture, Father Rameau came in. Not seeing Ric, who had chosen a side pew, he went through the ritual in a practiced manner. Ric had never seen a professional do it, with all the obeisances, and was impressed. His resentment began to ebb a little. The Bright Lady had a lot to do. She couldn't be expected to drop everything whenever he wanted to have an argument with her. The idea that he worshipped something large and impersonal was comforting to Ric, who had, after all, chosen to be a public servant. Watching Rameau made worship feel less like a relationship and more like a job. Ric was good at jobs.

Rameau rose and turned around; wiping his face after what had been an especially vigorous, or dusty, prostration. He caught sight of Ric. "Inspector Massey!"

"Ric."

"I'd return the honor, but nobody's called me 'Auguste' for so long, it sounds more formal than the title. Can I give you coffee? Breakfast?"

"I just ate — but you can give me something," Ric said, on a whim. "Just how much do you know about the Lady?"

"I'm learning." Rameau led Ric through the door to the right of the altar, into an office-cum-jumble-room. It contained a large wardrobe, three music stands, two stacks of unopened packing boxes with parts of a saxophone laid across them, a

448

desk with a surprisingly modern computer on it, and two chairs. It smelled of lamp oil. "What did you want to know?"

"I guess — does she have any morals? Any standards?"

"Ah," said Rameau, as if relieved by a question he could answer. "You mean, has She any concept of who deserves Mercy and who doesn't."

"Yes."

"No. She doesn't."

"That's what I thought," Ric said glumly.

"So who are you being asked to extend Mercy to, against your own judgment? If you don't mind my asking."

"A guy named Locullan. He called a demon into his own daughter, and it got out and took him. The Lady's been on my case ever since, because I was the one the demon reached round to grab him." Ric felt angry again. "It's not like I handed him to it! I'm not the criminal here."

"No, doesn't sound like it," said Rameau, leaning back in his chair.

"She shouldn't be harassing me."

"Well, look at it this way. You get to learn about Mercy from Her, and he gets to learn from the demon."

That took the wind out of Ric's sails. "Uh," he said.

"If you were going to find this guy, how'd you start?"

"Look up the demon. But I don't know its name — that would be in the official report. There's a weekly summary online."

449

"Fine," said Rameau, clicking at the computer. He swiveled it towards Ric and handed over the mouse. "Let's find out two useful things. It's good for the digestion."

Ric typed in the factory's address, clicking through to the Arcana section. He searched by date, and then by area. "There isn't a record in the demon database."

"Who files them?"

"The attending exorcist. That would have been Milicent Pasqueflower." The only report under Milicent's name was from the wrong end of town. Ric found his own report, scanned in from a departmental form, but the space for 'attending exorcist' was illegible. "This doesn't make any sense. I know we had an exorcist. Crap! Excuse me." He rubbed his eyes. "My memory's been pants ever since — that's not important."

"Could you have forgotten something that major?"

"No. I just don't remember things that happen right before I go to sleep. I'm on a dreamcatcher."

"Ah. How do you compensate?"

"I use a steno pad," Ric said, pulling out his little notebook. He riffled the pages. "It must have been going bad for a while," he said, surprised at how much was unreadable.

"Let's try searching for this Magister Locullan," said Rameau, reclaiming the computer. "Hm. He comes up often enough at the University of Selanto, but all the links are dead."

"NUR," said Ric. "Sorry, in-joke." He frowned at the floor. "How can I not remember that? It was first thing in the morning. We had the girl on the

450

lawn, with the sorcerer," he said, closing his eyes. "Derek was scouting the house. I was with the patrolman, waiting for the ambulance. Then it pulled in and … the driver was a guy, twenties, dark hair and a nose ring. Shotgun was a woman, forties. Exorcist was — I can't see it! I see the ambulance, the driver, but I can't see the exorcist! What the hell's wrong with me?"

"Go on."

"We're doing the rite — I still can't see the exorcist. Now we're letting down the pentacle, and there's a summons on the girl's forehead, half wiped away. The exorcist has to have done that, but they're not supposed to. You never touch the possessed. That must be it!" Ric said. A wave of cold went through him, nausea and a freezing sweat racing after it. "The demon took the exorcist, and I've forgotten it. Because of — I have issues with possession. That's why the Chief wouldn't let me work the rest of the case. Crap." He clenched his fists in his hair, fighting shame. "Useless!"

"The Bright Lady doesn't think so," Rameau said gently. "She seems to want you on this case."

Ric stared at the desk surface. His thoughts crept, in first gear. "I'll call my partner," he said at last. "He's the one with the memory."

Derek picked up on the first ring. "Ric! Where are you?"

"Rameau's church. Where are you?"

"Still in the cafeteria, waiting for Ligalla. I think I can see — gold flame on the steeple, right?"

"Right. Listen, Derek. The Locullan case — who was exorcist on it?"

"Porter."

"Porter's SIO. He's no exorcist."

"Sorry," said Derek. "What'd you want to know again?"

"Who was the exorcist?"

Silence.

"Did you hear me?"

"No, you keep cutting out."

"Exorcist, who was the exorcist?"

"What?"

Ric had his pad on the table. He paged through it, looking for a pattern in the parts he could read. "Derek, why are we here in Osyth?"

"To help get Endamos back."

"Why us?"

"Why not? We're as much use as anyone else."

Speak for yourself, Ric thought. "Fair enough," was what he said. "Do me a favor — write me out a timeline of what we did yesterday?"

"All right, but you better see a sorcerer if this is getting worse."

"I won't know how much worse it's getting until I compare your timeline to what I remember." Derek made worried noises. "You're right, this connection's bad," said Ric. "I'll be back by noon. Talk to you then."

"That didn't sound like a productive conversation," Rameau said, looking shrewdly across the desk.

"No. But it could just have been the connection."

"This place has the best reception in the city," said Rameau. He turned the computer back and clicked at its keyboard. Ric watched and thought about hands. The exorcist's hands, wiping that mark

452

off the girl's forehead. He could almost see them, or was he making it up? Pale hands, male or female, coming out of maroon sleeves. There was something embroidered on that robe in the same color. Curly dark hair. Ric saw the hands again, holding onto someone's wrist. Only now the red wasn't robes, it was blood. He jerked.

"It's not just my memory! If a demon had taken an exorcist, it would have been all over the weekly report! It would even have made the news over here."

"Hm. That makes sense."

"There was an exorcism, and an exorcist. I filed the paperwork on it. And I wouldn't be walking around with a broken transcriber!" He flipped the notebook around. "It's like a copybook. Until this sentence — that's not a random malfunction, dammit, it's blacked out! — and this one! It looks like government evidence. Something's messing with my memory, and my report, and my notebook. And my cell phone." Ric stood up. "I don't like being messed with."

It was only ten when Ric got back to the Public Health building. Instead of calling Derek he went straight to the fourth floor, where the receptionist recognized him.

"Inspector. I was just thinking about you, wonder why?" He frowned, obviously racking his memory, which was the last thing Ric wanted to watch. "Oh, well," the man said, giving up. "How ya doing?

"Not so good," said Ric. "Listen, what kind of memory work do you do for witnesses?"

"Depends. We have psychics, if the memories aren't clear enough to work with a facial reconstruction program. Why?"

"There's someone I need to remember," said Ric.

"Okay. Josephson in the back room doesn't have anybody with him."

Ric followed directions through the busy space, feeling homesick for his own desk at the factory. Josephson was a white-haired man with jowls. His office smelled of chicken soup. "Yeah," he said, rocking back in an old-fashioned wooden desk chair, "the desk called. You need to remember somethin'."

"An exorcism I was in a few days ago."

"Mm-hm. Just normal touch-up or memory loss?"

"Loss," said Ric. "I'm on a dream-catcher."

"Hokay," said Josephson. "Have a seat. Put your hands here." He held his own hands out palms up, surprising Ric, who had expected a computer pad.

"Uh — how's this work?" he asked, gingerly placing his hands on Josephson's warm, dry palms.

"I pick up stuff outa your mind, and throw it up on the screen," Josephson said, jerking his head toward the computer. "I'm goin' to have my eyes closed, so you'll have to watch the screen. When you see somethin' you want to save, say 'now.' Got it?"

"Yeah … but my problem is that I'm not thinking about the things I want to remember."

"You're thinkin' about everythin' all the time. Memory loss doesn't mean t'isn't there, just you can't pick it outa the noise. Now, gimme what you do remember about it."

Ric tried to obey. It was embarrassing, how short the fragments of sequential memory were when they flashed up onto the computer screen. They were mixed in with all kinds of other stuff. The vampire Queen reappeared too often. So did the demon that had possessed him, and the one he'd seen in the pentarium, and memories of sitting in that golden room looking at someone blurry in the center of the circle. There were also flashes of an airplane interior, and then something more useful — the hands in the red robe, with blood running down them. "Now!" Ric blurted out, and a number '1' appeared in the bottom of the screen.

As if he'd given it a clue about what to show him, the computer put up less garbage and more good stuff. Now he saw Locullan's house, lawn, and driveway. He saw the little girl and the ambulance driver. Derek drawing something on the driveway behind the ambulance. The patrolman with his hat full of power crystals. A magician sitting bump on the ground, his face gray. The red robe again, rippling like water in front of him as he raced across the lawn. An exorcism candle. The hands, wiping something off the girl's forehead. "Hell. I mean 'now'!" Something came loose inside Ric's head with a pop, and the man in the red robe turned around. He was pale, with green shadows under his eyes. His mustache rippled in the summer breeze. He was in the chief's office, on the plane, in the center of the pentarium. "Now, now, now." He was standing in the pentarium now, and his eyes were black as he said something that made Ric's head hurt so much that he jerked his hands back to press his throbbing temples. "Now," he groaned, pushing on his eyes. "Now, now –"

"No point," said Josephson. "That's it."

"I'm going to –" Ric didn't need to finish the sentence. Josephson handed him a wastebasket, and he used it. Afterward, he felt a lot better.

"We got a buncha images," Josephson said, scrolling down the computer. "Same fella in all of 'em. Red robe –" his voice trailed off. "What're you lookin' for again?"

"I found it," Ric said hastily. "Let me copy those. Do you have a stick I can borrow?" He dug in his pockets, as if a data stick would have magically appeared there, but all that came to hand was his pad. He riffled its pages. A lot was still blurry, but he could read the last words he had heard in the pentarium: "You never met me. I never even existed."

Ric stared at the words for a moment. Then Josephson spoke. "Did you want this?" He held up a stick drive with 'Osyth Public Health' on it in orange letters.

"Oh! Yeah."

"Fine," said Josephson, handed him the stick, and turned back to his computer. Ric thought the man was going to save the files for him, but Josephson paid him no attention as he stood there with the stick in his hand, feeling foolish.

"Um — could I save those files?"

"Who's stoppin' you?"

"They're on your computer."

"What?"

"You just did a reading for me," said Ric. "Don't you remember?"

"Get out."

"Yes, you did. There." Ric's heart raced until he found the images in a minimized window. He sighed out loud, and dragged them over to the stick. "There." He opened the files on the stick, making sure they were there before he pulled it out.

"I'll be dipped," said Josephson, peering at the screen. His amazement faded before Ric's eyes, though. He closed the window and went back to whatever form he had been working on; then he swiveled his chair back into the position it had been in when Ric first saw him. "Yeah? Can I do something for you?"

Ric opened his mouth and shut it again. "Who do I see to put out an APB?" he asked.

"Morgan. Third desk over."

"Thanks," Ric said, and left.

"He's from Selanto," Ric said, waving the data stick to show Morgan he was legit. "Missing person."

"Really? We get their alerts." Morgan looked worried. Maybe he always looked worried. He had very black hair and very dark eyes, their outside edges drooping.

"They can't remember him. He's cast a charm on himself," said Ric.

"Magician, huh? How'd it miss you?"

Ric shot his sleeve to show part of the glyph on his arm. "I'm all marked up — treatment for a possession. He didn't count on that. It makes me the only witness, though."

"Oh." Morgan still looked dubious, but he plugged Ric's data stick into his computer. The man in the red robe looked at them from the screen, half-asleep and supercilious. "He's not very memorable," Morgan admitted. He turned his chair away from the computer and shut his eyes, as if testing. When he opened them, he looked as if he'd never seen Ric before.

"I told you so," Ric said.

"Told me what?"

"I told you that guy –" Ric pointed to the screen "— had a forgetting charm on him. Told you ten seconds ago, and you've already forgotten what I'm here about."

"Damn," said Morgan. "This is a joke, right?"

"No joke," said Ric, pulling out his badge. "How do you put out an APB on someone nobody can remember?"

Morgan frowned. "Does that charm work on the arcana?"

Ric considered it. "I don't know. Why?"

"What?"

"The APB on someone people can't remember. What do the arcana have to do with APBs?"

"Oh! Yeah. The door-imps might spot him. They all talk to one another — and if they spot someone, they can trap him."

"Sweet!" Ric said, grinning. "How do you get them to cooperate? Door-imps work for the door owner."

"Yeah, but registered imps work for us as well. It's illegal to have an unregistered imp in Osyth."

"How'd you get that law passed?"

Morgan grinned, this time. "Dunno; it was before my time. It's sweet, though. I'll send this out on the network, and if he walks past an imp we'll know it."

"What if they forget him as fast as we do?"

"Forget who?"

"Never mind," said Ric. "Can you set incoming to copy to my e-mail?"

"Sure. What's his handle?" Morgan asked, turning back to the computer. Like Josephson, he closed the picture without seeming to notice it.

"I don't know."

Morgan had to be reminded what he was doing twice more before he finished. "That's it," he said, as he hit 'send.'"How can door-imps get e-mail?" Ric asked.

"Wireless."

"O-kay," said Ric. "Thanks."

Half remembering was almost worse than remembering nothing at all. It was like being half-through a sneeze; if Ric didn't move he was going to do something unwise, so he trotted along an institutional yellow corridor toward the stairwell door. All kinds of charms were stamped on it, over the handle. Ric stopped in his tracks.

When had he last stood like this, looking at charms and hoping they'd hold? Monday, day before yesterday, in the pentarium. He seized on the memory. They'd come over to look at it, and Magister Cinea had taken them in. Cinea. Tall, elegant older guy in a stupid blue smock. Office full of scrolls. Someone had watched those scrolls, like a cat about to pounce on the tassels. Ric stalked his own thoughts, a step at a time. Cinea had an office.

The office had a computer. Magister — Whin, her name was. She pushed Cinea away from his computer as if they were old friends. She typed something in. Cinea turned the computer around, and there were the hands again, over part of the screen...

He read through Derek's timeline of yesterday. Two o'clock was when they had met in Magister Cinea's office and waited for the rest of the magicians. He could picture them from their names, which was a relief; Whin, Regan, Inos, Torecki, Navanax, Vinca, Pim, Klimt, Hoth. But he couldn't remember which of them had laid hands on Cinea's computer screen, or why. He remembered the pentarium locker room, the shower, and Torecki asking about his glyphs.

Whin had done something in the locker room. She'd made wards. What was that about? She'd done two sets, one with Endamos's ring and one with — what? Ligalla had put something around her neck. The Endamos wards, those made sense. That's how they had called him back. Ric could remember him appearing in the middle of the circle and falling into Cinea's chair — why? Wasn't there already a chair in the center of the circle? He remembered Endamos' face blurring, and his coming together again. He even remembered what it felt like, to have someone come together in his arms. His shoulders remembered how the weight changed, second to second. His skin remembered how loose that body felt, as if the man's clothes held nothing but broken pieces, more liquid than flesh ... Ric's stomach twisted, but then his arms remembered how bone reformed itself, straight and

460

strong, and muscle formed solid over it, and skin, wonderful skin, held it all tight together in the marvel of a whole body.

He looked away from the paper, blinking. *I can't know how that felt,* he thought. *I never held Endamos.* Cinea had held Endamos; Ric saw them clearly in his memories. But Ric's arms didn't care what he thought. They knew what they knew.

***

One of the best things about drinking Fire was the lack of hangover the next morning. The opposite of hangover, in fact. Russell was still floating as he walked in to work. The floating feeling survived hallway encounters with his two most prickly faculty, and he indulged himself by creating twice as many sunbeams as usual in his office.

"Wow!" Teddy Whin said, looking at the shafts of light and the rainbows cast by his crystal window-wards. "You're in a good mood!"

"I am," Russell said. "What can I do for you?"

"Something's wrong with the e-mail."

Russell felt campus e-mail was not his responsibility, but to be fair, he had bothered Warren about many less controllable problems. "I'll get right on that," he said, "as soon as I have raised the average faculty member's IQ for Linus, made the Dean of Students like Patsy, and stopped the rain."

"The rain has stopped," Teddy informed him, bouncing into his office as if she'd had eight cups of coffee. "That's one out of three."

"Do you really think I can fix your e-mail?"

"No, but you can remind me what was in it. It's the one Rho sent me about that guy pushing the unused potential theory of magic. What's his name again?" Russell must have looked as blank as he felt, but fortunately Teddy didn't notice. Her glance fell onto his wastebasket. "There it is! I knew I wrote it down somewhere." The paper she retrieved was in Russell's handwriting, though. It bore some scribbled-out words, and then 'Gordon K. Remen of U. Kasidora at Sterne,' and then some more scribbled-out words. Russell squinted at the scribbling, but since he had both written and scribbled in red marker there was no hope of seeing what had been underneath. "Thanks, can I take this?" said Teddy.

"Sure. I don't remember writing it."

"We had a big day," she consoled him. "Make sure you look up the headlines! Besides, forgetting you wrote it is not half as weird as my never looking at that theory. Did you ever know me to ignore a major theory?"

"I didn't think about it either," Russell said slowly, searching his memory. "That is strange, isn't it."

"It's not like we give a rat's ass about what Chancellor Spurges decreed," said Teddy.

"No. I'm sure somebody's studying it — no?"

She was shaking her head so vigorously that her curls trembled. "Not a one. It's like we've all been brainwashed, or something. Don't you have that feeling that you're coming out of a haze?"

"Um, not particularly," said Russell.

"I do. Rescuing people is definitely good for my energy level," said Teddy, preparing to bounce out of his office.

"So what are you going to do?"

"Call up this Gordon K. Remen."

"More power to you," said Russell. "I, on the other hand, will try to make the Dean of Students stop hindering Patsy in her labors."

He dealt in a masterful fashion with the Dean of Students, answered six student emails, deleted a bunch of incomprehensible, static-filled voice mails, and drafted a tactful but to-the-point complaint about the latter to the brownies at the Academy's technology help desk. Then he indulged himself with five minutes' luxuriating in the headlines, until his phone rang again.

"Russell Cinea here," he answered expansively.

"Russell," said the Dean's voice.

"Yes?" Russell leaned back at his desk, grinning into the phone. Rescued an exorcist, didn't we? Deny us that line now, I dare you. *News reports layered over one another on his computer screen.* Demonology Department at Osyth Cleans Up After Botched Selanto Exorcism, *said the top one.*

"You're having a big week," the Dean said.

"Three days," Russell corrected. "Hard to believe. I'm not used to the fast pace of administrative life."

Then the Dean said the first thing worth listening to in Russell's experience of him. "Perhaps you should get used to it. I'm emailing you a scan of the Departmental Year in Review Form. Have a look. I can hold."

Russell opened the attachment and skimmed it with a sinking feeling. "It's accurate, as far as it goes," he said. But he was thinking about the time fifteen years ago when Warren had been in hospital for depression. This Dean didn't know about that, of course. "A bit negative, but that's how we all feel at the end of spring semester. If you want happy talk, you should make these things due in fall."

"Warren's been chair a long time."

"I'm not taking someone's job behind his back!" Russell declared.

"Then we'll talk about it when he's back. Just start thinking about it. He can't go on forever," said the Dean.

Russell's good mood was almost completely gone when he hung up the phone, and it should have been completely gone. There shouldn't have been this trace of self-congratulation, this subterranean confidence that he would indeed do a better job as Department Chair than Warren did, this glow at the Dean's noticing his superiority after only three days … "Drat!" he said. He pounded a fist on his knee in righteous indignation slightly marred by the knowledge that Warren would be grateful to anyone who took over as chair. "I don't do things like that," Russell declared, even more righteously and louder, but he still had that nasty feeling of guilt mixed with conceit. It lingered like the taste of something rotten. "Pompous ass!" he said to himself, pounding his knee in a more punitive fashion, and felt a little better.

Still, he re-read the report. *'Soul-less faculty are as effective on interdisciplinary committees as normal faculty.' 'A second way to destroy*

464

employees' talents.' He could hear these phrases in Warren's voice, an eerie feeling since he knew Warren would never have voiced them. Then he heard something else in Warren's voice, this time an authentic memory from the morning that form had been filed. *'A demon fed on me in my office,'* he had said, and then he had described faculty duties vividly enough to scare Nezumia.

Russell froze. New depths opened within him as he remembered Warren's mood on that last morning of invocation. None of them had taken it that seriously. None of them had known Xiphister was stalking Warren.

The phone rang again, making him jump. *Damn!* "Russell Cinea here," he said into it, far more sweetly than he felt.

"Russell dear! It's Bosie."

"Bosie! Did you talk to Warren yesterday?"

"Why, no, dear. That's why I'm calling. I didn't hear a thing from him. That sounds rather foolish, doesn't it, to be calling about nothing," said Bosie, "but people our age know that nothing is the most worrisome thing of all, don't we, and I remembered you had been concerned about that demon following him. Not that Warren is in any danger from a demon, any more than you are, but I thought it was only honest to tell you about it. I try to always admit when I've been wrong and someone else has been right."

Russell's guilt grew with every word, until it seemed to grow right out of his body. He stood as if guilt was lifting him up by the scruff of his neck. "Did you have any phone messages?" *Like the ones I deleted...*

465

"Only static," said Bosie. "Oh! You're thinking — I can't see why demons would interfere with cell phones. They've never had any trouble in the Magic Building, have they?"

"No, you're right," Russell said absently, for she'd put an idea into his mind that felt like a sunburst of hope and absolution. He hadn't checked for messages on his cell phone! Lilian would surely have tried there, as well. "They probably just got back too late to call you last night. I'm sure you'll hear from her today," he said. "Let me know as soon as you do."

"Well, of course I will," said Bosie. "You can be sure that if I turn out to be right after all, I will call to gloat. Fair is fair."

Russell agreed with this, saying whatever would make her shut up as he dug through his pockets for the phone.

Three messages, all left in the wee hours when Russell's phone had been off. All from the same unknown number, and all lost in static. Russell listened to them four times over, sometimes on loudspeaker and sometimes with the phone pressed to one ear and a finger in the other, before he gave up. Was it even a woman's voice? He could convince himself it was. He could make himself sure it was Lilian with one listening, and then be just as sure it was Warren's voice on the next. He called back, but got only an out-of-service message.

"Damn," he said, looking at the phone's imperturbable face. The floating feeling was completely gone, now, and the headlines on his computer could have been about a completely different, happier department.

For a moment, Russell felt a physical thrill. Then he realized it was his cell phone, set on 'vibrate' in his pocket. It was Bosie. "Any news?"

"Well, dear, it's odd but not really concerning," said Bosie. "I did get a message from Lilian. It must have been delayed somehow; my system says it was sent last night, but I promise there was nothing there when I called you a minute ago. It was very static-y, though. And it sounds as if they're having a fine time."

"Oh, good. What exactly did she say?"

"I couldn't understand much of what she said, I have to admit. And it's so unlike either of them, but there, you never can say what people will get up to on vacation, can you. She said they were hanging around with goblins and hipsters."

The sunbeams on his walls and ceiling mocked him. One flashed into his eyes, and Russell felt as if the flash hit his brain and jarred it into motion. He leapt up.

Teddy was hunched over her computer, in her dark cluttered cave of an office. It reeked of incense. She hardly looked up when Russell rapped on the doorframe.

"Remember what we were talking about last night?" he asked, trying to keep his voice calm. "About summoning Xiphister before it can bother Warren?"

"What — oh, yeah! Sure!"

"We'll do it today. You're in charge of getting the circle together."

Chapter 34
The Candidate

They were a full thirteen in the pentarium, with only a few *hours' notice*. That was how many people would drop everything to face a man-eater for Warren. Russell had actually been able to create an A team and a B team, and had offended Linus by putting him on the B team. If nothing else went right, that would be a crumb of comfort. But right now, Russell was looking around the pentarium, for the second time in two days, at the strongest group of magicians he had ever directed. Half the demonology department was there, along with the best sorcerers from Public Health, Vinca and Bill Navanax from Alchemy, and Inos Galder.

"Twice in one week," said Navanax, catching Russell's eye. "I should have a joint appointment."

"The boundaries are breaking down, aren't they. I have three wizards on the B team."

Navanax grinned. "The what?"

"Don't repeat that," Russell said hastily.

"Oh, I will."

"Ready," Teddy called from her side of the circle.

Cham nodded confirmation from the other side.

"All right," Russell said, and felt them come to attention. "You'll do the basic invocation and then let me call Xiphister itself. There's no point anybody else making an enemy of it." *Warren inside that thing* — he shook it off. Perhaps, tomorrow, Russell would be an aging magician who had taken on more than he could handle. Perhaps, tomorrow, he would be mourning a friend. Today he was the lightmaker, the exorcist-rescuer, the Acting Department Head, and any demon must come at his call.

The invocation rose through the golden room. Russell's chant cut across it like a knife opening a door into the netherworld, a door the demon stepped through as casually as if it had come a thousand times.

It looked different. Its eyes were more human, its face more creased. Its expression was less predatory, more distracted. "What can I do for you?" it asked, looking around the circle, and it did not seem to be mocking them.

"Did you eat Warren Oldham?"

"Oldham? The one with the book. Oh, yes."

"We want him back."

Xiphister grinned, looking more like itself. "He is better off in my care than in yours, I think. And it is hardly my place to solve your personnel problems. Or perhaps it is?" It turned, looking carefully at everyone in the circle. "You have changed your coven. These are not all demonologists."

"These are all people who want Warren back," Russell said. "Alchemy, sorcery, wizardry — all the magicians of Osyth will be your enemies, if you keep one of our own."

The demon nodded. "Perhaps we can find a solution that allows all of us to use our talents. I understood you were hiring," it said, "but I had thought only demonologists need apply." It reached deep into its chest and pulled out a scroll tied with unpleasantly fleshy-looking pink twine. "My credentials," it said gravely, holding them out towards Russell. He didn't move, so the demon unrolled its scroll before his unfriendly eyes. Russell read the first few centimeters. *Magisters in Demonology from Selanto,* he read. *Thesis topic: mechanism of flesh-based binding. Magisters of Magic from Kasidora: semantic structure of charms. Magisters of Magic, Selanto: Role of nuclear decay in ley-line fluctuations. Certificate of Proficiency in Enchantment* — now that, that was ridiculous.

"You didn't earn these degrees," he accused. His eyes had skipped downward even as he spoke, and each of the last few lines visible fell into his heart like lead. *Magisters of Wizardry, Osyth: Excavation into ley-lines, Geography of the infernal realms. Head, Department of Demonology at Osyth. Certified Public Scryer. First Prize Preserves, Minich District Fair.*

"Parts of me did," said the demon Xiphister, unwinding the next section of the scroll. "My teaching experience. Grants. Publications."

"We hire individual scholars here!" said Russell. "Not slaveholders."

"Perhaps that should be my area of specialty," the demon said thoughtfully. It looked over Russell's head, but its focus was obviously on something going on inside itself. Any faculty administrator, even an Acting Chair, knew that expression. "The meaning and nature of individuality … do two who have been intimately connected for years truly remain separate individuals? In what does this individuality reside?"

470

Russell felt the blood drain out of his face. He didn't even know why at first, until he shut his eyes and remembered the sight of his old friend's face looking out of the demon's chest, the sound of that scream. If he ever saw Warren so entrapped, becoming part of the monster that held him — "No!" he cried, opening his eyes. "Give him back! Let him choose for himself what he wants to become, or face us all united against you."

He scanned the circle and realized, with a nasty shock, that some of his faculty looked more intrigued than valiant. Teddy, especially, had the chewing-it-over face that Russell had thought only he, among the demonologists, could provoke.

"Warren's taken care of all of us," he said firmly, rallying the troops, "and we'll take care of him. If you have any interest in working with us, you'll free him and all the other prisoners inside you. Until you've done that, we're enemies. And I will do everything in my power —" (*as Acting Chair of Demonology*, said a sarcastic part of himself) "— to destroy you."

Xiphister nodded as if this were the way most of its conversations went. "Very well," it said, rolling its scroll back up. "What would you accept as evidence that my relationship with those I contain is one of mutual consent?"

"Let them out and see if they go back in," said Russell. "Go ahead. Show me."

"Would you not claim I was controlling them?" Xiphister waved the appendage holding the scroll in a dismissive manner. "No matter. I have something you need, and you have nothing that more than mildly interests me. And as I said, your personnel

471

problems are not my concern. I shall return to the business from which you distracted me." It bowed, and in the act of bowing it was gone. But it left the scroll behind, and Russell saw Teddy look at it with interest too eager for his peace of mind.

The B team was waiting in the pentarium shower room. None of them said a word as Russell and the A team filed back in, Teddy Whin in the rear carrying Xiphister's scroll. They all looked at Russell, their faces so many blurred ovals in the steamy room. Russell opened his mouth and found he couldn't speak. He shut his eyes instead, and turned to press his burning face against the cool tile. Someone put a hand on his shoulder. That would be Vinca. None of the others would know to do that. None of them would dare. But Russell couldn't stand and weep. He was Acting Chair; though he almost sobbed aloud at the thought … he straightened and turned back to the roomful of magicians.

"It has Warren," he said, fighting to keep his voice steady. "I believe it also has Lilian. It left a list —"

"A list?" Russell couldn't tell who spoke, nor did he care. The question had turned their attention from him to Teddy Whin, and that was a blessing. So was the habit that made Russell take off his gown and step into the shower. The rest of the A team followed him, except for Teddy who would not leave the demon's scroll to the mercies of the B team. She waited until Russell had dried and dressed, then handed it to him before heading in for her shower.

He had recovered himself during his minutes under the water, and now he could see the B team clearly. They were not people he knew well, with the exception of Linus — Russell was careful not to let his gaze, or his thoughts, linger on Linus. Yet something hot began to form inside him, and it was not entirely unpleasant. He would think about Linus later.

"The demonology department will meet at nine tomorrow morning," he said. "Bring your best ideas."

"Demonologists only, or are others allowed?" asked Vinca.

"Of course. Anyone willing to help is welcome. Anders, will you —"

"I'll call them," said Anders. "Of course."

There was too much quiet in the room; a withholding-comment kind of quiet. None of them thought Russell could do anything in tomorrow's meeting except start the process of replacing Warren, but nobody except Linus would be so tactless as to say so. And Russell did not want to speak to Linus. "Tomorrow," he said hastily, handed the scroll back to the still-damp Teddy, and pulled on his coat. He left so quickly he had no time to think about where he meant to go.

Habit should have taken him to his office, but instead he left the stairwell at the ground floor and walked out into the sweet-smelling glow of late afternoon. The shock of its beauty stopped him in his tracks. Only yesterday, they had been drinking Fire in triumph! He looked at slanting, golden light that Warren might never see again. Grief was a physical pain, through his chest from shoulder to

473

shoulder. It made him gasp. *And Bosie*, he thought, *I'll have to call Bosie* — the thought almost made him double over.

"Russell?" a voice asked, and turning, Russell saw Susan Teale standing beside the door, still in her blue gown. His voice failed him. He gasped again. "It'll be all right," she said, and her hand was on his arm, her arm around his shoulder. Trying not to cry hurt more than grief, Russell discovered. Yet her arms around him were some comfort. So gently, so kindly, she led him into the shelter of the spruce trees, where an Acting Department Chair could weep unobserved.

474

Chapter 35
Lost and Found

Ric was dismayed to find that Magister Endamos had a square face and thick white hair. He hadn't realized until that moment that he wanted Endamos to turn out to be the person he had forgotten. *Well, he's not,* he told himself. *He's still the man we're supposed to take back to Selanto.* Perhaps Endamos knew who the dark-haired man in the red robe was. Perhaps he'd tell them, on the flight back. When Ric saw him, however, he was asleep with a bundle of charms hanging from the pole beside his bed.

"They say he's ready to travel?" Ric asked Derek, looking askance at the charms.

"That's what they say."

"What's all the jewelry for, then?"

"Not a clue. I hope they're sending someone who knows how to work it."

"He'll be off those by noon," said the nurse at the nearest station. "They're diagnostic and enteral translocation charms. Feeding, water."

"Can't he eat?" Derek asked.

She grinned, showing a gap in her front teeth. "He's been eating like a starving griffin. Plus ET feeding and rehydration. Exorcists need a lot of refueling, but he'll be ready to go this afternoon, I promise."

Ric and Derek wandered the hospital halls until they found an exit. Then they stood around on the sidewalk. Ric had a cigarette.

475

"Guess that's it, then," he said. "Hop the Chief Exorcist's plane back to Selanto, turn Endamos over to the authorities, and we'll be back on the streets tomorrow."

Derek looked at him. "Not happy."

Ric shook his head before he thought about it. "Nah — Yeah, I guess. We leave here and I'm another ocean away from finding the guy I forgot about. Or maybe not. Guess I remember more about him from Selanto than from here."

"He'll be fine," Derek said. "You heard the nurse."

Ric wanted to put his fist through something. Through Derek, if it would make the man hear him! But there was no point. *Nobody remembers that guy except me,* he thought. *Good thing they can't hear me talk about him, or they'd think I was crazy. I'd think I was crazy.* Whoever wiped the dark-haired guy out of the world's memory had made a mistake, hadn't he? Because every time Derek acted like this, Ric got more convinced there was something real going on.

"We ought to check on the exorcist that took care of that little girl," he said now, just to make himself feel better. "You know, the tall young guy with the mustache and the red robe. The one who wiped the summons off her forehead."

Derek stood there staring straight ahead, for almost a minute. Then he blinked and re-set. "He'll be fine," he said. "You heard the nurse."

Just like that, Ric wasn't mad at him anymore. He was mad at whoever'd done this. *When I find the slag that screwed with my partner's brain, I'm going to rip his lungs out.* "C'mon," he said. "Let's

476

get lunch, before we have to head out." He turned, and a man stood up from where he must have been sitting when they came out, on the retaining wall next to the parking lot.

The man was a few inches taller than Derek, slight, with something frail about him. The green shadows around his eyes, Ric guessed. Curly brown hair floated out from his head in a short halo. A curly mustache perched like a butterfly on his upper lip; he had one of those pointy Selanto chins, a tan, and a black bruise on one cheek. He was clad from the waist down in expensive tailored trousers and glossy shoes, from the waist up in a bloodstained dress shirt and a torn vest. But his eyes were black, like holes cut in his head. Ric couldn't believe there was a person in there.

"I've been looking for you," the man said. An ache started in Ric's head, right behind his eyes. He squeezed them shut, and got the feeling he was forgetting something — he reopened them fast, and a man in a bloodstained shirt was standing in front of him. *This is him,* Ric told himself, but it didn't strike in. He felt drugged, thinking on the surface. As soon as he blinked, he would forget that this man was — *who?*

Derek walked past the man as if he hadn't seen anything, and just like that Ric was full of anger, as if it had been waiting inside him, growing bigger and stronger, for years. He stepped forward and took the strange man's shirtfront in his fist.

"What the hell have you done to us?" he yelled. That was better. Ric felt less fuzzy by the minute. He remembered a time when he'd been competent. He'd trusted himself to do whatever this man

477

needed. Even if it meant — the thought slipped, but it was a different slip, an I-don't-want-to-know-it slip. "What did you do?" he yelled again, to avoid that thought.

"Something stupid," said the man in the bloodstained shirt.

Derek couldn't believe any of it, and neither could Ric when he wasn't looking at the man. Gerald, that was his name. Gerald Manley. He wasn't on the internet, and wasn't that odd enough in itself? Everybody was on the internet.

But they could both believe the files they found on Derek's phone, the ones the Chief had sent them when they left Selanto on this errand. The ones that confirmed what Ric hadn't wanted to remember. *That's always the way. The bad crap turns out to be true.*

"The chief exorcist was going crazy," he said. "Do you remember reading this?"

"Yeah," Derek said. "Guess I set it aside when it turned out Rosemont wasn't with Endamos. Guess I was glad to." He scrolled down. Lots of parts blacked out, in this file. But not all of them. Not enough... Derek scrolled down past a section break, and a picture came up instead of text. A heraldic shield, with a crown sanguine and an unsheathed . Eight droplets fell from the sword's blade.

They held still for a minute.

"White Knights," Derek said.

"Yeah."

The report was dated two years ago. And its import was absolutely clear. *This was what I didn't want to remember,* Ric thought. *Nobody cast any spell. I made myself forget this.* He shut his eyes in shame. His face burned.

"We were supposed to kill him. If we found Rosemont with Endamos, we were supposed to kill him."

"Yeah," said Derek.

"And the guy in the bloodstained shirt —"

"Who?"

"He's part of this," said Ric. "I made myself forget about him, too. That means he's key."

Derek didn't answer.

Not going to touch that one, Ric thought. *Smart man.* "What do we do now?"

"Go back to Selanto. We didn't find Rosemont, did we?"

"No," Ric said. "But what if we did? If we knew where he was, would it be our duty to find him? Knowing this?"

"We weren't assigned —"

"I'm not asking you that," Ric said. "Tell me what you see. Tell me what you don't know."

Derek gave him a strange look, half-angry and half-desperate. He shut his eyes. His mustache drooped further than usual; there were bags under his eyes, and Ric had a horrible glimpse of what Derek would look like dead. Then Derek screwed his eyes tighter shut and drew down his eyebrows in a scowl, and the dead look went away. He rocked back and forth, slapped the side of his head as if to jar something loose, and then opened his eyes.

"We have to find Rosemont," he said. "He's on fire."

"What!"

479

"That's what I saw," Derek said miserably. "He was on fire. Just starting. But it's going to get worse, until it burns up — we have to find him." He wrapped his arms round his belly. "We have to find him!"

"All right," Ric said. "We'll fly back tonight and drop Endamos off in Selanto, and then we'll find Rosemont."

"How?"

"I have a — I have a snitch," Ric said. Making up a plausible story for the guy in the bloodstained shirt helped. Ric could half-believe the story himself. The guy — Gerald, that was it! — became possible. "Rosemont's working at the University of Kasidora extension in Sterne, under the name Gordon K. Remen. My snitch'll come back on the plane with us," Ric told Derek. "He can track Rosemont."

He stared at the phone Derek was still holding and the picture on its screen. White knights. And nobody would remember it. Nobody would admit it. *This is the end of us*, he thought, his chest so heavy that he couldn't imagine ever moving again. *We kill the chief exorcist, the most important person in the world. What's left for us after that? Show trial, if they let us live that long.*

"Promise me something. Blood oath."

They didn't have to actually shed blood, not between the two of them. An 'are-you-serious?' look was enough.

"Let me do it," Ric said. "Don't step in unless he takes me out."

Derek looked at him for longer than an oath usually took. The grey film that went along with

Seeing flickered in his pupils. Finally he nodded, but it didn't make Ric feel any better.

Chapter 36
Chairman's Holiday

Mama Simone could hardly breathe, her chest was so cold. *For heavens' sake,* she scolded herself, *you're inside this thing! How can being in the same room with it be worse than being inside it, head to tail?* But it was. She wanted to run out into the demon, to get away from being in the same room with the demon.

The demon Xiphister looked around the room. It examined every one of them, and then fixed on Warren, taking three steps toward him like a prowling animal. *He's just a little boy!* Mama Simone thought. She stood up, and so did Lilian. But the demon never took its eyes off Warren, and now Warren was standing as well.

"What do you want?" he asked in a scared little boy's voice.

"You are the one who brought all of this to my attention," said the demon. Its voice was just like its body: heavy, gray, with something dangerous lurking inside. "If you are so concerned with what people need, explain it to me. Begin with this structure."

"What?" Warren looked around. "This is — "

"A book," said the demon. "You made my book into this. Why?"

"It's a house," said Mama Simone. "Surely you've been in a house before?"

The demon looked at her, at last. *Not so unimportant now, am I?* she thought. Something touched her shoulder from behind and she started, then realized it was Lees' hand. *The nerve!* Yet she liked it.

"What is the significance of a house?" the demon asked her.

"It's where people live. Together. Where families live —"

"Social groups," Warren cut in, his voice urgent.

Mama Simone felt vexed and puzzled. *What was he afraid I'd say?*

Warren was going on, nervous as a mamma bird running away from a nest. "People live in social groups," he said. "We need each other's company."

"Ah," the demon said. It surveyed the room. "And places to sit down, I gather. Places to sleep."

"And eat," Arthur said, pointing down a side hallway which must lead to the kitchen. "Bathrooms. Would you like a tour?"

"I can see it from here," the demon said. "Why do you say people need these things? My people have survived without them."

"If that's all you cared about, you wouldn't be here now," Warren said. He was sounding much more confident. "You don't just want them to survive. You want them to thrive. Right?"

The demon considered this. "Perhaps," it admitted. "Very well. To thrive, humans need companionship. And for that, I infer solid form. Which would require these physical supports, such as food and water." It frowned. "This becomes a nuisance. What else?"

"Nature," Warren said firmly. "Landscape. Sunlight, weather."

"Freedom," Lilian said, startling Mama Simone.

"Moral worth," Lees said from behind Mama Simone, but she knew he was making fun of the whole conversation. Still, Locullan turned and glared at him. And now the demon was looking that way too, over her head as if she weren't even there.

"People need to be good for something," she said, not to be ignored — but as so often when people don't want to be ignored, she said more than she meant to. "They've got to have a purpose. To use their talents. They've got to matter to somebody." Tears welled up in her eyes, and then she wished people would stop staring.

"Health," Locullan said hoarsely, swinging back toward the demon. Had he thought of getting its eyes off her?

"Very well," said the demon, as if checking an internal list. "Anything else?"

What King Herrel said was in his own language and Mama Simone couldn't understand it. But it made Lees laugh. His hand shook where it pressed her shoulder. And that irritated her enough to dry her eyes. *Just a joke to him, the lout!*

"Love," Arthur was saying. "But that's asking for a lot, inside a demon."

"It's all asking a lot," said Lees. "A demon can't make any of that stuff. It doesn't even know what the words mean."

The demon gave him a long stare. *Easy for you to twit the thing!* Mama Simone thought. *What are you, a piece of soul? It can't rip you apart.* But the demon didn't rip anyone apart. It merely stepped back into the entry and opened the front door. It reached out into the gray place outside, and pulled something in.

"Begin with this one," it said. "Fix it." And it dropped a person on the living room carpet.

***

A girl! Warren thought. *A woman,* he corrected himself. *A small woman.* The huddled body was a woman in her twenties, with short black hair. He couldn't see her eyes, because she had them screwed tight shut. She was wearing a long black robe and had golden chains around her neck, golden cuffs around her thin wrists and ankles. A magician's robe, a magician's gold. The stuff one wore when invoking a demon. *A stupid woman,* Warren amended but did not bother saying.

He bent over and touched the woman's head. "Um — hello?"

"Move over," Lilian said, poking his shoulder. She sat down beside the woman, and Warren had a moment of *déjà vu*. When had she done this before? "You're all right," she said, putting a hand on the woman's shoulder. "You're in our house. I'm going to check and see if you're hurt." The woman didn't respond; after a moment's waiting, Lilian began to run one of the charms from the first-aid kit over her body. "Her hands are burned," she declared. "Sweetie, open your hands. I'll put something on them to make them better."

The woman still didn't respond, but neither did she resist when Lilian opened her hands — dirty

485

little hands, broken-nailed as if she had been trying to scratch her way out of a grave. She didn't react when Lilian put salve on the burned palms. Lilian knelt back and looked up at them. "I don't know what else to do," she said.

King Herrel knelt down beside her and took the woman's hands. He breathed on them and laid his own hands over them, palm to palm. Warren was entranced. This was what sorcery had been in the beginning — sympathetic magic, from one person to another.

"Is it fixed?" the demon said, from where it stood beside the door. "Are you ready for the next?"

"Fixed!" Lilian blazed up. "She's nothing like fixed! Look at her! She's catatonic! This woman needs a hospital!"

"Very well. What is a hospital?"

"She doesn't need you to build her a hospital," Warren said. "She needs you to send her to a human hospital, back in the physical world. She needs you to let her go." *Pointless.* He knew that closed-in, I'm-not-listening look from hundreds of faculty meetings and intro classes. The Gen Ed look, he called it. And indeed, the demon wasn't listening. It had pulled someone else into the hall, and this person was starting to scream. And then more, and more — people who huddled in lumps and had to be dragged or carried into the sitting-room, people who moaned and shrieked and wept. Until finally something came through the door upright, under its own control.

It was like nothing Warren had ever seen before: man-shaped, slender and graceful, with a long gray robe and great feathered wings. Its beauty was only slightly marred by its being on fire, outlined by a halo of blue-gold flame.

Eighteen. Warren had made a list, but it didn't have many names on it. 'Thin black-haired woman, magician's invoking robe, burned hands,' it read, and stuff like that. Few of the demon's captives had been coherent enough to give their names. Warren had only recognized one of them, besides Locullan — a Magister Dessennes from Selanto who had fought with him bitterly over the pentarium, but who thankfully showed no sign of recognizing the eight-year-old Warren.

"This is awful," Lilian said to him. "These poor people!"

"At least they're not screaming outside the house," said Warren. "We can do something for them."

"But nothing we do seems to matter! They don't need first aid. They need years of psychiatric treatment. That one guy –"

Warren knew which one she meant. The one trying to get out of the house, back into the demon stuff; he didn't like having a body. He tried to scratch it off his bones. *That's what could have happened to all of us,* Warren thought. *It still could.* "They're from all different eras, according to their clothes," he said, to change the topic. "The woman could be from any time in the last two hundred years."

"And that one on fire," said Lilian. "What's that?"

Warren could almost see the burning in the center of the pentarium, its wings half-raised and its

487

face earnest as it spoke to them out of the halo of flame around it — but not quite. "There's no *grue*," he said slowly, "but we're all inside a demon. I may be *grue*-d out. I think —" he stopped. There was no point in telling the burning thing that it was a demon. Who knew what it might do, if it decided to be evil?

"I just don't know," he said miserably.

Lili knelt down to put her arms around him, and he buried his face in her shoulder.

"Some vacation!" she cried. "What was I going to get you away from — demons, and magicians, and middle management? Hah! Some vacation!"

Warren thought he'd heard that before, as well, but he didn't know where.

Chapter 37
Interrupted Magic

The burning thing stood between the coffee table and the loveseat, while Grandfather prowled around it. Its wings stuck out so far that he had to detour out around the recliner.

"You don't appear to need any healing," he said.

The burning thing appeared to think this over. "I need to know myself," it said.

Grandfather grunted and took another turn around it. "Well, not a demon," he said. "No *grue* — right, boy?"

"There's no *grue*," Warren agreed. He stopped just before telling the burning thing that, *grue* or no *grue*, it was the most demon-y creature he had ever seen. "The mysteriosi, in Selanto," he said instead. "It looks like one of them."

Grandfather sniffed. He took another turn around the burning thing.

"What's a mysterioso?" it asked.

"They were supposed to be messengers of the gods," said Dad.

"Heroic," said Grandfather. "Swooping in to defend their followers from demons, and other nuisances."

The burning thing obviously liked this. It stood taller as Grandfather spoke.

Warren didn't believe for one minute that this was a mysterioso. It was a demon, and one he knew. He could almost see it in the center of the pentarium, its wings half-raised and its face mock-earnest as it spoke to them out of the halo of flame around it — but not quite. *I bet he knows it's a demon too*, he thought, looking at Grandfather. *He's just playing it.* But hadn't Warren been doing the same thing to Xiphister?

As someone who'd committed the same actions, Warren felt he lacked the moral high ground to criticize Grandfather. As a person who couldn't remember where he had seen the burning demon, he lacked confidence in his judgment. As a person who appeared eight years old, he lacked authority. So in the end, he said nothing. And that made him the person who noticed first when Xiphister reached into the room — without moving from its position in the entry — and picked up the woman in magician's robes by one shoulder.

"Hey!"

Xiphister did not bother answering Warren, or any of the other people who shouted at it. It carried the woman out through the door, not bothering with any nonsense like knobs or latches.

***

The Magic Building looked its best on summer mornings, when the sky was blue and the meadow separating it from the parking structure was dotted with buttercups and daisies. The sunlit sides of the building glowed white and slate-blue shadows outlining every door and window. The grass was dew-spangled, and even Russell's shadow wore a rainbow halo.

He had never loved all of this properly when it was his. But now he noted every splendid detail, because it was a gift. He was wrapping it all up in a package and handing it over to Warren and Lilian — every movement of the air, every bird song, every step of the stairs and the familiar, precious occupants of every office he passed — but the gift ended at his own office door. He was going to become the Evil Magician he'd been trained to be, after all, and an Evil Magician did not share his magical artifacts. Russell felt some dampening of the spirit as he surveyed said artifacts, but he choked it down and reached up to the very top of the honeycomb-like wooden scroll rack on his wall.

Up here the scrolls were not stored in fancy cases with tassels on their lids, but in cardboard packing tubes. A person not versed in the ways of Evil Magicians would have ignored them as unimportant, leftover documents from graduate school that were too rare to discard, but too insignificant to bother unpacking. A wiser person would have ignored them out of self-preservation. These scrolls needed no more protection than a cardboard tube provided.

What Russell pulled down now was obviously a mailing tube, with Russell's name and address written on the side in a jagged, sloping hand that neither experts, charms nor demons could have identified as his own. He had not needed to write in this hand for forty-one years, and seeing it now gave him a thrill of half dismay, half delight. He put his thumb over a blot at the end of the address and felt the scroll recognize him; still, he hesitated before he touched the plastic plug in the end of the tube, and held his breath at the instant his fingers closed on it. Nothing happened, and Russell exhaled as he pulled the end off the tube.

People took blood for granted nowadays. They said 'blood oath' as if it were a joke, made pentacles out of their own blood, saved it in blood roses, and bartered it to vampires. They treated it like an especially useful kind of ink, or wine. But there was another kind of blood, and that was life's blood.

It was obvious why nobody used it. If you drew a pentacle in your own life's blood you would never call a demon into that pentacle, because you would be lying dead beside it. Cast a love-charm with life's blood, and the subject would speak at your funeral. There was only one way to do magic with life's blood and survive, and that was to take it from someone else who shared your blood. This was why the dark magicians of antiquity had so few surviving family members. Russell felt, but was not sure, that it was the reason for quite a few letters of condolence he had written over the years to old acquaintances in Selanto. One didn't hint at anything of the sort, of course. But there was no denying that the person who gave Russell this charm had lost two children ... what would the ectoplasm in the hospital lab congeal into, if it were hovering over this scroll? No matter, the man was long dead. Russell unrolled the scroll in a businesslike manner that ill-befitted its contents, but that was part of being an Evil Magician, wasn't it?

The blood had turned brown with age, as had the outside of the scroll; it was mere paper, by no means the darkest of dark magic. Yet it tugged at things inside Russell. It was alive with the life that

492

had been given to write it, and longed to be spoken. "Not yet," he said, looking at the clock. It was seven-twelve. Almost two hours to plan, and then the department meeting, which would break his concentration. It would be afternoon before Russell would be ready to cast this spell in the pentarium. He would have to draw his own blood to set the lines, and write the linking symbols on both the floor and the scroll itself. Then he would need the summoning charm, to call Xiphister back to him. That might be easy. The demon would appear, expecting a job interview, and find itself trapped in Russell's web. Then the real battle would begin; the battle that would go on for the rest of his life.

He let the scroll snap shut again, and put it safely into its tube and the tube safely into its cubbyhole. When he stood back, his knees trembled and his mouth was dry. He took a deep breath, scolding himself, but it did no good. He was in no state to prepare the most important charm of his life. *Most important!* he jeered at the thought. *Most horrible, most miserable!* He looked around his office and love welled up inside him for all of it, from the silly ceiling lights with their gridded covers to the cross-shaped window through which he could see the mountains. He loved this desk, and this chair that he should have replaced a dozen years ago, and this armchair so many colleagues had sat in. He loved working with James and Teddy and Warren. What would he do, without Teddy bouncing into his office every day? Without light and warmth, color and friendship?

Stop! he told himself. *You got Warren into this. You talked him into becoming a demonologist. If*

493

you'd left him alone, he'd be head of Wizardry right now, with no greater problems than how to put up some building. You caused all of this. Payback's a bitch. But none of this tough talk made him feel any better. He finally turned to the last resort, the one he'd been keeping his mind away from for the last eight hours. He thought about Linus, and the thought rose up through his chest into his brain, hot and strong as hard liquor. There were things Linus deserved, and only an Evil Magician would be able to do them.

Russell strode into the Demonology Department meeting like the world's most powerful Evil Magician, because personal power really was the only payoff for becoming an Evil Magician — and why should he wait to enjoy it until he'd done the deed, bound the demon, and was paying the price? But nobody noticed his new attitude at all. They were too busy, he realized, ignoring one another.

The largest number were ignoring Linus, probably because they didn't want him to waste meeting time defending himself. Teddy, however, was far too preoccupied to bother with either Russell or Linus. She had the demon's scroll on the table in front of her, and was supremely important on the strength of it. Several of the department members were studiously ignoring her, therefore. People often felt that Teddy needed quelling.

Some people were ignoring Russell himself, he realized with a certain amount of pique. *Who's running this meeting?* He rapped on the table, but not everyone looked up. Anders Regan, for

494

instance, kept his gaze on the table, and Anders couldn't be blaming Russell for any of this … Vinca was looking at Russell, but with a grave, sad expression that was worse than not looking. Patsy Hoth gave Russell a warning look. Bill Navanax looked into space just over Russell's head as if, not being a member of the Demonology Department, he didn't have a right to point out the obvious. What was that all about? Russell rapped on the table again.

"The floor is open for suggestions," he said. "Let's list them first, no discussion at this point."

Uncomfortable silence ensued, during which Anders even more noticeably did not look at Russell and Vinca and Patsy even more noticeably looked at him. Teddy, bless her, leaned back in her chair and began ticking off suggestions on her fingers.

"We could bind the demon, or help someone from a country where demon-binding is legal to bind it. We could hire it and use the Academy's contractual charms against it. We could contact the magicians inside it and encourage them to rebel. We could use alchemy to take away its magic. We could send someone into it with a weapon. We could take over one of the magicians inside it and use him to destroy it."

Now everybody was looking at Teddy, even those who had thought she needed quelling. They probably felt that the expressions on their faces were quelling enough.

"Can you do all that?" asked Sorcerer Pim.

"No," said Linus, almost bursting with indignation. "It's the biggest load of nonsense I ever heard!" Since almost everybody was ignoring Linus, this statement had little effect.

"We are not at the evaluation stage yet," Russell said. "Next?"

"Could we enlist the local demons against it?" asked Sorcerer Pim. "They helped you get rid of the demon in Magister Oldham's grimoire, didn't they?"

"We might bribe it," said Will Harding. "Those fitness center privileges seem to be a hot item."

"Other faculty might have an opinion about that," Vinca said.

"We're not evaluating at this point," Russell said again.

"Sorry."

"Are the people inside the demon alive or dead?" asked Vinca. "If the latter, new options may open to us." He nodded at Susan and Necromancer Klimt.

Klimt began to twist his long fingers together. "If they're dead, I could perhaps turn their tissue into things," he admitted. "I'm not sure what kind of things would help us overpower the demon. Or how it would help the people inside it — if they're dead."

"We could try to contact them via a séance, if they are dead," Susan said reluctantly. "We have plenty of things belonging to Warren, for me to focus on." This cast a pall over the conversation. "Maybe we could send in something without a soul," she suggested, as if to make up for her last remark. "What happens if a demon engulfs a vampire? Does the demon have any influence over the vampire at all? What if we sent in an empty pig?"

Russell had been writing down all these ideas, and now looked around. "Any suggestions from Alchemy?" he asked, looking at Magister Vinca.

Vinca shook his head. "Alas, no. Anything we did would change the nature of demons in general, and proposals for changing the nature of demons would have to pass Guild approval," he said. "I fear our bureaucracy is designed expressly to prevent us from doing this sort of thing. Nor would those in disagreement with the Guild choose to make their stand on this issue."

"What about Arcane Arts?" asked Inos Galder, surprising everybody. "Representative magic? Influencing either the demon or those within it?"

Russell caught sidelong glances among the demonologists, most of whose ignorance about Arcane Arts was surpassed only by their disdain for it. He looked around, but nobody said anything more. "Very well," he said. "I will re-read the list of suggestions, and we will evaluate and prioritize them."

"Wait!" said Teddy. She bent over the demon's scroll like a dog on point.

"What?"

"Someone's just disappeared from this list," Teddy said. She shuffled through a pack of papers at her right hand. "Magister Amabeth Is-Halem, from Selanto. She was taken seventeen years ago. Her degrees were on this list when I came into the room, and they've just faded away." She held up the scroll to demonstrate the empty space on it, and looked around the group in growing impatience.

497

"She's not in the demon anymore! She's gotten out!"

***

Endamos lay in the bed Ric remembered as being full of blood. There was no blood in it at all, but that didn't make Ric feel any better. Nothing could make him feel better. He slumped in the window seat he had used when they flew from Selanto to Osyth and pretended to be asleep, while familiar feelings chased themselves in and out of holes in his memory.

I don't want to kill anyone, he thought. But the files on Derek's phone — what would happen to the world, if the Chief Exorcist switched sides? If he served the demons instead of the people? Ric didn't have any trouble remembering how it felt to have a demon inside himself. *The stuff I want to forget* — and that hadn't been a bad demon. There were far worse demons out there. If demons got an exorcist's power — that was why exorcists were never supposed to touch the possessed. The image of those pale hands wiping the summons off the girl's forehead flashed into his mind's eye, and sudden doubt seized Ric. *Whose hand was that? Was it Rosemont's, and that's how he got — no, it just happened a few days ago. Was it the guy in the shirt — Gerald? Is he the one the demon has control of? Then he'd be tricking me!* Ric sat up straight, his eyes jerking open, and saw Derek standing in the galley, doing something with a can. His heart stopped pounding. *Derek can't even see Gerald, and he said Rosemont was on fire.*

But now he was thinking, things got muddier by the minute. Perhaps Gerald was a demon, and he intended to destroy Rosemont. Perhaps the demon would leap from Gerald to Rosemont. Perhaps it was using Ric and Derek to get near Rosemont. But why would it need to do that? *Gerald's the only one who knows where Rosemont is. And nobody else can see Gerald.*

He doesn't need us to take him anywhere.

He looked at Derek. Derek finished whatever he was doing with the can, looked back, and nodded. *We have to find Rosemont,* Ric thought. *When we do, then I'll decide what I have to do. Arrest them both, and let the Chief sort it out!*

Relief surged through him, warm and solid. He closed his eyes again, and this time truly slept.

***

Teddy Whin held court in the conference room. Russell could call it nothing else. She had the scroll spread out on the table before her, and with her cell phone and laptop she was following, and providing live commentary on, the demon Xiphister's divestiture. Five magicians had disappeared from its résumé, and most of the demonologists were unable to settle to anything else with this excitement going on; they couldn't work five minutes without running down the hall to pop their heads in and see who had just been released.

"I can't confirm any of them," Teddy said, frowning at her cell phone. "I don't think the police in Selanto are taking this seriously at all."

"They ought to know to take you seriously by now," said Bill Navanax, who had not gone back to the Alchemy department after the meeting, but had remained in the conference room, tilted back in his chair with his feet on the table. Russell did not like Bill very much. Alchemists in general were full of themselves.

Russell stood in the middle of his office, at loose ends. He should have felt relieved at leaving this morning's scroll in its cardboard tube. But he'd begun steeling himself to become an Evil Magician, and that was the first step down the slippery slope. Compared with the things he might have been doing, departmental paperwork seemed stale and hollow. He scowled. Teddy was making the most of this, wasn't she? And Bill, avoiding whatever he ought to be doing over in Alchemy …

Russell scowled even harder, but now it was partly at himself. Was this the sort of thing an Evil Magician concerned himself with? Petty jealousy and backbiting? He feared it was. All the Evil Magicians he had known, and they were many, had wasted hours justifying themselves; worthless efforts, because anyone who looked at them could tell they were motivated by petty jealousy. *I could do a better job of it,* Russell thought, and for a moment the idea of becoming an Evil Magician took on luster anew. He'd show them how it ought to be done, without defensiveness and lying to oneself! But then, what was the point, if Xiphister did not need to be bound? He gave the scroll one last look, of regret mixed with relief, and left his office in search of someone to distract him.

Susan Teale was sitting at her desk, but not working. She had her chin in her hand, and was staring over the top of her computer monitor. She jumped when Russell spoke to her.

"Oh! I was woolgathering; sorry."

"We're all off balance," he said. "Not knowing what Xiphister's up to –"

"Yes, and I can't see us finding out," she agreed. "We hardly want to go invoking it, when it seems to be doing something good for a change. I feel sort of at loose ends, don't you? We could go over to Durrell's, but it doesn't seem right."

"No; I'm not sure I should leave the building, at this juncture." A shout down the corridor supported Russell's reasoning, and they both looked out to see Bill Navanax waving to them from the conference room's door.

"They've found one!" he called.

Teddy was on her cell phone, making notes on one of her papers. "May I put you on speaker?" she asked when Russell came in. "We have Russell Cinea here. He's a world expert on demon binding." Suddenly Russell liked her again, but he had no time to explore this feeling as she set the phone down on the table.

"This is Detective Porter, Selanto Guard," a voice said from the phone. Russell and Susan introduced themselves.

"We'll have the whole department in here before long," Teddy said. "Do you mind if we don't bother with introductions as they come in?"

"No," Porter said. "It'll all be public knowledge here in a half hour anyway. We found her in one of the lockers down in the pentarium complex. I'm guessing she'd been there since you reported her back this morning."

"Did the demon put her in a locker?" Teddy's tone was dubious, and Russell agreed. That was too high school-bully to fit a demon of Xiphister's standing.

"No, from the blood trail she put herself in there. It looks as if the demon left her in the pentarium. She has a lot of skin injuries, but they all look self-inflicted. Our guess is that she was trying to recreate the environment she's been used to for the last seventeen years."

Pain, Russell thought. *Darkness, restriction, helplessness*. Pity swamped him for a moment, and then professionalism took over. These were, after all, what demonologists who had bound demons expected, and feared. The longer you held a demon, the worse the dreams became.

"Can you communicate with her?" he asked.

"Not yet," said Porter. "She was pretty unresponsive until they took her out of the locker. Then she went wild, and had to be sedated. She's in hospital now. Maybe you can tell us what to expect?"

"She's the first person who's ever come back from inside a demon," Russell said. "But all demonologists who've bound them report the same dreams, which are widely regarded as premonitory. In the dreams, the victims float in darkness, unable to move or speak, while the demon inflicts pain on them as if from inside them. We think that while the

502

magician sleeps, the demon is able to access the brain and practice, as it were. Many bound demons have boasted that they were learning about the human nervous system."

"Holy –" Porter said. "Why does anyone –" he seemed to realize this was tactless, and stopped.

"We feel the same way," said Russell. "That's why demon binding is illegal in Osyth." He looked at Teddy, who shook her head. She hadn't told Porter of the Selanto Guard about Warren. *If we're lucky, we'll never have to*, Russell thought, and his heart leapt.

***

"It's gone that way," the kid said, looking into the blue bowl on the coffee-table and pointing toward the loveseat. "When it first brought her in here, it had gone that way" — toward the front window —" and now it's gone that way."

"But which way is that way?" asked Lilian, as if it mattered. *He's her husband,* Mama Simone reminded herself. *They've probably learned to care about the same stuff.*

"I don't know! I need a map," said the kid.

"Tell the demon that's what humans need, next time it asks," said Lees.

"It's easy for you to talk," Lilian snapped. "You don't need to be anyplace in particular."

"Simmer down," Lees said. "Patience is a virtue, possess it if you can."

"Seldom found in woman, and never in a man," Mama Simone pointed out.

"Do as I say, not as I do," Lees countered, grinning. Mama Simone couldn't think of an adage to shoot back at him; but anyway, the demon was back, in the entry. "Didn't bother knocking this time," Lees said.

It didn't bother speaking either. It reached into the upstairs, again without moving from the entry, and pulled out another of the damaged magicians.

"Now it's going *that* way," the kid announced into the emptiness it left after it went out through the door.

***

Five o'clock came and went, but nobody in the demonology department headed home for supper. Even Linus, who had maintained a stern disinterest in the goings-on in the conference room, was still in his office with the door open when Russell ran down to the second floor. Linus never left the door open ... he stuck his head out and looked 'round, doubtless having heard the stairwell door shut. When he saw it was Russell, he scowled and retreated back into his office like a hermit-crab, shutting the door with a bang. This would have been discouraging, if Russell had come down to see Linus, but he had merely been taking a constitutional and was just as happy to avoid what would have been an unproductive interview.

"They've found six," Teddy said when he looked back into the conference room. "Are you staying? We've ordered pizza."

"That depends on what's on the pizza. Any sign of its releasing Warren or Lilian?"

504

"Not yet." Teddy shoved the scroll toward Russell, who reread the bottom of it. Warren's and Lilian's vitae were still there. *I didn't know she made pickles,* he thought.

"It looks as if it's releasing them in the order it caught them," Teddy went on. "What's really interesting is the top of the scroll, where they used to be. Look at that!"

Russell unrolled the scroll back to the top. Teddy had annotated it with bright pink post-it-notes, recording the names of Xiphister's captives and the times they had disappeared from the scroll. The top ten inches were white and clean — but the paper was different. It had more texture and a shadowy pattern on it like a watermark. He held it up to the light, but it was too thick to see through. "Hmm." He squinted, tilted it so light from the corridor slid across the surface. "Leaves? Runes?"

"Your guess is as good as mine," said Teddy. "I photographed it and fed it into the charm bank, but no match yet."

"I didn't know demons used charms."

"This isn't your average demon."

"Hmm." Russell would have liked to spend more time with the paper, but doing what? He handed it back to Teddy. "You said they'd found six. How many has it let go?"

"Nine. But they're all over the world. People might have found them, and just not told me about it."

A thought struck him. "Earnest Steenberg. Has it let him go?"

Teddy sought down the scroll. "Steenberg — nope. He's still in there."

505

***

Milicent Pasqueflower was standing just inside the jetway when Ric, Endamos, Derek and Gerald came down it. But she only seemed to see the first three of them.

"Colin!" she cried, and caught Endamos in a big embrace. He stood stiffly until she let go. "Are you all right? It must have been horrible!"

"I don't remember much of it," he said.

Milicent looked over his head at Ric and Derek.

Derek shrugged. "He's been sleeping most of the time, and we had orders not to bother him with questions."

"Well — you must be starving," Milicent suggested. "Can I get you something to eat?"

"Honestly? I just want to go home to Kasidora."

Milicent looked nonplussed.

"What's the issue?" Ric asked her.

"Well — if Lord Stimms were here, I know he'd want to check Colin out, make sure he's all right, and find out all the details. But — oh, drat!"

"We'll take him to Kasidora," Gerald said. "We're going that way."

Milicent looked straight at him, frowned, and looked at Ric. "Who — oh, my head hurts," she said, and put a hand to her head. "I wish Rosemont would come back! As if he had a choice. He wouldn't be gone of his own free will. I so hoped he was in there with you, Colin."

506

Endamos shook his head. "Nobody was in there with me. I just want to go home and get back to work. Who's been taking care of my dogs?"

"We hired a pet-sitter," Milicent assured him. "I guess I could drive you home."

Ric looked at Gerald as Milicent turned her back, her arm around Endamos' shoulders, and felt a pang of sympathy at the man's expression. *He's lost his friends — and did he have a home? Pets?* "We'll do it," Ric said. "We have to see someone over in Kasidora anyway, after we file the paperwork."

Derek looked up from his phone. "I did that on the plane. Just sent it in — got us tickets on the next hop over and rented us a car, as well."

"Excuse us," Ric said to Milicent, and pulled Derek over to the side. "Listen, you stay here. I'll drive him over to Kasidora, while you get some rest. I slept on the plane."

Derek shook his head. "We're the White Knights," he said, his face fixed. "I'm not letting you go through this alone."

"What d'you think you'll add?" Ric said ferociously. "You can't even see my source. You can't remember anything I say about him. I'm telling you, stay here. I'll feel worse if this takes you down as well."

"My phone has the evidence to clear you if we end up — doing it."

"All the more reason it should be safe here."

Derek pinched the bridge of his nose and shut his eyes. For a few seconds he breathed fast, and then slowly. Then he opened his eyes again.

"I have to be there," he said. "We have to stop him."

"How?"

"I can't see that," said Derek. "I just know I'll have to do something my gut says is wrong."

Ric didn't move, because if he moved he was going to break something. Derek thought he was being reassuring, but what he was assuring Ric of was catastrophe. *Stop him — do something my gut says is wrong* — Ric thought of asking again, but found he couldn't face knowing any more.

Chapter 38
Together Again

What a difference two days had made in what Rho heard around the farm! Maybe all I needed was a little rest, *he thought, stretching in his bed.*

"This tree's taken," sang the blackbird in the maple tree. "My nest, my babies, my mate. This tree, this tree's taken, all others, all others keep out. I protect, I protect."

"Crow! Crow! Thief killer crow!" called another bird from the edge of the woods, and more voices took up the cry. They faded into the distance, doubtless pursuing the crow.

"Hey! Goat!" the horse neighed.

"Na na," jeered the goat.

"Out again, well I never, yes you did, she always does, ooh! Potato bug!" said the hens.

The rooster crowed from atop the chicken shed. "Morning on MY FARM! Mo-mo-MORNING!"

"Holy crap," Rho said, sitting up in bed. "I wanted this back?" But he was grinning from ear to ear. The house smelled of lemon polish, coffee, and pancakes.

Mama was in the kitchen drinking her coffee and reading the Minich Township News. "Morning," she said without looking up. "The batter's over there if you want to make yourself some. This is a busy town, isn't it?"

"I guess," said Rho, who had found Minich pretty slow after Osyth and Kasidora. "For its size."

"How big would you say it was?"

"You're the one who lives here, not me."

"I guess I've just never thought about how many people there were. Or how much different stuff they did. They're all — what d'you call it? This one's a student, and a basketball player, and he's in a band."

"Multitasking," said Rho. "I guess we never did much of that, did we?"

"It's a little far into town to do all that," said Mama. "Still, there's a quilting club that looks a touch interesting. Trouble is you'd have to quilt."

Rho grinned and poured his coffee. "I expect that's the general idea."

"I'd rather have a 'try everything' club."

"Start one. You could wear funny hats."

"You think I wouldn't," she accused him, but she was back in the paper. "How do you do these jumbles?"

"I never could. Ask Gretyl." Rho's good mood went away a bit when he thought of Gretyl. "She thinks there's something wrong with you," he said, with a feeling of plunging into something. "She thinks you've changed."

"Oh, there's no disputing that," said Mama. She looked down at herself. "I've changed a great deal."

"I mean just now. Since you burned everything and brought it back."

"Doing that can change a person."

"Are you magic now?"

"Yes."

Rho thought about this for a while, until his pancakes bubbled all across and were ready to flip. "Why weren't you magic before?"

"I didn't need to be," she said easily. "If you're just sticking in one place, doing the same thing every day, you don't need to be magic. But when it's time to change, you use whatever you have. Magic's just another tool. You don't let a tool run you; you use it when it's the right tool for the job, and otherwise you let it lay."

Rho didn't have an answer to this. He'd never thought of magic that way and neither, he bet, had any of the magicians he'd studied under and worked with. Magic was their reason for being. "I can't turn it on and off," he said at last, poking at the pancake. It had come out wudgy, crumpled in the middle. "You can?"

"It's not easy," she said. "Not like a light switch. It takes years to get it off and then years to get it on again. Unless you have help — and for that kind of help, you have to pay."

Rho thought of magicians who had given parts of themselves to demons. He thought of his own few days in Warren's grimoire with the demon, and shuddered. He'd paid then. But he hadn't wanted to get rid of his magic, had he? "What did you pay?"

"That's my own business," she said.

"Just tell me you didn't get it from a demon."

"I got it from an old lady just like me. She owed a favor to a friend of mine."

"Oh," said Rho. "Well, I hope it makes you happy." He made another pancake while Mama finished the paper. "I wonder who's better off, the magical or the mundane," he said at last. "Gretyl and Willett look like they have good lives, but I can't tell. They're always sour and suspicious

511

around me. Lilis doesn't have anything much, but she seems happy."

"What about you?"

"I don't know," said Rho. "I don't know anything."

She put the paper down and stared at him. "You look a lot like the old pictures of your father," she said. "I was going through the albums last night. He had that same scrawny cat look when he was young."

"He knew what he was going to do in life, though."

"He tried a lot of things, like the people in here," she said, shaking the paper. "Then I guess he had babies to take care of. He used to play the trombone, did you know that? Sometimes he'd go way out in the woods and play it. He'd make this noise like a mother bear. Woooaaaah! The trees used to laugh at him."

Rho sat down with his plate of nasty-looking pancakes. "I miss him," he said, surprised at himself. "I'm sorry I wasn't here to say goodbye. I shouldn't have done that to you." He felt a combination of terror and relief as he waited for her to answer, which took a while.

"I'm sorry, too," she said carefully, as if she too was discovering her feelings. "You're right, you shouldn't have done it. But it's hard to realize how short a man's life is until you've lived more of it. Now you'll know if anybody should ask you."

Relief emboldened him. "Why did he start with the pigs?"

"I don't know," she said, turning a page. "I wasn't involved in that decision."

"Are you going to keep them?"

"I don't know that either. Everything's different, now."

Rho chewed and thought. *He was angry*. The pig-shed, the pool of sewage — they were his father's anger, carved on the land. A message to the son who'd cared more for insects than for his own family. *He'd laugh*, thought Rho. *He'd laugh if he knew I depended on those pigs now*. The thought made him push his plate away half-finished. *What am I going to do? If I leave here, will my power go away again? Or will I be fine, as long as I can find some factory farm or breeding facility? Or kill kittens?*

***

Six different people tried to stop Gerald from following Ric, Derek, and Endamos onto the commuter flight from Selanto to Kasidora, but Ric could see all of them forget about the unticketed passenger almost as soon as they'd told him to get off. Gerald ignored them and sat down behind Ric and Derek, until people with those tickets got on and made him move. Ric watched his flyaway brown curls bobbing down and up again as he stole other seats and was rousted out of them until the doors finally closed and the plane took off for the twenty-minute hop. He wondered what Gerald's final seatmate made of it.

Endamos, next to Ric, leaned against the window and stared down. Ric looked out at a into towering castles of cloud with dazzling white tops, mist-blue caverns, slate colored bellies. He tried not to think, but that was a laugh! *Half an hour to get the car and drop off Endamos. Maybe an hour, if we get him settled. Does he have anybody we should call? No, or he would already have called them from Osyth.* He tried to remember Endamos' files. No family, no contacts. Lord Stimms was Power of Attorney, maybe for all the exorcists. *Bad idea, they need backups.* Ric brooded about exorcists. *Hell of a job. No friends; probably know demons better than they know people.* A fragment floated in his memory. *'I've made people feel so bad they killed themselves.' Who said that? And then something goes wrong, and you catch on fire —whatever that means — and they saddle jerks like me with the job of killing you. Half an hour to get rid of Endamos and two hours to Sterne — or wherever this Gordon K. is. If this flight ever lands.* As if it had been listening, the plane tilted downwards and sunlight blazed off its wings into Ric's eyes, a flash of fire.

It took exactly half an hour to get rid of Endamos, who was just as anxious to get away from them. Ric went back to the car first, to talk with Gerald.

"He's not in Sterne," Gerald said.

"What? How do you know that?"

"I called his office. He's at the extension campus in Minich — staying there tonight, rather than drive over the pass in the dark."

"Oh. That must have been a chatty secretary."

"People don't remember what they've told me, or why they shouldn't."

"Who's this?" Derek asked, looking in the window.

514

"My contact," Ric said. *"White knights. He's undercover."*

Derek blinked. *"I'll say."*

"Hop in. We're going to Minich."

Minich might have been one of those quaint villages nestled in the foothills, but it wasn't. It looked like an afterthought from some long-past mining era, kept alive only by the railroad terminal and a seed-and-feed store — and a surprisingly new-looking school complex, with a sign out front proclaiming the virtues of the Minich Eagles. The hotel they stopped at, next door to the school, had similar slogans painted on its windows. There was nobody at the desk; when Ric rang the bell, a receptionist in her twenties came out of the back room, dabbing a napkin at her chin. *It's suppertime!* he thought, surprised. The sun was still high above the hills.

"Did you want a room?"

"We're actually looking for someone," Ric said, showing her his badge. "Have you rented a room to this gentleman? Gordon K. Remen?"

She took Rosemont's picture with the tips of her fingers. "Oh yes. He checked in about an hour ago. Why, has he done something?"

"No, we need to get hold of him about an emergency back in Sterne. His cell phone's not working."

"Well, he asked me how to get out to Jeffries' pig farm. It's over on Rohde Hill Road. Here, I'll draw you a map."

***

515

Warren kept his eyes on the leaves swimming in the blue bowl. He watched them race from side to side, each time Xiphister reached through the walls and up the stairs to pull another magician out of their makeshift beds. What could the demon be doing, except letting them go? It was traveling from one spot to another, releasing its captives on their home turf. *Or not,* Warren warned himself. *It could be doing something horrible. It could be eating their families, to give them companionship. Or their colleagues, to give them work. Or something I have no idea of. Something that will teach me never to try reforming demons.* He held tight to the edge of the table, and the leaves swam back and forth. Lili knelt down beside him and took his arm; he was just the height to lean his cheek against the top of her head.

"What's your problem?" Grandfather said, but not to Warren. He was speaking to Xiphister. The demon did not answer, but Warren saw it feeling round upstairs with a vacant look, as if all its attention were on the seeking hand. "Lost something?" Grandfather asked. "I'll check for you." He headed up the stairs.

Warren and Lili ran after. The top of the stairs grew clearer as they neared it, and the three bedrooms, one bath that Warren had grown up in. But now they were filled with unhappy magicians. King Herroll, Dad, and Locullan moved between the beds, offering what? Who could fix the wounds being in a demon had created?"Something amiss up here?" Grandfather asked cheerfully, ignoring the cries, sobs, choking moans from all around. "The demon's reaching for something and not finding it."

"Small wonder," Dad said crossly. "It's making them all frantic. Probably someone nipped down the back stairs, and who'd blame him?"

Nobody had nipped down the back stairs. Somebody had gone out the window in the bathroom, and left a long scrap of his coat caught on it.

"The man in the tweed jacket," Dad said. "Squinty-faced guy, glasses."

Warren remembered him as the man who'd resisted coming into the house in the first place.

"He wanted to stay out there," Grandfather said, shutting the window on the swirling grayness outside. "Hope he's happy."

"Hey," said Locullan, and looked down. He shrieked. Warren looked and saw a black, three-fingered hand — Xiphister's hand — close around the man's biceps. Locullan cried out again. "Let go! Make it let go — don't let it take me again — I don't wa…" Then he was gone, right through the walls. His screams came up the stairs for just a second before they cut off.

Warren found he had his arms around Lili, and hers were around him. They reached right around, as if he was a child, and he should have felt safe in them. But he didn't feel safe at all.

***

The sun was half-way down the sky when Rho headed toward the pig shed. He tried not to think about the pigs. He thought about Gordon K., and how professionals had to stick together, and how it was tragic for a man to lose his magic. He thought

517

about Mama and how good it felt to be back on good terms with her and have the apologies over with, but that was not helpful. Having done one difficult right thing like apologizing made him feel he should make it a habit. He should do the next difficult right thing, but what would that be? *Those pigs wouldn't survive a day if I let them out*, he thought. *And even if I were going to, letting Gordon get some good out of them before I do it is the right thing, isn't it?*

Animals chattered around him all along the way. Rho had forgotten how full of them the countryside was, and how busy they were in June. Swallows almost ran into him as he walked up the lane. "Hurry up, hurry up!" they cried. "No time, mouths to feed!"

Near his feet, field mice bustled in the same rush. "Mine!" one of them told another, defending a dropped pig-nut.

"Give it here," the other said dangerously.

"Back off!" said the first. "Hey!" It retired, nursing a nipped ear and a grievance. "Get you back," Rho heard it mutter as it wriggled between the grass stalks.

A wren's indignant chatter rose from the nearest hedgerow. "Get –g-g-get owowowout! My place, my my my my, get –g-g-get owowowout!" Rho was not surprised to find that this challenge was directed at a black sheep a hundred times as large as the little warrior.

"Settle daaan," said the sheep. "Jest havin' a bite here and there. Dinna faaash yersel'."

The wren was not pacified, and kept up its scolding. Rho chuckled to himself as he climbed

518

over the stile …then he saw the pig shed in the distance, and all the pleasure leached out of him.

The path lay stretched out from where he stood to the shed where the pigs lived out their lives in crowded pens for his supper, his ham and bacon; was it any worse if he got magic from them, as well? Rho told himself he hadn't made up his mind. But a swallow swooped past his shoulder crying "Got it!" and the joy of magic flashed into him again. The world was bright and clear, the wind brisk, the animals' voices clamoring in his ears, and magic had made the decision for him. Hadn't it? Besides, didn't he have an appointment at the pig shed? He walked forward at a brisk pace

A white sedan came rattling up in a cloud of dust. *Gordon K. parked on the shoulder* and got out, dapper as ever.

"Good evening to you," he said expansively. "Would that be your facility?"

"That's it." Rho walked toward the pig shed, along the base of the waist-high berm that surrounded the waste lagoon.

"And what are they discussing?" asked Gordon K.

Rho listened hard. He didn't want to tell Gordon K. that he couldn't pick any words out of the noises inside. Finally he heard something, the same grumbly voice he'd heard before. "Late with food," it said. "Always late…"

"Food," he said. "The next feeding's late."

"Hm," said Gordon K. "That compares favorably with much of the conversation I am exposed to at work. Perhaps things are different on a main campus, however."

519

"Not that I remember," said Rho. He looked across the iron-gray surface of the waste lagoon, watching aspen trees shimmer in the wind, and tried not to think about the pigs he'd talked to and joked with on the farm — how lively and full of fun they had been, how much they had enjoyed their brief lives.

A mouse scurried by, its cheeks full of grain. "Left at the black rock, around the wild carrot, home," it mumbled to itself, and disappeared into the grass.

"Is your magic coming back?" Rho asked Gordon K.

"I don't know," said Gordon K. "You look pale. Are you dizzy?"

"What? No," Rho said, taking inventory of himself. Pale he might be, but dizzy? Not even a little.

"Perhaps pigs are not the right source for my sort of magic — Ah, we have company," Gordon K. remarked. Rho turned and saw a car coming down the road, a thin cloud of dust following it.

"They're probably going out to Topp Road," he said. "There's a trailer park up there."

"Ah. No, we appear to be their destination — unless they require directions."

The car had indeed pulled in at the drive. Rho heard gravel crunch under its tires as it came to rest. He expected the driver to roll down his window, but instead three men got out: one thin-faced, in a grey suit; one with a bluff young face, droopy mustache, and blonde sideburns; and one Rho just couldn't drum up much interest in. He had wavy dark hair and a mustache, but he didn't matter.

Grey-suit seemed to be the leader, but he also seemed reluctant to approach them. He walked over toward Rho as if it were his unpleasant duty. Rho just had time to begin imagining the things that it might be a stranger's unpleasant duty to tell him — Mama? His job? — when the man spoke.

"I'm looking for Gordon Remen," he said, and Rho relaxed for a moment, before realizing he ought to be sympathetic if Gordon K. was in trouble.

"I am Gordon K. Remen," said Gordon K. "To whom have I the pleasure of speaking?"

"Ric Massey," said grey-suit, pulling a wallet out of his breast pocket and displaying a badge. "Selanto Guard."

"Ah!" said Gordon K., and Rho imagined that he stood a little taller. "I believe I know what this might be about, Detective Massey."

"You do?"

"I do. And I hope to be able to accommodate you in the near future, but until then I would prefer to keep our business private —" he stopped. He was looking at the third man, the one Rho had forgotten about.

"Perhaps I am mistaking your purpose here," Gordon K. said to Massey. But his eyes never left the third man, and that made Rho look, too. Rho could think about the third man, just so long as he stared; when he blinked, it felt as if his eyelids were windshield-washers, wiping away drops of thought.

"That's magic!" Rho said. "That's a charm. Why's he casting a charm on us?" The man was young, not much older than Rho himself. He was slight and tall. His hair waved in the breeze, his mustache had curls in it, and he looked altogether lightweight and fluffy; plus, he had a sleepy expression as if he never paid real attention to anything. Rho wouldn't have liked him even without the charm … he blinked, and forgot what he had been thinking about, but he didn't like that young guy. There was something off about him, and he had a superior air.

The pigs behind Rho had heard the car, and were in a state of excitement.

"Food coming!" the grumbly pig squealed. "Food! Food!"

Other pig voices took up the chant. Some of them were just grunts and some just squeals, but some said "Food! Food!" as if it were the only word they knew.

Rho felt a hand on his shoulder, and suddenly all the pig sounds turned back into squeals and grunts. Sense emptied out of the world, leaving it full of no more than cheeps, squeaks, wordless cries from animals near and far. He whirled and saw Gordon K. looking at him with a bland, serious, slightly regretful face.

"What did you do to me?" he cried. "I can't — you stole it! You stole my magic!"

"The potential of animals may be enough for magic that works on animals," Gordon K. said, "but at this moment, I fear I must work on men. You understand."

And although Rho felt cold and sick inside with the sudden emptying-out, he found that he did understand.

***

522

"Stop that!" Ric said, and Rosemont let go of the little guy.

The little guy staggered. "What did you do to me?" he cried. "I can't — you stole it! You stole my magic!"

"The potential of animals may be enough for magic that works on animals," Rosemont said, "but at this moment, I fear I must work on men. You understand."

The little guy stared, his eyes bugging out; but Ric could tell Rosemont had convinced him. *The Chief Exorcist can make people believe whatever he wants them to believe*, Ric thought, and cold ran over him from glyph to glyph.

Rosemont stepped forward, and his eyes never left Gerald's; none of the rest of them mattered at all. Ric felt like nothing.

"You," said Rosemont. "Do you think you can control what I believe about you? Are you that strong?"

Gerald snorted, and this seemed to anger Rosemont even more.

"You are no match for me," he said. "You do not control who I am, or what I know."

"Don't I?" Gerald asked lightly. Ric could tell he was very angry. "You don't even remember my name."

Rosemont stopped. The two of them locked eyes. Ric could almost see their powers clashing. "I remember you," said Rosemont, triumph blooming in his face. "Gerald Manley! My good-for-nothing student."

"Really," drawled Gerald. "Was I good for nothing before I was your student, or only after you'd used me? Shall we ask your new protégé?" The two exorcists glared at each other.

Whichever of them wins, I lose, Ric thought bitterly. There was no way he could avoid his duty, now that Rosemont had shown his true colors by stealing the little guy's magic. And he had better draw and fire now, before Rosemont could turn. Shoot the world's Chief Exorcist in the back, for a reason nobody else would remember. Ric reached for his gun as if he were doing it in a play. He would fire, they would take their bows. But Rosemont's expression had changed.

"You told me — you called me — no, you Named me a demon!" he accused Gerald. "You made me into a demon, and then took my place. While I put all my skills to a demon's uses."

Gerald looked at Rosemont with more than his usual languor.

"Do you deny it!" cried Rosemont. "Or will you dare to say I deserved it?"

"I can't," said Gerald, his tone tight and ironic. "Do you truly want me telling you any more about yourself?"

"No," said Rosemont. "You've told me entirely enough about myself. Arrest that man, detective!"

"Um — for what?" Derek asked.

"For turning his teacher into a demon!"

"What demon?"

"Antimora. The possessor."

The names went off like fireworks in Ric's brain. Tingles spread across his chest as the dreamcatcher tried to deal with a year's worth of memories flooding back. *Antimora! The possessor — and he was Lord Stimms, Gerald Manley, he*

524

went into the alchemists' refuge after it. Then all the truckers went on strike. And the Lady appeared. Fuck! How are people walking around with all this chopped out of their minds?

Derek looked at Ric, his expression changing from bafflement to the one they used when communicating in front of insane people. "Tell you what," he said, "let's go someplace where we can take both your statements."

"I've done nothing wrong," said Rosemont. "He's the one you should be taking away!"

"I dunno," said Derek. "Seems to me, I just saw you steal this guy's magic. Isn't that what you said?"

"Yes!" said the little guy.

Rosemont turned toward him. "You don't mean that," he said, and Ric saw doubt steal back into the little guy's eyes. *Chief Exorcist*, he reminded himself. *The man who can tell people what they are. And the demon who told a dozen people to kill themselves ...* Ric had seen two of Antimora's victims after the demon finished with them, and wished he hadn't.

"Were you the demon?" he said, ignoring Derek's expression.

Rosemont turned back to him. "I had no choice. When an exorcist Names one –"

"Prove it," Ric broke in. "Tell me what you did to Agnes Heatherington."

Rosemont's eyes were looking into his, yet Ric felt no reshaping of himself. He was, if anything, colder than he had been a moment before, and more ruthless.

"I cannot win this game, can I?" said Rosemont. "If I cannot tell you, you will not believe Gerald made me into the demon. If I can, you will arrest me for murder."

I can barely think of it without retching, Ric thought, *but this man only sees it as a counter in some game. Either he didn't do it — either he knows nothing about it at all, as killer or exorcist — or he is a demon.*

"But if you did it, you are a murderer," he said.

"You can't think that," said Rosemont. It was a command. Ric felt it leaking into his head and turning his brain around, pushing his memories away again. It felt cold and greasy, and it ached right down into his bones. The world went into slow motion as Ric pulled his gun out of the holster. The effort of moving his arm against Rosemont's command tore things inside, muscle and nerve and into the soul ... he heard Derek shout, but it seemed to come from another world, far away. He raised the gun and took aim.

Just before he could squeeze the trigger something pulled on his sleeve from behind, so forcefully that his aim was lost. "What?" Ric yelled, whirling around, but he knew nobody would be there; and that, somehow, was the last straw. "What the hell do you want?" he bawled, tears of frustration blurring his vision. "How long are you going to jerk me around? What the fuck have I ever done to you?"

Nobody answered. Nobody even looked at him except the thing standing under a dusty tree at the edge of the driveway, not a meter away. It was Ric's height, slightly stooped, with a shiny black carapace over humanoid arms and legs. It looked at him with eyes that were half insect, half human, and all demon.

Chapter 39
The Forgotten Demon

"Aa—" said Ric, his voice sticking in his throat. The *grue* was so strong that he couldn't move.

The demon leaned forward, peering at him with an absent-minded kind of concentration. "Yes, you are the one," it said, as if talking to itself. "You are what he needs." Straightening up, it plunged one hand into its own chest, up to mid-arm. It wrinkled its brow for a moment, feeling around in there, and then pulled its arm out. Ric expected an organ of some sort, but the thing it pulled kept coming; bigger and bigger, unfolding and uncurling, until he saw that the demon had pulled a full-sized human being out of its chest. It held the man by the scruff of the neck, as if he were a kitten, and for a moment he hung passive as a kitten. Then the demon dropped him in a lump on the grass.

The man fell into action. His limbs were already moving when they touched the ground. He scrambled away from the demon, barreled into Ric's legs, and clung to them.

"Please," he whimpered. "Don't let it –" When he looked up into Ric's face, he shut his mouth.

Ric opened his own in surprise, then closed it and took a second to collect himself. He took hold of the man's arm and pulled him to his feet.

"Magister Ian Locullan," he said formally, "You are under arrest for the murder of Cynthia Locullan."

***

Rho would never have known the creature to be a demon except for the *grue*. It looked benign, like some kind of *walking tree cricket*, and something about its face reminded him of Warren Oldham. It turned round after dropping that man from inside itself at the detective's feet, and looked at their little group with a considering expression. And even though they'd been fighting and getting ready to shoot each other, all that seemed unimportant when a demon was standing two meters away from them observing.

"Perhaps I over-reacted," said Gordon K. Was he crazy? There was no over-reacting to a demon! But he was, insanely, talking about something else — what, Rho, couldn't quite grasp. "I should not be asking you to arrest someone you can't remember — someone who, in effect, no longer exists. Someone whose only skill was to influence people, and who can no longer use that dangerous skill in the slightest! Why, arresting this poor boy would be cruel. He has nothing but potential. He needs a place to live, and someone to care for him. Come along, Gerald."

Rho saw him reach out toward the dark-haired man. It wasn't a big movement, nothing to make anyone jump, but the blonde man with the sideburns did jump. He yelled and jumped as if he were trying to stop the world from ending, right in between Gordon K.'s arm and the dark-haired man. He knocked both of them off-balance, and Gordon K. lurched sideways. The blonde man stood between

529

them panting and gulping as if he were about to throw up.

"Gerald," said Gordon K. "He belongs with me," he told the blonde man, who looked even sicker.

"No," he said, and swallowed.

"Yes," said Gordon K.

Rho felt that word run through him from feet to head. There was nothing sure in this world except that Gerald, whoever he was, belonged with Gordon K. After all his agonizing over the pigs, moral certitude at last! He took an eager step forward, toward the blonde man, and saw Massey and his prisoner turn that way with the same relief on their faces.

"Step aside," Gordon K. said to the blonde man.

"No!" the man cried, clutching his head. He stepped forward, almost into Gordon K. — Rho would be able to reach him in just a few steps — and threw up, all over Gordon K.'s impeccable front. Now it was Gordon K.'s turn to dance to one side, almost into — how had Rho forgotten there was a demon standing right there? The *grue* came back so strongly he froze in his tracks.

The demon put one claw on Gordon K.'s shoulder. Rho was reminded of a cat he had seen dozing on his mother's porch, long ago. A ground squirrel had run across the porch, right into the sleeping cat's flank; this demon had the same air the awakened cat had, of not having sought this but of being too polite to reject it. The look it turned on Gordon K. was one of bemusement and distraction,

530

as if it were trying to remember what kind of thing he was.

Gordon K. was not intimidated at all. "You know me," he said, looking into the demon's compound eyes.

"I do," it said slowly. "I do have need of you." This close to it, Rho could see that its surface was like a hide swollen shiny. Was the black part of the hide, or was the coating transparent, letting him see the thing's black insides? As Rho thought this, he saw a hand reach up from the blackness inside the demon. Two hands, with a shimmer of blue fire around them; they reached towards Gordon K. Rho's throat stuck silent as the hands reached out of the demon and closed around Gordon K's upper arms.

"People need to know themselves, to be whole," the demon said. "I do not understand it, but I am told –"

"You're told wrong," Gordon K. said, pulling. He looked at the dark-haired man — the last person, Rho would have thought, that he could appeal to. "Gerald! Help me! Will you let a demon take someone right in front of you?"

"Alas," the dark-haired man said, with his eyes half closed and his face a mask of indolence, "I have, as you said, nothing but potential."

The hands pulled, and before Rho could take more than a step forward they had pulled Gordon K. right into the demon. The demon seemed to pull itself in after him until it disappeared entirely, leaving not even a smudge where it had stood. And the world burst back into speech around Rho.

"Monster! Monster!" twittered a titmouse from the tree under which the demon had stood.

"Mmm, good one!" a dragonfly mumbled, with its mouth full of grasshopper.

Another, precocious grasshopper chirped from the shorter grass behind it: "Hey girls, hey girls, hey girls…"

Far above, a lone hawk balanced on the wind. "Heeere," it screeched. "I'm over here."

Even the pigs in the shed had voices, now. "Food," they said. "Food now! Food!"

The people in front of Rho looked at him and he looked at them: Massey and the man he'd arrested, the blonde man who had thrown up and the dark-haired fellow Rho had trouble remembering.

"Are you going to tell me what's going on," Rho asked flatly, "having fed my friend to a demon and all?"

Massey and the blond guy looked at each other.

"He was the Chief Exorcist," said Massey. "He disappeared a while back. Don't you remember?"

Rho didn't remember, but this seemed addressed to the blonde guy with sideburns.

"I guess …" the blonde guy said doubtfully. "Why am I having trouble with this?"

"Because an exorcist can control what the world thinks about him," Massey said, more confidently. "I only remember because of the glyphs. He stepped down because he'd become a demon."

"Gordon K. wasn't a demon!" Rho felt outraged on Gordon K.'s behalf. "There wasn't any *grue*. He was a decent guy!"

"He took your magic, not five minutes ago. That's a crime, isn't it?"

"Not as big a crime as letting a demon eat someone!" Rho yelled, shaking. His chest burned, his bowels clenched inside him, and the next damned fuckhead who spoke up was going to get it right in the snoot — Rho was furious, enraged, as if he'd stored up all the anger he might have felt since February for just this moment. "I'm calling the police!"

"We are the police," said Massey, and held up a badge. "Look, what could we do? We didn't feed him to the demon. He stepped into it. We just weren't able to stop it from taking him."

"You didn't even try!" Rho didn't want to hear any more of their half-assed explanations. "You're on private property," he said. "Take your prisoner and your demon and whatever that guy is" — pointing at the dark-haired fellow — "and get the hell off my land."

The blonde guy looked as if he wanted to say something, but Massey was a better judge of people like Rho. He got them all into the car without another word, and they went back down the road in the same another cloud of dust just like the one they'd come up it in. But back then, Rho had been happy.

"Food," a grumbly voice whispered behind him. "Food now!"

Rho spun around, but of course all he saw was the pig shed. The padlock hung there, unlocked. Rho tore it off and jerked the door open. The movements inside shut off as if he had turned a switch.

533

He glared around the inside of the pig shed, not seeing much because the lights were off. It stunk, even with the heavy-duty ventilation that blasted a wall of rattling noise at him. Rho stood at the end of a row of low corrals, each with quite a number of pigs in it.

"Food!" they began crying, their snouty faces raised toward him, but as he came into the shed they fell silent and drew back. There was something about Rho, or the situation, that they knew better than to mess with. *And they are right*, he thought.

He walked to the very back of the shed, getting used to the darkness, and opened the gate of the furthest corral. He opened every one of them as he walked forward, and when the pigs looked afraid of him he wanted to hit them. He wanted to give them something to be afraid of. He grew angrier with every gate he touched.

By the time he got back to the door, he could hear movement behind him in the shed. The front corral held a dozen pigs or so. A big white porker crowded its way to the front of the corral.

"Food now?" it asked. It was the grumbly-voiced pig, and Rho was suddenly more furious than ever.

"No!" he said, and found himself shouting. "No food!" He snapped the gate open. "No food out there. Do you understand me? No food. You're better off in here being — mindless *things*! You're better off not talking. You're better off without it — " He choked and ran out the door of the pig shed, around the side of the waste lagoon. "Better off without it," he said as he went, though no pigs could have heard him.

***

"It took Locullan!" Warren shouted, pelting down the stair.

Grandfather, half a flight behind him, laughed. "That's the first time you've acted like an eight-year-old."

"We saw it take him," said the woman — Mama Simone. "It took the thing on fire, as well. And it's almost back where we were. Look at the leaves!"

Warren felt like an eight-year-old when he looked in the bowl and saw the leaves clustered near one side of it — not nosing against the china walls, but arranged in a snowflake floating just a little off-center.

"Can we cast the charm?" Lilian asked.

"This might be our best chance."

"King Herrel!" she called.

This is it! Warren thought, staring at the leaves clustered in the center of the bowl. Yet what was it? Would the home-ward undo anything? Would it get anyone out of the demon Xiphister? And what if he were out, his grimoire in his hands again — no longer a house, a living family, but a dead book? He shook himself, mentally. Losing the illusion of family was no reason to stay inside a demon. He was holding Lili's hand and that was all that mattered.

You were swallowed by a demon and found nothing worse than your grandfather inside it, he scolded himself. *Your wife was swallowed by a*

535

demon, and nothing bad happened to her either. For goodness' sake, was there ever a man with better luck? Appreciate it, you fool! He looked around the room, and while he couldn't have said he liked all the members of this unexpected little household, he couldn't have said he hated them either.

"I don't know what this charm's going to do," he said to Dad and Grandfather. "It might whisk us out of here with no time for good-byes."

"Well, that's true," Dad said. He had to bend way down to hug Warren. "It's been a pleasure seeing you again, son. And Lilian. Always a delight." Warren took deep breaths of the tobacco-and-aftershave smell. He held on as long as he could, but there was Grandfather behind Dad, with his hand outstretched.

"Good meeting you, kid," he said. "Nice to see the line's carrying on. And you found a better woman than any of us deserve. Hang onto her." But Grandfather's real interest was in saying goodbye to the farmwife with the trees — Mama Simone. He bent over her hand and kissed it. "Perhaps we will meet again, under more conducive circumstances," he said to her.

"Rascal!" was all she said, pulling her hand back, but Warren could tell she and Grandfather had each said just what the other one wanted to hear.

She has the right attitude, he thought as he sat down beside her on the loveseat, the grimoire on his lap. *Enjoy the encounter, without worrying about whether it'll happen again. Take the good—* he gripped Lili's hand tighter and saw excitement mirrored on her face before she let go and moved to

536

the chair opposite him. Mama Simone and King Herrel completed the circle. Warren took a last look around the room and returned Dad's nod. Then he lit the candle in the blue bowl and took a deep breath to begin the home-ward.

The front door opened and Warren almost didn't look up, so used to Xiphister's presence had he become. His casual glance turned into a fixed stare at, not Xiphister, but the burning thing. The mysterioso, he'd called it, but no more. What stood looking at them was no baffled creature searching for itself. It was a demon, and it knew what it was.

Chapter 40
The Lost League

Warren fought with his memory as he stared at the burning demon. *I knew that, once,* he thought. Where had his mind gone? Had he actually turned into an eight-year-old? *You're a full professor,* he scolded himself. *A magister, a department head...* and with that, his administrative self awoke within him and he knew how to handle this.

"We thought it let you go!" he said, with innocent surprise. "What happened?"

How often he had said that, and every time he had known exactly what happened long before the person responsible appeared in his office. But one must never let the miscreant know. The administrator was always, unaccountably, uninformed of faculty misdeeds. The administrator always heard them first from their perpetrators, and nodded and understood. So, now Warren looked at the demon and prepared to nod and understand, and felt parts of himself revive, and discovered he hated them. *I'm never doing this again!* he thought. It was not a decision but a discovery.

The demon looked at him with amusement. "Are you the leader of this little group, now? Well, then you should know that our host has changed its approach. Instead of putting us where it thinks we will thrive, it has decided to engulf those things we need. I hope none of you have mentioned your families. But your family is here, is it not."

Its mouth moved as it said these things, but Warren was watching its eyes. They were flat, distracted. The creature was feeling about it for the effects of its words. It fed on some emotion — fear, perhaps, or horror. Pain or sorrow. It cast out a web of words, tugging on each strand until it felt a struggle at the other end.

Should we feed it, Warren thought, *so it stops baiting us? Or would that encourage it?* He let himself think, just a little, about what it would mean if Xiphister had decided to keep Lilian here with him, trapped forever. The thoughts crawled out of where Warren had locked them, not even mentioning them in his mind lest Xiphister hear. They brought cold with them, and a sick, dry hollowness in his throat. But Warren was used to these feelings, and to setting them aside while he did the next thing that had to be done. *Thus far and no farther,* he said to them.

The burning demon sighed and stretched its hands out in front of it, as if to a fireplace. "Ah, I shall be comfortable here," it said. "For as long as I choose to stay."

Warren turned away from it, as if trying to deny the feelings he had himself called up.

"It's all right," Lilian said, putting her hand on his arm. "We'll find a way out." But he could tell she didn't believe herself.

"Of course," he said. It sounded like a lie. "At least, we can help King Herroll here cast his charm." *Though what it can do inside a demon —* he thought as loudly and miserably as he could, and the burning demon smiled. It stood next to them, attentive and tolerant, as he and Lilian set up their

539

(*futile, pointless,* he thought as if casting his own secret spell) home-ward. Warren's hand trembled as he lit the candle, and the first lines of the rune were wobbly where he wrote them on the outside of the bowl. *Focus!* he scolded himself, no longer sure what was play-acting for the burning demon's benefit and what was real.

The burning demon viewed the whole process with what looked like amusement until they finished the runes and light began to spread out through them, onto the tabletop. Then the quality of its attention changed. "That is wardage," it announced, bending lower to examine the pattern. "I am afraid I cannot allow that." It took Warren's arm and effortlessly pulled it away from King Herroll's, breaking the circle.

The demon's hand seared. Surely it had blazed right down to the bone! — but Warren saw his arm still whole, burned black where the creature grasped it at the same time that the *grue* froze his bones. He gasped, too hurt to breathe, and let go of Lilian on the other side.

"Finish it," he choked, jerking out of the way so she and Herroll could reform the circle. He fell off his chair and hung, off-balance, from the demon's grip on his arm. Now he had his breath, it was impossible not to cry out.

"Like hell I will!" Lilian said, starting up after him. "We're in this together."

King Herroll, however, grabbed her hand and pulled her back down, and so did the farmwife. Herroll raised his voice in the chant, urgent, and the web of light reformed, flowed toward Warren.

540

Lilian saw it move. Still looking at Warren, she joined in the chant.

Warren, meanwhile, resorted to every boy's style of fighting. He began to kick the demon in its shins, and bit its arm through the robe, which provided some protection from its flames. In fact, the *grue*'s chill in his mouth was some relief from the burning in his arm. Emboldened, Warren let the demon's grip take his weight and kicked higher, at what he hoped were its tender parts.

The demon laughed scornfully, but it also danced and dodged, into the edge of the homeward's light; Warren felt it freeze for an instant, gasping in shock as the charm touched it. Its grip grew weak as an old man's, just for that instant: he twisted frantically, pulled himself free, and lunged into the web of light. He flung his body onto the ground and scrambled between Lilian's and King Herroll's feet till he was huddled under the table itself. Safe! Home free!

***

Well! Mama Simone had kept her mouth shut, but it wasn't because there was nothing to say. You know, casting the spell would have been enough excitement for me, *she thought to whatever was in charge of all this. And it would have; she hadn't cast a spell since the twins were two, when she'd given up her magic as the price of getting rid of theirs.* And where did I get that idea that I couldn't have magic and family? *she asked herself, looking at Warren and Lilian, family people who cast this spell together every day. Then the thing on fire reappeared, and any fool could tell it had remembered it was a demon;* and we're inside another one, *Mama Simone thought. That told you all you needed to know about trying to balance magic and family, didn't it?* You made your point, *she thought to the invisible orchestrator.* But no, that wasn't enough for you, was it?

There was certainly plenty to be said about having one's husband turned into an eight-year-old, and pulled away from one by a fiery demon. Lilian's face, when she had stood up to go after him! We shouldn't look, *Mama Simone had thought, and had looked anyway. In fact, did she have to admit it, she'd been jealous when Warren said what had to be his goodbye.* At least he's told her what to do with herself! *Then Lilian had turned back to the table and let them pull her down, white as a sheet, while the demon was killing her husband behind her. Mama Simone had never ever felt so ashamed of herself. She kept her mouth shut, and set back to reading the charm so she could do her part, little as it was. She didn't let herself have any more inside conversations with whatever might be listening, but that didn't make her stop feeling, and she felt small, low-stakes, as if she'd lived a lazy little life and taken the easy road at every forking.*

She didn't see how Warren got loose from the demon, but she could imagine it. She'd tried to hold on to her share of eight-year-old boys, and seen plenty of them wriggle free and hide under tables. If she hadn't been busy, she would have cried with relief. This time, she had the decency to keep her eyes on the charm and not look at Lilian's face. The streaks and curls of light spread across the table, over all of them and out into the room, and somehow Mama Simone took hold of it and pushed it out further. *I'm doing magic!* she thought, and was thrilled. Then she felt it stop. The lace had stretched as far as it could go… a hand came up from under the table, two hands, and pried at hers where it held King Herroll's. She took Warren's sweaty little-boy hand and he backed out from under the table, squeezed onto the sofa close beside her when he could have had plenty of room, and she'd had plenty of little boys do that, too. His hand was sweaty and his voice shook, but he steadied up as he recited the charm. After all, they did it every day. Holding hands with him, hearing him and Lilian cast the charm in confident unison, Mama Simone felt bold enough to look up and see what it was doing to the room.

The strangest thing! *It's like fairisle,* she thought. Only more so. Because most people did fairisle knitting on a solid black background, even though they might use a variegated yarn for the pattern. That was a pretty effect, as if you cut the pattern out of a sheet of black paper and then laid it over a multicolored sheet. What Mama Simone was seeing now looked more like Aunt Dismas' fairisle. She had not been content with a black background: oh no, Aunt Dismas had knitted the background in one variegated yarn and the pattern in another, so you saw the pattern in red-to-blue on a background of yellow-to-green, or some such. So right now, Mama Simone saw another world showing through the web of light that the charm had cast, showing in black-to-blue against the living room's brown-to-tan. In the outside world, low houses against a summer sky; in this, a fiery demon that sometimes seemed an old man, with Lees getting in its way now that the danger was over, the scamp.

We're going away, Mama Simone realized, and jiggled her arm to feel that she had indeed put it through the bale of her bucket full of trees. The lines of light were spreading. They grew wider and wider; now black-to-blue was the background and brown-to-tan just a decorative pattern against it. Lees looked at her from a thread-thin lace of brown-to-tan, and winked. Then he was all gone, in a flash that made Mama Simone shut her eyes. The feel of a summer breeze against her face made her open them again, and she saw too many things at once.

She saw the lacy light pour across the landscape, toward the horizon, as if some magical craftswoman in the blue bowl were knitting like mad, pushing it out. She saw it blaze out of the mirror in the goblins' hole to where she sat with Lilian, waiting, and as it touched her she took one of King Herroll's hands, there in the goblin hole, and stood up. She leaned close to the mirror, trying to see through the light, and saw a man standing there, just as the knights stood in the other mirrors. He was a tall man wearing a raincoat too wide for him and too short in the arms, or was it a coat embroidered with silver leaves? His hair was rough, or were those the points of a crown? He was King Herroll, she supposed, though it was hard to tell from the light. A tall young oak tree stood beside him on either hand. The light shone through the trees' young leaves, through the man's ears and the thin bones of his wrists and hands, and he reached out to Mama Simone and Lilian. They looked at each other. Then they each took a hand, and climbed back into the mirror. The Mama Simone in the goblin's hole and the one sitting around the table both held tight to the king's outstretched hand, and in that moment she was all one person again, covered in the light of Lilian and Warren's charm. And she felt magic pour into her, as bright and tingling as first love.

***

The lacy light spread out from the bowl, the way it did every evening when they set the homeward. Warren felt it warm on his knees, his chest, then his face. Then it was all over him and spreading out behind him, up the walls as they said the final words of the charm. He knew this because he could see it behind King Herrel and Lilian. Through its pattern he saw — houses. Cottages, more like, set around a green village square: a street leading out of the square ended at a wall with an open gate in it, and through that gate Warren saw a bit of meadow and the snow-capped top of a mountain.

He saw this through the sitting room wall and the pictures, through the fiery demon, and through grandfather. That was a shock. Warren looked sideways for Dad. Dad was almost all landscape by now. A cottage door swung open and closed behind him, and it looked as if it were his heart beating. And now the breeze that was swinging that door hit Warren in the face. He glanced down and saw the grimoire beside him, but it was as transparent as all the rest.

545

Oh no! Warren thought, and with the hand that wasn't holding Lilian's he reached for the grimoire. As soon as he touched it, though, the wind increased. It was a gale, dragging at every part of him. It blew away from Lilian and towards Grandfather, who looked more solid.

"Warren!" Lili cried, tugging.

Warren tugged as well, trying to pull himself back towards her. He saw as if in passing that the leaves in the bowl were moving again, toward the edge of the bowl nearest Lilian; as if Warren and the grimoire, and everything the demon Xiphister contained, were moving away from her where she sat in the village square. *The demon's going somewhere*, he thought, *with my grimoire!* And for a moment he gripped the book tighter. He cast a last look around the room, at Grandfather and at Dad.

Dad smiled and moved his mouth, but Warren could hear nothing over the wind in his ears. Grandfather wasn't smiling. He was looking at Warren with what seemed like pity for someone clinging to childish things, and that made Warren angrier than anything Grandfather had ever done. *Pity me! There's nothing about me to pity!* he thought, and let go of the grimoire so fast he almost threw it down. And they were gone.

Warren, Lilian, Mama Simone and King Herrel were sitting on the grass in the village square. The door that had swung behind Dad's chest was still swinging, and the creaking of its leather hinges was the only sound Warren could hear. He looked down at his hand, clasping Lilian's. It was an old man's hand.

"Warren! We did it!" Lilian said, a little shaky. Her hand tightened on Warren's, and he knew she would never mention the way he had clung to the grimoire — or if she did, it would only be to say he'd chosen her. And she would be right. She was all right! They'd escaped from Xiphister, the man-eater! Warren, Lilian, King Herrel and a woman who called herself a farmwife had done one of the greatest feats of magic in modern history, with nothing except a home-ward.

Now that the horror was behind them, it seized him by the arm, burning up toward his shoulder. *What that thing would have done to us,* he thought, cold to the bone at the very thought of it. His head swam and breath came thick in his throat.

"It's all right," Lilian said. "Here, lie down." Warren lay back and looked at the sky. Sparkles ran across his vision, like tiny living things. The little oak trees' leaves waved over his face, and he moved his head so they blocked the sun from his eyes. "Is it your arm?" Lilian asked.

"I guess —" Warren said. But it wasn't just his arm, though that hurt like the very devil. It was all the fear he hadn't been able to admit when he had to face the fiery demon. The burning arm and freezing terror spread, fought each other to a standstill in his chest, and began a proxy war in his bowels. "I don't know," Warren said, and put his unhurt arm over his eyes.

Sightless, he could feel again. The summer breeze, the earth hard and strong under his spine. He could smell dust and grasses, and hear the air rustle in the leaves above him. He could feel someone take his hurt arm, and hear King Herroll speak in

Old Selantese. *That's a charm, and I'm missing it,* Warren thought. Tears of anger and self-pity prickled in his eyes. *I don't care! I'm allowed to miss something sometimes!* The burning in his arm faded away, then the turmoil in his guts. Warren had nothing to deal with except the thoughts in his head, and he couldn't let them worry Lilian any longer. He swiped his arm across his eyes and sat up.

"Thank you," he told King Herroll, forgetting the language barrier. The King smiled at him.

"What do we do now?" Lilian asked, sitting back on her heels. "I'm not sure where we are."

"In his kingdom. I think we'll have to follow his lead."

They all looked at King Herroll. He was as shabby as he had been before, and didn't seem the kind of person to whom folk would look for guidance until he stood up and the sunlight hit him. He looked — north, Warren supposed it was, and bowed to the distant mountains. Then he turned, bowing to each cardinal point, and stood as if waiting for the valley to acknowledge him. Would it do so with glory and furor? With some quieter blessing? Did the land, even the ley-line, care who claimed to rule it? *It should,* Warren thought. The land had a lot to lose when the wrong sort of people ruled over it. This valley just needed to look around to see what happened to such land.

But if King Herroll's valley realized that he was its best bet, it gave no sign. The wind continued to blow and the sun to shine. One of the cottage doors continued to sway open and closed, and something else clanked rhythmically in the breeze behind Warren . He had just realized that sound was new when King Herroll looked over his head with a smile. He turned and found himself facing knights on horseback.

There were eight of them, all in sparkling armor like pictures from a storybook, and their horses wore blankets in bright colors that winked out as they rode into the shadowed street and flashed back into color when they came into the square and formed a circle around Warren's group. The last of the knights led another horse, a dappled gray wearing a russet blanket edged with green. The corners of this blanket, at least the ones Warren could see, were embroidered with silver coronets, and scalloped swags of fabric looped from its bridle to its saddle. Warren had never been in the presence of this much glory — in fact, he had never been this close to horses — and he stood up to step back a pace, keeping Lilian safely behind him. Mama Simone, however, did not seem at all nervous.

"There you are!" she said to the knights. "We've been battling demons and you've been horse-stealing?"

One of them grinned. "Not stealing," he said. "Finding."

King Herroll stepped forward, reaching out his hand. The gray horse came to him, pressed the whole length of its face against his chest while he ran its ears through his hands and crooned to it.

"You 'found' them?" Mama Simone was chaffing the knight who spoke their language. Now that he thought to look, Warren could see a resemblance between that knight's face and the carved knight on the bier who had spoken to Ver. Like that carved knight, this one was not speaking

549

Warren's language, yet Warren could understand him. And the man was alive now, in his prime.

"They came to us," he said now, grinning at Mama Simone. "So we knew our lord had escaped the monster, and that they would take us to him."

One of the knights rode up beside King Herroll and leaned down, handing him a coat of green and russet. It was embroidered with the same silver coronets as the horse's blanket, and a wide silver border of intertwined oak and beech leaves ran around its neck and sleeves. When King Herrel put it on he was so changed that Warren could hardly believe he was the same man. Warren certainly would never have dared leave a lunch for this princeling, or donate him a used raincoat.

"These are my rescuers," King Herrel said to the knights. *Generous of him, since he did some of the rescuing,* Warren thought. Then he started. He'd understood the King!

"How can we understand you all of a sudden?" Lilian asked.

King Herrel ran a finger over the silver leaves embroidered on his collar. He tugged at the edge of the collar, pulling off three of them; two oak leaves and one beech leaf. He gave the beech leaf to Warren and the oak leaves to Mama Simone and Lilian.

"Thank you," said Warren, examining the leaf. The embroiderer had copied every vein, but the shimmer around it was not just silver and sunlight. Warren put it in his pocket.

King Herrel looked at him with amusement. "In my time, we wore our magic in plain view. Now

550

you hide it. Every farmwife is a sorceress, every man you pass on the path a wizard."

Warren flushed.

"What'll you do now?" asked the farmwife.

"What would you have me do for you?"

"Watch over my trees," she said immediately. "Keep them safe."

King Herrel looked at the saplings in the bucket. "They are the King's trees, that brought this land out of the demon's power," he said, a proclamation. He looked around the circle of knights. "None shall touch the King's trees. They are the health of the land. Should they fall, who knows what demons might return?"

All the knights nodded, and one brought his gloved hand to his helm in salute.

"What of you?" the King said to Warren and Lilian. "What boon would you have from me?"

"Oh –" Lilian said, and Warren knew she was going to say 'that's all right,' or something of the kind. She stopped herself, though. "Let me think a minute."

King Herrel was looking at Warren now, and for a moment Warren felt himself in a fairy tale, where any wish could be granted. *What nonsense!* But what if it wasn't nonsense? Then, of course, Warren should ask for his grimoire back — he didn't want to, though. He'd let go of it. To have it back would mean letting go all over again sometime in the future. It would mean using his wish to go backwards, keeping himself stuck in the past.

"I want to come back here and study," he said, quickly before he could overthink himself. "And my students, and my colleagues. Let us learn about your kingdom."

"You would walk the ley-line here."

"Yes."

King Herrel turned to the knights again. "The magician Warren has free entry to all our land, and the women Mama Simone and Lilian likewise. Any he sends to us we will treat as honored guests. This is the King's order."

They nodded, and this time two of them put their hands to their helms in salute, including the one who spoke all languages.

King Herroll looked at Lilian once more.

"I don't know!" she cried, a little desperately. "Or — I don't want anyone to hear me." She rushed forward, as if Warren would stop her, and whispered into the King's ear.

King Herrel stepped back and looked down at her, grinning. "That kind of wish, I understand," he said. "It will take more than a proclamation to grant it."

"Oh —"

"But I shall!" he said, bowing grandly. "It will be my quest, nor shall I rest until it is fulfilled."

Lilian looked very embarrassed.

King Herrel turned away from her, and swung himself up onto the horse. "Come," he said to the three of them. "We will show you on your way."

Warren felt uneasy as he looked up at the horses. "Is it walking distance?" he asked.

"Five hour's walk, more or less, to where we first met."

The knight who spoke all languages had dismounted with a rattle. Warren expected to be

552

hauled up like a sack of potatoes, but when he put his foot on the knight's hand, he almost flew into the saddle. *I didn't know I could do that!* he thought. But of course, it had been the knight's doing. Now the knight had leapt up behind him, and Warren was crowded toward the horse's neck, his legs forced apart by the width of its shoulders. He felt precarious until the knight's arms came up on either side, holding him in position. Then the grandeur of it all struck him. Knights and pennants, just like the story books! He looked around and saw Lilian sitting breathless before another knight, and Mama Simone before a third looking very matter-of-fact and gripping her bucket's handle with both hands. Then the horse was moving, and it wasn't as rough as Warren had expected.

They rode almost reverently down the street, with no sound but clopping and jingling. They passed three, four side streets on their way to the gate; the village was larger than Warren had thought. "Um — was this town here in your day?" Warren asked the knight behind him.

"It was," the knight answered. "It has seen hard days since. We have much to do here."

"Who'll live in it now?"

"I know not, as yet."

They went out of the gate and reined up in a group, looking over the wide plain. "Star Mountain," said the knight, pointing. "It means star in our tongue." Warren puzzled over this for a minute, before realizing the drawback of translation spells. "There –" the finger swung — "the Sheep League. Where we came through the gobin's door."

553

Warren thought of the tunnels and shivered. He didn't want to go back to the goblin hill. King Herrel was pointing in a different direction, though. The horse turned, the knight's arms came tight around Warren's sides, and they began to pelt down the hill like an avalanche for a few steps, and then the horse's gait smoothed out. Warren began to enjoy himself. This was the appeal of riding, this feeling that you were part of the animal and couldn't fall off if you wanted to. He looked back over the armored arm that kept him safe, and saw the other knights with Lilian and the farmwife perched before two of them; all of them racing across the plain, vivid and merry as part of a fairy tale.

***

Rho was halfway around the sewage lagoon when something happened to his vision. The view was — dappled was the only word he could think of. It was changing, one view appearing over another in little dots that grew larger and larger like one of those artsy slide transitions students liked to use in presentations. The mountains across the river looked as if they had been pulled backwards and a new range was appearing in front of them bit by bit.

"Hey!" an indignant voice yelled, from his right, just over the edge of the waste lagoon's berm. And looking upward, Rho saw a big crack opening at the berm's edge. The indignant voice didn't have to tell him to run. But having run, to the end of the berm and back up around it to the open pig shed, where a few tentative pigs saw him coming and ran back inside, he stopped. What was he supposed to do about — what, an earthquake?

"Who's in charge here?" the voice bawled.

Rho guessed that would be him. He went up to the top of the berm.

The voice kept yelling. "I got rights! Who owns this dump?" It was a very large voice, and it came from a very large mouth. "Who doing that?" the mouth yelled. Rho realized he was looking down into the depths of the waste lagoon, which had now broken all the way through on the downhill side of the berm and was rapidly emptying of waste. *Crap*, he thought, *that's going to get us in all kinds of trouble!*

The Gulper clung to one side of the draining lagoon, glaring up at him. It was a surprisingly bright indigo, Rho's size, and frog-like, with tremendously long, delicate digits. Its eyes came up on stalks and glared at Rho, and it opened its gigantic mouth again. "You messing with my garden?" It hollered. "I got rights. I got a lease."

Rho didn't know what to say and didn't have time to say it. The landscape's dappled effect had spilled over the broken edge of the lagoon and was spreading toward him. On the flat surface it looked like lace made of light, and Rho knew he'd seen something like it before. But that didn't make him dumb enough to let it touch him! He stepped back. The lights hit the Gulper, and it stopped its shouting and stood up, surprisingly tall on spindly legs. Its eyes peered forward and back.

"Oh, that place," It said. The words were grumpy, but its tone wasn't. "Bound to happen," it admitted, and squatted back down; before Rho could ask it anything it had disappeared below the surface of what fluid remained in the lagoon, and Rho saw its blue hindquarters ducking down a burrow. Then Rho was dancing back again to keep his feet out of the dappled light. It spread to just before the middle of the berm, and then stopped.

Rho stood on the top step, irresolute, but it seemed as if the light would come no further. Its lacy threads spread sideways instead, growing wider until they began to merge. Now he was looking at patches of tall grass in the waste, wherever the threads met; they spread more and more, until they covered the lagoon and it had been replaced by a field sloping down, quite a long ways, toward a wooded river valley. A big ridged mountain rose out of hills on the other side of the valley. The mountains Rho was familiar with seemed to have backed away from him and were only partly visible behind the new peak.

"New," the hawk cried from above him. "Big new place. Who's here? Who's here?"

"Big shake," muttered a vole from beside the path.

"What, what?" called a peewit, fluttering out over the new valley.

The songs of insects rose from the new grass: "Here I am, here I am!"

Rho stumbled backwards down the steps, never taking his eyes off the new landscape. He went past the edge of the waste lagoon, at a safe distance from where it was pouring down the hill in a viscous gray stream. Did it move faster as it flowed downwards? Had it begun to sparkle by the time it went twenty meters, and to babble by the time it had gone another twenty — was it, in fact, a rill of clear water by the time it reached the boulder at which Rho rejoined it? He looked, smelt, dabbled a grass blade in it and watched the crystal drops fall. By the time he looked up, he was no less baffled but recovered enough to think about himself.

It wasn't my fault! he thought, stomping downhill beside the brook. *All I did was apply for a job! How was I to know that Kasidora hired a black magician to run their extension office?* What kind of idiots — of course, his own degree was from Kasidora, so that somewhat limited Rho's critique of them. On the other hand, it gave him first-hand evidence to support any critique he cared to make; and now he wondered, considered, and decided that everyone he had met in Kasidora had been as bad as Gordon K. in all that mattered. They had all valued Rho for his potential and what they could make of it, not for himself. That was what he had left a good home for. To be a tool, a plaything, used and thrown away when he was used up ... Rho had to stop walking at this point, because rage choked him. *You're the idiot!* he told himself. *Treacherous, ungrateful ass, letting anyone who looks like a loving parent screw you over, when you had loving parents at home all the time!* "Daddy," he said out loud, and was so horrified at the whine in his voice that he sat down in the grass.

The valley spread out before him, the long slope running downward in ridges and dips until it ended at a river. On the other side of the river Rho thought he could just see a village in the flat bottomlands, and beyond the village the other side of the valley rose, covered with forest, into the

557

foothills of the Sheep League. But the south end of the new valley, to Rho's left, opened wider and wider around the base of the great star-shaped mountain. The river spread there, into a scalloped bay, and islands dotted the calm water —

Rho realized he could not see any of this except the mountain and the light filling that end of the hazy valley, yet he knew it was there. He had looked at a map of it hundreds of times over the last semester. It was the Alchemists' prison, the most magical place on earth, and it lay spread out right in front of Rho, between his pig-shed and his hedgerow. On his land. His!

Rho spread out his hands in the grass on each side of him as if to balance himself. *If there was ever a time to actually think,* he told himself, *this is it!* He lay back and looked up at high, thin clouds. *What would a normal, sensible person do? Someone whose life had more in it than worrying about himself and his magic? What would Daddy have done?*

He lay looking at the sky for only a few minutes, because the answer was so obvious. He pulled out his cell phone and made calls; to the police, to Russell Cinea in Osyth, and to Mama at home.

***

"Fuck," Ric said. He pulled over at the dusty roadside and put his forehead on the steering wheel. "We just fed a man to a demon."

"We did our duty," said Derek. He didn't look even slightly upset about what had happened to Rosemont.

"Are you serious? You think that's all right?"

"I'm not talking about what I think. I'm talking about what I know."

Ric kept his face on the wheel for a few minutes, thinking about nothing. What would it be like to just know? It would be like that moment when Rosemont had called him to move Derek out of the way. That one instant when it had been clear and the only true thing in the world, that Gerald belonged to Rosemont. That all the new Chief Exorcist's potential belonged to the old Chief Exorcist. That's the sort of thing I 'know,' *Ric thought.* Whatever the strongest exorcist tells me to believe.

He looked sideways at Derek's face. Soft and young, with the stupid mustache that made him look like an old guy trying to look like a young guy. But Derek had known what to do all by himself. He'd stood up to Rosemont.

"You're a scary man," Ric said. He sat up and started driving, and suddenly everything to his right went into spots. He hit the brakes.

"What?"

"My eyes," Ric said, but then he saw Derek and Locullan and Gerald looking in the same direction. The spots were real. They spread and fused together, and a new vista appeared, the mountains pulling back and away from him as if they were on a conveyor belt. "What the—" Ric said. "Did we do that?"

"I didn't," Derek answered. "Did you?"

They sat and watched the new land appear. Ric wondered if he should pull off further to the left, but it didn't reach the road, and after about ten minutes it seemed to be over.

When a new kingdom appears out of nowhere, spreading whole mountain ranges apart, what does your traveling detective hear about on the local radio? Broken power lines. Ric tried three stations before giving up in disgust. He could tell more than that just by looking out the car window!

The new land spread to their right, a wide valley north of the Kasidora River; it had cut them off from the Kasidora Mountains and their path back to the airport, so Ric drove east along its edge looking for a way across. He was beginning to think he had chosen the wrong direction, for the valley seemed to go all the way to the sea. Shafts of light and blocks of purple shadow poured over its edge from between mountains on the other side, the Kasidora side he was trying to reach, and made a blur that swallowed up the bottom of the new valley. Ric couldn't tell whether there were houses and farms down there.

"What is it, ten kilos wide? A hundred kilos long? The landscape spreads out ten or a hundred kilos, and all they notice is that the power goes out."

"They don't have the resources out here," said Derek. "If this were the city, somebody's traffic helicopter would be flying over it."

"Wait!" Ric said, turning the volume up. "Here's somebody who knows something."

"—right between the house and barn," said an elderly man's voice. "I was just bringin' in the tractor, and all of a sudden it herks me a kilo back from my drive, and a bygod river startin' up in between us. I just got crost before it was too deep. Now I gotta put in a footbridge just to feed my cattle, an' how I'm getting' the tractor back to the field, who knows?"

"He should have left well enough alone instead of taking it through the river in the first place," said Ric. He felt spent, on edge, and was looking for someone to find fault with.

"Stop here," Lord Stimms said from the backseat. Just like that, Ric hit the boiling point. But while he was still drawing breath to explode with, Derek said the same thing.

"Stop!"

Ric hit the brakes. The road ended a hundred meters ahead of them: just stopped, as if its builders had gone home and never come back. A wide meadow replaced it, sloping down into the new valley. Halfway down the slope it cast up what looked like a newborn stream with a fringe of willows along its banks.

Ric got out and walked up to the end of the road, all alone. He stood with his arms folded and glared at the valley. He really could not have said what he was so mad about ... being jerked around, he guessed. Having his memories messed with; thinking he had to assassinate the Chief Exorcist; arresting Locullan instead; having Rosemont take him over like that — his eyes blurred, and he rubbed them with one hand. When he took it down, someone was standing beside him. Fuck!

"What?" Ric snarled, turning towards Gerald. He stood looking out over the valley. An evening breeze riffled his hair.

"Perhaps this is where I should leave you," he said.

"You're kidding."

"Would you rather have me scrounging around Selanto? You'd get reports every day of stolen wallets nobody could remember setting down, or used hotel rooms they couldn't remember renting. I haven't the stomach for it, myself."

Ric hadn't thought about that. Gerald's problems actually made him feel a little better, by comparison. "You really want to wander through that valley?"

Gerald shuddered. "Where else do I belong?" he said bitterly, and stepped off the road.

Ric grabbed his arm, without thinking. The minute his fingers touched Gerald's sleeve, knowing poured into him. His fingers knew what that arm felt like even when it was coming apart. His eyes knew what it looked like with blood pouring down it. His heart knew what he had felt, seeing Lord Stimms' hands cling to Derek in his sleep; his mind knew what it was to think yourself worthless and to be reassured. *That's what mercy is*, he thought.

"What?" said Gerald –no, Lord Stimms. But he didn't pull away.

"You're not going down there," Ric said. "You're coming back to Selanto with us." He felt bigger with every word.

"To do what? Stand trial for turning the Chief Exorcist into a demon? Nobody will remember the evidence."

"We'll figure that out when we get there," said Ric. "The Guard will find something to do with an invisible informant, and I have a spare room. The lady using it will share."

"Oh," said Lord Stimms, with a little of his old manner. "And you're in charge of me because?"

"Because," said Ric, "I'm the White Knight. That's why." He took one last look into the valley before shepherding Lord Stimms back to the car. Was it a glint of water he saw in the far-off bottomland, or the glint of armor? Was it a deer or a palfrey in the tall grass? Ric did not care. He knew what picture he was carrying in himself as he turned the car around and drove north.

Chapter 41
Going Home

They rode along the bottom of the long slope Warren had walked past the first time he followed the ley-line. Where he had met King Herroll on the path, and wondered what lay below. The cottages he had looked down on must be on the other side of the valley, now. King Herroll turned and led the way upward, and Warren saw the great beech tree above them at the crest of the ridge. They reined up under it.

It was then that he discovered that Mama Simone came from the other side of the valley, near the village.

"You've come all this way out of your way!" Lilian said.

"I'm not so sure of that," Mama Simone. "I wasn't thinking about going home."

"You're sure?" Lilian said. "Warren and I can drive you back. It's just a little way to our cottage."

"I'm sure," Mama Simone laughed. "I'll be fine."

"We will take you," said King Herrol. "It was my error."

Warren could see Mama Simone start to say no and then change her mind. "All right," she said. "You can take me as far as the village, and show me where to get across the stream. I think I'll be able to see my way from there." Warren tried to conjure up the map. Her farm must be just across the Kasidora River from their cottage - across what would have been the Kasidora River in the old geography that was. Now the new valley spread between them.

He knew he was not thinking clearly about this woman, who had come into a demon to rescue him. He also knew that when he did think clearly about her, he would think about mothers taking the magic out of their babies and storing it in oak trees, and whether a person like himself was obliged to report things like that, and if so, to whom? So he was never going to think clearly about it.

"I'm sorry," he said to the woman. "You helped save me, and I can't even remember your name. What were you doing in that demon again, with those trees? It's all getting fuzzy."

She gave him a sharp look. "It'll be clear in the morning."

Warren shook his head. "It'll be worse in the morning," he said. "I'm going to forget it all if I don't write it down — and I haven't any paper."

"What?" Lilian asked, giving him a sharp look.

"I don't remember what those trees were, do you?" Warren asked; turning and looking back at her with his eyebrows raised. They had perfected this sort of communication back when they had children, so Lilian nodded almost immediately.

"What trees? I think being in a demon does something to the memory," she said. "I'm not forgetting your name, though. And don't you forget mine. Anything we can do for you, ask right away. I'll never forget what you did for us."

"I will," said Warren. "Here's my card."

"I didn't do anything for you," Mama Simone said. But she put the card in her skirt pocket.

565

"I guess that's a matter of opinion. Any time you need my help, call. Any time."

"What, even after you've forgotten all about me?" Mama Simone put her foot in a knight's hand, and vaulted back up onto the horse. She looked down at her skirt with a frown, but the knight handed her the bucket, leapt up behind her and turned his horse back toward the river.

"No goodbyes," King Herrel called as he wheeled the gray horse, "for we will meet again, when you come to study here. Blessings go with you until then!" He looked up at the beech tree spreading above Warren and Lilian, and grinned as if a sudden thought had amused him. "May those who go take strength and courage, and those who come find rest and shelter," he said, in Old Selantese, and Warren was again delighted to know the reply.

"And may those who dwell be a blessing to all," he answered. He stood with his arm around Lilian, watching the knights ride away in the sunlight.

"You wanted it for that Rho," she said.

"What?"

"A research — monopoly. You want it for him, don't you? All the rest of your people can compete."

"Well," Warren admitted, "he did come to mind. But look at it!" He gestured at the grand sweep of the valley, down to the star-shaped mountain. "It's the place Teddy and Russell have been searching for all spring. I couldn't let it get away from them."

Lilian's sniff said everything her words didn't, about Teddy and Russell. Then she stiffened. "Oh, no! When we were up on the mountain I called Bosie and told her to tell Russell –"

"Tell him what?"

"That you were hanging around with Xiphister! I thought he'd know what it meant, and it wouldn't scare her."

"He's probably having a fit," said Warren. It was funny for just an instant. Then he thought about how Selanto magicians dealt with demons. "We have to call him," he said, trying to keep his chill at the idea of Russell binding Xiphister out of his voice. But Lilian must have heard something of it, because she handed him the cell phone right away.

Warren sat below the beech tree and made his phone call. He got answering machines at Russell's office and home.

Lilian scowled down at him. "I forbid you to sit there worrying about Russell. Or Rho, or any of the rest of them."

"It's just that he might do something extreme."

"All right, I'll try Bosie." Lilian looked amazed when she actually got through on the phone. "Bosie! Do you have Russell's cell number with you? Thank you —" she jotted on her palm. "Warren wants — yes, he's right here."

"Warren, dear!" Bosie's voice scratched through the cell phone. "Lilian tells me you've been having a gay time. Well, what passed for a gay time in my day."

"Um — what did she tell you?"

"Oh, all about your new friends. Goblins and hipsters." Bosie laughed. "I haven't heard anyone use that word in a dear's age. Wherever did you pick it up? Or are things that old-fashioned down — wherever you are; goodness, I've no idea."

Warren opened his mouth, just to let the air in. He felt himself grow light as a bubble, filled with air and sunshine. "You told Russell we were with hipsters?" he asked, and saw Lilian's mouth go into an 'O'.

"Yes, dear, he found it as amusing as I did. Though he was too much of a gentleman to point out that I'm old enough to use the term. Always such a pleasure to talk to Russell, you know."

"So he's doing all right."

"Oh, I believe so, dear. A little bird told me he has a new candidate for one of your positions. But otherwise, I can't say I've heard any real news from your department. You haven't been gone a week, after all. They can't have gotten up to all that much."

"That's good," Warren said. "Thank you, Mama. I love you."

"Well, I love you too, dear. But let me talk to Lilian again, I want her to tell me what to do about the garage door opener. It keeps opening all on its own, dear, in the middle of the night."

Warren handed back the cell phone and leaned back against the beech tree's smooth trunk. For the first time in his vacation, he relaxed completely. Lilian finished talking to Bosie, hung up, and sat watching him with a considering expression.

"Here I've worked like mad to keep you from being worried by that department, when all along you needed to know they were all right before you could relax!" Warren gave her a shamefaced smile.

"You know you won't be really happy until you've called Russell again," she said, and handed him the phone.

Russell's cell phone also put Warren into voicemail. "Um, Russell, it's Warren," he said, and had almost left his number when he saw Lilian's face. "Everything's fine here. Hope it's all going well on your end. Well, um, I'll try you later." He handed the phone back.

"Do you want me to find out Rho's cell number, so you can check on him too?"

"What? No! He's only had a few days away from us. Let the poor man recover."

Lilian sniffed and grew tart, as she always did when thinking of Rho. "Let him recover! He's not the one who just climbed out of a demon. Oh, I shouldn't have sat down. I don't think I can get up again."

"You know what I really want to see? That trollop of a bed. Cushions and sheets. A hot bath, and then sleep for — how long?" Warren grunted his way upwards along the tree trunk until he was upright, and bent down to pull his wife to her feet. By the time they caught their first glimpse of the cottage, the sun was almost down to the far side of the new valley. He had long since given up thinking about anything except supper and bed.

"Oh, look," said Lilian. "It was waiting for us!"

As they approached the porch, the door swung open wide and Warren could see firelight within. He smelled roast meat and fresh bread. The gray cat walked into the middle of the doorway and sat down in a shaft of slanting sunlight. "Yow!" she said. She went on at some length while they bustled into the room. Warren found it a welcome distraction as he got his bearings.

"Look at this," Lilian said, standing at the kitchen table. "Champagne! And — what are these?"

"I don't know," Warren said, looking at the round, brown objects. Each sat in its own fluted cup on a golden tray, beside the glasses. "Truffles?"

"It's gold," said Lilian, rubbing one of the fluted cups. Her voice stopped before the last word was over. She didn't move.

Warren put his hand on her shoulder and turned her to face him. "You came after me," he said, tilting her chin up to look into her face, crumpled with oncoming tears. "You came into a demon to get me back." He kissed her once before the flood, and then he held her and let her cry.

**

Russell's cell phone rang just as he'd locked his office door after a long day of, it must be admitted, doing little except hanging on Teddy Whin's every word as she sat in the conference room, relaying more and more depressing reports of Xiphister's ex-tenants. They were not doing well, according to Teddy, not well at all... and then she had gone home and taken the scroll with her. All in all, Russell was not in the mood to find that he had locked the cell phone in his office. But he could not just let it ring. He was Acting Chair, wasn't he? "Oh, for –" he said, reopening the door and retrieving the phone from the desk. "Yes? Cinea here, Demonology Department."

"Oh, Russell!" Bosie sounded surprised. Who had she expected? "Dear, I said I would call to gloat, and here I am gloating."

"What?"

"Lilian just called me, and she says she and Warren are doing just fine. He had a lovely birthday cake, and they went shopping in Sterne."

Russell was thunderstruck. "What! But the demon said it had Warren!"

"What? A demon said that? Well, Warren is a match for any demon," said Bosie. "I've always said he was. That's why I'm gloating. I'm not precisely sure just how one ought to gloat over the telephone, I must admit, but consider me gloating."

"Well, for goodness' sake," Russell said, quite inadequately. "Are you sure? Can we call her back?"

"She hasn't given me her number, I told you that. Do you think I don't know my own daughter-in-law?"

"No, no," Russell said. He had just realized that this most important news had come to him before Teddy noticed it, and now he could think of nothing but getting Bosie off the line. "I consider myself thoroughly gloated over, Bosie, and I shall buy you a bottle of wine the next time we see one another."

"That's handsome of you," said Bosie. "Of all the gentlemen I've known, I must say you are the most gracious loser."

Russell called Teddy's number almost before Bosie's voice had stopped.

"Yup?" she answered, after several rings.

"It's Russell," he said, holding his breath for fear she would break out into news.

"Russell? It's work," she said to someone. "Has something happened?"

"Yes," Russell said, rejoicing. "Bosie just called me to say Lilian called her to say they were both fine. Lilian and Warren, that is. They're celebrating his birthday. With cake."

"What?" Teddy fairly squeaked. "But Xiphister —"

"Maybe Lilian phoned from inside it? What does the scroll say?"

"Oh, crap!" Teddy said. "I haven't unpacked it yet. I was taking a shower. Crap, crap — hold on." Rustling and unclear exclamations, in two voices. "Let's see," she said, picking the phone up again. "Wizardry, Selanto, Sorcery, Selanto — that's it! No Wizardry from Osyth, no Magic from Osyth, no department chair, no scrying — no first place pickles either, that must have been Lilian's too. They're out! They have to be out! Oh —" she stopped short and Russell, who had been grinning in enthusiasm, now shared the letdown. Did they actually dare to believe news this good? He looked up at the scrolls on his top shelf and shivered. Had he come that close to abandoning all his ethics, on evidence this flimsy?

"Did Bosie get Lilian's number?" Teddy asked.

"No," said Russell.

"Wow," said Teddy. "Do you think we dare believe it? Lilian should call one of us, she really should. She left Bosie a message about it, after all — doesn't she think Bosie would tell us?"

"After talking to Bosie, she's probably sure of that."

572

Teddy was silent a moment. "We'll just have to wait," she said. "Darn! When are they due back?"

"Wednesday evening."

"It's like not being able to sneeze. And do we have to offer Xiphister Rho's position, if it gets rid of its captives?"

"It won't be qualified any more, if it gets rid of its captives."

"That sounds like a bait and switch. Wow," said Teddy, "You're actually making me feel sorry for a demon!"

Russell felt suspended in mid-reaction as he hung up the phone. Was he to rejoice over Warren's escape, prepare to bind Xiphister, notify the Dean about any of it? What did an Acting Chair do in a situation like this? He swiveled his chair around, glaring at the papers on his desk, and finally drew a legal pad toward him. The least he could do as chair would be to draft a draconian departmental policy about faculty leaving contact numbers when they went on vacation.

The sun had set by the time Russell finally put down his pen and left the office, having created a policy that would stand forever as a reminder and reproach to his irresponsible colleague. Demonologists for generations to come would wonder at its strictures, and be told the cautionary story of Warren and Lilian. Thus would they live on in infamy ... he picked up his cell phone and it blinked at him. *Missed call — Hiram Rho.*

Rho sounded as if he were laboring over the choice of every word in his message. *A big valley just opened up over the Vinchifer ley-line,* he said, and Russell thought of sinkholes. *It spread the mountains apart, I'd say five kilometers or so, and I can't see how long it is. And, um, part of it's on our property. You can get into it from my farm. I'm in there right now. So I guess that gives the department an in — I don't know what you want to do about it. Call me back, I guess — anyway, that's it.*

Russell stood with his mouth open. He played the message back three times, writing every word down on a sheet of paper. Then he sat down and read it.

He knew he should call somebody about this. A Very Virtuous department head would call the department's geomancer. But Russell was not a Very Virtuous department head when it came to Linus; he was a borderline Evil Magician on that topic. Linus could wait and find out with everyone else, on the morning news — or better yet, when one of his rivals in the field forwarded him a preprint.

He turned his computer back on and began to search for verification of Rho's story, which was easy to find. A helicopter from Kasidora had flown over the new land, live-streaming video, and Russell recognized every feature. The source of magic from Teddy's map. The Alchemists' prison from Vinca's.

"There are some people down there," the narrator said over the helicopter's *whup whup*. "They look like they're riding horses."

But Russell didn't care. *It's on Rho's land,* he thought. *It's ours! And that's solved his problems. His job's safe. He'll probably end up running a field station there.* Leaning back in satisfaction, he noticed that the cell phone was still blinking. *Blink all you like,* he thought to it. *There's no way I'm deleting that message!* But when he picked it up, it was blinking about something else. A hidden number had left a message, at almost the same time as Rho's. "I get three calls a year on this thing, and they all come at the same minute," Russell complained, re-opening his voice mail. It was doubtless some nuisance call, but still — *Um, Russell, it's Warren*, the voice mail said. Russell started so violently he almost fell out of his chair. *Everything's fine here. Hope it's all going well on your end. Well, um, I'll try you later.*

Russell righted himself and stared at the phone. "Try me later! That — the nerve! 'Everything's fine' — at least he didn't say 'wish you were here' — " Speech failed him as he snatched up his office phone — no more cell phone calls were going to slip by him tonight! — but he knew it would not fail him when Teddy answered.

***

Mama Simone's skirt was bothering her. She'd always claimed that a decent print dress was good enough for any situation a respectable woman got into, but riding astride a knight's warhorse was proving her wrong. She tugged, and got one edge almost halfway down her thigh before beginning to go off-balance — not that she could fall, with the knight's strong arms on either side.

"What did women in your kingdom wear to go riding?" she asked the knight.

"Doeskin breeches," he answered.

575

That sounds awful comfortable, thought Mama Simone. Why did doeskin sound softer than buckskin, and either one sound softer than deerskin, and that sound softer than deerhide? She could almost feel the soft leather — no, softer than leather. Soft, yielding, but strong enough to keep pinchy harness and scraping saddle edges away from a lady's legs. She could feel it, and when she looked down that was because she was wearing it. She had a jerkin of the same stuff. They were tan, and as she looked at them embroidered patterns started to appear, the way pictures sometimes did when she shut her eyes at night. They would flash before her, faces changing into one another or scenes zipping past as if she were on a long car trip, or garden flowers — the blur of images on her own clothing made Mama Simone feel ill, and she closed her eyes. *Leaves,* she thought. *That's all I want.* When she opened her eyes again the clothes had settled down. There were little embroidered leaves scattered over them, green and russet against the tan leather. Mama Simone looked at them critically. *Some silver ones,* she thought, and they appeared. *No, just silver-edged.* She didn't want them to get confused with the one King Herrel had given her. *And longer sleeves — elbow length.* She felt as if her hands were pulling the sleeves down and tracing the leaves onto the fabric, but it was all happening inside her mind. Her thoughts were making the clothes. *They don't feel like thoughts,* Mama Simone thought, and pinched the breeches. The fabric was supple and thick between her fingers.

She glanced to one side and saw the King riding at ease beside her, his eyes amused.

"Can everyone here do that?" she asked him.

"Not in my day," King Herrel said. "You are a sorceress." Had the knight carrying Mama Simone stiffened his arms a little in alarm?

"Not in my day," said Mama Simone.

"There is magic here," King Herrel said. "Nöon's magic. Alchemists' magic. It lay unused, and now it rises. Like water, it will find a channel."

Mama Simone thought about this. *I'm a channel,* she thought. *But maybe only in here...* they topped a rise in the plain, and she saw the village not far away, in the middle of a sunny, windswept plain. Beyond it, the foothills of the Kasidora range and her empty farmhouse, with the tree-Mama Simone somewhere between here and there...

"Could a respectable widow lady rent one of those village houses?" she asked King Herrrol. "Once you get the place redded up, that is."

"A widow lady might seek safer quarters. A sorceress — who am I to advise a sorceress?"

Mama Simone looked sideways at him. "You're the man who might give the sorceress a little guarding, until she learns just how much she can do for herself. Or do you have a castle to live in?"

"My castle was in another country, long ago. When Nöon ruled here, he lived in the mountain." King Herrel leaned down and plucked a blade of the grass that grew almost up to his saddle. He chewed it as he looked at the village. "Many people suffered there."

"All the more reason to clean it out."

"Or burn it."

Mama Simone shuddered. "That doesn't get rid of things," she said. "It just hands them over to something else, to use against you."

"Ah? Well," King Herrol said, spitting out the grass blade, "let us seek counsel." He reined in and turned his horse, waiting for the other knights to catch up. "Men of Storn, what shall we do with yon village?"

He wouldn't ask them if he really wanted to burn it down, Mama Simone thought. *They don't know anything about what happened in it, do they? They were asleep in the goblin's mountain.*

She was right. Each knight in the circle gave another reason for claiming the village as their own, and it seemed as if King Herrol sat straighter with each reason.

"I saw many suffer in this village," he said when they had all finished, "but your presence will cleanse it for me. Let us lay new memories over the old."

"Hah!" shouted the youngest of the knights, the one with an easy grin and a wild look in his dark eyes. He rose in his stirrups and began a charge down the slope toward the village.

"Hyah!" Mama Simone's knight said as well, and the horse got bouncy under her and then stretched out in a gallop. They were all racing, flying across the grassland, and didn't rein up until they reached the gates. Like a parade, still filled with the excitement of that dash, they rode in single file into the center of the square.

"That house," she said, pointing at a cottage close to the square. "That's the one I want."

The blonde knight was not impressed. "It'll need work," he said. "That roof's a mess."

"All of their roofs are," said the young, dark-eyed knight. "That's for us, Herrol! The merchants' hall, or what-say-ye. Large enough for a king's banquet below and ample room by the fire."

King Herrol had not taken much heed. He was pacing out the square, and now he seemed to have found the place in it that he wanted to squat down in. *He better not be doing what I think*, Mama Simone thought, fixing his back with a squinty eye. When he stood up, she saw that he had planted something — the beech sprig he'd been carrying when she first saw him as a dirty tramp. He stood back, looking at it, and the sprig began to grow. Before her eyes, it stretched tall and wide. It was knee-height to King Herrol, waist-height, tapping at his chest, stretching over his head. He stood and looked at Mama Simone's chest — no, at the bucket she was still carrying.

"There, and there," he said, pointing to two other spots in the square. Together, they planted the two oak seedlings. She stood beside one of them and saw it spring up, to her own height — it tapped a leaf against her cheek — then taller, until its branches waved over her head.

"Hist!" one of the knights said from behind her. They all went silent and melted into the shadows. *Trained warriors*, Mama Simone thought. Not to be outdone, she stepped into her cottage, peeking through a crack in its wall.

The newcomers' shadows came into the square long before they did. There were two of them, gigantic as shadows are around sunset; for the sun

579

was almost gone to bed, stretching out his rays and yawning. The shadows reached to the scorched place in the center of the square, and then to the merchants' hall the knights had claimed. Mama Simone knew there were horses somewhere around that building and armed men in every one of its archways, but nobody could have told. The shadows didn't notice. They flowed into the archways, but their sister shadows must not have told them anything about what was hidden within, and they went on up the building without discovering the knights.

Then a flash of light came into the square, and Mama Simone realized that one of the shadows' legs had entered. Sunlight came between them every time the shadow took a step; a man, or someone in trousers. The other shadow was skirt-solid, then flickering beneath a hem. And then the two people had entered the square themselves, walking more carefully than their shadows.

One of them was smallish, scrawny, with tow-colored hair that stood out sideways and would have two cowlicks in back. He would eat Cousin Mirelda's marmalade cake in big bites, and never know what to say in company, and seeing him like this, unexpected, made Mama Simone's heart jump in her chest. She took a deep breath and tightened herself up to make that first step out toward him, and then the other person came into view.

The second person was respectable, in the kind of print dress that would do for any occasion. She walked fast because she had long legs. She stepped hard because she wore wooden shoes, the kind you kick off beside the back door. But they were shoes

580

and a dress that Mama Simone had burned. Mama Simone froze. The tree-woman had finally caught up with her.

Robin and the tree-woman stopped and looked around the square.

"It's empty," Robin said. "There were people here, though. The birds say so."

The tree-woman looked around as well. It looked straight at where Mama Simone was standing. "Yes," it said, in a girly voice that could not have been like Mama Simone's own. "Nobody lives here. We should go home."

Mama Simone pressed herself against the tree, weak in the knees. *That thing took my place!* she thought. *What'll it do to the children?* But that was not really what she meant. That was a mother's lie, one of the things you trained yourself to think so that nobody, not even yourself, would know how you really felt. Underneath it, some cold clever part of Mama Simone was thinking, *She'll take care of them for me.*

"It's on our land," Robin's voice said. "It's the biggest news in magic in forever! Just walking in it, I can hear the animals better than I ever could — and it's on our land! People from Osyth are going to be all over this."

"I thought you were working in Minich this summer," said the tree-woman.

"I am," said Robin. She could hear him take a deep breath. "I owe Gordon K. that much. He was good to me, up till the end."

That doesn't sound good! thought Mama Simone. *What's he been doing? Letting himself be used by some older magician* — but she was never

581

going to find out, was she. He'd told the tree-woman. The tree-woman knew Mama Simone's son, and had all the fun of knowing him. They would be the ones laughing together in the kitchen over supper, or working together in the garden. He'd tell his stories about work to the tree-woman...*But you're magic here,* said the hard part of her. *Will you give it up again?*

Mama Simone sagged against the wall, but then the image of Lilian and Warren flashed into her mind. Lilian and Warren walking back to their family lives without giving up their magic — Lilian scrying and walking into demons one day, scrapbooking and cuddling grandchildren the next. "No!" she said, and everything in the square went silent. "I don't have to choose. I'll have both." She took a big breath, put down the bucket she'd been carrying for half her life, it seemed, and stepped out of her cottage just as the sun gave one last yawn and slid his toes under the far horizon.

Epilogue

Warren and Lilian looked both tired and rested as they came up the concourse. They made no objections when Russell commandeered their wheeled bags.

"We don't have any checked baggage," Lilian said.

"Fine," Russell said. "So. When you two take a vacation, you don't fool around. One demon and one world are enough for most of us stay-at-homes."

"That's why they call it vacation," Warren said, smugly. "It's bigger and better." He looked up at the coral sky with appreciation. "So, did you have a good week? I see you got rid of the rain."

"I wish I could claim credit for that," said Russell. "Not much since you called. We got the Dean's official okay to hire for Neil's position, and picked up a few candidates for Rho's — but it looks as if he may be back after all. He sounded pretty good on the phone yesterday. Linus is furious that I didn't call him about the Alchemists' prison."

"You sound happy about that," Lilian said.

"I am." Russell opened the front door for her.

"A gentleman and a scholar," she said.

"So, um, you enjoyed being chair?"

Russell only had to think for a second. "It was the most frightening week of my life," he said. "But once I accepted that, it was a wild ride. I had no idea what you put up with."

"It's not always so eventful."

"I don't know about that. The Dean showed me your end-of-the-year report."

"Oh," Warren said from the back seat, and Russell, merging, dared not check his expression in the rearview mirror. "What did the Dean say about it?"

"It's what you say about it that matters," said Russell.

Silence from the back. Was Lilian listening? She looked asleep in the front seat, but Russell didn't believe it.

"It's actually what you say that matters," Warren answered. "Do you think you could survive a few years of it?"

Was Lilian asleep or not? If she were awake, surely she would react to that. But if she were asleep, why would Russell feel this glow from where she sat, as if sunshine had filled the passenger seat of his car? *That doesn't matter,* he told himself. Because the same glow was filling the driver's seat. *I didn't know I wanted this job,* he thought. Was that true? *I've wanted it for years. I just didn't want to take it away from him.*

"I think I could. If you don't mind stepping out for a while."

"I have to. I was managing people, even inside a demon. After a while you lose yourself in the role."

Russell thought for a while. *I almost did,* he thought. *Not Warren's role, but a role* — "I have a few scrolls you'll need to lock up for me," he said. But there was no answer except a murmur, and then a snuffling noise. He concentrated on the interchange's twists and turns for a few minutes, and when he got out onto the clear highway and was free to glance at his passengers, he saw Warren, like Lilian, leaning back with his eyes shut. Russell decided not to disturb them. He was Chair, after all, and they were under his care.

www.ingramcontent.com/pod-product-compliance
Lightning Source LLC
Chambersburg PA
CBHW010252030726
47497CB00010BA/3184